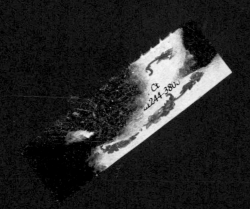

And This Too Shall Pass

ALSO BY
E. Lynn Harris

INVISIBLE LIFE
JUST AS I AM

And This Too Shall Pass

A NOVEL BY

E. Lynn Harris

DOUBLEDAY
NEW YORK LONDON TORONTO SYDNEY AUCKLAND

PUBLISHED BY DOUBLEDAY
a division of Bantam Doubleday Dell Publishing Group, Inc.
1540 Broadway, New York, New York 10036

DOUBLEDAY and the portrayal of an anchor with a dolphin
are trademarks of Doubleday, a division of Bantam Doubleday
Dell Publishing Group, Inc.

Book design by Terry Karydes

This novel is a work of fiction. Any references to real people,
events, establishments, organizations, or locales are intended only to
give the fiction a sense of reality and authenticity. Other names,
characters, and incidents are either the product of the author's
imagination or are used fictitiously, as are those fictionalized events and incidents
that involve real persons.

Library of Congress Cataloging-in-Publication Data
Harris, E. Lynn.
And this too shall pass: a novel / by E. Lynn Harris.
p.   cm.
1. Football players—Illinois—Chicago—Fiction.   2. Chicago (Ill.)—Fiction.
I. Title.
PS3558.A64438A53   1996
813'.54—dc20   95-38844
                                                                              CIP

ISBN 0-385-48030-X
Copyright © 1996 by E. Lynn Harris

10   9

Dedicated in Loving Memory

FOR MY GRANDMOTHER, BESSIE ALLEN HARVEY
(1912–1995)
FOR HER LEGACY OF UNCONDITIONAL LOVE
AND FOR TEACHING ME THE POWER OF PRAYER

and

FOR CARNEY "BUTCH" CARROLL
(1955–1995)
FOR THE JOY OF FRATERNITY AND FRIENDSHIP,
FOR BEING MY BROTHER AND IN THE END
TEACHING ME THE MEANING OF COURAGE

IN MEMORY
Ellis H. Smith, Jr. • *Anthony F. Rogers*
Marcia Phillips • *Michael Buckner* • *Keith McDaniel*
Pearline Morris • *Stephen Corbin* • *Teddy L. Morris*

ACKNOWLEDGMENTS

For much I am grateful, to many I am thankful. My faith: I am grateful to my Lord Jesus Christ for His many blessings in my life and for being the center of my joy. My family: My mother, Etta W. Harris, whose pride, support, and unconditional love came not with my literary success but with my birth. My aunt Jessie L. Phillips, for being the best aunt in the world and the best friend I've ever had. My uncle, Attorney Charles E. Phillips (who came up with the book's title), for being a role model in every sense of the word and one I can talk to. My sisters, Anita, Zettoria, and Jan, for being wonderful mothers to my nieces and nephews, who bring much joy and love in my life. Also Wanda McAdoo and my special godson, LaMark. And to the rest of my large and supportive family, most especially two cousins, Jacquelyn Y. Johnson and Kennie L. Phillips, two wonderful people I want to be like when I grow up.

My friends, who in many respects have become part of my family: Tina and Joneé Ansa, who inspire me as artists and humble me as being among the finest people I've ever had the pleasure and honor to call my friends. Vanessa Gilmore, Lencola Sullivan, Robin Walters, Cindy and Steve Barnes, Tracey and David Huntley, Overtis Brantley and Regina Daniels, who have been there for me for more than a decade and surround me with friendship and love. My boys, prime examples of the three out of four we never hear about: Timothy Douglas, Troy Danto, Keith Thomas, Carlton Brown, Kevin Edwards, Jerry Jackson, Bill Britton, Martin Christopher, Brian Chandler, Ken Hatten, and Anderson Phillips.

My agent, John Hawkins, who has to be the best in the business, for his support, guidance, and being the type of man I am proud to call my friend. Special thanks to members of his staff, Moses Cardona and Sharon Freidman (my audio agent), for their support with a touch of class. I am blessed to have a publisher who supports me in every way possible: Martha Levin not only discovered me, but publishes me with great care and wisdom and remains one of my staunchest supporters. Also at Doubleday: Steve Rubin, for his support and leadership at a company I'm proud to be associated with. Emma, the receptionist, who has always made me feel at home, even when I hadn't sold a single book, and who makes sure I get all the wonderful letters. My publicists, Tracey George and Sherri Steinfeld, for two successful tours; and Janet Hill, for being a friend I always know I can talk to. And even though he doesn't like clichés, here is one that's appropriate: last, but certainly not least, I give many, many thanks to my brilliant Doubleday editor, Charles Flowers, not only for his valuable editing skills, but for being the type of person with whom I would trust not only my words, but my life. Who said you couldn't find friends in this business?

I have to thank all my escorts who make the road bearable, most especially Esther Levine, Kathleen Livingston, Lenore Markowitz, and Lorraine Battle. Thanks to the many African American booksellers who have become my friends and family (you know who you are —read the novel closely). Thanks also to Linda Chatman, Wayne Kendall, and Taurus Sorrells for much needed support. A special "You're the Best" Award to Laura Gilmore and Runabout Errand Services for keeping my chaotic life in order. I'm grateful to my bankers, Gwen McCants Allen and Allen Jones, at NationsBank for realizing that I'm still a struggling artist, and to my special friends who provided assistance with the book's technical facts: Deborah Crable, Dyanna Williams, Michael Richmond, Lajoyce Hunter, Dr. and Mrs. Arthur Smith, and Attorney Rowana A. Williams. Special thanks to Delta Sigma Theta, Alpha Kappa Alpha, the Arkansas Razorbacks Basketball Team, and the Radiojocks who pump up the volume about my books: Tom, Paula, Sybil, Bonnie, and Wendy.

Writing is a lonely job, so I know how blessed I am to have

friends whose input I trust and admire. They help me pull it together, hold it together, and make sure I am never really alone, so special thanks to Phyliss Perry for our wonderful coffee talks and a new friendship I treasure. And a **Standing Ovation Award** to Blanche Richardson, whose love, friendship, and novel surgery are appreciated more than she will ever know and make me wonder how I managed life before I met her. The **E. Lynn Harris Music Awards** and special thanks to Toni Braxton ("You Mean the World to Me"), Kevon Edmonds and After 7 ("Till You Do Me Right"), and Vanessa Williams ("The Sweetest Days"), for their support and wonderful music to listen to while I write. And a **How Do You Mend a Broken Heart Award** to Everick, for being a blessing in my life and giving me a loving and safe place for my heart. Maybe a house and a dog aren't such a bad idea.

Finally, a **Simply the Best Award** to all of you who have supported me from the very beginning by purchasing my novels, spreading the word about my work, writing me letters, and keeping me in your prayers. I'm humbled by the support and love you have shown me. I will try to the best of my abilities to never let you down. Thank you and hold tight to your faith, family, friendship, and the power of prayer.

CONTENTS

And This Too

Shall Pass

Where there is fear . . . faith cannot exist . . .

PRELUDE

Zurich had dreams. Tamela had secrets. Sean had questions. Mia had demons. And MamaCee had answers. Dreams of passion he had never known. Secrets she had never shared. Questions about love and God. Demons, deep and dark. And MamaCee had answers.

CHAPTER 1

SHE DEAD!

Another grueling football practice was over and Zurich Robinson's pumpernickel-brown face was a shower of sweat. As he opened his locker, he heard the voices and laughter of his teammates echoing against the cement walls of the locker room, the snapping of towels against skin, the slamming of locker doors. His stomach began churning like a washing machine when he saw the note inside his locker instructing him to report to the offensive coordinator's office. Instead of heading to the showers, as he normally did after practice, Zurich removed his gray practice shorts, put on his jeans, pulled a mesh T-shirt from his locker and slipped it over his massive shoulders. He did not make eye contact with any of his teammates as he raced toward Coach Kennedy's office.

When he reached the dingy area that served as a makeshift office for the coaching staff, Zurich stepped into the first open door, where he saw Dave Kennedy and Gene Tolbert, the head coach and general manager, sitting on the edge of a large gray desk. He became even more nervous when he saw them talking in hushed tones with grim looks on their faces. Zurich knew something was up, something that concerned him and his career with the Chicago Cougars, an NFL expansion team. Was his dream of becoming an NFL quarterback about to come to an end? Would he be going back to Canada, where black quarterbacks were as common as black running backs? He believed that he was practicing well. He was number two on the depth charts, and roster cuts, to the final fifty-three players, were more than a week away, after the final exhibition game against the Chicago Bears. But who knew when the coaches would make up their minds?

"Have a seat, Z-man," Coach Kennedy said.

"If you don't mind, Coach K, I prefer to stand," Zurich replied. Standing, he could make a quick exit in case any tears welled up when he received the bad news.

"Suit yourself," Kennedy said. He looked toward the Cougars' head coach and asked, "Are you going to give him the news or should I?"

"You do it," Gene said.

Kennedy nodded and looked Zurich straight in the eye. "Zurich, we've made a very important decision. A decision we think will have a big impact on our inaugural season in the NFL."

"Yes, sir," Zurich mumbled.

"Well, you might wish you had taken that seat, but here goes. Coach Tolbert and I have decided that you're going to start against the Bears." Now both coaches were smiling broadly, and Zurich's muscular legs suddenly felt like Jell-O. Had he heard his coach correctly?

"What do you say, Z-man?" Coach Tolbert asked, as he slapped Zurich on the shoulders.

"I am, I am . . . I'm starting," Zurich stuttered. It was not a question, just a statement of disbelief.

"You will be the starting quarterback the first time two Chicago professional teams play each other on the field. You, Mr. Robinson, will become a part of history." Zurich decided he needed some support after all. He slowly slid his body onto the black metal chair near the door. He felt a tear forming in the corner of his eye and then suddenly broke out into infectious laughter.

"I don't believe this. This is a joke . . . right?" he asked as he clasped his hands together and quickly released them, pointing toward his coaches. "This is a joke?" he repeated.

"It will be a joke if you don't perform," Coach Tolbert said.

Zurich leaped from his chair and started to hug both his coaches, but opted for firm handshakes instead.

"Thanks, guys. I promise not to let you down," he said as he raced from the office. Zurich had some calls to make.

He located a pay phone in the dim hallway, but Zurich couldn't decide whom to call first, his agent, Dan Cunningham, or his father. He remembered Dan was on the West Coast with one of his more prominent clients, so Zurich dialed his father's number and when the operator came on the other line, he said, "This is collect from the NFL's newest starting quarterback."

"Excuse me?" the operator said.

"Collect from Zuri," he said.

"Thank you," she said.

After a few rings, the answering machine came over the line. As he listened to his father's cheerful voice, he wondered where his father could be. He knew his father had finally convinced his sometime live-in lady friend, Rhona, of the merits of golf and they played often. His father had spent most of his life as a caddy at one of Tampa's country clubs and was enjoying his early retirement. He now had his own caddy, thanks to his savings, the Florida lottery, and the generosity of his three working sons. But at times like this when he needed to talk to him personally, Zurich regretted giving his father a fancy answering machine. He would always leave him messages saying he was thinking about him and things were going great, even when they were not. If his voice sounded depressed, it never failed that his father would call him back and say, "Remember, son, it's only a game."

"Sorry, sir, but there's a recorder picking up," the operator said.

"Thanks anyway," Zurich said in a dejected tone.

"Well, I'm happy for you," the operator said.

"Thank you. Thank you very much," he said.

"What's your name so when you become rich and famous I can tell my grandkids I talked to you?" she asked.

"Zurich Thurgood Robinson." Saying his name out loud made him remember how MamaCee, his grandmother, had chosen the middle name of the Supreme Court justice because she had dreamed that Zurich, too, would become a judge. His mother got his first name from a postcard his father had sent from Switzerland, when he visited the country while serving in the Army. It looked like such a beautiful city, she told Zuri later, and she knew her newborn would be beautiful, too. It was one of the few memories Zurich had of his mother. Leola Robinson had died of breast cancer when he was only six years old.

"Ooh, I love your name! The best of luck, Zurich Thurgood Robinson," she said.

"Thank you. Thanks a lot," he said as he hung up. A broad smile crossed his face. He knew MamaCee would be home and happy with her grandson's exciting news.

MamaCee picked up the phone on the first ring. She, too, had an answering machine, which he had given her, but she refused to install it and was firm about leaving the machine in its box in her closet alongside several other unused electronic gadgets.

Zurich could hear the excitement in MamaCee's voice when she told the operator, "Of course I'll accept the charges; that's my grand-baby."

"MamaCee."

"Hey, baby. How you doin'?" MamaCee asked.

"I'm doing great!" Zurich said. But before he could share his news, MamaCee had some news of her own.

"Baby, you 'member Miss Bertha Joy?"

"Miss Bertha Joy. Naw, MamaCee, I don't think so," Zurich responded.

"Yeah, you 'member her. She lived down the road from me. You know, in that terrible-looking pink house, the one with them dirty gray shingles on the front. You know, baby, cross the creek, where you boys used to play all the time."

"Naw, I don't remember her. Guess what, MamaCee?"

MamaCee ignored Zurich's question.

"You got to 'member her, Zuri. Bertha Joy weren't that pretty of a lady, not 'xactly ugly either, even though ugly was spread pretty even through that family of hers. She moved up to Detroit, but then she moved back home with her mama, six months after she followed that man up there, you know, that skinny fellow who used to collect bottles and sell them up at the Piggy Wiggly. Laroyce was his name; man wasn't big as a Georgia peanut. But he was a real city slicker, him being from Detroit and all. I don't think he's been back down here since he moved back up North. I wonder what happened to him?" MamaCee paused for a second, but before Zurich could get in a word, she continued her story.

"Well, anyhow, when she got up to Detroit, Miss Bertha Joy found out that fool was married. A couple of months later his wife pulled a gun on her when she found out Bertha Joy was messin' round with her husband. It was a shame 'fore God. That's when Bertha Joy moved back home. Everybody down here was talking 'bout it. You know peoples in Warm Springs like to mind other folks' business. But not me. I wouldn't have known 'bout it 'cept her own mama told me the whole story. I really felt sorry for her. Them kids of hers gave her so much trouble. Miss Mabel Joy, you know that's Bertha Joy's mother, used to say all the time, 'The good Lord gave me all these bad-assed kids just to mess with me.' Not like my babies. I tell my friends all the time, none of my children or my grandbabies ever gave me an ounce of trouble. Can't say that 'bout some of them women my sons married though."

"I still can't remember her, MamaCee. What about her?" Zurich asked. By now he realized it would have made more sense to say he remembered Miss Bertha Joy. Instead he leaned back against the wall and enjoyed the animated buzz of his grandmother's lively conversation, or as his father called it, *Mississippi storytelling*. Sooner or later he would be able to share his good news.

Zurich pictured MamaCee, whom everyone in Warm Springs called Miss Cora, wearing some floral print dress with her slip and bra strap showing, well-worn flip flops, most likely yellow, sitting on her favorite sturdy, wooden stool in the cluttered kitchen of her home, talking on the black wall phone with the rotary dial. She was probably looking out the screened door at her vegetable garden, gently tapping her ample hips with an old flyswatter she held in her other hand. MamaCee was a robust woman, a true size eighteen, with smooth raisin-brown skin and plain features that lit up like a movie marquee when she smiled. And she smiled a lot. Miss Cora was proud of the fact that she was seventy-five years old and still had most of her own teeth. She had one gold tooth, right up front, that sparkled with an aura of wisdom when MamaCee was doling out advice to her friends and family members. She still pressed her concrete gray hair with a pressing comb her mother had given her, but on special occasions she wore one of the two wigs she had purchased from a wig mail-order house.

After his mother died, Zurich had spent most of his youth in Warm Springs, chasing his brothers through MamaCee's garden. It was in that garden and in the field beyond that he learned he could run fast and throw a football further than most boys his age and even his older brothers. At times, he longed for MamaCee's dirty white five-room clapboard house, sitting under a sky of the purest blue and protected by trees that struggled to produce a few feet of shade during the summer. He missed the front porch, which always seemed drenched in some type of divine sunlight, with its swinging bench and MamaCee's spit cup resting beneath her favorite rust-colored lawn chair. The cup stayed there even after MamaCee had given up dipping snuff.

"She dead," MamaCee said calmly.

"What?" Zurich quizzed. Did she say this lady he couldn't remember was dead?

"She dead," MamaCee repeated.

"Who's dead?"

"Baby, didn't you hear me? Miss Bertha Joy. She dead."

"She died?"

"Dead as that fish I fried last night," MamaCee said. "Miss Mabel Joy been dead for 'bout five years. The mailman found Bertha Joy laid out on the floor of her kitchen. She hadn't been dead long when he found her, 'cause she still had her color. Doctor said she had a stroke. You know she was never the same when she came back from up North. Started drinking, hanging in juke joints, sleeping with anything with three legs. But I don't think she suffered much pain," MamaCee said. She let out a short sigh and continued, "I guess the way she died was just as good as dying in your sleep. You know I have asked the good Lord, if it's His will, that my last days will be my best and that I die in my sleep."

"I'm sorry to hear that," Zurich said. How he loved the stories his grandmother could tell, no matter how long, but he sure didn't like to hear her talk about death so casually.

"Yeah, they gonna have the funeral tomorrow evening down at the church. I'm ushering. I hope them kids of hers don't act a fool. Them girls of hers are young, but they some big heifers and you know how we can act at funerals. It don't matter if we like the folks or not. I hope y'all don't be actin' no fools when I've gon' on to glory." She paused for a moment, as if she was taking a minute of silent prayer that her family would behave without her. After a moment, she remembered Zurich was the one who called, not her.

"What news you got for me? That team you playin' for treatin' you right? 'Cause if they ain't, you tell them don't make your grandma charter a plane up there to git them straight," MamaCee joked. It didn't matter that MamaCee had never been on a plane of any kind and had turned down every opportunity her children and grandchildren had offered to fly her anywhere.

"You don't have to do that, MamaCee. Matter of fact, I got some great news today," Zurich said. At last.

"What's your big news, baby?"

"I'm starting against the Bears," Zurich said proudly.

"That's wonderful, baby. Even though I don't like my baby playing that brutal he-man game, I'm happy for you. Who are the Bears? I bet they're paying you a nice chunk of change for that . . . huh, baby?"

"The Bears are Chicago's other professional football team and yes, I'm doing all right," Zurich said, remembering the bonus in his six-figure contract if he started an exhibition game and another bonus if he started during the regular season.

"You watchin' your money right, baby? Giving your ten percent to the Lord? Can't forget Him. He's brought us from a mighty long way," MamaCee said.

"I'm being real careful. But I've got to run, MamaCee," Zurich said.

"You been praying, baby?" MamaCee asked.

"Every day. First thing in the morning and right before I go to bed," Zurich said.

"That's my baby."

"Well, I've got to run. I love you, MamaCee."

"And I love you, too, baby. Have you talked to your daddy? I haven't talked to him in 'bout a month. Every time I call down there I get that answering contraption. What 'bout your brothers. You talked to your brothers?" she asked.

"No, ma'am, I haven't talked with my brothers. I've been real busy with practice. Did you leave a message for my dad? I just tried calling him," Zurich said.

"Naw, I don't like talkin' into that mess," MamaCee said.

"If I talk with him soon, I'll tell him to give you a call."

"Okay. But tell him not to call tomorrow. I'll be at the funeral.

And then I'm going to take a case of Co-Cola over to Bertha Joy's house. Maybe I should make some tater salad and take that over there too. I know it won't go to waste. They may be in grief but them heifers still like to eat."

"You do that, MamaCee. Please give the family my regards. Tell them I'll be praying for them," Zurich said.

"See, I knew you 'member Bertha Joy," MamaCee laughed.

"I love you, MamaCee. Bye."

"Bye, baby."

Zurich looked at his watch and raced back to the locker room where he saw a couple of players getting taped by trainers and a few others sitting in the whirlpool. He tried to identify a friendly face with whom he could share his good news. Mark Traylor, a huge offensive lineman with golden blond hair and crooked teeth, walked up and patted Zurich on his shoulders. "What's up, Z-man? How's my favorite rookie doing?"

"Mark, guess what? I'm starting against the Bears," Zurich said.

"Get the fuck outta here. That's great, man! Cool. Yeah, that's real cool." He gave Zurich a powerful embrace, which startled him. Pleased at Mark's affection, Zurich stood stiffly in front of his locker, as several of his teammates started congregating around Zurich, patting him on his shoulders and butt, and offering their congratulations. For the first time the Cougars' locker room was festive. The team was 0–3 in their first exhibition season, and football pundits had not expected them to win any games against established NFL teams, though they had surprised people when they actually came close to winning their second game against San Diego in overtime. Zurich had played a few downs in each of the losses, but didn't really feel as if he was making a contribution to the team.

Chicagoans were excited to have two professional teams like rival New York City. The NFL had surprised everyone when it awarded Second City the franchise over Memphis and St. Louis. Even more surprising, the city and the Chicago Bears' management had agreed to let the team share Soldier Field with the Bears until a new stadium was built on the city's North Side, facing Lake Michigan. The first game between the soon-to-be city rivals was the hottest ticket in town and had been sold out for over a year. Scalpers were selling tickets for no less than two hundred dollars apiece. There was even talk that the

NFL commissioner was going to attend, which was unheard of for a preseason exhibition game. It was also going to be shown nationwide by ABC, with its regular Monday night crew announcing the game.

"With you starting, maybe we'll have a chance against those punk-ass Bears," said Mario Hunter, the team's first-round draft pick from the University of Michigan. Mario and Zuri had been friends since their first meeting at a high school all-star football camp before their senior year. Zurich had tried to convince Mario to attend his alma mater, Southern Florida Tech, a small Division II black college in south Florida, but Mario had decided on Michigan. Zurich, too, had been recruited by some of the country's top universities, including Michigan and Florida State, but none of them could promise he would play quarterback.

"Thanks, Mario. You think I'm up to it?"

"Do I think you're up to it? Man, don't worry 'bout what I think. 'Cause you know what I think. You the man . . . my dog. Now gimme some love," he smiled as he moved toward Zurich.

Zurich gave Mario a bear hug and turned to see Craig Vincent walking toward them. A tall and gangly white guy with brilliant red hair, Craig had started in all three of the Cougars' preseason games. He had been in the NFL as backup quarterback for the Dallas Cowboys for four years and was expected by everyone to be the Cougars' first quarterback. He had not started the season off that great, but no one put the blame on him, especially since the Cougars' offensive line was inexperienced even by college standards. He had not been that talkative with Zurich on the field during practice or in team meetings. As a matter of fact, Zurich could count the words they had exchanged on one hand. Craig was from Miami, and he and Zurich had been rivals in high school. Zurich was All-City in Tampa, while Craig was All-City in the greater Miami area. Craig went on to become the starting quarterback for the University of Florida during his sophomore year and had led the Gators to two Sugar Bowl victories. Named All-SEC quarterback in his junior year, Craig had finished in the top five in the Heisman Trophy voting. It was Craig who was drafted in the first round, with a million-dollar signing bonus. Zurich was left with nothing but impressive statistics. Despite losing only once as a starter while in college, Zurich was ignored by the NFL in the draft. Several teams had encouraged him to go the free agent route if he was willing to try another position, like wide receiver or free safety. Pro scouts often commented that with his speed and that chiseled six-four, two-hundred-and-twenty-five-pound body he could play many positions in the NFL, just not quarterback.

Zurich realized professional sports had an unwritten racial code. They justified their racism by pointing out the many blacks hired in other positions and how well paid they were. When it came to quarterbacks, blacks who had led their teams to victory in high school and college suddenly had their intelligence challenged. Then there was the dubious question of whether the fans would accept a black quarterback. Athletic ability versus strategic skill hovered over any young black man who aspired to play quarterback on the professional level. Black NFL quarterbacks like Warren Moon and Rodney Peete were the exception. Black quarterbacks in the NFL were still as rare as black players in the National Hockey League.

Zurich ignored the advice and subtle racism of NFL coaches and stayed an extra year at Southern Florida Tech, taking classes and assisting the coaching staff while working out daily and honing his already impressive skills. He also managed to get his degree in Communications and made the dean's list every semester. When Zurich graduated and the NFL was still unimpressed, he headed to Canada, where he led Montreal to two Grey Cup Championships. And now, it all seemed to be coming together.

"Congratulations, Zurich," the white quarterback said stoically.

"Thanks, Craig," Zurich replied.

"But don't get too comfortable 'cause I'm right behind you."

"That's fine. I welcome the challenge," Zurich said.

"We will see," Craig said with a slight edge.

"Come on, Gee, let's go celebrate with some brews," Mario said.

"I'll buy," Zurich said.

"Cool. We can get you some milk or Kool-Aid or whatever it is your square ass drinks. I might even arrange to get your timid ass some pussy," Mario said.

Zurich looked at Mario and shook his head, but he was used to the constant ribbing about his clean lifestyle. Zurich reached into his locker for the keys to his rental car and noticed Craig sitting alone at the opposite end of the locker room. Craig stood up, ripped off his mesh practice jersey, slammed his fist against the metal lockers, and yelled, "Oh, fuck."

As happy as he was, Zurich empathized with Craig. He knew how it felt to be rejected by a team. Zurich removed the coach's note from his locker and briefly considered sharing his feelings with Craig, but he realized maybe now was not the best time. He tucked the note in his wallet to save and show to his father, and walked briskly out of the locker room and into the brilliant sunlight.

CHAPTER 2

I SHALL NOT BE MOVED

Tamela Coleman had some major decisions to make regarding her personal and professional life, but she decided to start with a minor one. On the last Friday in August, she broke a precedent for her five-year legal career. She did not show up at her office nor did she call in sick or inform her secretary she was taking a personal day.

Instead, Tamela muted the ringer on the phone, turned down her answering machine so low she couldn't hear incoming calls, and with a feeling of pure defiance laid her uncombed head against six fluffy pillows on her king-sized bed for her first annual "I've Had It Up to Here Day."

When the "Today" show ended, Tamela used her remote control to switch to Chicago's own "Oprah Winfrey Show." Miss Oprah was looking good, Tamela thought as she reached under the covers to see how much fat she could grab on her own hips. She stopped before her hands touched her skin. No, she was not going to worry about her weight today, as she did on occasion. Besides, her refrigerator was filled with ice cream, half a chocolate cheesecake, fresh fruit, and leftover hamburger pizza, all of which she planned to devour during the day.

Tamela's hips were rounder than those of the models she saw on television and in fashion magazines. She knew they could be reduced a little without harm to her supple, sistah girl figure, which she assumed was about twelve pounds too much for her five-six frame. But she refused to allow thoughts of health club and StairMaster to spoil her day.

Tamela was a subtle, almond-colored beauty, with intense brown eyes, high cheekbones, and full lips. She changed her hairstyles with the seasons. Summer found her hair swept into a sophisticated french twist. Fall would be dangling curls.

She had a wicked sense of humor, with a tongue to match, but very few people were aware of her acid wit. The good girl in her didn't want to hurt other people's feelings. Sometimes in conferences with clients, especially those talking about how much wealth they had, she would have a concerned, interested look on her face, but in her head she would be thinking, *Bitch, don't nobody care how much money you got.*

In the overcast of the morning, Tamela settled into her comfortable bed and surrendered herself to her thoughts, soothed by her bedroom's pastel haze, which she had proudly painted herself. Her favorite childhood dolls and stuffed animals watched her from an old-fashioned overstuffed chair, as she lazed through the morning with the craziness of the guests on Montel, Sally, Rolonda, and Ricki. So this is what went on during the day, and where did they find these fools, Tamela thought. And why did the majority of them have to be black? "Telling all their business like somebody cares," Tamela said, laughing out loud at some of the antics of the guests. She could not believe one young black girl with blond hair would let a talk show put her name up on the screen over the words Self-Proclaimed Mall Whore. When an older black woman from the audience asked the teenager how could she be on television talking about going to malls and picking up men to have sex, the young lady told her, "You need to sit down and mind your own business. How can you be on TV lookin' like a box of Fruit Loops?" The audience hooted and hollered in support of the fast-talking young lady.

In the afternoon, Tamela flipped by the soap operas because she didn't dare become hooked on "All My Children" again. When she'd been an undergrad, she'd almost failed her biology lab class because it was at the same time as her soap. So Tamela put the television on mute and began to read from cover to cover all the magazines she only thumbed through during visits to the bathroom. Later she picked up the Walkman resting on her nightstand and listened to the last of

Ruby Dee's narration of Zora Neale Hurston's *Their Eyes Were Watching God.*

Afterward, while savoring the comfort of her bed and half asleep, Tamela suddenly sat up straight. What if her superiors decided to fire her for taking the day off without telling anyone? Maybe she would beat them to the punch and walk in the office Monday morning, dressed to impress, and hand them a letter of resignation. For months she had been unhappy with her position at MacDonald, Fisher, and Jackson. She had dreamed of a private practice since her first day of law school, but always came up with more reasons why she shouldn't than why she should strike out on her own.

What would their reaction be? Would they be pleased or would they be concerned about how they were going to replace a double minority?

Five years ago she had joined the prestigious firm with high hopes. After finishing in the top quarter of her class at Northwestern Law School, Tamela had done the unthinkable at MacDonald, Fisher, and Jackson when she failed the Illinois bar exam twice. It did not seem to matter that she scored the fourth-highest grade after she passed on her third try. The firm usually made a big deal when associates scored in the top five on the test, but in Tamela's case, they simply seemed relieved that she had finally passed.

Failing the bar had surprised everyone who knew Tamela and it had left her in a state of shock. Tamela had graduated from Southern University magna cum laude with a dual degree in Political Science and English. She had always done well on standardized tests, but she had psyched herself out on her first attempts at the bar by a recurring dream that had started weeks before the exam.

In the dream a heavyset white man with long white hair was sitting at a large bench with a gavel in his hand. Tamela gave him her completed bar exam and without even looking at it, the man started laughing and pounding a large gavel across her exam.

She didn't understand the dream and couldn't get it out of her mind during the second time she took the exam. When she told Desiree Brown, her triple G—(good-good-girlfriend)—about her dream, Desiree had advised, "Girl, you need to forget about that dream and go in there and kick ass and take names, like I know you can." There were no dreams before Tamela's third try.

Still, she knew that in the minds of the partners and other associates, Tamela Coleman didn't have the right stuff to become a member of Chicago's legal elite. She feared it was only a matter of time before they informed her of that fact.

She had chosen the firm because it was one of the few large practices that had not only another minority woman, an Asian-American, but a black partner as well. Never mind that Tim Franklin was a black Republican who was clueless when it came to his racial heritage. A Yale Law School grad, Tim was constantly embarrassing the few blacks employed by the firm, mostly paralegals, secretaries, and mailroom clerks. Tim would comment on their clothes and was fond of saying, "Excuse me," at the top of his lungs when they used what he considered substandard language. To make matters worse, he only did this when white associates were in earshot of his reprimands. Once, when a couple of white partners were close by, he said to Bettye, one of the senior and most popular black secretaries, "It's a shame you didn't take English as a Second Language while you were in high school." He pulled stunts like that on almost every black person working at the office, except, of course, Tamela, who had given him a *don't-go-there* look the moment he fixed his mouth to comment on one of her new braided hairstyles.

There were other reasons Tim didn't come after her. In her first six months at the firm, Tamela had made the error of dating Tim for a short period. Huge mistake. She almost laughed out loud the first time she saw his chubby body in boxer shorts. He strutted around her bedroom with knock knees and titties bigger than her own. Throw in his IBM (itty bitty meat), and Tamela felt as if she were with a woman while he grunted and flapped on top of her. This educated Negro couldn't even grind good. Initially, Tamela was attracted to him because he was so damn smart when it came to the law, but she soon learned he had no common sense. Her father used to say all the time, "You can have all the book sense in the world, but it don't mean jack if you ain't got common sense." At times she wanted to just haul off and pimp-slap him when he started talking Republican nonsense and bragging about his boy Clarence Thomas, make that Justice Clarence Thomas. She made a point of reminding him she still had her I Believe Anita buttons.

He didn't protest when she suggested that their dating was not such a good idea with him being a senior partner and especially in their field, with the constant worry about sexual harassment claims. Tamela figured he had some white woman stashed away in his Gold Coast condo, since he had never invited her there during the three months they dated. Their misguided attempts at sex had always occurred at Tamela's apartment. She found herself pleased at the possibility of some white woman having to put up with Tim's dumb shit. Regardless of their personal relationship, however, Tamela still respected Tim's skills as a lawyer.

After a day of mindless talk shows, Tamela went to her bathroom to draw water for a soothing evening bubble bath, complete with candles. As Tamela relaxed in the warm bath, her thoughts went from her possible resignation, her own practice, and finances, to the absence of a decent male companion. She leaned back in the water, and drank some wine, relaxing as a warm buzz spread through her body. Tamela had enough in her checking, savings, and money market accounts to last maybe four months before she would have to consider moving back to her parents' Hyde Park home. Her only major expense besides rent and her student loans was her Marshall Field's account. Moving back home would not be that bad since her mother, Blanche, was her best friend and her daddy, Henry, was the most remarkable man she had ever known. To the best of her knowledge he had been a faithful husband to her mother for over thirty-five years and had been a wonderful father to Tamela and her brother, Hank Junior.

But what about her sex life? That probably wouldn't be a major problem since Tamela had decided two years ago to remain celibate until she found the right man. All the STD's floating around and the threat of AIDS scared the hell out of her. She had never had sex in her parents' home and since she was very vocal during sex, Tamela couldn't foresee doing the *nasty* there. Besides, along with a clean bill of health and condoms, Tamela wanted a man with his own place. Men who lived with their folks or who boasted of their permanent potential or protested using a condom didn't get far with Tamela Faye.

But Tamela was getting ahead of herself. One day off wouldn't solve the shortage of black men, so maybe she should concentrate on making sure she had money in the bank. There were still a number of medium to small firms interested in her services, although as she had said to Desiree, she didn't want to have to get used to some new white folks or stuck-up black folks for that matter. If she made a move then it would be to her own suite of offices. Even though Tamela hadn't discussed opening her own practice in detail with her parents, she knew she could count on their support.

Blanche had wanted to be a lawyer but settled for a career in teaching when she married a month after graduation from college. She taught English at Southside High, one of Chicago's most danger-ous high schools. But nobody messed with Blanche because they knew her husband and her massively built son were just minutes away, coaching the Washington High football team. She was elated when her firstborn decided on a career in the legal field, instead of becoming a starving artist, painting, or attempting to write the great American novel.

Tamela had to decide what she was going to tell her parents about wanting to quit such a good paying job. Well, she thought, the truth might work. Her parents could always tell when she and her brother were skirting the truth. She would tell them how the firm showed her no respect and treated her like a first-year associate.

Most of her time was spent on what Tamela referred to as shit work—the few personal-injury cases the firm took, trust accounts, and probate work for the firm's pampered clients. These clients were usually rich, old, gray-headed white ladies whom none of the men wanted to work with. The assignments were always very tedious and required a lot of paperwork, but very little court time, and Tamela loved her moments in court. One of her lead cases had involved repre-senting a prominent African-American woman suing a white fran-chise beauty salon for damaging her hair when they left a relaxer in too long. The partners assigned her the case when she mentioned in the staff meeting that she, too, had experienced problems with the product in question. After only two meetings with the attorneys rep-resenting the salon and hair care company, Tamela was able to re-solve the woman's case for a nice six-figure settlement. She took a little extra pleasure in the fact that it wasn't a black-owned hair care company, but a white counterpart trying to exploit the lucrative black hair care market.

But after that settlement, it was back to the ladies, wills, and paperwork. The only cases that brought her in front of a judge were the many pro bono cases she handled from the overworked Legal Aid Society or the legal assistance Tamela provided for members of her church who couldn't afford an attorney. Most of these cases were criminal matters, and Tamela loved the challenge and rewards they provided. These cases made her feel as if she were making a contribution to her community.

She was confident that her parents would understand her thinking and feel that she was making the right decision by leaving. The thought of having their daughter at home in this dangerous city would also influence their support. Even though she was thirty years old, her father called her almost every night after the news to make sure that she was safe. He would always say something like, "I just got through watching the news and saw where this girl had been raped. I just wanted to make sure that my pumpkin was all right."

After her bath, Tamela brushed some of the day's food crumbs from the light blue sheets. She arranged the pillows carefully for neck and back support and climbed back into her bed. With her remote, she changed the channel to WGN's "Evening News" with Allison Payne, the beautiful black anchorwoman whom both her daddy and brother had secret crushes on. Reminded of her father, Tamela reached for the phone and hit the speed dial button for her parents' home.

"Hello, Coleman residence," Tamela's mother said.

"Hey, woman. What'cha doing?" Tamela said.

"Hey, baby. I was just thinking about you," Blanche said.

"Something good I hope," Tamela said.

"Of course. How was your day?"

"Just wonderful," Tamela said.

"Oh. What happened? Something good at work?"

"No. Nothing happened. I didn't go to work. Matter fact, Mama, I didn't leave my apartment today and it was wonderful."

"What? You're not sick, are you?" Blanche asked, concerned with her little girl's health.

"Naw, Ma. I just needed a day to make some decisions about my life. What I'm doing with my life and where I'm going," Tamela said.

"Oh, baby, you've got the rest of your life."

"Not really. You've forgotten that your baby girl turned thirty this year," Tamela said.

"You're still a baby. So did you come to any conclusions?"

"I think so. But I want to talk with you and Daddy about them. Is he there?"

"No. He and Hank Junior went bowling," Blanche said.

"You mean Daddy and Hankie are missing their girlfriend Allison on the news?"

"Oh no, your daddy got me taping the news. I was expecting him back by now. He didn't even eat dinner and you know he will want me to fix him something when he comes in. And he will want me to sit there and watch him eat every bit. I certainly have spoiled that old man," Blanche laughed.

"And you love it," Tamela added.

"You think so? Well, I guess you're right. You want us to call you when he comes in?"

"Naw, Ma. It can wait," Tamela said.

"You sure?"

"I'm sure. I love you. Tell Daddy I called and that I love him," Tamela said softly.

"We love you, too, darling. And whatever decisions you make, you know your daddy and I will support you. We are very proud of you," Blanche said.

"I'm going to hold you to that. Night, Ma."

"Sleep tight, baby. Don't let the bedbugs bite. Oh, baby, I forgot I needed to ask you something," Blanche said.

"What's that Ma?"

"You remember Dora Lee Morris?"

"Dora Lee? No, what about her?"

"Remember, she used to teach Sunday school with me," Blanche said.

"Naw, come on, Ma, don't go there," Tamela said.

"Go where?" Blanche laughed.

"Don't give me Dora Lee's history. Net it out. Why did you ask me if I knew her?"

"Her son, Pede, is in trouble and she asked me at church if you could help out. They don't have much money," Blanche said.

"What kind of trouble is he in?"

"Well, he slapped his girlfriend and the DA is talking about prosecuting him for assault. Pede is a good kid, only sixteen, and his mother is worried about him going to jail and having a record," Blanche said.

"How did the DA get involved in a slapping?"

"One of the teachers reported it and then the principal demanded that the police come to the school and arrest Pede."

"It sounds like he not only needs a lawyer, but some counseling too," Tamela said.

"Yes, I feel the same way. But he's really a good kid; it just seems like to me the DA is overreacting. The girl doesn't even want to press charges."

"I don't know what I can do, besides calling over to the DA's office and seeing who's handling the case. I could talk with, what's her name, Dora Lee?"

"Yes, Dora Lee Morris."

"I'll talk with Mrs. Morris and her son, if we can agree that he's going into some type of counseling. These young boys have to realize they just can't go around slapping people," Tamela said.

"You're absolutely right. I will call Dora Lee tomorrow. Is it okay if I give her your number at the office?"

"Sure, Ma, that will be fine. All right, it's bedtime. I love you," Tamela said.

"Thanks, baby. Expect Dora Lee's call. I love you."

When Tamela hung up the phone she felt an overwhelming sense of serenity. It had been a perfect day. No matter what decisions she made, life, like the day, would be blessed.

CHAPTER 3

PEOPLE AND PREACHERS

"I *believe* in God. It's preachers and people I don't believe in. That's who I have a problem with," Sean said.

"But come on. Just come once. Give my church a chance. It's different. Trust me," Anja pleaded.

"Your church . . . do they have a preacher?"

"Yes, dufus. You know the guy I'm dating, Reverend Wilder. He's great!"

"First of all I'd be nervous 'bout a dating preacher. But that's a whole other conversation. They do have people at your church, right? People as in ushers who roll their eyes at you when you don't want to sit in the tight-fitting pews they point you to? People as in deacons who are always begging for money like ugly men beg for pussy, and people in choir robes who jump up shouting and waving every time your Reverend Wilder says something negative about certain groups? People as in members whose mission is to get heaven to keep other people out?"

"What's your point, little brother?"

"My point, big sister by only two weeks, is that I know you mean well, but I have had my fill of organized religion. Let's not talk about this anymore. Okay, baby?"

"Can we at least pray over the phone before you hang up on me?" Anja asked.

"Sure we can, but it will have to wait until tomorrow."

"Why, may I ask, Sean?"

" 'Cause someone is knocking at my door," Sean lied.

"I'll pray for you."

"Good, then I'm covered. Got to go. Peace out, my sweet sister."

Somewhat troubled by the conversation with his sister, Sean hung up the phone and spread himself over the plaid sofa under a hanging lamp, one hand on his exposed stomach, the other nursing a luke-warm beer. He wanted to take a nap so he set the bottle on the hardwood floor, crossed his legs, and nestled his head in his hands behind his neck. Sean couldn't fall asleep. He opened his eyes and stared at the cream-colored ceiling, listening to the sounds of the city coming from his open window. Though it was one of summer's last humid days, the large room was cool, flooded in a gentle breeze, aided by a small portable fan.

Sean's midtown Manhattan studio apartment was untidy. The sign of a brilliant writer, he told himself. With a name like T. S. Elliott, he was destined to become a writer. Even though he spelled his surname differently from the famous poet's, he had on occasion written poetry, but he made his living writing about arrogant and overpaid athletes. The curtainless windows were dusty, the floor un-swept, and stacks of books and old magazines filled each corner. Empty beer bottles and dirty clothes littered the floor. He started halfheartedly to get up and straighten the place, but decided he could better use this time to map out a strategy for finding work. When drowsiness clouded his thoughts, he decided that maybe a short nap would give him the extra energy he needed to plan out the next cou-ple of months.

Sean was not your typical unemployed black man. He chose not to be on the payroll of a large organization. A year ago, he had left a good paying job as a senior sportswriter at the conservative-minded *Atlanta Chronicle* to take a chance in New York City. He was drawn by the lure of lucrative freelance assignments, problems with his prior position, and the chance to be close to his half-sister Anja and nine-year-old nephew, Gerald. He had plenty of freelance articles lined up when he moved to New York City, but the baseball strike had erased some of his richest possibilities. At first he didn't mind because, though he loved baseball and had played himself for a year in college, Sean found the players extremely boring. The Age of Athletic Arrogance he liked to call the current professional sports climate. A group of clueless prima donnas who put their own goals above their teams and the sports they played.

During his down time, Sean had found a New York literary agent and written a book proposal on racism in professional sports management. It was not the book he wanted to write, but his agent had convinced him that such a book was a potential best-seller. And Sean was about making money. He had developed friendships with several professional players in the hope of one day ghost writing one of those premature, quick-to-the-press memoirs that publishers sometimes churned out.

In many ways, Sean was relieved that fall and football were approaching. He knew his phone would begin to ring off the hook with assignments—or at least he hoped so. Even though he liked New York City, he was ready to visit other great cities and spend nights in hotels much nicer than his Tenth Avenue walk-up apartment. For the right assignment, he was even willing to return to his hometown of Decatur, near Atlanta. Decatur stirred up many memories for Sean, both good and bad, but recently, every time he thought of his hometown, he obsessed over the bad memories.

After six years of award-winning work, Sean had resigned from his newspaper job there when a promised column of his own failed to materialize. The paper's management made feeble attempts to keep him, assigning interns and cub reporters to work under him. But, when they failed to give him a definite timetable for a column, Sean decided it was time to leave. He just could not understand why his editors had failed to see the merits of such a column, a column he had wanted to write since he was a freshman at University of Georgia's School of Journalism. Editors at the paper said they didn't understand Sean's constant complaining and explained that they only had room for the two sports columnists who had been at the paper for decades. They pointed out that Sean had one of the most coveted beats, covering the Atlanta Falcons, as well as the Atlanta Braves, the hottest team in Atlanta.

But a column would give Sean an opportunity to explore important issues that the two other columnists never addressed, like institutional racism, and the images of African-American athletes, the good and bad. He knew that people in decision-making positions in the sports world read columns, while hardly noticing regular coverage. They only cared that articles reported the scores right and spelled their names and those of their star players correctly.

The *Chronicle*'s rival newspaper, the liberal and larger *Atlanta Journal-Constitution*, employed two widely read and respected African-American sports columnists, and the few times the *Chronicle* had let Sean write columns, the paper's fax machine and mailroom were swamped with praise. Of course, the *Chronicle* never knew that much of the praise came from Sean's friends. Even so, the letters and faxes didn't seem to help. Ironically, when the O. J. Simpson case began to dominate the op-ed and sports pages, Sean's former editor called and offered big money for him to become a guest columnist covering the Simpson trial. They felt it would make more sense for an African-American to write a biweekly column on the highly sensitive and racially charged trial. Sean declined. He also declined to write columns about Mike Tyson and the burning of football player Andre Rison's country club mansion, a fire started allegedly by his rap-singer girlfriend. Sean felt very strongly about the image of black men in the media, and was a card-carrying member of the Please Don't Let Him Be Black Club, when bad things happened. He worried that if he stated the sometimes obvious, that some black sports heroes did bad things, black athletes and the black community would shun him. He didn't want to be labeled an Uncle Tom like other African-American journalists who wrote pieces going against the community. Once, while in college, Sean had written a piece on several star black athletes involved in pulling a sexual train on a black female student. It was almost a year before any of the black players would speak to him again. Although the article put Sean in a difficult position with his peers, he felt that as a minority journalist he had to report the rape. He knew that black-on-black crime, especially violations against women, couldn't be ignored. He felt that the same story in the hands of a white reporter would sidestep that issue, and instead blame the incident on all black athletes in one fell swoop.

While Sean had not decided on the guilt or innocence of Simpson, he had other reasons for not joining in the circus of Simpson commentary. Sean knew professional athletes could become violent when the cheering stopped. His own father, Travis Senior, had beaten Sean's mother, Laura, often, when an injury prematurely ended his potential Hall of Fame baseball career. Unable to play, his father started to drink heavily and dabble in drugs. Many times Sean and his older brother, Travis Junior, had had to pull their father off their mother, wash him up, and put him to bed.

It was during the height of his career that Travis Senior met Beverly Watson in New York City. Travis had to be in New York City several times a year to play ball and an extramarital affair quickly developed. Travis and Beverly were expecting the birth of their daughter at the same time Travis and Laura were anticipating the birth of their second son. Anja was born in New York's Harlem Hospital two weeks before Sean was born in Atlanta's Grady Hospital.

It was ten years before Sean, his brother, and his mother found out about Anja. Sean would never forget the look on his mother's face when Beverly showed up drunk at their home, nor would he forget the beating his father gave Laura when she dared question his morals.

Anja did not accompany her mother down South, but Sean saw the picture of his half-sister Beverly had left with Laura. From the photo Sean could see they shared the same smooth cinnamon skin color, golden brown eyes the color of brandy, high arching eyebrows, and a toothpick-sized gap when they smiled.

After decades of putting up with countless affairs and abuse, his mother finally divorced his father when Sean finished high school. Her leaving forced Sean's father to finally get himself together with drug and alcohol treatment and therapy. Recently, his parents, who had somehow remained friends, had started dating again. Sean's father had had no further contact with Beverly, who, Sean later learned from Anja, was also addicted to drugs and alcohol. Sean and his brother were hopeful their parents' rekindled affair would lead to remarriage. Despite their father's previous problems, Sean and Travis Junior loved their father and believed that he had changed. But Sean would never forget those violent nights during his youth. So while he despised the attention men like Mike Tyson received, he was relieved it brought attention to a problem he had experienced firsthand. He wanted to believe there was always some good hidden in evil.

While a teenager, Sean vowed never to hit another person in his life. This created problems when his older brother used to hit him if Sean beat him in basketball, and when his peers wanted to display their manhood with their fists instead of their playground finesse. These memories convinced Sean to play baseball because it was not as physical as basketball and football.

When they were teenagers, Anja wrote to Sean and they became pen pals, writing each other at least once a month, exchanging school photos and poetry they had written. Through Sean, Anja was able to collect bits of information about the father she had never known, much to the dismay of Sean's mother. It was only in recent years that his mother would even say Anja's name.

They finally met face to face during Sean's first visit to New York his sophomore year of college. They were amazed at how much they had in common. Anja and Sean both wanted to become writers, they both loved sports and read and collected baseball cards and *Archie* comic books.

While Sean followed his boyhood aspirations, his sister's dreams were sidetracked by the birth of her child during her junior year at Hunter College. She and Gerald now lived in Brooklyn, though Anja worked in Manhattan as a customer service supervisor at Chase Manhattan Bank. She took writing classes at the Learning Annex when time and budget allowed.

Six months after Sean moved to New York, Anja began dating the Reverend Theodis Wilder. She had seemingly dedicated her life to the Reverend and his nondenominational church. While Sean was happy with his sister's apparent religious bliss, his attitude toward organized religion was definitely, "Been there, done that, got the soundtrack."

Sean opened his eyes from a two-hour nap to find evening had fallen. Rubbing his eyes and wiping tiny beads of perspiration from his upper lip, he noticed a picture of a smiling Anja and Gerald on his desk. Maybe he had been too tough on his sister, he thought. She was only trying to help. Sean got up from the sofa, popped in a Phyllis Hyman CD, and went into the kitchen and poured a big bowl of Frosted Flakes. While eating the cereal, he leaned his back against the sink and moved his head with the music. The CD was a gift from Anja and his thoughts moved from the tasty cereal and music to his sister. He placed the empty bowl in the sink, reached for his phone, and dialed Anja's number, but after several rings, her answering machine came on and informed callers that she was at prayer meeting at

Brooklyn Eastern Church. The message ended by inviting callers to join her and the Reverend Wilder.

Sean smiled to himself as he hung up without leaving a message. He had a meeting to go to himself, where there was a different kind of praying going on.

CHAPTER 4

Am I Black Enuff for Ya?

The ivory silk nightgown dropped smoothly and swiftly to Mia Miller's ankles. She stepped out of the gown and into her glass-enclosed shower, where the heat and water pulsated in a steamy mix. Mia was savoring her time in the shower so much that she washed her chestnut brown hair three times with strawberry-scented shampoo. She covered her body with an almond bath scrub and backed up against the wall, using her hands to shield the water occasionally and then stepping directly under it to feel the force of the shower as it rinsed away the granular substance.

This was a big day for Mia, and she wanted to enjoy every single moment. Today she would appear with the Channel 3 FiveAlive anchor team as the first African-American female sportscaster at the Chicago Fox affiliate. Mia had joined the station two years prior, as the substitute sportscaster and host of "Mornings with Mia," a talk and news show that required her to report to work at 5 A.M. With her new position, Mia was not due at the station until 3 P.M. unless there was some major sports story breaking.

After her shower, Mia blow-dried her hair. When she saw that it was only 6:15 A.M., Mia thought about climbing back into bed, but she was wired. Her body clock hadn't adjusted to her new schedule, so she went downstairs to the kitchen of her townhouse and heated water for a cup of herbal tea. She looked in her refrigerator and pulled out a plastic bag containing a day-old bagel. Noticing a half-empty bottle of Mumm's champagne, she decided to make a mimosa to celebrate her new job. Mia put the bagel in the small toaster oven and reached into the freezer for some concentrated orange juice. The can was covered with icebox frost, so she slipped it under warm water to speed up the melting process. She poured the champagne into a large black coffee mug and took a gulp to see if it still tasted as good as it had the evening before. It did.

Mia took a seat on a metal stool and gave herself a big hug. She was so happy with her new position that she wanted the rest of Chicago to wake up and join in her joy. Her promotion to the main sports anchor was unexpected to many people at the station. But not to Mia, who was not a bit surprised. When the station's regular five o'clock man, Jonathan Nelson, had been offered a position with the new Fox football pregame show, the station's general manager brought in five different candidates for the slot, all men and all white. Mia had started kissing up to Helen, the general manager's secretary, while the interviews were taking place, sending her catered lunches and flowers. Helen kept Mia posted on the potential candidates, and even slipped Mia copies of some of their audition tapes. After viewing the tapes, Mia became even more confident that her time had come. When the GM had called Mia into his office two weeks ago, she'd wanted to shout what took you so long, but instead she acted shocked and even shed a few tears. She thought they were happy with her work, but in television you could never be sure. Electronic media personalities were subject to Q ratings and invisible Nielsen families who decided who got to keep their jobs and who might consider career changes.

Nevertheless, Mia knew people were watching her and enjoyed what she was doing. People stopped her in the local market, at the coffee shop where she read her newspaper and took notes for story ideas. Even though she enjoyed the attention, like school age autograph seekers, there were times when she resented the intrusions, especially when she was out on dates or makeup free. She was neither as warm as she appeared on television nor as cold as some of her former classmates thought. Despite working in a city where national talk show hosts, aside from media mogul Oprah, were almost as common as store clerks, local newscasters still had their fans.

As much as Mia loved Chicago, she had visions of bigger opportunities. She planned to be the first black female national sportscaster since Jayne Kennedy. People had often told her she looked like the younger, pre-marriage and -childbearing Kennedy, which she considered a compliment, but she certainly didn't see herself ending up doing infomercials for a psychic service. Mia was also quick to point out that she had hazel eyes, tinged with green, while Jayne had plain, though warm, brown eyes.

Mia Renee Miller was a beautiful woman, and she had the pictures to prove it lining the walls of her two-bedroom townhouse. Mia as a homecoming princess . . . Mia at the prom . . . Mia posing with the family dog. Only her parents had more pictures of her. She was tall, slender, and elegant, with a head full of hair. In high school she had made varsity cheerleader two years in a row, not because of her jumping and tumbling abilities, but because, as Mia put it, "I can slang my hair with the best of white girls." She had mixed feelings when people described her as light, bright, damn-near-white, or as one former boyfriend called her, "Mariah Carey lite." Mia often used darker shades of makeup on the air and in public so people would stop asking if she was all black. She recognized the recent trend in dark-skinned beauties in movies and on television, but Mia was not about to let a trend put a roadblock in her plans.

In her new position she would have her own hair and makeup person, and she had her agent make sure it would be a black person, who would understand her special makeup concerns. Mia's agent had negotiated a new six-figure contract, which included a thousand-dollar-a-month clothing allowance, with an out clause that would allow her to leave the station if she were offered a network position, or a job in New York or Los Angeles. After two coffee mugs of champagne, the second with a sip of orange juice, Mia spread apricot jelly over the burned bagel and took a couple of bites before she went upstairs, climbed back into her bed, and turned on her television to see how Shelly Alexander, a cheerful blonde, was doing in her former position. Just as she was lying dreamily on the pillows, the phone rang. This early in the morning Mia knew it could only be one person.

"Hello, Mother," Mia said.

"How did you know it was me?" her mother laughed.

"Who else would be calling me this early?"

"Well, how does Chicago's newest super sportscaster feel?" Emma Miller asked.

"I'm doing okay, but just between me and you I'm kinda nervous," Mia said.

"Oh, that's normal. But remember how well you did in Mississippi. I bet those people at that station are still talking about how great you were," her mother said.

"I guess so," Mia said as she watched Shelly with the mute button on.

"What are you going to wear?"

"I don't know. I'll find something in that closet of mine."

"Something from your closet! No, darling, you have to go out and get something new. I don't care how much it costs. Send your dad and me the bill."

"You don't have to do that, Mother. They gave me a clothing allowance," Mia said.

"Good, then listen to your mother. Go to that store in the Water Tower you like so much and get something jazzy. Where does Oprah Winfrey shop?" Emma asked.

"Anywhere she wants," Mia laughed.

"I know that's right. I knew I should have gotten you something and FedExed it to you. You know we do have some new stores in Dallas that can compete with that stuff you guys have in Chicago. Now don't forget to tape the show tonight, especially the opening when they show you doing your thing and overnight me the tape. Your daddy and I can't wait. We'll add it to our collection."

"I won't forget, Mother. But it's not like you and Dad haven't got enough tapes of me on television. Tapes of me graduating, me playing soccer, me doing ballet."

"We're proud of our daughter. And this is special. You've been talking about this job ever since your first day at Northwestern," Emma said.

"I know, Mother, and thanks for calling, it means a lot to me," Mia said softly.

"Well, I wasn't gonna let this special day come without me being the first one to wish you good luck. You don't have anybody there with you, do you?"

"You're dipping now. But the answer is no. No new prospects," Mia said. She started to inform her mother that getting a man had never been one of her worries.

"Maybe with your new schedule, you'll have time to meet some of those fine Chicago men you used to tell me about," Emma said.

"Maybe. Maybe not. That will have to take care of itself. I gotta go, Mother. I love you and Dad very much."

"And we love you too, baby," her mother replied. "Oh, Mia, before I forget. Derrick called here the other night. He wanted your new number."

"I wonder what he wants?" Mia asked as she looked toward the closet that housed audition tapes, and pictures and letters of former lovers, including Derrick Smith, the Mississippi businessman she had almost married. A month after she had accepted his engagement ring, and after a heavy night of partying, Derrick had slapped Mia across the bedroom when she had refused to participate in anal sex. Mia wanted to make sure that his first slap would be his last, so she filed a police report and had a restraining order issued against him. Derrick had called her day and night crying and begging, promising Mia that nothing like that would ever happen again. She accepted his apology, advised him to get help, and never saw him alone again.

"He said something about being up in Chicago soon and wanting to get ahold of you."

"You didn't give him the number, did you?"

"Oh no, baby. I know better than that. I don't give your number to anyone. Sometimes I will see some of them girls who used to give you such a hard time in high school. They will come over at the beauty shop or mall and say how they heard you were a big television star and do I have your number, just in case they're ever in Chicago. I want to tell them, of course I have her number. I am her mother, you dumb bunnies. But I just smile and ask for their number, explaining that I will let you get in contact with them," Emma said.

"That's good, Mother. That's what you should do. Isn't it time for you to get ready for your day?"

"Yes, darling, it is. Are you trying to get rid of your mother?"

"Of course not, Mother," Mia said.

"Well, bye, Mia."

"Bye, Mother."

Mia hung up the phone and pulled her knees up to her breasts, wrapping her delicate arms around herself. She thought how blessed she was to have her parents. Parents who didn't have to love her but had chosen to after her natural mother had given her up for adoption, just hours after her birth in Dallas. Mia was born in the same Parkland Hospital where President Kennedy had died exactly two weeks later. She never knew why her mother had given her up or who her natural father was, and she had convinced herself that she didn't care. She told herself she wasn't rejected, but wanted. Ellis and Emma Miller told her about her adoption when she was twelve years old, when one of her playmates teased her that she didn't favor her parents, grandparents, or her younger sister, Tanya.

Her parents had even offered to help find her birth parents, but she had declined. Emma had told her that her mother was a teenager when Mia was born, but that was all she knew. Emma and Ellis had decided to adopt when they were told they couldn't have children, but three years after they had brought Mia home, Tanya was born.

Mia and Tanya were close, but they had had their moments of sibling rivalry. When they were teenagers they fought over clothes, telephone time, and the pink Volkswagen their parents had bought for them to share. In recent years they didn't see each other that often. Tanya had moved to Paris to pursue her career as a designer and every now and then Mia would receive letters, clothing, beautiful handmade ribbons, and expensive bottles of French champagnes. Mia, in turn, shipped her sister frozen Chicago pizza, magazines, and videotapes of "Soul Train," as a reminder of their childhood.

After "The Morning Show" and "Oprah," Mia decided to take her mother's advice and spend some money on a new outfit. She put on her gym clothes for a quick workout before heading to the Water Tower shopping center. Just as she was picking up her keys from her dresser, the phone rang again.

"Hello," Mia said.

"LaDonna in the house," Mia's best friend sang into the phone.

"Hey, girl. What are you doing calling me so early? What time is it out there?"

"Oh, child, it's early but I just got in. I went to a sneak preview of this new movie with that fine Allen Payne and Miss Jada whatsherface," LaDonna laughed.

"How was it?"

"Oh, it was all that. Mr. Allen Payne had an ass from heaven, girl."

"You so crazy. Was it work-related?"

"Oh, honey, everything I do out here in La La Land is work-related. I'm trying to get an interview with Allen, but he has this publicist from hell handling the movie. But you know me: I ain't giving up. Are you excited about this evening?"

"Naw, I'm okay. Ain't nothing left but to do it," Mia said casually as she looked at her nails and wondered if a manicure could wait one more day.

"I know that's right. Well, I'm getting ready to go to bed. But I just wanted to let you know that I was thinking about you," LaDonna said.

"I appreciate it, girl. I'm going to the gym, then to shop, and then it's on," Mia said.

"Well, knock 'em on their butts. Bye, M & M," LaDonna said.

"Bye, LaDonna. Thanks for thinking about me."

"Oh, Mia, before I forget. That good-for-nothing Derrick called me at home and at the station, trying to get your number. Said something about a big business deal he was working on in Chicago. I told him I thought you and your new boyfriend were going to be in Europe visiting Tanya."

"Thanks, LaDonna. He called my parents' home, too."

"You know for a brother with all them degrees, Derrick is stupid. If he really wants to get in contact with you, all he has to do is call the station and leave a message for you."

"I know, honey. But that's Derrick. What he's doing is trying to play one of those old, tired-assed mind games. You'll see, he'll put it out in the universe that he's trying to get ahold of me, hoping that I will call him, or that one of my family or friends will tell him that they've talked with me and I would love to talk with him. I'm glad you told him that little lie that I was dating someone."

"Got to look out for my sister. Girl, that bed is calling my name. See ya."

"Bye, LaDonna. I will talk with you later this week."

"Deal," LaDonna said.

Mia picked up her address book and turned to the Smiths. She would call Derrick and tell him that she was going to be out of town and to stop bothering her family and friends. She was also going to ask him what his new fiancée had to say about him trying to contact her. After dialing the area code for Mississippi and the first three digits of Derrick's office number, Mia stopped and hung up the phone. She knew Derrick. He would have some cute little answer that would be an out-and-out lie. This was her day and no one was going to spoil it.

CHAPTER 5

TRADE ALERT

Tamela walked out of the Starbucks near her office with a steaming cup of coffee, no sugar, no cream. Coffee without pretense that would do what she wanted it to do. Wake her up and give her the caffeinated courage to follow her plan. Her situation had changed slightly since her Friday holiday of complete bed rest. There was no letter of resignation in her camel-colored leather briefcase, just a plan of action carefully mapped out on a yellow legal pad.

She had reviewed her options on Saturday night with her parents and her best friend Desiree, a teacher at the Chicago Magnet School for the Arts. Tamela and Desiree had been tight since eighth grade when they both made the B-team cheerleading squad. In high school, they had consoled each other when they failed to make the varsity squad, whose only two black girls were regulation light-skinned. They did make the drill team and Desiree convinced Tamela to run for senior class president, which she did, becoming the first black and first female student to hold the position. It was during her stint as class leader that Tamela first considered the law or politics as possible career choices. Until that point, she figured she would become a schoolteacher like her parents.

Even though they went to different colleges, Tamela to Southern and Desiree to Fisk University, they spent all of their holidays and school breaks together. As adults they had a Sunday ritual of church and then champagne brunch at one of Chicago's fancy hotels along Michigan Avenue, followed by window shopping along Mag Mile. They were members of a black women's literary club and Delta Sigma Theta, which they had both pledged in college, and were now active in the local alumnae chapter.

Both Desiree and Tamela's folks thought Tamela should have a secure job offer or a strategy for opening her own office before turning in her resignation. They agreed she needed to make a change, especially if she was not happy, but the three of them were more practical than Tamela when it came to decisions. "Headstrong," Tamela's mother sometimes called her. They all told her that no matter what she decided they would support her. Desiree even offered her spare bedroom, which was something for her because she loved her privacy. But the two of them had always agreed that rooming together might damage their friendship. Having witnessed several best friends turn mortal enemies after becoming roommates, they didn't want that to happen to their relationship.

Desiree's voice of reason made even more sense when she informed Tamela that she, too, might be out of a job soon. There were serious talks of cutbacks in the school system's budget and her principal had told her that arts programs were at the top of the list when it came to cost-cutting measures. Even if the dance department did survive, there would be no pay increase. Desiree was so worried about her job security that she had spent Sundays combing the Help-Wanted ads and had researched several temp agencies. She had also put out feelers for roommate possibilities just in case Tamela stayed put. Unlike her best friend, Desiree said she would move into a convent or a homeless shelter rather than back home where her mother would constantly nag her about finding a suitable young man to date and eventually marry.

At Trinity United Methodist on Sunday, Tamela had run into Cassandra Crater, another one of her sorority sisters, who was working for a small black law firm on Chicago's South Side. Tamela had recently read an article on the firm in the *Chicago Legal Times,* which sounded as if they were really up and coming. Cassandra told Tamela that they were looking to expand at the beginning of the year and she would love for her to talk with her partners.

While talking with her soror, Tamela thought it might be exciting to work for an all-black firm, but realized it wouldn't be problem-free. If she worked for a predominantly black firm, she wanted it to be a firm she started herself, or one she'd been involved with from the beginning. She thanked her, wished the firm continued success, and promised to keep in touch.

Tamela walked into the huge suite of downtown offices of Mac-Donald, Fisher, and Jackson, smiling and speaking to familiar faces like the maintenance man and the firm's receptionist, Sonia. Instead of going to her office, she headed toward the area where most of the partners' offices were located. As she turned a corner, she bumped into Tim Franklin. Just the man she wanted to see.

"I need to speak with you, Tim," she said boldly.

"We missed you on Friday, Ms. Coleman," he said sarcastically.

"I was taking a personal day," she said.

"Why don't you let us know in advance the next time?" he smiled. "You never know when a big trust or probate client will walk through the doors looking for someone with your skills." Tamela couldn't tell if he was being serious so she looked to see if there was anybody around. She wondered if Tim was the only one who'd missed her since no one from the office had called to check on her whereabouts.

"Oh, you didn't get my message?" Tamela asked innocently. Her tone and arching eyebrows gave away the fact she had not called, but Tim just stood there with a sly smile on his face.

"Maybe I did, maybe I didn't," he answered. "Come on into my office. I have something I need to talk with you about."

Tamela followed him into his office, one of the largest in the firm. A huge maple desk dominated the room, with a mismatched swivel leather chair. During her interview, Tim had told Tamela the desk belonged to his grandfather, one of the first black Republicans in Chicago. His walls were lined with shelves filled with all types of books, both legal and nonlegal, while pictures of Illinois Republican governor Jim Edgar and Justice Clarence Thomas held prominent places on his walls. Tamela didn't sit down, but walked over to the huge window behind Tim's desk. Lake Michigan spread out, gleaming and flat in the morning sun. The dozen or so sailboats that dotted the water looked like miniatures from her lofty perspective.

"Can I say you look nice today or is that considered sexual harassment?" Tim asked.

"You tell me. Isn't that your area of expertise?" Tamela asked.

"Yes, it is, and that depends on how you take the compliment."

Looking down at her well-tailored, blue pinstripe pleated skirt with matching jacket over a collarless silk shirt and simple strand of fake pearls, Tamela replied, "I'll take it in the spirit it was given, so thank you, Mr. Franklin." Tamela played with her pearls as she thought that something was up with Tim. He wanted something, but so did she.

"Let's talk," Tim said.

"What do you want to talk with me about?" Tamela said as she took a seat. For a moment she chose to forget that she needed to talk to him.

"Well, you know I'm a member of BMU, right?"

"Black Men United? Yes, I remember when you joined," Tamela said. Black Men United was a national social and service organization founded in Chicago in the mid-sixties by a group of African-American physicians and lawyers. It was a way to get many black men from different fraternities together for a common cause. Tamela's father had been invited to join the group, but the one-thousand-dollar initiation fee was more than his budget could stand. Nevertheless, he had attended some of their events with his Omega brothers who were in BMU. In recent years the group had made efforts to expand the somewhat elite organization by recruiting more men like Tamela's father and young men graduating from college. Their Boys to Men mentor program had been recognized by former President Bush as one of the Thousand Points of Light, after Tim made someone in the Bush administration aware of this group of well-connected black men.

"Well, we are having our big fund-raiser for the scholarship program at the Swisshôtel this weekend." He paused to gauge Tamela's reaction. "And I've been nominated for president for the next calendar year," he added proudly.

"That's great, Tim, but what has this to do with me?" she asked.

"I know we agreed it might not look good, the two of us dating. But I'm in dire straits here, Tamela, and frankly I need a date. I don't think it would look good me coming alone," he said.

Tamela smiled to herself. Tim was about to ask her out on a date.

Should she go knowing how much she disliked being around him in a social setting, especially a black function where his being a nerd was even more apparent?

"So you need a date, huh." Tamela beat him to the punch. She was smiling on the inside saying to herself, *Naw you ain't asking me out. Where is that white lady you got stashed away?* she wondered.

"Yes, I need a date."

"How bad?" Tamela smiled.

Suddenly Tim's voice sounded shaky and nervous, like a sweaty schoolboy asking the homecoming queen to the prom, when the homecoming queen didn't even know he existed. Tamela quickly decided that she would go, but first she was going to string him along. The BMU was one of the most powerful organizations in Chicago and one of the few all-male organizations besides the fraternities. If nothing else, Tamela would be able to make some valuable connections, both professional and personal. If the truth were told, she and Desiree had already talked about buying the two-hundred-dollar tickets and going without male escorts. Even though they both thought such social events were a bit tedious with all the frontin' that could be expected.

"Yes, I know it's late, but I would forever be in your debt," he said, trying not to stoop to begging.

"What if I'm dating someone?" Tamela asked, playfully.

"I could call him and explain my situation and tell him it's not like a date-date."

"That won't be necessary, Tim. I'm not dating anyone. But before I agree, I have a favor to ask you."

"Shoot," Tim replied, now feeling as if he were on third base with the team's home-run hitter at bat.

"I don't know how aware of this you are, but I'm really concerned about my future here. You guys have only given me what I consider busy work, the shit stuff," she said.

"Tamela, everybody here is pleased with your work. We're always getting great reviews about your work from clients."

"But, Tim, anyone right out of law school could do the probate work and personal injury. I want to work with the big boys," Tamela said.

"What type of cases are you talking about?"

"Well, you know I've been doing a lot of pro bono work over at Legal Aid?"

"Yes. But I thought that was only for six months," Tim said.

"They still needed me when the exchange was over. Which is part of my concern. If you didn't know I was still doing work over there in my spare time, then I know the other partners aren't aware of all the criminal work I've done," Tamela said.

"You do have a point there. I didn't realize you were so interested in criminal work."

"It's not just criminal work, because from what I've seen, we don't get that many criminal cases in the office."

"Agreed."

"But there are other high-profile cases that would get me more courtroom time," Tamela said.

"I hear you. What can I do?"

"What I need is for you to see what you can do about getting me a good case to work on. I don't care what kind of case it is. Corporate, criminal, or whatever. I'm willing to do whatever it takes to prove to these people that I can hang with the best of them."

"I'll see what I can do," Tim said. "I'd like to think they would listen to me."

"I hope so. I mean with all the money they pay you," Tamela said.

"What do you know about how much money they pay me?" Tim joked. Tamela wanted to say what she never said in public, *Nigger, plezze.*

"Tim, now come on. You're wearing a Rolex Presidential watch, driving a convertible Jaguar, and wearing very expensive suits. You can't do that with what they pay me," Tamela said.

"I guess I do okay."

Tim walked over and sat on the sofa beside Tamela. His voice changed, suddenly confidential and intimate. He was so close she could feel his breath make contact with her lips. Tim lowered his voice and said, "I tell you what. You help me out with the BMU function and I promise that when the next high-profile case comes in, you will get the chance to show us what you can do."

"Can I get that in writing?" Tamela smiled.

"Now, Ms. Coleman, you know I can't do that. But you have my word." Tim relaxed and leaned back in his chair.

"Your word."

"My word."

As Tamela was deciding whether or not Tim could be trusted, the voice of his secretary flooded his office on the intercom.

"Mr. Franklin, Warner Mitchell wants to move your lunch meeting to one o'clock," she said.

"Tell him that's fine and I'll meet him in the reception area," Tim said.

"Yes, sir."

"So do we have a deal?" Tim asked.

"Leave me a message with all the details about the dance," Tamela said as she got up from the sofa, shook Tim's hand, and headed back to her office.

"Consider it done. Have a productive day, Ms. Coleman," Tim said.

"I already have Mr. Franklin," she said. "I already have."

The sound of his own voice woke Sean from a restless sleep. His answering machine was on, announcing that he was unavailable and instructing callers to leave him a message. After the beep, Sean heard the familiar gravelly voice of his agent, Don Thomas.

"Sean, give me a call ASAP. I've got a wonderful assignment for . . ."

Sean quickly grabbed for the phone from his sofa bed. "Don, hold on. Let me turn this thing off." He reached down to the floor where his machine was resting and clicked it off.

"Sean, sounds like you're still asleep," Don said.

"No, no, I'm wide awake," he said, trying to clear the morning fog from his mind. "What's this great assignment you're talking about?"

"It's with *Sports Today*. You know *ST*. They want you to do a feature on the sudden emergence of black NFL quarterbacks. They saw the profile you did on Warren Moon."

"Oh, great. That was one of my best pieces of work. But what 'emergence' are they talking about?" Sean joked.

"Stop giving me shit, Sean. Have you ever done any work for *ST*? You know before you signed up with me."

"No, but I've sent them plenty of query letters."

"The job pays well. They are offering 5K for seventy-five hundred words. In addition . . . are you sitting down?"

"Yeah, yes . . . I'm sitting." He was actually lying down but his agent didn't need to know everything.

"They're picking up expenses," Don said.

"No shit . . . expenses too?"

"That's right. I talked to the editor directly."

"Where do I sign? When do I start?" Sean quizzed.

"I was so confident you would want this that I asked them to send the contract ASAP. After I've had a chance to look at it, I'll messenger it over," Don said.

"That's great, Don. I'll hang around the basement until it's delivered."

"Fine. I'll tell my assistant to send it right away. The editor suggested you start with this Zurich Robinson kid in Chicago. I think he's with the new expansion team."

"Zurich Robinson, Zurich Robinson. Why does that name sound so familiar?"

"You must remember him. He's from your neck of the woods. Used to play quarterback at Southern Florida Tech," Don said.

"Oh yeah. I don't think I ever met him, but I do remember him vaguely. I didn't cover any of the small black colleges when I was in Atlanta."

"Well, he is supposed to be the hottest young quarterback in the NFL. *ST* is sending over some bio information on him with the contract. They said they didn't have much, but I told them to send what they had. You should already have info on Warren, Randall, Rodney, and Vince."

"Vince?"

"Sean, wake up, man. Vince Evans."

"Oh shit. I forgot he still plays for the Raiders. My man Vince still kicking butt at forty. He's gonna be a black George Blanda," Sean joked.

"See I do know something about sports," Don boasted. "You may be my only full-time sports journalist, but I've been doing my homework."

"I see. I stand corrected," Sean said.

"Okay, Mr. Elliott. Give me a call when you're up and about."

"Sure, soon as I shower, shit, and shave," Sean said.

"Good enough! I'll talk with you later. Congrats," Don said.

"Thanks, Don. Peace out."

Sean hung up the phone and smiled to himself as he rubbed the overnight growth on his usually smooth face. He was thinking about the five thousand dollars and being able to bill someone else for his food when his thoughts were suddenly interrupted by a deep male voice very close to him.

"Say, Gee, can I take a quick shower before I leave?"

Sean turned to face the lanky, but muscular, brown-skinned stranger. He had forgotten the name of his overnight guest. This familiar loss of memory often occurred with Sean after a night of drinking, and especially when it came to his sexuality, something he did not like to spend a great deal of time thinking about. It usually only entered his mind when the alcohol took control. When dealing with people, his personal policy was, don't deny it, don't advertise it.

Sean had discovered his sexuality at a summer baseball camp when he was twelve. One of the sixteen-year-old counselors was instructing him on his batting swing and when he pressed his muscular body against Sean's backside, both of them got erections. In Sean's case it was the first erection he ever noticed and he felt its throbbing power. That night, when the lights went out, Sean discovered the joy of masturbation, his mind clouded with thoughts of his camp counselor.

During his senior year in high school, Sean realized his attraction to men wasn't just a passing fancy. When his prom date, Millicent Thomas, offered him more than a good night kiss, his sex failed. He felt embarrassed then just as he did now with this nameless trade. They were different types of embarrassment, but neither one made Sean feel good about himself.

"So, Gee, me takin' a quick shower won't be a problem. I don't want to 'cause no extra problems," the stranger said.

"Oh no. Sure, man, you can take a shower. There are some towels outside the shower," Sean said as he pointed toward the bathroom without looking at the stranger.

"You don't even remember my name, do you?" the stranger smiled.

"Of course I do, but you need to get busy, 'cause I've got to be downtown in 'bout thirty minutes." Sean lied on both counts.

"Cool," the stranger replied.

As the guest walked nude toward the bathroom, Sean slowly moved from the bed to look for his wallet and watch. He breathed a sigh of relief when he found them both in his normal hiding place, a wastebasket covered with fake trash. Sean spotted the stranger's clothes piled next to his bed and he quickly rifled through the blue work pants, trying to ignore the dirty, yellow-used-to-be-white briefs and the thick basketball socks with huge holes. He found a thin, worn black wallet, and inside a New Jersey driver's license with the name Gregory Johnson. Sean put the wallet back into Gregory's pants and looked around his apartment and shook his head. More than ten beer cans were scattered throughout the room. The cans explained his nagging headache and case of cotton mouth. On top of one of the cans were the small remains of a joint. Sean did not use drugs himself but kept a small amount for special guests. Sometimes the trade Sean found attractive needed a little bit more stimulation than beer or wine to get in the mood. In his boxer underwear, Sean started picking up the beer cans, when Gregory walked out from the bathroom. He had a towel wrapped around his waist and was using another to briskly dry his hair as he walked toward Sean's computer.

"So you a word processor or something like that?" Gregory asked. Sean did not remember meeting Gregory, never mind if they had discussed careers. And he wondered what did people call him, Gregory or Greg.

"Oh yeah, I am a word processor," Sean lied, sort of. Sean spotted his favorite pair of baggy jeans and put them on with an Atlanta Braves' jersey.

"You make a lot of money doing that?" Greg asked.

"I do okay," Sean replied.

"Don't forget you said you would lend me some money to get back home. I can't leave you my home phone number but I got a beeper number in case you want to get together sometime. I'll give you a special code so I'll know it's you," he said.

"Sure," Sean mumbled as he pulled a twenty-dollar bill from his wallet and pressed it into Greg's large, ash-covered hands.

"Thanks, Gee, this sho helps a brother out," Gregory said.

"Dang, look at them caps you got. You collect 'em or something?" Greg asked as he noticed the collection of professional sports baseball caps Sean had gathered over the years. He wore a different one every day.

"Yeah, I do," Sean replied. He was hoping Gregory wouldn't ask for one of his caps.

"Do your friends call you Gregory or Greg?"

"Ah, man, peoples call me Greg. Sometimes my moms call me Gregory," he said, still eyeing the caps.

"Cool. Look, Greg, I don't mean to be rushing you, but I've got to get out of here," Sean said.

"Hey, homes, I understand. Got to git to that J.O.B.," Greg said as he put on his blue work uniform, an outfit he had removed the previous night with the agility of a quick-change artist. Sean gazed at Greg instead of enjoying the morning sunlight that flooded his fifth-floor walk-up. Memories of the previous night were returning. Sean had met Greg at a seedy bookstore slash nude bar called the Stargate between Forty-second and Forty-third on Eighth Avenue. The Stargate had managed to survive the city's efforts to clear the area of all the sex shops, gay bars, and prostitutes—male, female, and shemale. They had chatted briefly before Sean invited him back to his apartment. Sean thought Greg was handsome in a brutal, masculine sort of way and he liked the fact that he wasn't the brightest bulb in the lamp. All he talked about were the cars he fixed and washed in a nearby Manhattan garage. He remembered Greg telling him he could not stay long because he lived with his common-law wife over in Jersey City and she would raise all kind of hell if he stayed out late. Sean did not have to ask him if his wife knew where he was.

Sean liked the Stargate. You didn't have to waste a lot of time with the courting and the chase. They didn't have clubs like this back in Atlanta, at least as far as Sean knew. Atlanta didn't even have adult bookstores. Most of the men in establishments like the Stargate came there for one thing and one thing only. The joint was popular with black and Puerto Rican hustlers, whom Sean tried to stay away from, but he was not totally opposed to giving trade a few dollars to help out. What he liked most about this seedy establishment was the anonymity and the lack of commitment among its colorful clientele. There was no pretense of love, of maybe moving in together, buying a dog, and living happily ever after. Sometimes, if the sex was great, Sean would see the trade again. But it had to be stupendous, not just good. And if the man showed signs of appreciating Sean for more than sex, then it was see ya. Sean had done the I Love You More Than Life thing and wanted no part of that ever. He had convinced himself that it was next to impossible for two black men to have a long-term, totally committed, loving relationship. He imagined that such relationships existed, but it just hadn't happened to him. When the time in his life came where he needed loving affection, Sean had told his sister, he would buy a puppy. And yet, as difficult and as lonely as being black and gay could be, Sean struggled not to live the life of the *tragic black homosexual,* despite the many days when he didn't know which part of his being weighed heavier, being a black man, or being gay.

But with the majority of Sean's encounters with men like Greg, he had mixed emotions afterward. Partly because he knew it was just fucking, and not the lovemaking he was too stubborn to admit he desired. The minute Sean would reach his climax, a wave of sickening guilt rushed over him and he suddenly hated being attracted to this type of man. Maybe it was time to leave New York where men like Greg were a dime a dozen. Make that twenty dollars apiece.

CHAPTER 6

VBD'S

It was a good week for Mia. As soon as the FiveAlive sports segment opened with its fight song light anthem, Mia launched into her new assignment. Her first sportscast went so smoothly that the crew of cameramen applauded Mia when the newscast had gone off the air and the anchors had removed their microphones. She looked great; her makeup looked as if it had been applied by a skilled plastic surgeon; and her hair hadn't moved unless Mia wanted it to.

There were positive phone calls from viewers to Channel 3's voice-mail comment line and even a few faxes of praise for the new addition to the FiveAlive news team. Ratings during Mia's first week were up slightly, which was not surprising with the hype Channel 3's PR department had generated on Mia's behalf. There were new promos featuring Mia, a mention in Kup's column in the *Chicago Sun-Times,* and Mia's face plastered on several of Chicago's city buses and El stations.

Everybody at the station seemed pleased, with one notable exception, Carolyn Moore, an almond-colored anchor woman who had been at Channel 3 for more than five years. Not only did she not appreciate all the attention Mia was receiving, Carolyn was also a bit miffed that she was not consulted about promoting Mia, a courtesy the general manager had promised and in the past had kept with every new addition to the team. The FiveAlive newscast was Carolyn's domain, and she was not happy about sharing her throne. Especially not with a beauty like Mia Miller. While the blond anchorman eagerly welcomed Mia on her first day, Carolyn had given her a dry, "Yes, welcome, girlfriend." As if she just couldn't say Mia's name. At a very early age, Mia had learned to ignore the rudeness of people jealous of her, and she was quick to recognize condescending friendliness, perhaps because she often used it herself.

When the rest of the news staff took Mia out for drinks and dinner at Houston's restaurant after her first broadcast, Carolyn politely declined, saying she had a standing manicure appointment that she did not dare cancel. At dinner, Chip Winston, the weather guy, told Mia that Carolyn had hit the ceiling when she found out the Oak Street clothing store that supplied her with an occasional outfit wanted to do the same for Mia. Even Mia's mother commented on Carolyn's ice princess act after viewing tapes of the first couple of shows that Mia had sent, as promised.

"What did you do to her?" Emma asked when they talked late one night.

"Would you believe nothing?" Mia responded.

"Then why does she have her panties in a bunch?"

"Don't know . . . don't care," Mia answered. She really didn't understand Carolyn's attitude. Carolyn was well respected, and Mia had heard she was among the highest-paid media talents in Chicago. She had been nominated for a local Emmy for three years running and was supposedly happily married to a successful Chicago businessman. One evening at the Eastgate health club, in the building next door to the station, Mia bumped into Carolyn at the bank of Stairmasters and Lifecycles. Dressed in a black Lycra midriff top and neon pink biker shorts, Mia had just finished signing an autograph for one of the young ladies who worked at the health club's information desk. Her long hair was pulled together in a loose ponytail, giving her the look of a high school cheerleader rather than a professional journalist. Carolyn had looked tired in a gray warm-up suit and without her standard pancake makeup. She had rolled her eyes at Mia without speaking, then turned to whisper and giggle with an overweight friend whom Mia did not recognize.

At first, Carolyn's chilly treatment bothered Mia, but then she decided she had seen this movie too many times to be worried about the ending. She was used to it, especially when it came to black

women. It didn't matter whether they were light-skinned or dark-
skinned, they would give Mia the blues. It happened in junior high,
high school, and college, especially after she became the first black
girl to pledge Tri Delta at Northwestern. From then on, the sisters in
the black sororities gave her the silent treatment at Greek activities
and when she saw them on campus. When Mia pledged Tri Delta, it
was history-making news on campus, and naively, Mia had thought
her black peers on campus would be proud. In Dallas, a few blacks at
her high school were excited for her when she was named homecoming princess and a member of Keyettes, a previously all-white service
organization. Throughout college, it didn't seem to matter that she
had a black roommate before she moved into the sorority house or
that she was dating one of the most vocal and popular black athletes.
No one seemed to take into consideration the rumor Mia had heard
through a former roommate. Namely, that she would never make line
with the AKA's or Delta's, especially after she had gone out with men
their members had dated. But the men had asked her out, she hadn't
asked them. Mia felt the women's behavior toward her was childish,
and even though her mother was somewhat disappointed that she
didn't pledge a black sorority Mia felt she could do without the extra
hazing she had been warned about. She was growing tired of black
people saying she "talked white" and "acted white," simply because
she spoke English correctly and had been seen tossing her hair like a
white girl. Besides, the sisters in Tri Delta were excited to have Mia in
their organization, even though they were always asking questions
about why black folks did this and why they did that, as if she were in
charge of all the black folks on campus. Mia would always respond,
"I don't know, why don't you ask them?" Many of her sorority sisters acted nervous when Mia's dates, always black and usually very
dark-skinned, arrived to pick her up. When they tried to fix her up,
the guys were usually light-skinned and nerdy. Mia didn't have the
heart to tell them that when she said she liked black men, she meant
blue-black. Though Mia loved her sisters at the Tri Delta house, she
lived there for only one year, before getting an off-campus apartment
with the sister of her then-boyfriend.

Mia was under the impression that this type of treatment was
over for her, especially after she met LaDonna when they were both
working in Jackson, Mississippi. LaDonna Woods was her first close,

black female friend other than her sister. Even though Mia had been cold toward her on their first meeting, because of her previous experience with black women, LaDonna won her over when she declared, "You got only twenty-four hours to be shady, Miss Thing. I'm LaDonna, the official pretty girl's best friend." They had been friends ever since.

In many ways Mia had hoped that Carolyn would treat her like a good friend rather than an enemy, especially since they were the only two black women employed by the station as on-air personalities. Mia decided after the first week of Carolyn's icy treatment that she was not going to allow Carolyn, or anyone else for that matter, to ruin something she had worked for and deserved. The other employees at the station treated her with great respect and even the usually uptight manager had joined the group for drinks and dinner to celebrate Mia's successful evening debut.

Forget Carolyn! In the weeks and months ahead, Mia wanted to get to know some of Chicago's leading sports personalities like Michael Jordan, Scottie Pippen, Shaun Gayle, and B. J. Armstrong on a first-name basis. She hardly ever had problems forming friendships with men. Keeping them as friends was another story.

It was also during the first week that Mia got the plum assignment of interviewing both head coaches of Chicago's NFL teams and their starting quarterbacks. The main six and ten sports anchor and sports director had a family emergency so he gave Mia the interview assignments. Mia was excited about the interviews, and after visits to her health club, she spent the evenings studying press guides, clippings, and all the information she could get her hands on regarding the two coaches and their starting quarterbacks. One of the things Mia loved about her new job was going to bed late and not at the usual seven o'clock bedtime she had been accustomed to with her previous anchor duties.

Instead of reading the front pages of the *Tribune, Sun-Times, Defender,* and *USA Today,* Mia would find the sports section and read it from front to back in the morning and again at night before bed. She replaced her nightstand copies of *Essence* and *Cosmopolitan* with *Sports Today* and *Sports Illustrated,* moving the first two magazines to her bathroom for skimming. Mia had always read the sports magazines, for her job and because of her love of sports, but now she studied them as if they were textbooks or notes for an important final exam. She knew who was making news in the world of sports as well as what was hot and trendy in the fashion world and how to find a suitable mate.

At night she no longer turned on her CD player to let Janet Jackson, Vanessa Williams, and Boyz II Men serenade her to sleep. Instead she kept her tiny clock radio tuned to SPW, the twenty-four-hour sports call-in show, and made notes of the comments from callers to use for future interview suggestions to her producer. Television was out of the question unless it was ESPN.

One evening while she was studying her notes for the interviews with the Cougars and Bears, Mia decided to call her voice mail at the station to see if the two quarterbacks had called her back to set up interview times.

Only one had. When Mia heard Zurich Robinson's voice, the tiny hairs on her arms felt as though they were standing at attention. What a deep, sexy voice, Mia thought. She wondered what he looked like, if the voice matched the face. She was trying to recall if she had seen pictures of him at the station or in press info, when she suddenly heard Derrick's voice. "Mia. I've been trying to get ahold of you, girl. You're a hard woman to reach. But I guess that's what happens when you become a big star. Anyway, your mother and LaDonna wouldn't give me your home number, so I figured I could reach you at the station. I'm going to be in Chicago for most of September and October and I want to take you to dinner. I don't know where I'm going to be staying. You got any suggestions? I promise I won't snore. Pretty please. Give me a call when you get this message. My number is 309-555-3495 and my cellular is same area code 555-2349. Be sweet," Derrick's voice said.

Mia immediately followed the instructions of the automated voice: "Press K, the 5 key, to keep this message or D, the 3 key, to discard this message." Mia couldn't hit 3 quick enough.

Mia went to her kitchen, pulled a wine goblet off the overhead rack, and poured herself a hearty glass of red wine. She took three long swallows, refilled the glass, and went to her living room, trying to get her mind off Derrick's call and back to her work. She sat down on the sofa, took another swallow of wine, and pulled out the photo of the Cougars' new quarterback. When she saw the head and action shots of the man with the sexy voice, Mia almost choked on her mouthful of wine. She was startled by the handsomeness of this truly over black man. He was Phine, not the regular f-i-n-e. She laid the pictures next to each other on her salmon-colored sofa and clapped her hands and smiled. In her life, Mia had seen fine men of all races, at school and work, but Zurich Robinson made Mia appreciate something LaDonna said all the time. "Mia," her girlfriend would say, "the boy was so fine that I wanted to go over to his house and slap his mama." As Mia gazed at the pictures she figured Zurich Robinson's mother had been slapped many a day.

"Take my card, just in case you change your mind," the bespectacled photographer said to Zurich.

"Sure, I'll do that. I'll give it to my publicist, Gina DeMarco," Zurich said.

"Oh, Gina DeMarco is your publicist?"

"Well, we're trying each other out on a trial basis," Zurich said. "Do you know her?"

"I don't know her, but I've heard great things about her. By all means give her my card. Here, let me give you two so that you'll have one also." He smiled as he pulled two slightly dirty cards from his camera bag.

As the photographer walked off, Zurich smiled at the all-too familiar encounter. He had been walking down Michigan Avenue toward his new publicist/manager's office when the man had approached and asked him if he was a model and if he was interested in doing some "art type nude shots." He could not keep track of the number of times photographers had approached him in recent years. Today, as he always did, Zurich politely declined the photo sessions, especially when the words "nude" and "art type" were included in the proposals.

He was still not used to people commenting on how he looked, and although he did not understand the hoopla about something he had no control over, he had resigned himself to the unwanted attention his features attracted. At times, Zurich thought it was funny. No one had ever mentioned his looks from the time he was a young boy through his freshman year in high school. Girls where he grew up and where he spent his summers only seemed interested in fair-skinned boys with light eyes and curly hair. Now all of a sudden his dark skin color and shaved head seemed to attract attention wherever he went. In Canada, a sportswriter had written that, "Zurich Robinson, the roughly handsome Montreal quarterback, appears to have a body so solid you could strike a match off it." Zurich had been taught by MamaCee and his father to always treat people the way he wanted to be treated, so mutual respect was more important to him than how a person looked.

Still it was hard to ignore his straight, paper-white teeth when they revealed a smile that was pure innocence and yet promised something entirely different, something *sensual*. Throw in his desert-brown eyes and smooth head, and, well, it caused quite a stir when his picture was on the front page of the *Tribune*'s sports page during his first week of practice.

After the picture appeared, Zurich started getting about ten to fifteen letters a day from all types of women, and a few men, with pictures and suggestions on how they would like to personally welcome him to Chicago. He was constantly getting phone messages from cousins and long-lost girlfriends whom he knew nothing about. It was during times such as this that Zurich was happy Gina DeMarco had entered his life.

Although he didn't understand why he needed a publicist/manager, Gina DeMarco made him an offer he couldn't refuse: her services free of charge until she brought in endorsements and other opportunities for Zurich to make money outside of football. He was impressed with her go-get-it attitude and everyone he talked to, like Mario and one of his coaches, had nothing but praise for Gina.

One of the first things she did was to get her secretary to answer his mail, with thank-you notes and autographed pictures. This allowed Zurich the chance to concentrate on more important things; like getting ready for the Bears and making sure he had all the plays of the complicated Cougar offense down. He was stopping by Gina's office to drop off the twenty-plus letters he'd received in two days when he met the photographer. He walked into Gina's pink-and-green-decorated office; her face was covered with a huge smile. Gina DeMarco had a striking presence, skin the color of the sweetest maple syrup, round hips, a small waist, breasts and legs she was apparently proud of, judging by the tailored suits and short skirts she wore. When she walked into a room, people noticed. Gina enjoyed laughing and would end almost every sentence with "Am I right or am I wrong?" Then she would just go on with her next thought without waiting for anyone to respond.

"We got our first offer for an endorsement," Gina said.

"Already? That was quick. Who with . . . Nike? Puma? How much are they offering?" Zurich asked.

"None of the above. And you'll get a big kick out of this," Gina said.

"Who is it and what's the product?"

"Well, like I said, this is funny. Some guy who saw your picture in the paper thinks you would be the perfect model and spokesman for a line of underwear he has developed. They are supposed to be on the market just in time for Christmas. We should at least look at it. Am I right or am I wrong?" Gina said.

"Underwear. Somebody wants me to model underwear?" Zurich thought about the many times MamaCee had told him and his brothers, "Don't be walking around this house with your ass out," when they would parade in their Fruit of the Loom's as teenagers.

"Yes, and get this," Gina laughed. "You will never guess the name of these specially designed drawers for black men," she said as she grabbed her side from laughing so hard.

"What are they called, Gina?"

"VBD's," Gina said.

"VBD's?"

"Yes, VBD's," Gina smiled slyly.

"Is that the designer's initials?"

"I don't think so because his first name is Justin. You really don't know what it stands for?"

"No," Zurich said seriously.

"The first two letters stands for *very big.*" Gina paused and then said, "The last part begins with a D and ends with a K." She laughed. "Can you hang my brother?"

"Oh . . . shit. I mean . . . oh, man. You're kidding, right? You're just messing with me," Zurich said as he burst out smiling.

"See for yourself," Gina said as she gave Zurich the letter and a diagram of the proposed underwear.

"I don't believe this. I know a whole bunch of my teammates who would buy them, whether they needed them or not," Zurich laughed.

"I know that's right. I might even have to get a pair for my husband. Now that's a man who needs them," Gina boasted.

"I think we should pass on this," Zurich said. "And it's not because I'm not up to the task," he said sexily.

"I ain't mad at'cha, Mr. Robinson. And I thought you were some kinda square. You and I are going to be cool. We can hang. Am I right or am I wrong?" Gina quizzed.

"You know you're right, Gina. What have you come up with in regards to charities?" Zurich asked. He had asked Gina to scout out charities that he could volunteer for without fanfare.

"Well, I know Big Brothers would love to have you. I'm also talking to some people with an organization of black men called BMU, who have an excellent mentoring program that I think you would be great for," Gina said.

"Did you check into the local AIDS group?"

"No, I'm still looking into that. I have heard of one that provides food services for patients. I could find out about it and maybe you could send them a check," Gina said.

"Yeah, I'd like to do that and whatever else I can do. I mean I just don't want to send a check," Zurich said.

"Fine. You know that's very admirable of you. I don't know if I've heard of any athletes, with the exception of Magic Johnson and a few tennis players, who wanted to be associated with AIDS charities. More of them need to, though. Am I right or am I wrong?"

"Right again. It's a terrible disease," he said mournfully.

"What's that you got?" Gina asked, noticing the notebook Zurich was protecting with his life.

"Oh, just some more letters and my playbook," Zurich said. Everywhere he went, he carried the black Chicago Cougars' playbook, which weighed ten pounds and held more plays than there were names in the Chicago phone book. At least it seemed that way. When he was not busy with two-a-day practices, Zurich would spend time studying his playbook or weight lifting, though it was apparent his body did not need any new muscles.

When he'd arrived in town, Gina had also helped Zurich find an apartment on Michigan Avenue near her office, convenient to Grant Park, Soldier Field, and several restaurants. The apartment building was a modern structure, with a crystal chandelier dominating the lobby, which was adorned with smoked-glass mirrors, a concierge desk, and a doorman station. The apartments themselves were comfortably large with marble foyers, fireplaces in the bedrooms, and spacious kitchens. Gina seemed to take care of everything for Zurich, including getting the apartment furnished. He was happy to move from the crowded dorm the Cougars had provided during training camp. As much as he enjoyed being with his new teammates, Zurich appreciated the silence a new apartment without roommates would provide.

The only activity he had managed that was not related to football and not under the direction of Gina was finding a church. Mario and a couple of his teammates were always teasing him when he showed more interest in finding a church than finding the hottest night spots. All his teammates seemed to talk about were their business deals and going, as Mario called it, "Looking for new pussy."

Zurich's Southern Baptist roots were an important part of his life. The most important part, he told himself, even though in sports it was hard to talk about your faith without making God sound like a celebrity best friend. Zurich had seen many a player talking about what the Lord meant to him when the cameras were rolling and then acting like Satan's only child after a few drinks.

Sweet Harmony Baptist Church was located at the end of Hyde Park. A small church by Chicago standards, with only two hundred and fifty members, it reminded Zurich of the church MamaCee attended in Mississippi. A church, like most Southern Baptist ones, where the deacons, all singing off-key, would gather around the offering table on their knees, singing "I Love the Lord He Heard My Cry." Zurich had often heard MamaCee singing this song as she inspected Zurich and his brothers before they went to church. MamaCee would have the Robinson boys in attendance three times a week, for Sunday school, Wednesday prayer meeting, and regular Sunday service. If they did not want to go, well, that was fine with her. But she had one rule that could not be broken, don't go to church and you couldn't leave the front porch until you had been to church again. Zurich and his brothers agreed that two hours in MamaCee's church was a fair trade for being able to roam outside and play football and basketball until their bodies gave out.

Zurich was so soothed and impressed by the church that he marched down the tiny aisle and joined the moment the Reverend Dr. Darwin Russell opened the doors of the church for new members. The burly minister with the high-pitched voice recognized Zurich from the *Tribune* picture and made a big deal out of him, leading the church in a special prayer for Zurich and his football career. In many ways, Zurich considered Gina DeMarco an answered prayer. He trusted her to guide him as he did few people. When Zurich left Gina's office, he headed for his new apartment. He walked slowly down Michigan Avenue and enjoyed the long summer twilight, his eyes hidden by sunglasses, his hairless dome covered by a Florida Marlins baseball cap, and his ears adorned with tiny silver loops that he never wore at practice or while playing. When he walked into his lobby a half-hour later, the pale, redheaded concierge gave him his keys and a fax he had received from Gina.

Beneath a headline of z-man strikes, the fax informed Zurich of an interview request she had approved for him after the Chicago Bears' game with the sports anchor Mia Miller from Channel 3's FiveAlive program, and her number for Zurich to call and confirm. She also mentioned a request for an in-depth interview with *Sports Today,* but she needed to get more information before deciding if it was something he should consider. He smiled to himself as he headed toward the elevator and thought about what MamaCee would say if he called her with all his good news. "Boy, you've got an abundance of blessings. The good Lord must have found out where you live," she would say. Now if only his blessings would continue against the Chicago Bears.

CHAPTER 7

THE LADIES WHO LUNCH

Tamela and three other members of the SRB (Sisters Reading Books) Literary group exchanged mischievous glances as the two waiters placed plates of fruit-covered waffles, fluorescent-colored pasta, and chicken wings on the maple tabletop.

It was the first Saturday afternoon in September, and the summer wind had started to cool. Fall was closing in on Chicago, and Tamela's curls were flawless!

Desiree, Karen Rice, and Stephanie Jackson were also all members of Delta Sigma Theta Sorority. They had agreed to meet Tamela at the Bennigan's across the street from Grant Park and the Art Institute of Chicago. Officially, they were meeting to come up with recommendations of novels their group would read for the rest of the year. Unofficially, they wanted to catch up on what was going on in each other's lives since there was never time for such talk when the full twenty-plus group met once a month. After they exchanged tiny samples of each other's entrees, Desiree pulled the fork from her brick-red lips and said, "So, Tamela, tell the ladies your big news."

"What? You met somebody?" Karen asked.

"No, it's not news yet. Miss Big Mouth," Tamela said as she looked at Desiree cross-eyed.

"It might be," Desiree said. "Go on and tell them."

"What Miss Big Mouth is talking about, well, I'm thinking about starting my own firm," Tamela said and looked at her friends for a reaction. Karen and Stephanie broke out in huge smiles and said, "You go, girl."

"Nothing is official yet. I'm just checking into it," Tamela said.

"Sisters got to do it for themselves," Stephanie said. "You got any good leads on office space and clients?"

"Like I said. I'm working on it. I met a lot of people last night at the BMU dinner-dance," Tamela said.

"Yeah, T, how was that?" Desiree asked. She had decided not to go alone when Tim invited Tamela.

"It was okay, but you know how those things can be," she said.

"How so?" Karen asked.

"You know, uppity wannabe Negroes putting on airs," Tamela said.

"Oh, I know, don't you just hate it?" Stephanie asked.

"Sho you right. By the time the night was over, I was so sick and tired of frontin' Negroes coming up and asking me, 'So what do you do? Where do you live? Did we meet at the Black Ski Summit or on the Vineyard?' I started to say I ain't never been skiing, but maybe we did meet in the backyard." Everyone started laughing and exchanging dainty high fives with each other.

"I know that's right, but what's a diva to do?" Desiree asked.

"But I decided to have some fun when this friend of Tim's came over and asked me what I did, knowing full well that I worked with Tim," Tamela said.

"What did you do, soror?" Stephanie inquired.

"I told him I was a doe hoe," Tamela said as she took her fork and lifted some pasta from Desiree's plate.

"A doe hoe?" Karen said with a quizzical look on her face.

"That's the same look he had," Tamela said as she pointed her fork toward Karen's face.

"What is a doe hoe?" Desiree asked.

"You see that white girl over there?" Tamela questioned as she pointed toward a pretty teenager seating customers as they came in and marking their names off the lunchtime waiting list.

"Yes," Karen and Stephanie said at the same time.

"Well, she is a doe hoe," Tamela laughed. "You know, like close de doe."

"Girl, you are so crazy," the three others said in unison.

"I know it, but it helped lighten up the evening," Tamela said.

"Did you meet anybody interesting?" Karen asked.

"Just a bunch of politicians and lawyers. All trying to figure out how they can win back City Hall from Daley," Tamela said.

"They can forget it," Desiree said. "There won't be another Harold Washington in this city for a long time."

"I don't know," Karen said. "If Marion Barry can make a comeback, anything is possible."

"Tamela, you should run for mayor. We could work it like we did in high school," Desiree suggested.

"Please, don't you even go there. I'm busy enough just trying to keep the job I got," Tamela said.

"I know that's right," Stephanie said.

"Oh, I did meet . . . well, not exactly meet . . . but there was this fine busboy or waiter that kept looking at me and smiling. He was so pretty I assumed he was probably gay, you know, but before the night was over he slipped me this napkin with a sweet note on it," Tamela said.

"What did it say?" Desiree asked.

"It said, 'I just want to tell you how beautiful you look tonight,' and he drew one of those little happy faces with a little curly 'fro and signed his name, Caliph," Tamela said.

"He didn't have an Afro, did he?" Stephanie asked.

"No," Tamela said.

"Caliph. Spell it," Karen said.

"C-A-L-I-P-H, Caliph," Tamela said.

"That's an unusual name, sort of strong-sounding," Karen said.

"Did he leave a phone number?" Stephanie asked.

"No, he did not," Tamela said, as she brought her soft drink to her lips.

"Then he was probably gay," Stephanie said. "They seem to be able to appreciate a good-looking sister better than the straight ones."

"As my mother always says, tell the truth and shame the devil," Tamela said as she slid her index finger around the top of her water glass.

The women finished their food and all ordered coffee while Karen asked to see the dessert cart. Karen loved Bennigan's dessert cart. She was a little stocky, but not fat, and she loved clothes too tight for her powerful thighs and thick waist, which explained the black mini skirt she was wearing.

"I know you're not," Tamela said.

"What?" Karen asked, looking at Tamela with a sneaky smile.

"Ordering dessert."

"Maybe," Karen replied.

"Girlfriend, you keep eating like that and you are going to be a charter member of the Big Panties Club," Desiree teased.

"I'm sorry. But I ain't trying to be no fashion model," Karen said.

"I know that's right," Stephanie added. Of all the women sitting at the table, Stephanie was the one to most likely be mistaken for a fashion model. She was exquisite-looking with a Tater Tot brown skin, an oval face surrounded by neck-length black hair, carefully styled.

Desiree pulled out rolled-up copies of *Essence* and *Emerge* magazines and opened them onto the table. She had large paper clips on a page in each magazine.

"Let's just recommend the books on these best-seller lists," she suggested.

"But I've already read all of those books," Stephanie said.

"Me, too," Tamela interjected.

"So, what are we going to do? We decided that we were only going to read books by black people," Desiree said.

"Yeah, but what about Africans?" Karen asked.

"They are black, aren't they?" Tamela smiled.

"Yes, I guess you're right," Karen said.

"Why don't we get the lady at that bookstore under the Wabash El tracks to recommend some books?" Desiree said.

"That's a great idea. And we would be supporting a sistah too," Tamela said.

"You know we ought to go in and buy a couple of those books on tapes for some of the books we've been avoiding," Desiree said.

"Oh yes, those are great," Tamela said.

"I'll check into it," Stephanie said.

The women had refills on their coffee and chatted about books that would be tape candidates, sorority business, and, eventually, men.

Karen was finishing a hot fudge brownie when she turned to

Tamela and asked her what she thought of all the coverage the O. J. Simpson trial was receiving.

"Honey, like I tell the people in my office who are always asking me what I think about it, I don't think about O. J. Simpson ever. But I will say this, black folks need to turn off Court TV and if they got to watch television then they need to be watching C-SPAN so they can keep their eye on Congress," Tamela said.

"I know that's right," Desiree said.

Just when Tamela was getting ready to suggest another topic, Desiree swiveled her head and let out a delightful squeal.

"Speaking of black men, look at that tall glass of chocolate milk," Desiree said as she stared at a tall, attractive black man walking into the restaurant.

"A tall glass of what?" Karen asked.

"Chocolate milk," Desiree repeated.

"And we're always complaining how men talk about us. Listen to yourself, Desiree. You ought to be ashamed of yourself," Stephanie said.

"I'm not shamed, he is fine," Desiree giggled.

"He's okay," Tamela said as she looked toward the door.

"Oh . . . oh . . . oh . . . oh," Desiree said, as she held her mouth as if she was trying to prevent something from falling out.

"What is your problem?" Tamela asked.

"Don't you know who that is?"

"Should we?" Stephanie asked.

"He does look familiar," Karen said.

"That's the new quarterback for the new football team. Zurich Robinson is his name. Honey, he is Shaft fine, muther-shut-your mouth. I could do a stank butterfly with him," Desiree said, recalling the latest dance craze.

"Since when did you get to know so much about sports?" Tamela asked.

"Since they started having players that look like that," Desiree said.

"Who do you think he's waiting on?" Stephanie posed to the group.

"Would you ladies like some more coffee?" the waiter interrupted.

"Yes, but you can also bring the check," Desiree said. The waiter gave Desiree a grateful smile.

The women were silent for a moment, gazing toward the hostess station where Zurich Robinson was standing. He noticed them looking at him and smiled as he looked at his watch.

"Please, dear Lord up above, don't let him be waiting on a white girl," Desiree said as she looked toward the ceiling with her hands in a prayer position.

"Chile, get a grip and calm yourself down," Tamela instructed. She wanted to say, You girls act like y'all ain't never seen no fine men and he ain't even all that.

"Girls, I have a confession to make," Desiree said.

"What have you done now?" Tamela asked.

"Yes, girl, tell us what you did," Stephanie said as she removed her square-shaped glasses.

"I wrote him a letter and sent him a picture," Desiree said as she mockingly held her head down in shame.

"No, you didn't," Karen said.

"Oh yes, I did. Look at him," Desiree said in a defensive tone.

"Honey, are you that desperate for a man?" Stephanie asked.

"It's not about desperation. It's about trying to meet a fine, smart man who also has the potential to make a lot of money. I read in the paper where he is single, a college graduate, and was on the Dean's List," Desiree said.

"What did he major in, Recreational Management?" Tamela asked sarcastically. *That's what they major in at Southern,* she thought.

"No, the paper said some type of journalism. I think broadcast," Desiree said.

"Oh, that's different," Karen said. "And, ladies, you know how cold it gets in Chicago. Better meet a man now when the weather is warm enough so that you can see what you're getting. When it gets cold, you know how men cover up those horrible bodies some of them can have."

"Ain't that the truth, girlfriend," Desiree said.

"Did he write you back?" Stephanie asked.

"No, not yet. It's only been a couple of days," Desiree said.

"You should go over there and tell him that you wrote him,"

Karen suggested. Tamela had a Please don't go over there and make a fool of yourself look on her face. Desiree saw this but ignored her friend's caution.

"You think so?" Desiree asked.

"Yes, you wrote him a letter. Go over there and tell the brother you think he's fine. If you don't, then I will," Karen said and she rearranged the pink scarf adorning her neck.

"How do I look?" Desiree said, as she pulled out a tiny compact from her purse. Her lips were still brick red and her eyes were large and dark in a round face, surrounded by pencil-length dreads.

"Are you going to go over there?" Tamela asked.

"Yes, I am," Desiree said, as she closed the compact and slipped it back into her purse. As soon as she made sure her blue silk blouse was tucked neatly into her starched jeans, Desiree slid out of the booth, turned to her friends, and said, "Wish me luck, sorors."

"You go, girl," Stephanie said.

But just as she started to walk toward the door, Desiree saw an attractive black woman come in and go directly up to Zurich Robinson and begin talking to him. Desiree assumed that it was someone he knew and the person he was waiting for. They seemed to be enjoying each other and the woman, who looked familiar to Desiree, was looking up at Zurich like a schoolgirl with a serious crush. Dejection set in, and Desiree slid back into the booth.

"Well, sorors, it looks like I'm not going to meet my husband today."

"Isn't that the new sportscaster, Mia Miller?" Karen asked.

"It sure does look like her," Stephanie said.

"Yeah, that's her. She was at Northwestern when I was there for law school. She didn't hang out with sisters too tough, but she always had a fine black man on her arm," Tamela said.

"Is she nice?" Desiree asked. "And what is she doing with my body?" she joked.

"She's sometimey. Sometimes she speaks and then sometimes she acts like she doesn't see you. A lot of my sorors at Northwestern thought she was a bitch," Tamela said.

"Wait a minute. I have an issue here," Desiree said as she held her hand up in a stop-in-the-name-of-love fashion.

"What is your problem?" Tamela asked.

"Didn't we say we were going to stop calling each other names?"

"Yeah," Karen said.

"I didn't call her a bitch. I just said some people I know think she's a bitch," Tamela said.

"I just don't like the word," Desiree said.

"Well, what do I say when it applies? I'm all for sisters treating each other with respect and all, but let's face it, some of us *are* bitches," Stephanie said.

"I got it. I got a better term," Tamela said.

"What? Let's hear it," Desiree said.

"Let's just say she's a DD," Tamela smiled.

"A DD. What's a DD?" Karen asked.

"Defective Diva," Tamela said.

"Oh, I like that," Stephanie sighed.

"Me, too," Desiree said. "A DD. Defective Diva."

"See, look what we've accomplished today. An alternative to that terrible name," Tamela said.

"But back to my dream boy and Miss DD. Is she all black?" Desiree asked.

"Now how am I supposed to know that? I did not go up and ask to see her papers," Tamela replied. "Anyhow, what difference does it make? She got some black in her and so, guess what? That makes her black."

"Hello," Stephanie said, lifting her tea glass as if she was toasting Tamela's response.

"Why do we have to claim all the mulattoes?" Desiree asked with a smile.

" 'Cause we that kind of peoples," Stephanie said.

"I think she's black. Although she pledged a white sorority," Tamela said.

"She did what?" Desiree asked.

"Yes, girls. Miss Thing pledged Delta Delta Delta," Tamela said.

"Was it some kind of affirmative-action pledging?" Stephanie asked.

"No, she just went through rush and they gave her a bid. She didn't come through the real Delta though," Tamela said.

"I know that's right. Is there any other Delta, besides Delta Sigma Theta?" Desiree inquired.

All the women gave each other high fives and sang, "Delta sho nuff Delta."

"She kinda looks like an AKA," Karen said.

"There you go with those sorority stereotypes. Something else we have to work on," Tamela said. "But that will have to wait till next time," she added.

The hostess led Zurich Robinson and Mia Miller past the area where the women were sitting. Both Zurich and Mia smiled at the group as Zurich pulled out the chair for Mia at a table about ten feet away. The women were silent when the waiter came and said, "Can I get you ladies something else?"

"Yes," Desiree said as she lifted her hands and pointed toward Zurich. He was still standing and was wearing pocketless black silk trousers molded to his round backside. When he turned to take a seat in front of Mia, the ladies could see his muscular upper body testing the strength of his beige knit shirt.

"Desiree, please," Tamela said as the waiter smiled and picked up the small brown tray with the money.

"Chile, he ain't wearing underwear," Desiree said.

"How can you tell that?" Karen asked.

"Did you see him when he bent over slightly? No line, girl. And look at that ass, honey. You can set a full tea service on it," Desiree said as she gave Karen a circle snap.

"Let's go before this potential DD embarrasses us all," Tamela said. She looked at Zurich's ass and privately agreed that it was nice. Maybe he was all that. *But why waste a body like that on tea. That is a family reunion slab of barbecue body.*

"You can talk about me all you want, but I'm going to meet that man," Desiree said confidently, as she followed her sorority sisters out of the packed restaurant. Outside on busy Michigan Avenue, the women exchanged hugs and cocktail kisses and all four went their separate ways.

Back inside the restaurant, Mia and Zurich settled in for a three-hour lunch. When Mia had contacted Zurich through his publicist, Gina suggested they meet and go over some of the questions Mia planned to ask during her profile. For the station's hour-long Sunday-night sports shows, she wanted to interview him before and after the game with the Bears.

Gina DeMarco thought Mia Miller would be a good friend for Zurich to have in the press, so she granted her exclusive access to Zurich before he talked with sportscasters at Chicago's other major stations. With Mia being somewhat new, Gina knew she wouldn't be as jaded as some of the other fat-faced sportscasters, with their bad hair and ties. Gina had also watched Mia's career closely and felt that, like her client, Mia Miller was going to be big in the Chicago sports community. Maybe one day soon, Mia Miller would need a publicist/manager, too.

Mia was struck not only by how handsome Zurich was (better than his pictures, she thought) but also with his command and delivery of the English language. He seemed confident, friendly, and ready to answer the questions Mia had prepared. Zurich took note of how beautiful Mia looked in her form-fitting peach linen dress. They ordered sandwiches, and Mia clicked on her tiny black cassette recorder. But before she asked her first question, Mia called the waiter.

"Would you change that iced tea to a white wine?" she asked as she clicked off her recorder.

"Sure. And you, sir, do you still want the iced tea?"

"Yeah, I'll stick with the tea," Zurich said. Mia gave a quick toss of her hair, smiled at Zurich and the waiter, and turned the recorder on once again.

"So, when did you know that you would one day be the starting quarterback for an NFL team?" Mia asked.

"When Coach K told me," Zurich laughed. "No, just kidding with you. Well, I was always the quarterback when I was a kid. It didn't matter if I was playing in the fields behind my grandma's house with my brothers and friends or on an organized Pee Wee football team down in Florida. I knew that quarterback was the only position that I wanted to play," Zurich said.

"Did you have any doubts when you were overlooked after graduating from Southern Florida Tech, despite a stellar career?"

"No, not really. With SFT being such a small school, I didn't get a lot of press coverage. Just the local papers. But I knew my chance would come one day. I just had to be patient and make sure I was prepared," Zurich said.

"Was there any defining moment when you knew, despite being black, that you would be given a chance?"

"Watching Doug Williams when he quarterbacked the Redskins in the Super Bowl was really special for me. I was twenty-two and had just been ignored by the NFL draft. When Doug entered the league, they did not give him his props. But in the Super Bowl game, well, it was so exciting for me. I was there with Doug on every pass, every run, even the plays that did not go well. I knew then that the same thing could happen for me. His performance helped me to hold on to my dreams of playing in the NFL, during a time when it would have been real easy to give up," Zurich said.

"So, Doug Williams is one of your role models."

"I respect his talent and what he accomplished, but my role models are my father and grandmother. People I can talk with every day if I need to and people I can hug," Zurich said with a big smile.

"They sound like special people," Mia said.

"Yes, they both are. My grandmother practically raised me. Up until I entered college, I spent almost every summer and sometimes the whole year with her in Warm Springs, Mississippi," he said.

"What does your father do?"

"He's a professional playboy," Zurich joked. "No, he's retired. But he was a caddy for an exclusive country club right outside of Tampa. About five years ago he started playing golf himself. Keeps trying to get me to start playing."

"I guess your father is proud of you," Mia said as she acknowledged the waiter bringing her wine.

"I think he is proud of all his sons," Zurich said as he picked up his water glass, which looked frail in his massive hand.

"How many brothers and sisters do you have?" she asked as she took a drink of her wine.

"Four brothers, no sisters."

"Where do you fit in? The oldest or are you the baby?" Mia smiled.

"No, I'm next to the baby. My younger brother is a student at Morehouse."

"What about your mother?"

"What about her?" Zurich asked in a terse tone that Mia didn't notice. She was too busy looking at Zurich."

"Is she still alive? Does she work?"

Zurich began to look uncomfortable and cleared his throat several times before taking a big gulp of water and then finally answering Mia's question.

"No, my mother is dead. She died when I was young and I don't know that much about her," he said in an uneasy voice.

Mia let Zurich take a break from her questions as she eyed him thoughtfully. His voice was comforting, gentle yet strong, even more appealing than it sounded on the phone message. She drank the last sip of her white wine and signaled the waiter to bring her another glass.

While Zurich took bites from his tuna sandwich, he prayed Mia wouldn't pursue questions about his mother or brothers. He assumed Mia had a wonderful relationship with both her parents and wouldn't understand the loss of loved ones. At times, he felt the loneliness of a man separated from his family. But Zurich kept these feelings hidden, a secret he held to despite his closeness to his father and MamaCee.

After a few moments of silence, Zurich pushed thoughts of his mother out of his mind and tried to focus on the eager woman before him.

"So, Mia Miller, let me ask you a question. How did such a beautiful young lady like yourself get involved with sports and those brutes who play the game?" Zurich asked as he playfully twirled the ice in the bottom of his now empty water glass.

"Well, that's a sexist question, Mr. Robinson, but let's just say when I decided on journalism as a career, the area of sports interested me the most. My father did not have any sons, so he took my sister and me to games and my mother took us to the ballet. We took both ballet and soccer classes when we were young," Mia said.

"Is your sister in the media, too?"

"No, she's a fashion designer. She lives in Paris," Mia said.

"That must be exciting," Zurich said.

"Yes, that's what Tanya says," Mia said as she took a long swallow of her wine.

"Where did you grow up?" Zurich asked.

"In Dallas. And you? Did you say some place in Mississippi?"

"I went back and forth a lot. My father was sometimes working two jobs and interviewing potential new wives. I was born in Tampa, but I spent a lot of time in Warm Springs after my mother died. It's a little country town about sixty miles south of Jackson," Zurich said.

"I used to work in Jackson, at the ABC station there. Does your grandmother still live there?"

"Yeah, she does."

"Do you still visit her a lot?"

"Uh-huh."

"What about Tampa? Do you go to there often?"

"No, not a lot. I've been busy with my career and following up on some other career plans," Zurich said.

"I've never visited Warm Springs or Tampa," Mia said.

"So what's your favorite sport?" Zurich asked, trying to steer the discussion away from his family.

"Football, basketball, tennis, and in that order," Mia replied quickly.

"And your favorite ballet?"

"*Firebird* performed by the Dance Theatre of Harlem," Mia smiled.

"Oh," Zurich said quietly. His face again shifted to a more serious look.

"Are you okay?" Mia asked, noticing the far-off look in Zurich's eyes. She tried to read his face, but couldn't.

"I'm fine. I was just thinking about something. I'm sorry," Zurich said.

"You mentioned other career plans a minute ago. What do you plan to do when your playing days are over?" Mia asked.

"I'd like to do what you're doing. I have a degree in Communications and I plan to become either a sportscaster or a play-by-play commentator," Zurich said. "I'm a big fan of Ahmad Rashad because he was able to make the transition from player to sports announcer with a lot of class."

"Yeah, NBC's got a good thing with him. I think you'd probably be a great sportscaster or play-by-play man," Mia said.

"You think so?"

"Yes, I do. Matter of fact if we're still friends after my report, I'll invite you down to the station and show you around and introduce you to some people," Mia teased. Of course, they would be friends, she thought, great friends.

"I would like that. Thank you, Mia," Zurich said softly.

"No problem. I'm sure the people down at the station would love meeting you. Can I ask you something off the record?" Mia asked as she turned off the tiny recorder.

"Off the record? Gina warned me 'bout this," Zurich smiled.

"It is not about sports and it's . . . well, it's a personal question," Mia said, blushing.

"Personal?"

"Yes, personal, Mr. Robinson," Mia responded.

"Okay. I think I'm ready," Zurich said in a jovial tone.

"I know from your bio that you are not married. But are you dating anyone or otherwise engaged?" Mia asked.

"No, to both questions," Zurich said. They both smiled a little self-consciously, before Zurich looked down at his empty plate and Mia looked on the floor for her purse. When she removed her wallet from her purse, Mia was smiling both outwardly and on the inside. Zurich started to ask Mia about her marital status, simply because she had asked him, but he didn't. Instead he was thinking about her offer to introduce him to people at her station and how things in Chicago were falling right into place.

Mia gazed at Zurich and hoped he would ask her if she was married or dating anyone seriously. If he did, Mia would know he might be interested in asking her out for a date. Yes, she thought, as she and Zurich waited in silence for the waiter to bring the check, Zurich Thurgood Robinson was quite a remarkable young man.

When the waiter brought the check, Mia placed her credit card on the brown tray and finished the last of her wine.

"So what do you have planned for the rest of the day?" Mia asked.

"I'm going to study my plays and maybe go down to the weight room and work out," Zurich said as he stood up and moved over to help Mia with her chair. As he stood over her, Mia felt a rush of warmth throughout her body when his large hands touched her shoulders. When the two of them walked outside to say good-bye, Zurich thanked Mia for lunch and the conversation and extended his hand. Mia smiled and playfully slapped his hand away so she could reach up and hug him, and then kiss him on the cheeks. Slightly startled, Zurich said good-bye and headed north on Michigan. Feeling light from the wine and Zurich's presence, Mia headed south. Walking in opposite directions, Mia and Zurich were both thinking about their lunch. Zurich liked Mia and felt she could be a good contact. Mia adored Zurich and couldn't remember meeting a more perfect man. As Zurich stopped at a light, he decided he wanted Mia as a friend. That was all. A block away Mia stopped to look in a travel agency window and decided she wanted Zurich for herself. And that too was all.

CHAPTER 8

Room with a View

Sean awoke in the comfort of a king-sized hotel bed in a not-so-windy city. Then again it was still technically summer and Chicago was cooler than New York City. He had arrived late Saturday night after deciding at the last minute to attend the exhibition game between the Bears and Cougars. He hoped to conduct his initial interview with Zurich Robinson after the game on Sunday.

Since he knew very little about Zurich Robinson and the new Chicago franchise, he planned to stay in Chicago for a week and then head to Cincinnati to meet with Jeff Blake, another black quarterback, who had suddenly become the leading candidate to direct the Bengals' offense. He had added Dallas to his tour when the world champion Cowboys signed Rodney Peete to back up their golden boy quarterback, Troy Aikman. Sean was ecstatic that the number of black quarterbacks with starting potential had doubled in less than a year.

But Sean had even more on his mind. During the plane trip, he drank four beers as he looked out of the tiny window of the 737 aircraft and considered the sad state of his life. He knew very soon his lack of steady income was going to become a big problem. Sean had had such big plans when he moved to New York, first and foremost helping out his sister with Gerald's development. He wanted to send his nephew to private school, and take him to Met and Giant games, movies, and possibly send him to summer camp. He wanted to be a positive image for Gerald, but sometimes he felt his life and sexual orientation made that impossible. And with Anja's new man, Sean felt his sexuality might become a problem for his sister, who in the past had been supportive of her brother's homosexuality. Lately she had been dropping hints about how prayer and the laying on of hands could change Sean. A couple of days after her first Reverend Wilder sermon Anja had asked Sean, "Have you ever been sexually attracted to a woman?" Sean had answered with the same question, "Have you ever been sexually attracted to a woman?" "No," Anja replied quickly. "Same answer," Sean said. He knew she meant well, but he also understood that no one person could completely understand another's life. Even though he had convinced himself he didn't want a serious one-on-one relationship, he knew he could no longer take a chance with his life every time his libido showed up by picking up men like Greg. In order to be a good role model for his nephew, Sean wanted to eliminate the things from his life that embarrassed him. He was not ashamed of being gay, just disconcerted by his choice of partners.

Sean showered, dressed, and went down to the lobby of the Embassy Suites. He stopped in the gift shop and picked up copies of the *Chicago Tribune* and the *New York Times* and walked into an adjacent coffee shop.

While standing in line to purchase coffee and a muffin, Sean listened to patrons talk about the Bears-Cougars game as if it were the Super Bowl. He knew the baseball strike had made sports fans a little bit more eager for the football season to start, but he could not recall this much excitement and hype surrounding an exhibition game, a game that would probably be a blowout for the Chicago Bears. These people had to know there was no way a team that had only played three games and lost them all could match up against the Bears, a team expected to battle Minnesota for their division title.

Sean made his purchase, walked outside, and had the hotel doorman hail a taxi to take him to Soldier Field to pick up his press credentials. It was a pleasant morning, the air felt crisp, the sky was cloudless, like an even blue mural. Sean felt an exhilaration that made him forget his problems for a while. Traffic on Michigan Avenue seemed heavy for a Sunday, with long lines of cars driving bumper to bumper.

"So, who do you think is going to win the game?" the taxicab driver asked, interrupting Sean's quick skim of the *Tribune* and *Times* sports pages.

"I don't know. What do you think?"

"Well, I kinda hope the new team wins. You know with them having a black quarterback and all," the middle-aged black man said.

"You know it takes more than one person to beat a team like the Bears, even if it's just an exhibition game," Sean offered.

"Yeah, young man, I know you're probably right, and regularly I'm a Bear man. But they ain't been right since they got rid of the Fridge, Payton, and that Ditka coach guy," he said.

"The Fridge had run his course here, don't you think? And Walter left when he was on top."

"Yeah, I guess you right, but they didn't have to get rid of the coach. I kinda like that guy," he said.

"So you like the Bears' former personnel and the Cougars' new black quarterback . . . huh?" Sean quizzed.

"Personnel?" the driver asked, not quite certain what Sean was talking about.

"I mean the players you mentioned," Sean said.

"Oh yeah, personnel. You know that black quarterback looks like he is going to be a good one," he said.

"Well, I hear he is good," Sean said as the cab pulled into the empty parking lot of the large stadium. Sean looked at his watch and noticed he had two hours before the three o'clock kickoff. Maybe he could meet Zurich before kickoff.

"I just hope they give him a fair shot," the driver said as he turned the meter off and turned to face Sean. "That will be seven dollars, young man. You need a receipt?"

"Yes, sir, and keep the change," Sean said as he placed a ten-dollar bill in the driver's hand.

Sean wished the driver a good day, walked briskly through the parking lot, and located the press office. Included in the packet of information he received was a note informing Sean that all requests for one-on-one interviews with Zurich Robinson must be approved by his publicist, Gina DeMarco. Oh great, Sean thought, as he looked at the note. A quarterback with a personal publicist, shades of Deion Sanders, he thought. This was not a good sign. Zurich Robinson had not completed a single NFL pass, and he had already moved to the head of the prima-donna class of players. Suddenly Sean wished he had started on the West Coast with Vince Evans.

After applying the last of her makeup, Tamela raced from her bathroom to her living room and pushed the intercom button.

"Yes?" she said into the little white box.

"I'm downstairs, pumpkin. You ready?" Hank Senior asked.

"Yes, Daddy, I'm ready. I will be right down," Tamela said as she grabbed her purse, trying to decide whether or not she needed the jacket she had pulled from her hall closet. Even though she did not care that much for football, Tamela was excited about spending Sunday afternoon with her daddy. They had decided a month ago that this would be the day for their annual daddy-daughter outing, which was usually a Chicago Bears football game. They always chose an exhibition game because Tamela had gotten very ill once after sitting through a Bears game in cold weather one late October. So now, it was Hank Junior who braved the Chicago cold, not once, but twice, during the football season. Their mother had decided that though she loved spending time with her husband, his Friday night high school games were enough football for one woman. Hank Senior loved the Bears and the occasional college game because he did not have to coach. He could relax and holler like the rest of the people in the stands. He did not have season tickets, but for more than a decade, he had bought three sets of tickets to the Bears games once the season ticket holder requests were filled and tickets went on sale for the general public. With the new team in town, he was seriously considering breaking down and purchasing season tickets for the Cougars, but he wanted to wait and see how good, or probably how bad, the Cougars would be during their first season.

"So how's my baby girl?" Hank Senior asked as he gave his daughter a hug and a quick kiss on her made-up lips.

"I'm fine, Daddy. You ready for the game?" Tamela asked.

"And you know it," Hank Senior replied.

Tamela looked over at her daddy and smiled. He was game ready with a Bears sweatshirt over his white cotton dress shirt and binoculars hanging around his neck. Hank Senior was a short and thick man, with a melon for a belly, a little pad of extra skin under his chin, and a receding hairline. He had often teased his wife and kids that he was thinking about cutting off what little hair he had so that he could "be like Mike," referring to the popular Michael Jordan commercial.

During the drive to Soldier Field, Tamela and her daddy talked about sports and the law. When her father asked her if she had been watching the O. J. Simpson trial, her quick and terse "no" let him know that she did not want to talk about it. This was one of the many times that Tamela reminded him of his wife of over thirty-five years. If they did not want to discuss something they would let you know with a quick word and a rolling of their eyes.

Tamela changed the subject by asking her daddy what kind of team he was going to have and which team he would cheer for today. Hank Senior thought his team might have a chance to compete for the city title, but he had not made up his mind between the Bears and Cougars. "I'll wait until I get inside the stadium," he said.

"I don't understand why they have to have two professional teams in the same city, Daddy," Tamela said.

"I think it's great. Now Chicago is just like New York. Besides since the Cougars are going to be headquartered up in Evanston, they will probably have all the white folks in the burbs pulling for them. As if this city isn't already divided enough. But I sure do like that quarterback the Cougars have," he said.

"The black one?" Tamela asked.

"Yeah . . . Zurich Robinson. I'm going to try and get him to come and talk with my kids if I can figure out a way to contact him," Hank Senior said.

"Just call their public relations department. I'm sure they can help out. We saw him yesterday at the Bennigan's on Michigan Avenue. Desiree is all in heat about him. And guess what, Daddy? She wrote him a letter and sent him a picture of herself!" Tamela laughed.

"What kind of picture is that girl sending out?" Hank Senior asked with fatherly concern.

"I'm sure it was strictly legit, Daddy."

"I hope so. But maybe I should have taken Desiree to the game since she's so interested in the players," he said.

"Oh, she knows as much about football as I do, and our interest level is about the same. She would only be watching that quarter-back," Tamela said.

"Now, daughter of mine, don't tell me you don't know something about football. After all these years, something had to seep into that pretty little head of yours. What are you gonna do when you have a future Bear or Cougar?"

"Daddy, come on now, don't spoil the day by talking about something like children," Tamela said.

"Yeah, you're right. You got to have a husband first," Hank said.

"Daddy. Just find a parking spot, please."

Hank Senior parked in a large remote lot near McCormick Towers, and they caught a shuttle bus to Soldier Field. Once they entered the stadium, Tamela grabbed her daddy's warm hands and whispered in his ear, "Thanks for bringing me, Daddy. You know how much I look forward to being with you."

"Me, too, pumpkin, me, too," her daddy said as he stopped and gave his daughter a big hug. "Maybe this time you'll learn something about the game."

Zurich Robinson walked into the Cougars' locker room a bundle of contradictions. He was calm but nervous, excited but tranquil. This was a day he had dreamed of since the first time he'd thrown a football and his father said, "Boy, you got an arm on you. If you keep that up one day you might end up playing in the NFL."

Now that day had arrived, and Zurich was concentrating on staying focused, on making the butterflies populating his stomach work for him and not against him, as they had in the past. Like the time when he was in the tenth grade, playing for the varsity, and his first three passes were off the mark. "You're just nervous," his coach had told him. "Make those butterflies work for you. Don't lose your cool," he'd added.

Zurich looked cooler than an ice cream cone on a hot summer day, dressed in white pleated gabardine slacks, a white oxford shirt accented by royal blue suspenders, Italian loafers without socks, and carrying a black leather bag. Zurich found solitude sitting in front of his locker as he reached into his bag and turned off his portable CD player. He took out the Warren G disc and placed it in a protective plastic cover.

It was almost an hour before the kickoff, and he slowly removed his clothes and carefully put them in his locker, placing his pants and shirt on wooden hangers he'd brought from home. He folded his underwear and removed the silver loops from his ears, dropping them in his loafers.

Wearing only a pair of black compression shorts and his teal and gold jersey with the number 12 and the name ROBINSON on the back, Zurich put his body through several stretches to loosen his tight, tense muscles. The locker room was filled with the sounds of slamming locker doors, all types of music, from rap to country, and the voices of several Cougar players shouting things like, "Let's go kick some Bear ass," and "Let's not self-destruct, Cougars."

Moments later as Zurich was tightening the strings on his gold football pants, Mario walked up, smiling and comically moving his head from side to side, as if he was dancing to the latest pop tune.

"Whatsup, Gee?" he asked as he exchanged slaps with Zurich with a cupped hand.

"You the man, Mario. You the man," Zurich responded.

"You nervous, Gee?"

"Naw, I'm ready to go," Zurich said as his stomach began to churn with a reservoir of anxiety.

"Gee, just get me the ball," Mario said while he positioned his arms as if he were waiting to catch an invisible football.

"And you know it," Zurich said as he cocked his arm in a passing motion.

"It's all good," Mario said, and walked back toward his locker.

Zurich started lacing up his shoes and several of his teammates stopped by his locker to wish him good luck. When he was completely dressed in his Cougar uniform, Zurich found his way into a private stall in the bathroom, locked it, and kneeled and prayed. In his silent prayer he asked the Lord to give him the strength to do his best, and that every player, both Cougars and Bears, would leave the field in the same condition in which they began. When he left the stall, he was calm, no longer nervous, relieved and ready.

———

The first half flew by and a few minutes after the third quarter started, the sun disappeared and a cool wind blew into the packed stadium. Tamela suddenly wished she had brought her nylon sorority jacket; she had forgotten how close Soldier Field was to Lake Michigan. She looked at the scoreboard and tried to estimate how much longer she would have to sit on the aluminum bleachers as goose bumps appeared on her arms. The game was close, 14–14, at halftime, and Tamela knew her daddy would not want to leave early. So just as she'd done when she was a little girl and the minister became a little long-winded, Tamela whispered to her daddy, "I'm going to the ladies' room." Without moving his eyes from the field, Hank Senior mumbled, "Okay, pumpkin."

Tamela found her way to the crowded ladies' room and decided she could wait until she got back to her own apartment. As she walked from the place where so many women had sought refuge, she smelled popcorn, hot dogs, and strong coffee. Tamela went to the concession stand and purchased two cups of coffee, a hot dog, and some popcorn and started back toward the stands. While trying to balance the cardboard box that held her food, Tamela accidentally bumped into a hard male body in a blue uniform. When she looked up toward the tall stranger, she noticed a shining silver bar with the name TAYLOR engraved on it. Then Tamela heard a baritone voice say, "Looks like you got your hands full."

Tamela realized that she had bumped into one of Chicago's finest. A straight-standing and sinisterly handsome policeman who looked vaguely familiar as he smiled boyishly down at her.

"Excuse me, Officer," Tamela said.

"No problem, miss," Officer Taylor said. As Tamela walked away the officer's thick eyebrows arched as he tried to figure out why Tamela looked so familiar. "Excuse me, miss, but have we met?" he said. Tamela turned around. "Are you talking to me?"

"Yes. Have we met before?"

"I don't know, but you do look familiar," Tamela said.

Tamela was trying to figure out where she had seen this man as she took note of his clear complexion, the color of heavily creamed coffee. His skin was flawless, and his full lips barely moved under his thick light brown mustache.

"My name is Caliph Taylor," he said as he extended a neatly

manicured hand toward Tamela. She glanced to see if his fingernails were clean.

"Caliph . . . Caliph. You're the busboy!" she said, suddenly realizing where she had seen him.

"And you're the fine lady in the fancy gown with the stuffed-shirt boyfriend. I think the dress was blue," he smiled.

"No, he's not my boyfriend. And yes, my gown was blue," Tamela said.

She could smell his aftershave as he moved closer to her, trying to avoid being bumped again by other fans. That's when Tamela noticed his eyes were light blue-green, as though he had mixed the colors himself from a child's watercolor paint set.

"So, do you mind sharing your name?" Caliph asked.

"What?" Tamela asked, as she suddenly heard the roar of the stadium crowd. Somebody must have scored, she thought.

"Can you hear me?" Caliph said as he raised his voice. "What's your name?" The cheering had subsided and this time Tamela heard him perfectly.

"Tamela Coleman," she replied.

"Is that Ms. or Mrs. Coleman?" he asked.

"My mother is Mrs. Coleman, and I'm Ms. Coleman," she said.

"Oh," Caliph said, placing his left hand to his chin. No ring, Tamela thought as she looked into Caliph's eyes. Tamela felt a sudden rush as if her insides were a bowl of ice cream just covered with hot fudge.

"So, are you a busboy or a policeman?" Tamela asked.

"Who says I can't be both?" Caliph smiled.

"So you're a smartass! Come on, tell me, are you a busboy?" she asked.

"Would that make a difference?"

"A difference regarding what?"

"A difference if I was to ask you for the digits," Caliph said.

"The digits?" Tamela asked coyly. She knew full well what he was talking about. He had asked in that mack daddy tone she loved and despised. Loved when men like Caliph talked that way, but hated when nerds like Tim tried to use the tone to impress a woman.

"Excuse me. May I have your phone number, Ms. Coleman?" Caliph asked politely.

"I tell you what. Why don't you give me your phone number? I'll think about whether or not I want you to have my number and I'll call you," Tamela said. Tamela knew that if he gave her his phone number without hesitation, it meant he really was single. If he stumbled, it would warn her to stay away.

"You got a piece of paper?" he asked.

"No. Don't you have the paper you write tickets on?" Tamela asked.

"Yes, but that's property of the city," he smiled. "Oh, here, I see something I can write it on," he said as he reached for the top flap of Tamela's popcorn box. "You don't mind, do you?" he teased. She was happy she had bought the box instead of the bucket of popcorn. He couldn't write his number in a bucket.

Tamela responded with a half smile. Caliph took a pen from his shirt pocket and wrote down his phone number, including a beeper number. Tamela looked at the home number and realized his exchange was the same as her parents'.

"So you live in Hyde Park?" she asked.

"How did you know that?" he asked.

"I'm psychic and my date is probably getting worried about me," she said as she smiled again and started toward the tunnel.

"You sure are cold. But I like that!" Caliph shouted after her.

When she reached her father, the coffee, hot dog, and popcorn were cold, but since Hank Senior was into the exciting finale of the game, Tamela set the cold food down on the concrete and cheered along with her daddy. Only Tamela had no earthly idea who she was cheering for or who was winning. She simply felt she needed to cheer. She let out a high-pitched scream that even took her daddy's eyes from the field for a moment. "What are you so happy about?" he asked.

"I'm just happy to be here with you," Tamela said as she grabbed her daddy's arm. She squeezed it tightly and laid her head on his shoulder.

Spectacular. That was the only word that could describe Zurich Robinson's NFL debut. In a game that shocked the 77,000-plus people packed into Soldier Field, the Chicago Cougars defeated the Bears 38–31, thanks to a last-minute eighty-six-yard drive engineered by Zurich Robinson. The game was tied 31 all with fifty-three seconds remaining, when the Bears were forced to punt. Like a seasoned NFL veteran, Zurich led the Cougars down the field with the skill of a heart surgeon. Sure it was only an exhibition game and the Bears used a lot of rookies, but a win was a win. And this win was big!

Zurich had completed his first eleven passes, including a seventy-seven yarder to his friend Mario. He finished the day with 483 yards passing, completing 27 of 33 attempts, a new NFL record for a rookie in a debut, exhibition or regular season. In addition, he rushed for 92 yards, eluding a Bears defender for a 44-yard run in the final drive. A run that prompted one of the announcers covering the game to remark, "Zurich Robinson was faster than a hiccup; this kid is going to be a great one."

Zurich could not believe how well he had played and how solidly his young offensive line had protected him, especially during the game's winning drive. He could not wait to shower, dress, and get to a phone to call his father and MamaCee. But first he had to meet the press. Under the lights of the camera Zurich's shaved head gleamed. The scene was chaotic. More than twenty reporters crowded around, nodding and smiling as they held tape recorders and microphones under his mouth and shouted out questions.

"How did you start your day, Mr. Robinson?" a reporter asked.

"I went to early morning church services and prayed that I would have a great game and that my team would win. And that no one would get hurt," Zurich added as he flashed a big smile.

"Looks like your prayers worked. Are you going to do that for every game?" the reporter asked.

"I pray every day," Zurich answered confidently.

"What about your chances against Atlanta?"

"How many games do you think the Cougars could win?"

"Is this sweet revenge against the NFL for not drafting you out of college?"

Zurich's eyes were darting around the locker room looking for help; finally he shouted, "Fellas, fellas, one at a time, please."

The questions were coming fast and furious, as though all the reporters in Chicago had gathered around Zurich's locker. Mario's 157-yard rushing effort and his other teammates' hard work didn't seem to matter. When he gave his teammates and coaches credit for the win, the reporters simply thought Zurich was being modest.

"Will you always be this modest, Zurich?" a plaid-shirt-clad sports reporter asked. Zurich waited for a moment and was surprised at the silence. Clearly, this was a question the other reporters wanted him to answer.

"There is no room on this team or in this game for arrogance. Football is a team sport and no one person can be successful alone," Zurich replied.

"A humble quarterback. What will they think of next?" the reporter joked.

"Excuse me, excuse me," said a familiar feminine voice. Zurich looked over the reporters and cameramen and spotted Mia Miller pushing her way toward his locker. It did not dawn on Zurich that he was standing in front of his locker naked as a jay bird, having removed his uniform and jock en route to the shower, until Mia stood directly in front of him, moved her eyes downward, and then quickly lifted them and stuck a microphone in his face.

"So how does it feel to have such a fantastic debut performance, Mr. Robinson?" Mia asked.

"Zurich. Please call me Zurich. But it feels great," Zurich said, suddenly feeling a little uncomfortable standing completely nude before a woman he had just had lunch with. As MamaCee would say, showing the world all your stuff.

"Ted, my man, would you get me a towel?" Zurich said to one of the locker room attendants. Zurich caught the white towel in mid-air and quickly wrapped it around his waist. The towel was not big enough to cover him entirely. His left hip was still partially exposed despite the efforts of his left hand.

"Thank you," Mia mouthed.

The moment was a little uncomfortable for Mia also. She had been in locker rooms before while in Jackson, but there the rules were different. Female reporters covering college sports had to wait until after the players had showered and dressed before asking questions. But the NFL and the Chicago Cougars would have none of that double standard, so Mia and a couple other female reporters were allowed in the Cougars' locker room at the same time as their male counterparts.

The atmosphere in the packed room was upbeat, as if they'd won the division title in their first year and were on their way to face the Dallas Cowboys or San Francisco 49ers in the Super Bowl. Players of all shapes and colors were playfully engaged in butt slapping with wet towels and exchanging high fives with a youthful exuberance. The locker room smelled of old footballs and funky masculine sweat. Mia cringed at the slamming of lockers and inhaled the sexy scent but tried not to enjoy it. That was hard especially while she was standing in front of Zurich. She was impressed with the way he was handling all the attention, although at times his dark brown eyes moved quickly from side to side, like a small trapped animal, caught between the proverbial rock and hard place. Mia seemed to have developed a fan club of her own. One of the Cougars' offensive linemen, also buck naked, had noticed her when she walked in and followed her over to Zurich's locker, shouting, "Hey, Miss Sports Woman. Let me take you out to dinner?" He was a big guy, muscular, with a slight gut and dark short hair. His face had a sleepy, dumb look and his mouth hung open as though he was surprised. He fully expected Mia to acknowledge his presence and question. He was making her extremely nervous. But she realized this was part of her job, and she had to remain calm and professional.

"I'm sorry, this is my first game covering you guys. What is your name?"

"Darnell Pickens," he said. Mia could have sworn that Darnell was getting an erection. It wasn't that she was looking, but from the ribbing Darnell's teammates were giving him, she knew she'd better not look.

"Hey, big guy, Ms. Miller is talking to me right now. Your locker is down on the other side, right?" Zurich asked.

"Yea, Z-man. You know where it is," he said.

"I tell you what, Darnell. Why don't you go and take your shower, get dressed, and when Ms. Miller finishes with me, I will bring her down to your neck of the woods. How does that sound?"

"Cool, but be swift, Z-man," Darnell said as he gave Mia a toothy grin. Mia felt slightly uncomfortable and dwarfed by Darnell's thickness. Darnell turned his naked ass to Mia and Zurich and started toward his locker, taking his teammates with him. Some of the other reporters followed the naked brigade of players, and Mia was left standing face to face with Zurich.

"Thank you. I think you saved me from something," Mia smiled. She loved the way Zurich had leaped to her defense.

"No problem. Darnell is harmless. I'm kinda surprised to see you in here," Zurich admitted. He grabbed a bigger towel from the top of his locker and quickly replaced the smaller towel with it, hanging the smaller one around his neck.

"Hey, Zurich. I'm Sean Elliott from *ST*. Great game," Sean said, as he maneuvered himself between Zurich and Mia. He had been standing there for a while observing the interaction between Zurich and Mia. Zurich smiled and extended his hands toward Sean and said, "Thanks, man. I think Gina mentioned you."

"Yeah, I'm supposed to see her tomorrow and set up a time when you and I can spend a couple of hours together on this story I'm working on," Sean said. "But we could get together when you get dressed if that's cool with you."

"I'm sorry, but Zurich already has an interview booked," Mia interjected, positioning herself closer to Zurich. Sean looked at Mia and gave her one of those Who is this bitch looks. He did not like women reporters in the dressing rooms, especially when they were as pretty and aggressive as Mia appeared. Why would a player like Zurich want to have a one-on-one interview with him when he could be doing the same thing with an attractive member of the opposite sex? Sean felt they had an unfair advantage with most players, especially the single ones.

"Excuse me. I don't want to get you mad," Sean said as he lifted his hands in a defensive position.

"Sean, why don't you give Gina a call and have her set up a time when we can talk, my brother? Gina will work something out I'm sure," Zurich said.

"Cool," Sean said as he looked directly into Zurich's eyes. He started to say, That's what I was told to do anyway, but didn't. He's not bad at all, Sean thought, nice-looking, great body, and does not use the word "be" as a verb. Sean shook Zurich's hand and started toward some of the other players he wanted to interview, when Zurich called out his name. "Sean, nice meeting you. I look forward to our interview." Sean smiled and said, "Same here." Not bad at all, Sean thought.

Zurich looked at Mia and said, "Close your eyes while I remove this towel and then we can go to the interview room and talk." Mia smiled and playfully closed her eyes; she had already seen his body, a body that provided an impeccable view from any angle.

"You can open your eyes now," Zurich said.

"I wasn't going to see something I haven't seen before," Mia said boldly. Maybe not this good, she thought.

Zurich realized that she was just innocently flirting, or at least Zurich assumed she was. Women flirted with him all the time even after he told them he was saving himself for marriage. He realized that many did not believe him or didn't want to believe him. Once when he explained to a female admirer about his premarriage celibacy plans, she told him, "That's all well and good, sweetie, but from the looks of you . . . trust me when I say there will be plenty left for you to save."

Mia, in turn, was looking into Zurich's face and saw a man she could easily fall in love with. When she followed him to the VIP press area, she tried not to notice his smooth and clear back, accented by a white towel around his neck, or notice the white underwear rim creeping from underneath his tight jeans. All week Mia had hoped his clothing hid some minor deformity, a small dick, bad skin, or perhaps hammer toes. But now she knew better.

CHAPTER 9

AM I RIGHT
OR AM I WRONG?

Zurich ended the day of his NFL debut alone and in the dark where he felt safe and protected. The only light in Zurich's apartment came from the other buildings and the thin illumination of the moon hovering over the city. He sat on the blond floorboards, which slanted in different directions. The apartment's high ceilings made the room feel airy, but intimate. The air in his living room was warm and still.

After the game and the countless interviews, he turned down invitations to go out and party with his teammates and a dinner invitation from Mia Miller. Instead he came home and called his father and MamaCee. His father had watched the game on television and was quite proud. He talked about their upcoming game with Atlanta and how he had already made hotel reservations and how he was going to bring Rhona and her son. MamaCee was overjoyed to hear from Zurich. It was Sunday and she had missed one of her three church services to watch him on television.

"Your team won, huh . . . baby?" MamaCee asked.

"Yeah, MamaCee, we surprised a lot of people," Zurich said.

"MamaCee wasn't surprised. I told Mr. Thomsen, you know the white man I used to do day work for, that y'all were going to win. Yes, sir, I said, ain't no way my grandbaby goin' to be on a losing team. You member Mr. Thomsen, don't you, baby?"

"Yeah, MamaCee, I remember him," Zurich said. He knew if he said no, he would get Mr. Thomsen's entire history.

"You know last Christmas, he bought me a little twelve-inch color television with a remote control thing. I put it on top of my old black and white one, which is bigger than the color one, and I watched my baby run and throw that ball. I was so happy for once that Mr. Thomsen gave me that TV," MamaCee said as she paused for a second and took a deep breath.

Realizing this might be his only opening for a while, Zurich piped in, "I'm happy, too, MamaCee. I didn't know you still had that old black-and-white one."

"What am I going to do with it? Ain't nobody want to buy a black-and-white television. I started to give it to this old man down the road that's always collectin' junk and selling it to somebody. I don't know who," MamaCee said.

"I'm getting my television and furniture tomorrow. Gina, the lady who's been helping me, went and picked out all my stuff," Zurich said.

"Oh, that's good, baby. Who is this Gina lady? Is she pretty?"

"Gina's my publicist, and she's been helping me get organized. And yes, MamaCee, she's very attractive and very married," Zurich said.

"What 'bout them girls with the short-shorts? Pants so tight they look like they ought to hurt 'em," MamaCee said.

"Those are cheerleaders," Zurich laughed.

"What size kitchen do you have?" MamaCee asked.

"It's medium size," Zurich replied. He wondered where she was going with these questions but knew better than to ask.

"You got any big pots?"

"No."

"What 'bout a big black cast-iron skillet? You know the kind I fry my chicken, chops, and gizzards in," MamaCee said.

"No, I haven't had the chance to go shopping," Zurich informed her.

"That's too bad," she said.

"I'll be fine. With practice and all, I'll be eating out a lot," Zurich said.

"Well, you don't need to be eating all that junk food. Tell that Gina lady that your grandmama said to get you some pots and git somebody to come in and cook you some real food. Them folks don't think you got so big eating that junk food, do they?"

"Don't worry I'll be fine." *Please no chitterlings in the mail,* he thought.

"What if I cook you up some chitlins and collard greens and send them through that express mail thing?" MamaCee asked.

Zurich laughed at the thought of chitlins and collard greens going through the mail. "Naw, thanks a lot, MamaCee. Just save them for when I come for a visit."

"Okay, baby. I need to git off this phone. I got some mo scriptures I need to read with me missin' one of my services," MamaCee said. "And talkin to you done gave me a taste for some chitlins, you know what I mean," MamaCee laughed.

"Yeah, MamaCee, I know. Take care."

"You too, baby. You talk to your brothers? Call them and keep praying, baby," MamaCee said.

"I will. Love you, MamaCee," Zurich said as he hung up his phone and smiled. Moments later, his phone rang. It was Trey, his younger brother, calling to congratulate his big brother.

He had watched the game with his suite mates at Morehouse College. Trey told him he was really looking forward to the game against the Falcons and asked his brother for a couple of extra tickets and a check, since his Pell grant money was late. When Zurich asked why it was late, Trey admitted that he was a little late getting the form in. He said he was going to ask their father, but MamaCee had told him not to be worrying their father about money. Zurich said he would think about it, knowing full well that he would be putting a check in the mail the next day.

After talking with Trey, Zurich got up and walked to his bathroom, where he removed his jeans, underwear, and T-shirt and turned on the shower, turning the dial all the way to hot. He glanced in the vanity mirror and decided his head and face would need a shave in the morning. While waiting for the water to get hot, he went to his bedroom and found some pajama bottoms and a jock. Then he stepped into the Plexiglas shower, which was just steaming up, and let the hot, pounding water spray his tense body. He enjoyed it so much that he stayed in the shower for over fifteen minutes before applying soap. After drying himself and putting vitamin E oil all over his body, he looked at the pajama bottoms he had pulled out before his shower, but decided not to put them on. On some nights he didn't sleep in pajamas, but relished the coolness of the sheets against his naked skin. Zurich walked into his bedroom and got his compact CD player with Natalie Cole's *Take a Look* disc already inside, and returned to the darkened living room. He felt the coolness of the floor on his butt as he sat quietly against the wall for back support.

As he listened to the sweet ballads, Zurich closed his eyes and replayed the game in his mind. It had been everything he'd imagined. He fantasized about future games, with his family in the stands cheering him on. He thought how blessed he was to be living his dream. His heart raced again with excitement as he remembered throwing his first successful pass early in the game.

But after he replayed every down of the game, a bout of melancholy descended upon him. Part of him felt lonely. Despite his success on the gridiron, he was missing something. Someone. His life was in a very strange place, unexplored yet familiar, and while the music piped into his ears, a warm wave of the blues washed over him. He thought of all the fears he carried alone, the words unspoken and the stories untold.

Mia Miller sat on a kelly green chaise longue in her bedroom and finished her third and final glass of white wine. She was feeling a little light-headed, not drunk, but not entirely sober, either.

Already in her nightgown she crawled into bed, first arranging the pillows very carefully and then sliding between her satin sheets. She picked up her portable phone and dialed Los Angeles. LaDonna picked up after the first ring.

"Talk to me," LaDonna said in her casual California tone.

"Hey, girl," Mia said.

"Mia. Whatsup?"

"Oh, just sitting here in my bedroom all alone," Mia said.

"What time is it?"

"Almost midnight," Mia said softly.

"Are you all right, Mia? You sound depressed," LaDonna said.

"No, I'm fine. But I do have a problem," Mia said.

"What type of problem? I thought they were treating you right at the station."

"Oh, everything is great at work," Mia assured her.

"Then what?"

"Man trouble," Mia sighed.

"Man trouble. That fool Derrick isn't messing with you, is he?"

"No, I haven't talked with him. He did leave a message, but I didn't call him back. Besides I'm not worried about Derrick. This is about someone else," Mia said.

"Okay, I'm glad to hear that. So tell me about this new man and what's the problem?" LaDonna asked.

"The problem is this guy I'm interested in doesn't seem to be taking my hints," Mia lamented. She could not think of admitting that Zurich had not fallen under her spell.

"Who is he? Does he have a name, and what's the matter with him?"

"I met him through work. He's the quarterback for the Chicago Cougars," Mia said.

"Oh yes . . . yes. I saw him on television earlier today. Home-boy might be blue-black, but he is fine. And I almost fainted when I saw those teeth," LaDonna said.

"LaDonna, that ain't the half of it. I actually saw him naked," Mia said.

"Where? How? When?" LaDonna quizzed.

"Well, as a member of the sports press, I get to go in the locker room the same time as the men," Mia said.

"What's wrong? Is he married? More important, honey, how was the beef?" LaDonna asked.

"No. I just think he's kinda shy. And the beef, well, he's got that and some more," Mia said. LaDonna let out a squeal of delight. "Calm down, LaDonna. I know you've seen some big beef in your day," Mia laughed.

"And you know it. So what are you gonna do? I think you need to go on and tap it, you know, see if he can use his equipment the way he throws that football."

"You are a fool, but you have a good point," Mia said.

Mia confessed that she was going to suggest to the station manager that Zurich would be a perfect candidate for guest commentator on their Sunday sports show, which she was going to co-host every other week. The other anchor was using one of the Chicago Bears and Mia thought it would be fair if she used one of the Cougars. That way, she said, she and Zurich would have to spend time together and somehow he would get the message.

"He has a degree in Communications or something and he wants to be a sports play-by-play man when he's through playing, so this would be perfect for us both," Mia said.

"Well, I wish you luck, girl. But you might ought to do what I do," LaDonna said.

"What's that?" Mia asked.

"Invite homeboy to dinner at your place and then make him an offer he can't refuse," she suggested.

"I couldn't do that," Mia said.

"Why not?"

"What if he says no? I would be embarrassed beyond belief. Besides, I invited him out to dinner tonight after I interviewed him, but he said he had to go home and call his folks," Mia said. "I've got to come up with another plan."

"Oh, that's great. He's close to his family. That's a good sign, that is, if he's not too close with his mother. You know how mothers can be. But somebody should warn homeboy you're working on a plan," LaDonna chuckled.

"You think so?" Mia laughed.

"Hello . . . hello, Miss Thing, this is LaDonna and I know you. If I were you, I would get off this phone and call him right now. Invite him to dinner, and if you still can't cook, get a caterer or take him to some fancy restaurant. Believe me, men like it when women take control. Then you will see how shy he is," LaDonna said.

"For one thing, I don't have to worry about his mother," Mia said.

"Why not? I thought you said he was close to his family."

"He is. But his mother is dead and his grandmother raised him," Mia said.

"That's too bad. But at least grandmothers aren't as bad as mothers can be," LaDonna said.

"I hope you're right. Well, I'm going downstairs and make me some coffee or tea. Maybe I'll put a taste of brandy in it," Mia said.

"You know that sounds great. I'm going to do the same thing. Night, Mia."

"Good night, LaDonna."

Mia hung up the phone and threw off the covers on her bed. She sat up, then stopped suddenly. A vision of Zurich standing in front of his locker nude flashed across her mind. The thought caused a warm and welcome rush of pleasure between her legs. She thought how she had been surrounded by all those men in the locker room, yet amid those male bodies and voices she had noticed only Zurich Robinson.

She could be falling in love with him, if love meant thinking of someone all the time. Zurich could love and protect her. She spent 99 percent of her time daydreaming of him taking her away, traveling around the world, maybe skiing or making love on sand-swept beaches.

She decided against the drink, and lay back down, after turning off the tiny lamp next to her bed. She chose to follow LaDonna's advice and ask Zurich to dinner late in the day, after practice. Mia fell asleep and began to dream. And in her dream he said "yes."

"Should I call him?" Tamela asked as she finishing putting in the last of her plastic rollers, the only kind that could get her hair just right. She was sitting cross-legged in her bed in what she called her grandma nightgown, an off-white cotton, knee-length garment with pink and yellow flowers all over it. Tamela had called Desiree to tell her about running into Caliph and was seeking her advice. Months before, they had made a pact not to get excited about any man. They had decided to concentrate on their careers, and felt that men and relationships would get in the way. They had also agreed if they did get involved with a man, he would be just a "basic boy type," average-looking, with an average job and life. That way they wouldn't have to put up with all the problems good-looking and successful men brought. Since Desiree had broken the pact by writing some man she would probably never meet, Tamela thought it was okay to be remotely interested in Caliph. So here they were, both interested in two very attractive and seemingly successful men.

"What harm can it do?" Desiree said softly. "Call him."

"But I'm not really trying to meet anybody," Tamela said.

"Then don't call him," Desiree replied with a sudden edge to her voice. Tamela realized that while she was going on about some man she had just met, something more serious was on her friend's mind.

"Desiree, are you all right?" Tamela asked.

"Yeah, I'm okay. I just got a disturbing call earlier this evening." She sighed.

"What's the matter? Is your mother all right?"

"Yeah, as far as I know. It's about my job. I heard from my union and it looks like they are going to cut programs deeper than we thought," Desiree said.

"So what does that mean?"

"Tamela, it looks like I might be out of a job. And while I'm worried about that I'm even more sad about the students. I have some students that really have a chance to dance professionally someday. But they've got to get the training now."

"So does this mean they could do away with the dance program?"

"I'm the only one teaching jazz and ballet and if I'm gone, then what's gonna happen?"

"Is there anything I can do?"

"Naw, not unless you got a job for me," Desiree said.

"Can you wait until I open my own firm? Until then, well I can look around. You know, ask some people at the office. Do you have a game plan?"

"I have a list of temp agencies. I'm so glad I took ninth-grade typing and that Windows course last year. I guess I will be doing that while I look for something else. But you know maybe this is a good time to consider another career. Maybe go to grad school."

"But you love dance. What would you study?"

"I still love dance, but I've got bills to pay. Maybe I'll go get an MBA or something like that. Shit, who knows, I may follow my best friend's step and go to law school. Then we could open up a firm together. I just don't know. I don't guess I'll know until they tell me I no longer have a job. But you know what?"

"What?"

"Somehow I will survive. You know me, girl, I'm like roaches.

You can get rid of me for a couple of days, but you know I will be back," Desiree said. Tamela was glad to hear Desiree sound more positive and hopeful.

"And you know it, but please, honey, get your head examined before entering law school, trust me when I say that. And I know I don't have to say this, but you've got a place to stay if you need it," Tamela said.

"I know. Thanks for just listening, Tam."

"I'm here for you," Tamela said.

"I know. Well, let me go. Maybe now I need to get down on my knees and pray," Desiree said.

"And so will I. So will I."

Early Monday morning, Sean headed to Gina DeMarco's office to discuss his assignment from *Sports Today*. He had almost overslept. He'd returned to his room at around 3 A.M., after spending the evening drinking brandy at a black gay cruise bar downtown. Located directly under the El tracks, the bar was affectionately called the Stop and Stab, because of its clientele. It had been a disaster for Sean. He had struck up a conversation with the one decent-looking guy, clean-cut-looking-for-trouble type, while sitting at the bar. Even though Sean was convinced they were both looking for the same type of man, he felt adventurous. Maybe, just maybe, he thought, he had met someone whom he could talk with after they made love. But the guy, Steven something, was a complete stuck-up jerk. When Sean asked him, "Steve, where did you go to college at?" he had replied in a very clipped, smart-ass faggot tone Sean despised, "I attended Dartmouth where they teach the correct use of prepositions." Sean responded quickly, "Oh, excuse me. I intended to ask you where did you attend college, asshole?" He did not give Steve a chance to reply, as he left the bar horny and with a quiet rage. A rage that simmered every time he thought about how black gay men treated each other. He thought they spent too much time worrying about white gay folks and straight black folks and never talked honestly about something they could attempt to change.

At Gina's office, Sean was greeted by a receptionist who seemed more interested in her colorful nails than in announcing visitors. From the way she was laughing on the phone, and saying "I heard that," and "Girl, that's deep, too deep," every other sentence, Sean knew she couldn't be talking business. After waiting about ten minutes Sean went over and stood directly in front of her.

"May I help you?" she asked.

"Yes, I'm waiting to see Ms. DeMarco," he said.

"Oh, I'm sorry. Let me buzz her," she said.

But before she could figure out which button to press, Gina opened the huge maple door that shielded a suite of offices from the reception area.

"Sean, I was wondering what happened to you," Gina said.

"I was here at nine on the nose, just as we agreed," Sean said as he moved his eyes in the direction of the receptionist, whose attention had turned back to her nails and her phone call.

"Come on back to my office," Gina said as she rolled her eyes at the receptionist.

"Thanks, I really appreciate your seeing me on such short notice," Sean added.

"Oh, no problem. I'm just glad I had a little time in my schedule," Gina said.

Once seated in her office, Gina asked Sean to excuse her for a second. She picked up her phone, hit a few buttons, and said, "Felicia, this is Gina DeMarco in the Jefferson Suite. Yeah, yeah, I'm doing fine but I've got a problem with Miss Thing out there in the waiting area. She has got to go," Gina said. "Well, I'm not surprised, please add my name to the list of people who want her gone." She paused before adding, "I thank you for your attention to this."

While Gina was on the phone, Sean noticed all the pictures on her wall of Gina with different celebrities in the music industry; some of the people he could make out, some he couldn't. Her office had an art deco flavor, and the suite was decorated with a pink leather chair and a green sofa. Everywhere Sean looked, he saw the Alpha Kappa Alpha insignia: on the card holder, the wastebasket, and even on a beautiful embroidered wall hanging with the AKA monogram.

Gina hung up the phone, shook her head, and said, "My peoples, sometimes we can be so wrong we're right."

She pulled out a compact and lipstick from her desk, pressed her lips together, and as she applied the rum raisin shade to her lips, started to quiz Sean on what his article was about and what he thought of her new client.

"You see this?" She held up a pile of pink message notes. "All these are requests for Zurich. Is he hot or what? Am I right or am I wrong?" she said while she closed her compact and put it in her top desk drawer.

But before Sean could answer, Gina laughed to herself and said, "You were in the dressing room yesterday, weren't you?" She paused before asking, "Is Zurich Robinson the finest specimen of a man you have ever seen? Am I right or am I wrong? Shit . . . if I wasn't married, I might have to give him some. But I wouldn't leave Clarence, that's my husband, to go to heaven. Am I right or am I wrong?" Gina laughed. Clarence must be some kinda man, Sean thought. But he liked Gina and thought Clarence might turn down a trip to heaven, too.

Gina DeMarco enjoyed hearing herself talk and hearing herself laugh. After a few more comments about Zurich, all ending with her "Am I right or am I wrong?" Sean finally got a question in.

"So, Gina, I guess you are an AKA?" Sean asked. He realized that was a dumb question. Of course she was, with the way her office was decorated.

"Honey, till the day I die! Are you greek?"

"No, the fraternities on my campus were crazy. It was in the day when hazing was part of the norm," Sean said.

"Yes, it was that way when I pledged. So I guess that tells you I'm no spring chicken," Gina laughed. Sean smiled back at Gina, and started to tell her that she couldn't be that old, but decided he had better get on with the business at hand.

"So do you think it's possible for me to see Zurich this afternoon? I'm only in Chicago for a week and I wanted to get started on the story and see if my editor wants me to expand Zurich's part, since it looks like he's going to be a big star."

"You got that right, Sean," Gina said. She pushed the intercom button on her phone and told her secretary to get Zurich on the phone and see what his schedule was. A few minutes later her phone buzzed and Sean could hear Gina talking with Zurich. She toyed with one of her large, gold clip-on earrings, looked at Sean, and asked, "Do you play racquetball?"

"I haven't played in a while, but . . ."

"What time do you have the court reserved, Zurich?" Gina asked over the phone. She put her hands over the mouthpiece of the phone and said, "Can you meet Zurich at the Chicago Health Club at two-thirty? And be on time," said Gina.

"No problem," Sean said. He wondered if he still remembered the rules of racquetball and whether he'd brought tennis shoes.

"How much time do you need?" Gina asked Sean, this time placing the phone against one of her ample breasts.

"About two hours," Sean replied.

"He needs about four hours, Zurich," Gina said as she smiled at Sean and winked. When she hung up the phone, she wrote down the address of the club, looked at Sean, and said, "I did that 'cause for some reason I like you. I don't know why, but I do. You must remind me of somebody. I don't know who, but don't worry, I'll think of it."

"Thanks, Gina, I appreciate that. Can I ask you something?"

"Sure."

"Why does a man only in his first year in the NFL need a publicist and manager? I mean, no offense to you, but when I first heard Zurich had a publicist, I was worried I might be dealing with a real prima donna," Sean said.

"Good question, and to be honest, and just between you and me, he doesn't need a publicist-manager yet. But you're correct that he's going to be a big star and the agent he has really doesn't work for him. I have big plans for Zurich," Gina said.

"Are you interested in becoming an agent?"

"I knew I liked you for some reason, maybe because you're smart. Yes, I plan on becoming a major agent. I've spent a great deal of time researching what it takes to be a great one. A lot of these agents, mostly male and white guys, sign up these players right out of college, sign them with big money and then leave them alone. Nobody shows them that signing the big contracts is just the beginning. They need to know how to manage their money, and have the opportunity for commercial endorsements without being a Michael Jordan or Shaq. I want to make sure that my clients have careers after they're through using their bodies," Gina ended as she got up from her chair and sat on the edge of her desk facing Sean. She sounded as if she were doing the closing argument in a Perry Mason trial.

"Have you always wanted to be an agent?" Sean was intrigued.

"You sure do have a lot of questions. No, I started out as a manager and publicist for a well-known declining diva who shall remain nameless. It was great, being exposed to the high life. Fancy hotels, room service, first-class air travel, limos. Because of her, I was living large. But one day I realized that it was her life and her shit. I wanted my own shit and starting my own business was one way of getting it. My husband is really supportive and I never stop working and I never stop thinking."

"As they say, Ms. Gina DeMarco, it's all good," Sean said smiling.

Gina smiled back, gave Sean a low five, and said, "Am I right or am I wrong?"

CHAPTER 10

ONLY HUMAN

Sean eased his badly bruised ego and aching body slowly into a seat next to Zurich, who sat sipping orange juice at the bar at the Chicago Health Club. Sean followed suit and ordered a tall glass for himself. Zurich had just beaten Sean unmercifully in five games of racquetball. Though he realized he was not in the same shape as he had been in college, he was not prepared for the whipping he took from Zurich or the complete exhaustion he felt after two hours of chasing a tiny rubber ball. Strongly built and just under six feet, Sean knew he was about ten pounds overweight. His body was so limp that instead of showering after the final game, he slumped to the floor of the locker room with his eyes closed and his back against the wall, while Zurich showered. He was, as they say down South, dog-tired. Sean thought even his hair was hurting.

"Is there anything you can't do well?" Sean asked.

"Well, I can't play golf that well," Zurich said. He seemed completely serene.

"Then next time I'll meet you on the golf course!" Sean said.

"Oh, you weren't that bad. At least you made it competitive," Zurich said. He didn't want Sean to resent him, and on some level, he admired Sean's style on the court, the way he never gave up, despite the beating Zurich handed him.

Sean reached into his black gym bag and pulled out a tape recorder and a black-and-white reporter's notebook. He laid the recorder on the counter, looked at Zurich, and said, "So, you ready to get started?" Sean really wanted to go back to his hotel and crash, but he had to do this interview to get paid. The juice was helping him recover a little, but what he really wanted was a massage and a cold, cold beer.

"Okay, Blackman. Start quizzing," Zurich said.

"Before we get started, I have a question, not related to the interview. How in the world did you meet Gina 'Am I wrong or am I right?' DeMarco," Sean asked with a broad smile. Zurich smiled back and laughed as he tapped the bar.

"Gina, she's my girl. She saves my life. When I first signed with the Cougars, and flew to Chicago, she met me at the airport. She was in a limo, dressed like a movie star. Came up to me, introduced herself, and then said, 'Zurich Robinson, I think you're going to be as big as Michael Jordan, Walter Payton, and Shaq combined. Am I right or am I wrong?' "

"What did you say?"

"What could I say? She was so confident and forceful. But not in a pushy way. I liked her style. So I said, 'I think you're right,' " Zurich said with a hearty laugh.

"What happened next?"

"Well, she had this presentation all prepared with companies she would contact on my behalf and how she would help me with people like yourself. The media. She has really been a blessing. And you know, I'm seriously thinking 'bout firing my agent and letting Gina handle all my personal affairs, including Cougar management," Zurich said.

"You must really trust her," Sean said.

"She makes it easy to trust her," he smiled.

"I got that from her, too. She's a firecracker with a touch of class," Sean said as he prepared to turn on the tape recorder.

"That's a great way to describe her," Zurich said. "Say where did you get that Negro League baseball cap from?" Zurich asked as he admired the tan baseball cap with several of the teams' emblems on the front.

"A friend of mine in Austin, Texas, has a store where she sells them. She knew I collected baseball caps, so she sent it to me. You want me to see if I can get you one?"

"Sure, I'd like that and I'll get you one of the Cougars' hats," Zurich offered.

"Thanks a lot, I'd like that. Now, this is for the interview. I want to know if you consider yourself a role model?"

"For who?" Zurich asked.

"Well, for young kids," Sean said.

"Maybe for my nieces and nephews. But not for other people's children. I think children should find their role models where they live. People they see every day. People they can talk to and get some instant response to their problems. People like their parents and older siblings. Now I know a lot of us come from dysfunctional families. Where maybe the mother or the father isn't a good role model, but there is usually somebody in the family, say a grandmother or uncle, that can provide support. I don't think because I can throw and run with a football that I have a right to be a role model to somebody I don't know," Zurich said thoughtfully. Just as he finished talking and started to take a sip of his orange juice, one of the locker room attendants came over with a towel and asked Zurich to sign an autograph for his son, telling him how he was one of his son's heroes. Zurich quickly agreed and exchanged a polite smile with the attendant as he signed the towel.

"So, I guess you've thought about this," Sean commented.

"No offense to you, but athletes get asked that question a lot."

"Point well taken. So let's talk about the game against the Bears. Did you expect to play so well?"

"I had hoped I would play well, but it was one of my best games ever. Everything just fell into place. Also, my offensive line was on," Zurich said.

"Do you think the Cougars can compete for the division title in their first year?"

"You want a PR answer or what I really think?"

"What you really think," Sean replied.

"Now, you know, Mr. Expert, that's next to impossible to predict. The team was well aware that the Bears used a lot of players that are not even on their roster right now. We will be lucky just to stay competitive and make the games interesting," Zurich said. "Like our racquetball game," he smiled.

"Touché," Sean said. He thought that maybe Zurich was becoming a little more relaxed.

Sean and Zurich talked about his time in the Canadian Football League and how difficult it was learning the rules of Canadian football after leaving SFT, where the running and passing were about half and half. Sean was impressed with how thoughtful and open Zurich was with his answers. After two hours of questions concerning football and Zurich's future in the NFL, Sean's questions became more personal. He wanted to know about Zurich Thurgood Robinson the man. He realized he had been given only a limited amount of time and he was pretty sure that his time was almost up.

"So, you're from Florida?"

"Yeah, grew up in Tampa, but my brothers and I spent a lot of time in Mississippi, where my father grew up."

"What part of Mississippi?"

"A little town near Jackson called Warm Springs. My brothers and I used to play football near Alcorn State University," Zurich said.

"I read where you have four brothers, no sisters. Is that right?" Sean said.

"Yes, that's correct," Zurich said, dropping his gaze.

"Are you close to your brothers?"

"Yes," he said quickly, now avoiding eye contact with Sean.

"Tell me about them," Sean said.

"I thought this interview was about me," Zurich said sharply. It became clear to Sean that he had stepped into dangerous territory.

"It is about you, but I want the story to reflect the complete Zurich Robinson, how he feels and how he became who he is. But if you don't want to talk about your family, well, that's cool," Sean said.

"I'm sorry, I didn't mean to snap. It's just that my family didn't choose to be in the public eye. So out of respect for them, I try not to discuss them. But don't get me wrong. I love my family. Two of my brothers are married with wonderful children and live in the Miami area. And I have a little brother who attends Morehouse College, majoring in English, and he walked on the football team. He's also a pretty good tennis and racquetball player," Zurich said.

"So, that's who you practice racquetball with," Sean smiled, making a mental note to ask about brother number four later.

"Yeah, sometimes. Actually he plays at about the same level as yourself," Zurich said.

"So, he's not that good," Sean laughed.

"You're a nice size, Sean. Did you ever play any sports?" Zurich asked, changing the subject.

"Yeah. I played a little baseball and ran track," Sean said.

"Where did you attend school?"

Before Sean could answer, he had a brief flashback to his Stop and Stab encounter. He smiled to himself.

"I attended the University of Georgia in Athens," Sean said.

"Were you any good at baseball?"

"Average," Sean replied. "What about your parents? Are your mother and father still living?"

"My mother is dead," Zurich said abruptly. He had hoped he had been clear about not wanting to talk about his family.

"I'm sorry to hear that. Let's move on and talk more about your education," Sean said as he realized to probe further might be hazardous to his health. Brother four would have to wait. "Did I read somewhere that you majored in Communications?" Sean asked.

"Yes," Zurich said proudly. "I want to be a sports announcer one day, and the opportunities for former players are usually in larger cities like New York and Chicago," he said.

Sean started to point out that Zurich was not alone in his desire to move to the announcer's booth, but he decided not to burst his bubble. Besides, he thought, Zurich just might be able to make the transition. He was handsome and well spoken, but Sean thought he might have to grow his hair back so he would look less threatening to Middle America.

"Is Gina gonna help you with becoming an announcer?"

"I know it's up to me, but Gina is well connected. But I don't know if I want to live in Chicago forever. I really want to live in the South," Zurich said.

Sean looked through some of his notes and the press information Gina had given him. The night before, he had noticed that there was a year missing from Zurich's résumé.

"Zurich, I see from the information I have that you stayed at SFT an extra year. Was that to complete your degree?"

"No, not exactly. I was scheduled to graduate on time, because my father had stressed the importance of education. When I wasn't drafted, I decided to stay an extra year and work on my skills. I thought about going into coaching, maybe on the high school level."

"When you weren't drafted, did you think about giving up?"

"No. I knew one day I would get my chance," Zurich said confidently.

"What about 1992?"

"What about it?" Zurich asked with that terse tone.

"Well, I see you were with the CFL in 1991 and in 1993. It doesn't say anything about you being cut. Did you go back to SFT?"

"No, I took a year off. I had some things I needed to work out," Zurich said.

"You want to talk about it?"

"About what?"

"The year . . . shall we say, of reflection," Sean said.

"No," Zurich said. He looked away from Sean, finishing off the glass of juice. Sean felt that Zurich was slipping away, but he was not quite ready to let him go, he still had a few more questions.

"I didn't see it in the information, Zurich, but are you married?"

"No."

"So, you're enjoying all the extra benefits of a single professional football player . . . huh?"

"Not really. But my teammates are making up for it. I mean those guys can practice all day and play all night. But not me. Right now, I'm concentrating on being the best quarterback I can be. To win as many games as possible, with the help of my teammates, of course."

"Understood. Is there anything else you'd like to share with our readers? Maybe something reporters haven't asked that you've wanted to comment on?"

"No, I really haven't had that many interviews, but I think with Gina that will probably change," Zurich said.

"I think you're right. Thanks a lot for your time and if you're ever in New York, please give me a call. I'd like to show you around," Sean said, handing him a business card. Zurich took the card, studied it for a moment, and then said, "I would like that. And the same thing if you're ever in my neck of the woods, maybe we can hook up."

Sean and Zurich both stood up and shook hands. Sean couldn't help but notice the rounded curve of Zurich's muscled arms as he pulled the sleeve of his red polo shirt in place. Zurich suddenly placed his finger to his lips and said, "Sean, I do have something I'd like your readers to know."

"What's that, Zurich?"

"That athletes are human. We make mistakes. We have the same type of problems other people have. Football, basketball, on the professional level is a job and people just get to see us do our job," Zurich said. "They're really not seeing the whole person," he added.

"Is there anything else?" Sean was a little mystified by Zurich's sudden shifts in mood, from terse to tender.

"No, just make sure you get in the human part. Make sure they know that."

"I will, Zurich. I'll make sure they get it."

CHAPTER 11

TAKE A LOOK

The work week was over. Early Friday evening, Mia Miller scooped up her diamond stud earrings from the glass surface of her vanity and placed them in her ears. She pressed her lips together to make sure her lipstick was still in place and dabbed her wrists with Donna Karan perfume. The coolness felt good against her skin and calmed her. In less than an hour she would be meeting Zurich Robinson for dinner and an evening of light jazz. She also hoped that she would end the night in his arms. It didn't matter if that meant her place or his. But just in case, she had bought new polished cotton purple and black sheets and lightly sprayed them with the same scent she was wearing. She had her paisley silk robe and a nice red silk camisole resting on the back of her bathroom door. Her dress was a sexy, black-and-white Barbara Bates silk dress with tiny spaghetti straps, from a boutique on Oak Street. Her hair was pulled back with a burgundy and black velvet ribbon, studded with tiny pearls. She had on a burgundy handmade silk brassiere with matching panties. The ribbon, panties, and bra were all gifts from Tanya, who had sent them from Paris. Mia slid her hands over her breasts to make sure they were secure in the special bra. She was proud of her breasts. For most of her life they had been small and elfin, ensuring her membership in the i.b.t.c. (itty bitty tittie club). But when she reached twenty-eight, suddenly, and without the help of a surgeon, her breasts developed, bountiful and full, among the best in Chicago television or in Chicago period, for that matter. She didn't mind that she had also gained weight in a few other places, because with a trainer's help she was able to shift the extra pounds to their proper place, rounding her once slim hips.

Mia took one final twirl in the mirror before heading to the downtown restaurant where she was to meet Zurich. Right before she got ready to bounce downstairs, she lifted her dress and sprayed perfume on her panties, rubbing the scent on her inner thighs. After she finished spraying, Mia had a horrible thought—maybe she had overdone it. She didn't want to smell like a whore with too much perfume. Mia started to jump in the shower, to remove the expensive perfume, but realized she didn't have the time. Besides, she thought, the combination of perfume with her own scent had driven grown men crazy in the past. Why would tonight be any different?

Mia had convinced Zurich to agree to an evening on the town, under the guise of talking about a position as a commentator on her station. She had talked with the general manager about Zurich and felt that when he met Zurich, he too would be impressed. There was no way he could not be bowled over by Zurich Robinson. Initially, Zurich had declined her invitation, saying he needed to rest for his upcoming game with Atlanta. But Mia had been persistent and had placed a call to Gina DeMarco. Zurich had finally called the night before and agreed to meet with her, after Gina told him she thought the meeting might help his future broadcasting career. Mia assumed that Zurich really did want to spend the evening with her and was just playing hard to get. If that was the way he wanted to play, then Mia Renee Miller was game. She was the queen of playing hard to get.

While Mia searched for her car keys, the phone rang. Mia wasn't going to pick up but thought it might be Zurich, calling to say he was running late.

"Hello, this is Mia Miller," she said, forgetting for a minute that she was at home and not the station.

"Mia," the familiar male voice said.

"Yes."

"How you doing?"

"I'm fine, Derrick. How did you get my number?" Mia said coldly. Mia thought, *What does this fool want and how did he get my number?*

"I have my ways. Didn't you get any of my messages?"

"Yes."

"Looks like Chicago is treating you right," Derrick said.

"Yeah, right, I'm doing fine. Look, Derrick, I was on my way out the door," Mia said.

"Oh shit. I was hoping I could take you to dinner tonight. I made reservations at Mason's," Derrick said. The same restaurant where Mia was going to meet Zurich, she thought. Since it was too late to change, Mia prayed Derrick wouldn't show up there and make a fool of himself.

"So you're in Chicago?" Mia asked. She could tell he had not lost his nerve.

"Yes. I thought I said that in my messages," Derrick said.

"Oh, did you? Look, I've got to go. I hope you enjoy your dinner," Mia said sarcastically, as she playfully stuck her finger in her mouth in a gagging motion.

"What about later on tonight? Maybe we can meet somewhere for coffee," Derrick said. "I could come by your place."

"Gotta go and I'm going to be out real late," Mia said and hung up the phone slightly flustered.

Mia had resumed the search for her keys when the phone rang again. Annoyed, she reached down and yanked the phone plug from the wall, but she could still hear the upstairs phone ringing. She marched upstairs to pull out the plug, but by the time she reached it the phone had stopped ringing. Mia took a deep breath and decided she was not going to let Derrick ruin her evening. But how had he gotten her number? Mia picked up the phone and dialed LaDonna's number. After a couple of rings LaDonna answered the phone and before she could say hello, Mia said, "LaDonna, please tell me you did not give Derrick my phone number."

"Hold up, Miss Thing. Now you know better than that. I would never give out your number, especially to that no count Derrick," LaDonna said. *Has this bitch lost her mind? Here comes Miss Thing's inappropriate behavior,* she thought. But she would remain calm— somebody had to.

"Then how did he get it?" Mia shouted.

"Mia, now hold up. Get a grip on yourself. Derrick's a businessman. He could have gotten your number from several places. You know how slick he is. Calm yourself down and let's think about this," LaDonna advised.

"I know you're right. I'm sorry. It just sort of shocked me when I picked up the phone and there he was on the other end of the line," Mia said. She felt bad when her temper flared up like an overly sensitive car alarm and she directed that fury toward her friends and family.

"I know, but Derrick is just country stupid. Just tell him you don't want to be bothered. And if push comes to shove, then you can just get your phone number changed."

"Yeah, I know," Mia said.

"I thought you had a big date tonight with that football player. What's his name?"

"Zurich. Yeah, I was on my way out the door when Derrick called, but I need to calm down. I am not going to let Derrick spoil this night for me," Mia said.

"I know that's right. Listen, have yourself a glass of wine and chill out and then go out and dazzle that man," LaDonna said.

"Yeah, you're right. I'll talk to you tomorrow. Are you still thinking about coming up here soon?"

"Yeah, I'm going to talk to my travel agent first thing Monday. I can't wait to see you, darling," LaDonna said.

"Me, too. Bye."

"Bye, Mia. And, Mia . . ." LaDonna paused.

"Yes?"

"Please have fun tonight, okay?"

"I will," she said as she hung up the receiver.

Mia looked in the mirror and touched up her makeup. She saw the tension in her face and quickly made a conscious decision to calm down, relax, and return to her former good mood. She dabbed her underarms dry and went downstairs and poured herself a glass of wine. As she drank the wine she thought about what LaDonna said about Derrick being just stupid. Maybe she was right, there had only been that one incident of violence, but she still wanted him to stay out of her life. Mia gulped down the last of her wine and found her keys. As she was walking toward the door, she stopped, made a U-turn, and plugged her phone back in. She dialed LaDonna's number once again.

"Hello," LaDonna said.

"Hey, girl, it's me again. I just wanted to tell you that I'm sorry for accusing you of giving out my number. I know you wouldn't do that. Will you forgive me?"

"There is nothing to forgive. I know how you are and I know you're uptight about this big date. Just get on out of that house and have a good time," LaDonna said, amused by her friend's occasional hissy fits.

"I will. I love you," Mia said.

"I love you too, doll," LaDonna said.

Mia hung up the phone and was thankful that LaDonna always had a way of making her feel better. And the wine didn't hurt either.

Mia pulled her royal blue Mercedes 190SL into the restaurant's valet area and handed her keys to the young black parking attendant with an eraser-topped haircut. He gave her a big smile, like a kid with an all-day pass to Disney World and said, "Hey, ain't you the sports lady?" Mia smiled and said, "You got that right." He grinned. "I love watching you on the tube." Mia made a mental note to give him a big tip when she picked up her car, especially after she heard him tell one of his co-workers, "Man, look at her. Look at that walk. She's all that and a bag of chips. She is over."

When she walked into the elegantly designed Creole restaurant, Zurich was standing at the hostess station. He looked quite handsome in an eggshell white suit, carefully tailored to his massive body, and a black cotton turtleneck. When he saw Mia, he gave her a broad smile and extended his hand toward her. But Mia reached up, placed her hands on his shoulders, and kissed him quickly on the lips. Zurich looked a bit startled and they both seemed to pull away from each other awkwardly.

"Mia, it's great seeing you," Zurich said. He was blushing something serious, as his dimples deepened in his face. Mia had never noticed his dimples before.

"Thank you, Zurich. It's good to see you. I'm not late, am I?" Mia asked as she looked at her Rolex while giving him a slow once-over.

"Oh no," Zurich said. "I just arrived."

The hostess came over when she saw Mia and said, "Mr. Robinson and Ms. Miller, your table is ready." Mia loved the fact that people gave her special attention when they recognized her, like the valet parking attendant.

Zurich pulled out Mia's chair and waited for her to be seated, then gently eased her chair closer to the table. Having Zurich so close, and smelling his Joop scent, made Mia want to simply start kissing him from head to corner toe. When he was seated, Zurich glanced around and complimented Mia on her excellent taste in restaurants.

"I love this place. The food is great and sometimes they have a jazz combo that's super. But I thought we might go over to the Intermission Jazz Bar over in Printer's Row after dinner," Mia said.

"Don't forget I have to catch a plane to Atlanta tomorrow. I really shouldn't have let you talk me into doing this until sometime next week," Zurich said.

"Oh, come on, relax. I promise to have you tucked in on time," Mia smiled.

The waiter came over, gave Zurich and Mia menus, and placed a wine list in front of Zurich.

"Not for me, thank you," Zurich said. The waiter looked in Mia's direction. "And you, miss?" Mia looked at Zurich and thought he wasn't drinking because of his big game on Sunday. She was hoping he wasn't one of those athletes who abstained from everything good for you before a big sporting event.

"What kind of wine do you have by the glass?" Mia asked.

"May I suggest one of the excellent California whites?" the waiter said, pointing to the list.

"Let me have a glass of house white," Mia said.

"And for you, sir?" the waiter asked Zurich.

"Just let me have an iced tea," Zurich said.

"Would you like to order an appetizer?"

"Sure, why not?" Mia said. She leaned over, touched Zurich's knuckles, and said, "Please get what you like. Channel 3 is paying for this," Mia lied. Her general manager knew nothing about her dinner.

"Oh, a beautiful woman, and with an expense account," Zurich said as he surveyed the menu and tried to relax. He could feel tiny beads of sweat gathering in the small of his back, a sure sign that he was nervous. He didn't know why Mia made him so nervous.

"You are too sweet," Mia giggled. She hoped her wine would arrive soon, so she could relax. She couldn't recall being this nervous about a date before.

Zurich ordered a cold shrimp appetizer and fried calamari and said to Mia, "We can share." Mia smiled and was relieved that at least Zurich ate fried food. So he hadn't given up all the good stuff.

"So how has your week been?" Mia asked.

"It's been busy with practice, meetings, and more practice. Atlanta has a complicated defense, so I've been staying late and going over plays with our offensive coordinator. I'm really nervous because I think my father and his lady friend and my little brother are going to be at the game."

"Don't tell me you're nervous after the game you just played," Mia joked.

"You bet. That was an exhibition, the Atlanta game is the real deal, and if I play badly on Sunday, I will be old news. My backup does not enjoy being a backup," Zurich said.

"I think he better get used to it," Mia said as she took a sip of the wine the waiter had finally placed next to her. She savored its wonderful taste as it spread a warm glow through her body.

"So, tell me about this commentator's position," Zurich said in a suddenly businesslike tone.

"Well, I don't have all the details. But I know you will be perfect for the job," Mia said as she took another sip of her wine. The glass was almost half empty.

"I would like to hear more about it. And I would have to talk it over with Gina to make sure it won't conflict with some of the companies interested in me endorsing their products. But this position is something I'd like to pursue." Zurich wanted to express interest, but not appear too eager.

"So are you hearing from a lot of companies?" Mia quizzed.

"Yes, we are. Shoe companies, sportswear, cereal, and even underwear. But I want to make sure I'm not overexposed," Zurich joked.

"I wouldn't worry about that. It's not too often that sponsors have a chance to have a good-looking, intelligent, black quarterback represent their products. Lord knows we need men like you," Mia said as she finished her first glass of wine. She asked the waiter for another glass when he brought the appetizers.

Zurich plunged into his calamari, while Mia toyed with the shrimp dish and gazed at Zurich. Realizing Mia was staring at him, Zurich stopped eating for a moment to ask, "Is everything all right?"

"Oh, everything is fine. Just fine," she said, looking away as she took a long sip of wine. An awkward silence fell over the table until the waiter brought out their dinner salads.

Mia acknowledged the waiter as he placed the salad before her, and then looked back at Zurich.

"Does my looking at you make you nervous?" Mia asked.

"Oh no," Zurich lied as he dived into his salad.

"If you just weren't so damn fine," Mia laughed, as the wine began to talk for her.

"Mia, you're awfully nice to say that. But what do the young kids say? I'm not all that," Zurich said.

"Please. You are all that. You know you're fine," Mia said. She wanted to break through his shyness and let him know that she was definitely attracted to him.

Zurich looked at her and saw how attractive she was. He knew she was just flirting, but it was making him uncomfortable. Besides, he had been under the impression that this was a business dinner. A dinner that could enhance his future in broadcasting. Zurich thought that Mia was drinking too much and too fast. But he knew that broadcasting was a cutthroat business. She probably needed a couple of drinks just to unwind. Besides, Mia wasn't his sister or his girl-friend. She wasn't even his type. A personal comment about her drinking could be misinterpreted. Zurich knew to keep his business separate from his personal life and this dinner, in his eyes, was strictly business.

The waiter brought Zurich's lobster and Mia's pasta and the two of them chitchatted over their entrees. They talked about sports, Mia's career, and how Zurich was adjusting to life in the Windy City. Zurich was enjoying his food while Mia picked at hers. Several times, restaurant patrons came over and asked the two of them for autographs. One, a matronly-looking, fat woman commented on what a handsome couple Mia and Zurich made. They both smiled and then giggled like school kids out on their first date. Mia giggled because she was thinking how great being a couple would be, while Zurich's laugh was more diplomatic, the raction he thought was expected of him. It was a part of his unique charm. His incredible ability to flow with people, not against them. By the time dessert arrived, Mia had finished her fourth glass of wine and had ordered Kahlúa and coffee, telling Zurich he didn't know what he was missing. When Zurich offered Mia a taste of his cheesecake, she smiled and leaned closer to him, and whispered, "What I have is sweeter." Zurich looked at her, puzzled, and Mia laughed nervously. "I meant the Kahlúa and coffee," she said. Mia brought the cloth napkin to her mouth and tried to wipe away the embarrassment she felt, hoping Zurich hadn't taken her last comment the way she had intended. Didn't he think she was sweet, that she would taste sweet? She took a sip of the piping hot coffee, hoping it would sober her up just a bit.

Mia seemed to regain her composure and turned the conversation to the television show, much to Zurich's delight.

"Have you ever done any commentating on television before?" Mia asked.

"Yeah, I did a couple of guest spots with a station in Canada," Zurich said as he finished his cheesecake. He had taken his fork and was playing with the lone strawberry that had adorned his dessert.

"Do you have a tape?"

"A tape?"

"Yes, a tape of your broadcast?"

"I think so. Matter of fact, I think I have one in a box my father just sent me," Zurich said.

"Do you think I could get it and make a copy of it?" Mia persisted.

"Sure. I'll get a copy made for you when I get back from Atlanta," Zurich said.

"No, I need it sooner than that. It would help if you would let me take the copy you have. I can get another copy duped while you're in Atlanta. We can stop by your apartment and do the jazz thing at a later date." Mia started to relax because it seemed her plans were finally taking shape. Just as she had dreamed, they would be alone and she knew he wouldn't resist her.

"Okay. But then why don't you let me drive you home?" Zurich offered.

"Oh, don't worry, I'll be fine. But I could ride over to your apartment with you and then you could bring me back to get my car. Do you have a VCR?"

"Yeah," Zurich said.

"We can take a quick look at the tape to make sure it's what I need," Mia said.

"Sure, no problem," Zurich said as he motioned for the waiter, glad to see Mia hadn't completely forgotten the purpose of their dinner meeting.

"Now, don't forget, I'm paying for this," Mia slurred slightly as she reached for her purse and took a last sip of her coffee. Zurich looked at her with his eyebrows raised, but she didn't seem to notice his concern. He hoped that the composed, professional Mia would be the one that went to his apartment to view the tape.

When the waiter returned her credit card, she and Zurich walked to the front of the restaurant, and the valet brought his car. Minutes later, they arrived at Zurich's apartment and he offered to run upstairs and retrieve the tape, but Mia wasn't having it, informing Zurich she wanted to "see where he slept." Again, that uncomfortable feeling stabbed Zurich. As he gently pushed the revolving doors, Mia managed to negotiate her way into the lobby. Zurich nodded at the concierge and Mia waved toward him and said good night, as if she herself lived there. When Mia and Zurich were on the elevator heading to his apartment, they were both silent. Zurich was thinking about packing for the trip to Atlanta, while Mia was wondering if she would have problems getting her car from the valet the following morning. As the elevator approached the twentieth floor, Mia finally broke the silence. "What floor do you live on?" Mia asked.

"The twenty-second floor," Zurich said.

"Then we're almost home," she said.

Zurich didn't comment as the elevator came to a stop. Mia walked out first and asked, "Which way?"

"Left."

He slipped his key into the door with 2239 in polished brass across the top. He held the door open and stepped aside as Mia walked in. Once inside Zurich pushed a beige dimmer on the wall and the room filled with a soft muted light that enhanced the magnificent view of the Chicago skyline that dominated the tastefully decorated room.

"Have a seat, Mia, and I'll get the tape," Zurich said as he headed toward his bedroom.

"Do you have any wine?" Mia asked.

"No, but I have juice," Zurich yelled from the bedroom as he rummaged through one of his footlockers. When he could not find the tape, he looked in the closet, with no luck, and then in his underwear and sock drawer. Still no luck. Zurich walked back to the living room, rubbing his cheeks with both hands. "That's strange," he said. "I could have sworn the tape was in the box my father sent me."

"Oh, sure," Mia joked. "Anything to get me up to your apartment."

"No, for real. I know he sent me that tape," Zurich said.

"Don't worry about it. I can get it later. Come over here and talk to me," Mia said as she patted the sofa next to her. Zurich gave her a strained smile and said, "You sure I can't offer you some juice?"

"No, thank you."

"I think I'll have some," Zurich said as he walked into his kitchen. Mia felt a little shaky as she stood and walked over to the entertainment system against the wall. She flipped through the CD's that were opened and called out to Zurich, "I see you're a big Natalie Cole fan."

"Yeah, I love Natalie," Zurich yelled as he placed the juice container back into the refrigerator.

"Do you mind if I play one?" Mia asked as Zurich walked back into the living room with his juice and an unpeeled banana. "No problem. Here, I'll put it on," Zurich said, peeling his banana.

"Great. Where is your ladies' room? I'd like to freshen up," Mia said.

Zurich placed his glass on the coffee table and finished the banana in two huge bites. "Let me make sure it's presentable," Zurich said as he went to his bathroom. It looked fine except that the lid was off the dirty clothes hamper. He placed the wicker top back on the basket and warm water over the bar of soap that rested in a ceramic dish on the sink, giving the soap a barely used quality. He hastily arranged the face towels hanging outside the shower and returned to the living room. With a sweeping motion of his arm, he announced, "It's all yours." Mia grabbed her purse and gave Zurich a mock curtsy as she passed him and went into the bathroom.

Mia took a quick look in the bathroom mirror and pulled her lipstick out of her purse. The color had left her full lips, but her cheeks were quite flushed. She applied fresh lip gloss, tightened the bow on her hair, and decided that she still looked pretty good. Mia realized that it was getting late and if she was going to make a move on Zurich, it was now or never. He did have a plane to catch the next morning. Mia wished she had just one more glass of wine to boost her courage. She even thought about telling Zurich to call the liquor store she'd spotted at the corner and have them send up a nice bottle of chardonnay. A bottle they could take to the bedroom.

From the bathroom, Mia could hear Natalie's soulful voice fill the apartment. She checked to make sure her bra and bikini panties were in place, but then Mia did something she felt would ensure a night of passion with Zurich. She removed her panties. She balled them up and opened her tiny black leather purse. But there was no room for them, with her credit card holder and her makeup. She started to put them back on, since these were special panties, when she spotted the wicker hamper, where she thought the panties would be safe for the night. She could put them back on when she left the following morning. She got a little thrill tossing her panties into the same hamper with Zurich's masculine-smelling T-shirt, socks, and underwear. She took one last look in the mirror and then sexily sashayed back into the living room, where Zurich was sitting on the sofa gazing out the large picture window.

"Did you miss me?" Mia asked. Zurich answered with one of his boyish smiles. Mia sat down on the sofa and enjoyed the way her naked bottom felt on her silk dress. This was a nice feeling, she thought, as she gazed at Zurich with an *I've got a secret* look. While Natalie sang her heart out, Mia and Zurich sat in polite silence. For the second time this evening perspiration formed at the small of Zurich's back.

Zurich rose from the sofa and walked over to the window. The night was clear and cloudless, and the light from a full moon cast an eerie glow over the room.

"I hope I'm not making you nervous," Mia lied while she drank in every curve of Zurich's muscular frame.

"No," he said as he turned and faced her. "Not at all," he lied back.

"Then dance with me," Mia said.

"Dance?"

"Yes, sir. Dance with me," Mia said as she stood and walked over to Zurich. She placed her slender arms around his neck and looked into his dark brown eyes, which almost seemed black. Zurich froze. Mia leaned closer to him, their bodies touching, and she could smell the freshness of his body. His clean, masculine scent soothed her. She felt safe in his arms. Mia started to sway against him, but he still did not respond. For a moment, he seemed carved from stone. She began to massage his shoulders, and felt the tenseness and rigidity in his neck.

"What's the matter?" Mia asked.

"Nothing," Zurich mumbled.

"Then dance," Mia commanded. He forced a smile, but his eyes expressed something other than pleasure.

Zurich allowed Natalie's voice to dictate his movements. Mia rested her head against his chest, and it seemed to her that Zurich was pulling her closer to him. The music saturated the room and Mia whispered, "This feels nice." She let her hand glide down Zurich's back to his sleek waistline. Zurich became even more tense. He stared at the wall, watching their shadows embrace. The music played on. Mia began to move with a little slow, seductive grind, lifting her abdomen up toward Zurich's midsection. She wanted to release his stiffness. "I thought you told me you were a great dancer," Mia said playfully. Zurich avoided her eyes and seemed only to move his legs . . . one . . . two and back. Mia realized that she was going to have to take matters into her own hands. This man was too shy. She searched for his heavy fingers and moved them toward her buttocks. Zurich quickly moved his hands back to her waist. He felt his sex betraying him as it gained weight. Zurich wished he was wearing a different type of underwear, rather than the Lycra-cotton blend that provided no support for an expanding muscle.

"What's the matter? You don't like the way it feels?" Mia teased.

She felt his hardening sex pressed against her. She thought she was almost there.

"I just don't think my hands should be there," Zurich said without looking at Mia.

"They should if I put them there."

Suddenly Mia kissed Zurich on the lips, and his own lips responded automatically. Her lips were soft, her breath full of wine. Zurich tightened his lips together and pulled away, holding Mia at arm's length.

"Mia, maybe we shouldn't be doing this. I think I should take you home," Zurich said.

"Why? What's the matter? I thought you liked me."

"I am fond of you, Mia. I think you're a very nice person. But I think you've had a little too much wine," Zurich said softly.

Her voice changed, laced with anger. "If I'm so fabulous, then why am I single and having to force myself on you?" Mia demanded. Zurich did not answer. Instead his heart started to race and a cold sweat covered his body, chilling him.

"Well, let's at least finish the dance," Mia said, as though her angry outburst had never happened. Zurich reluctantly moved closer to Mia and placed his hands around her firm waist. Mia took Zurich's hands, and this time, more forcefully, slid them under her dress onto her naked buttocks. She held them there, before Zurich could pull them away. Her body was as hard as a dancer's and for a split second, Zurich's hands lingered on her buttocks, enjoying their firmness despite himself. But when he realized that Mia didn't have any underwear on he jerked his hands away and pulled back from her with a shocked look on his face. How could he have gotten himself in this situation? He had taken great effort to avoid compromising situations that might jeopardize his promising career. His older brothers, his father, and MamaCee had all warned him about women like Mia.

"Mia, like I said, this is getting out of hand." He was trying to be firm, but polite. He didn't want to hurt her fragile feelings.

"What's the matter with me?" she shouted. Mia felt hot tears welling up in her eyes.

"Nothing's wrong. It's just that . . ."

"It's just what . . . ?"

"This is just too fast. Mia, we need to talk about this," Zurich said.

"Talk? Talk about what? I want you. Isn't that talk enough?" she demanded.

"But you don't even know me," Zurich said.

"I know I want you," Mia said.

"Come on, Mia. Let me take you home," Zurich said, reaching for her.

"Take me home. Fuck that!" Mia shouted, throwing his hands off her. Zurich was shocked at her language and her tone. He looked at her sympathetically.

"Where is my purse? I can get my own ass home," she said as she looked around. She retrieved her bag from the floor next to the sofa, and screamed at Zurich, "You don't have to take me anywhere. I can get my own ass home. Just please forget that this ever happened. Forget that we ever met. Because that's what I'm going to do about you." The tears spilled from her eyes and Mia covered her face with one hand. Zurich walked toward her to try and comfort her. Suddenly her sobs turned into heaving sighs and then she started screaming, "Let me the fuck alone! Leave me the fucking ass alone! I don't need your pity, you sorry ass mutherfucker. Leave me the hell alone."

"Mia, come on. Please stop crying. I'm sorry. I'm sorry. I didn't mean to hurt you." Zurich reached out to pull her to him and Mia's nails cut a bloody trail across his massive hands. Zurich looked at the deep scratches, while Mia bolted out the door.

Zurich started after her, but realized he needed his apartment key. He ran to his bedroom, snatched the key from the dresser, and raced out of his apartment toward the open elevator door. Zurich caught one last glimpse of her tearstained face as the elevator door closed just out of his reach. Zurich quickly pushed the down button and within seconds the other elevator door opened. He jumped in and hit the button marked "L" and silently prayed that he would reach the lobby before Mia left. When his elevator door opened, he saw the back of Mia's black dress pass through the revolving door.

"Mia, wait! Please come back. I'm sorry. Let's talk about this." The elderly white doorman and the concierge looked at Zurich but neither said anything, just exchanged puzzled glances. Zurich reached the sidewalk outside just as Mia jumped into one of the waiting taxis that were lined up in front of his apartment building. He stood at the curb as the taxi sped away. He placed his hands on top of his head and let out a long sigh, then walked back into the lobby.

Upstairs, frustrated and exhausted, Zurich lay his body across the sofa, repeating to himself, "What the fuck happened? What happened?"

Zurich pulled off all his clothes and stood buck naked in his living room. He walked over to the wall unit and hit the CD replay button and Natalie Cole's voice started to soothe him. He turned off the lights, walked into his bedroom, and climbed between his clean sheets. He wanted to sleep, but not dream. His eyes were wide open and he sat up and looked at the phone. Maybe he should call Gina and tell her what had just happened? But it was too late. Maybe he should call MamaCee? She would know what he should do. No, too late to call her. Zurich pulled Mia's card from his wallet on the nightstand and dialed her number. Maybe she was home by now. After five rings the answering machine came on, and when the mechanical beep sounded, Zurich said, "Mia, I'm sorry. I never meant to hurt you. Please call me when you get this message, so I know you got home safely."

With his hands clasped together and resting behind his head, and his eyes open, Zurich prayed silently. He had started to climb out of bed and get on his knees, as he did every night, but he was still pretty much in a daze from the evening's events. Zurich prayed that Mia would someday understand why he had rejected her, and that one day, maybe he too might understand her behavior and his own.

When he finally fell asleep, he dreamed. A bad dream. The kind where Zurich appeared just outside his body, watching himself, unable to stop what was happening to him and return where he wanted to be.

Zurich was on a football field, totally naked, except for his football helmet and mouthpiece. The rest of the team was also in the dream, but they were all in full uniform and didn't seem to notice Zurich or his nudity. They neither talked nor signaled to him, as they normally did during games. Zurich took his usual position behind the center. Each time he took the snap, he would drop back, and throw the ball perfectly into the hands of the same opposing player. No matter how hard he concentrated, the ball always ended up in the hands of the opposing player. When he tried to talk to his teammates, they acted as though they didn't see him. They would take their positions after each interception and Zurich would again throw the ball to the opposing player.

Just before his dream ended, Zurich took the snap and while looking for a Cougar receiver, he saw something that shocked him. Standing in the end zone, waving his hands wildly and shouting, "Zurich. Throw it to me, you dummy. Throw it to me," was a mirror image of Zurich, in full Cougar uniform, but without his helmet.

CHAPTER 12

Lips, Hips, and Fingertips

It was early Saturday evening and Tamela was bored. So despite her better judgment, but on the strong advice of her mother and Desiree, she decided to call Caliph. She hoped he had an answering machine so she could simply leave a message and then pray he returned her call. Although she had called men before, it was not something she wanted to become habit forming.

She climbed into her bed before calling the first of the three numbers Caliph had given her. He picked up on the first ring.

"Good evening."

"Good evening. Is Caliph in?" Tamela asked, suddenly feeling as if she were back in junior high calling some hormone-raging boy for a possible date to the ninth-grade prom.

"Caliph speaking," he said. His voice boomed across the receiver with a commanding resonance.

"Caliph, this is Tamela Coleman. I met you at the football game last week at Soldier Field," Tamela said.

"Of course. What did I do to deserve this call?"

"Well, actually, I was doing some interviewing for a PNB," Tamela said, fighting off a nervous laugh.

"What, may I ask, is a PNB?" Caliph asked as he smiled to himself. He was used to women calling him, but Tamela was one he had prayed would call.

"You don't know what a PNB is?" Tamela asked, laughing into her cordless phone as she pulled one of her pillows close to her. She leaned back in her bed and gazed dreamily at the ceiling as Caliph pondered her question.

"No, I'm sorry to say I don't know what a PNB is, and if you're interviewing me for the position, don't you think it's only fair that I know what it is?"

"Okay, I'll tell you. But like I said, I am just considering interviewing you for the position. Nothing is final yet," Tamela said.

"Okay, give it to me," Caliph said. He liked her sense of humor, that is, if she was playing.

"Potential New Boyfriend," Tamela said. "A PNB is a potential new boyfriend," she repeated.

"Oh, so you think just because I gave you my phone number, and by the way I didn't think you were ever going to call, that I might be interested in being this PNB?"

"No, I didn't say that. You asked me why I called," Tamela replied, thinking for a brief moment that maybe it wasn't such a good idea calling Caliph. Why did she listen to her mother and Desiree when it came to men? she wondered. After her cute opening Tamela didn't really know which direction to go in next.

"Well, let's say for the sake of further discussion, that I'm interested. One of the first things we would have to do is to change the name, because I haven't been a boyfriend in a long time. I'm only interested in being somebody's man friend, their significant other, their nigger, and maybe, someday, somebody's husband," Caliph said.

"You've already answered the first question on my application," Tamela said.

"What was the question?"

"Are you married?"

"Now, why would I give you my home phone, my beeper, and my cellular phone number if I was married?"

"I don't know. Why do men do stuff like that?" Tamela asked. She wanted to say dumb shit like that, but she didn't want to give Caliph the wrong impression. She was impressed that he hadn't used any cuss words with the exception of nigger, a term her brother and other black male friends used all the time.

"Well, I can't speak for all my brothers, but I personally am not married or otherwise engaged. I don't have the time," Caliph said.

"Which leads me to my next question. How many jobs do you have?"

Caliph let out a generous laugh over the telephone lines. Tamela loved the way he laughed. It reminded her of a kid telling a joke and breaking out into laughter before he got to the punch line, which usually became lost in the laughter.

"What's so funny?" Tamela asked.

"I was just thinking about that skit about the Jamaican family they used to do on 'In Living Color.' You know the family that had all the jobs," Caliph said.

Tamela joined in his laughter. "Yeah, I know the family. So how many jobs *do* you have?"

"Only one officially. That being an officer with the Chicago Police Department. But sometimes I moonlight as a security guard at sporting events 'cause I get in free, and I can put the extra money into the catering business I co-own with my older brother," Caliph said.

"So you own the business and you're not a busboy?" Tamela asked.

"Yes, I co-own the business and if I have to be a busboy, then I'm a busboy. But before we finish this application, let me ask you a quick question, Tamela."

"Sounds fair," Tamela replied.

"You're not one of these stuck-up sisters who will only go out with a brother with a bunch of degrees and a lot of money in the bank? A brother like the one you were with at the dance?"

"If you're asking me if I'm stuck up, then the answer is a definite no. If you're asking me if I like my men to have a job and a little money in the bank, then the answer is yes," Tamela said.

"Well, I do have my own checking account," Caliph joked.

"That's a start," Tamela replied quickly. She wasn't sure how long she could keep this silly chatter up.

"Naw, on the serious tip, Tamela, I'm really glad you called. Since you didn't give me your digits, I was kinda worried that I might never get the chance to speak with you and find out what's behind that beautiful smile of yours."

Tamela smiled to herself. Maybe her mother and Desiree did know what was best.

"Are you still there?" Caliph asked.

"Oh, I'm sorry. What did you say?"

"I was saying, and hoping you would agree, that maybe we should complete this interview in person. Say Sunday at Gladys's for breakfast. Or do you call it brunch?" Caliph was hoping she wouldn't call a meal at Gladys's brunch or ask what Gladys's was—a popular soul food restaurant on the South Side where he had breakfast often with other policemen.

"It depends on what time it is. Are we talking before or after church?"

"It's your call, Tamela. Should I wear a suit?"

"A suit to Gladys's?" Tamela quizzed.

"Well, this is an interview."

"It doesn't sound like you have time for another job," Tamela joked.

"If it's a good job, then I'll quit a couple of the ones I already have," Caliph said.

"Okay, why don't we meet at Gladys's at one-thirty on Sunday?" Tamela suggested.

"That's tomorrow."

"Great, you know the days of the week," Tamela said. As soon as the words came out of her mouth, she hoped he didn't take the statement the wrong way.

"Okay, Miss Smartass, that's fine, but don't you want me to pick you up? And what about the digits?"

"Thanks for asking, but I can find my way to Gladys's. And my number, just in case you get a more attractive job offer, is 555-2079," Tamela said.

"Bet. I'll see you Sunday."

"Fine. Have a good night."

"You too," Tamela said.

"Tamela," Caliph said.

"Yes."

"Just so you sleep okay. I do have a college degree," he joked.

"Stop playing with me," Tamela said.

"Good night."

"Good night, Caliph."

She smiled to herself as she got up from her bed, brushed her teeth, checked her door, and then climbed back into bed for a peaceful night's sleep.

The New York night was cool and refreshing, so Sean decided he would walk home from the posh East Side hotel. As he dodged between a bus and limousine at Seventh Avenue and Fifty-second Street, Sean began to laugh out loud at the predicament he had found himself in just moments before. It was as though he had just walked out of a bad porno movie.

Sean had gone to a bachelor party for Keith Meadows, a defensive end for the New Jersey Warriors. He hadn't wanted to go, but figured it would be good for business with all the players he could meet. You could never tell where you might meet a budding superstar. Keith and Sean had become friends when Keith called him to compliment him on a story Sean had written for the *New York Times* on the amount of money top defensive players were currently being paid. Sean also knew star players, like Keith, were always looking for experienced writers to help pen their *This Is My Life Up Till Now* memoirs. Books that the players and publishers felt the public couldn't live without. Keith was all set to marry his college sweetheart in a double-ring ceremony at Harlem's Canaan Baptist church on Sunday, and his friends were giving him a night to remember. When Sean walked into the two-bedroom hotel suite, he was somewhat surprised at what he found. Keith's best man, Basil Henderson, a wide receiver with the Warriors, had hired three women from a local strip club to come and entertain the troops. About thirty men, in various stages of undress, were lined up at the two bedroom doors and one of the bathrooms to be serviced by the ladies, whom Basil had described as not-your-everyday-garden-variety hoes. He had referred to them as top shelf, women who made their living as exotic dancers but also turned a few tricks on the side. Sean couldn't help but notice how handsome Basil Henderson was. His tight-fitting vest suggested a body of stone, with a chiseled face and honey-colored complexion highlighted by perfect rows of teeth. His eyes, a seductive gray, were mesmerizing, not only because of their color but also because of their intensity, demanding attention.

When Sean told his hosts he would pass on the party favors, Basil looked at him and said, "Man, what's wrong with you? Are you some kind of faggot?"

Sean started to tell him, "Hell, yes," but instead he reverted back to his high school mentality and said, "Which room is the sister in?"

"She's a beauty, Sean. She's holding court in the master bedroom," Keith said, pointing to a closed door down at the end of the hall.

"Then that's where I'm headed," Sean said.

"Okay, but just so you know. The blond with the big titties is in the bathroom and the Asian with the killer head is in the other bedroom," Basil said.

Sean looked toward the master bedroom and saw that there was no longer a line. An attractive, well-built black man had just walked out buck naked with his penis still erect and a big smile on his face.

"Man, you're in for a treat," he said to Sean as he walked into the other bedroom. Sean didn't say anything, but simply gave the man a smirk, trying not to look at his stiff manhood. Sean knocked tentatively on the master bedroom door before entering. He heard a delicate voice say, "It's open."

When Sean opened the door and walked in, he was surprised to see a slender, elegant, red-clay-colored woman, totally nude, propped up on a four-poster queen-size bed with her legs wide open. She was twisting her shoulder-length brown hair and smiling like a flight attendant at the end of a long flight.

"Come on in, baby. What's it gonna be? Lips, hips, or fingertips?" She smiled.

"I haven't heard that saying in a long time," Sean said as he made sure the door was locked.

At first, Sean was going to go for oral sex and just pray his sex wouldn't fail him, but he suddenly decided that he didn't have to do this if he didn't want to. And there was no doubt he didn't want to. He looked around the room, decorated with a duo of armless chairs, an oval-shaped marble table, and cherry wood nightstands and TV cabinet. He noticed an opulent display of pink roses in a big crystal vase. The room smelled of lilac air freshener and sex. There was a trail of condom wrappers scattered just under the four poster bed. At least these bozos were having safe sex, Sean thought. Sean raised his voice an octave into a stereotypical gay lisp, so there wouldn't be any misunderstanding with the young lady. He wanted her to know the deal.

"Now, Miss Thing, you know I don't want none of that," Sean said, pointing at her triangle of pubic hair. So that's what all the uproar's about, Sean thought, as he twisted his head slightly to get a better view.

"What you saying?" the young lady asked.

"I don't want no pussy. What part don't you understand?"

"Oh, you one of them . . . huh?"

"One of them? If you mean that I'm gay, then the answer is yes," Sean said.

"Don't go there. Homos are cool with me. My uncle is gay and to tell you the truth I could use a break. Usually at parties like this and when they have a white bitch with blond hair and blue eyes, I get little or no action, but I've been getting plenty here tonight. Maybe them dummies realized Miss Blonde's titties are fake and mine are real," she said proudly, lifting her breasts toward Sean. "You want to touch them and see? Mind if I smoke a joint?"

"Naw and no, just knock yourself out," Sean said. "What's your name?"

"Marlene," she said as she reached for a silk robe and a little purse that was sitting on the nightstand.

"And yours?" Marlene asked.

"I'm Sean."

"You don't look like no homo," Marlene said.

"Look, Marlene, if we're going to be friends, then you got to use the politically correct term and call me gay," Sean joked.

"Okay. You don't look gay."

"And you don't look like a hooker," Sean said. In fact Marlene looked like one of the beautiful black models he saw in magazines. She was actually quite pretty.

"You know there was another one like you at the beginning of the party. He might still be out there. And Sean, he was phine. I mean make me write bad checks fine, work the graveyard shift at 7-Eleven," Marlene laughed.

"How do you know he was gay?" Sean asked.

"I could tell. His stuff wouldn't get hard. He didn't want to touch me. And when I tried to give him some head he jumped back so quick, you would have thought I was some kind of blood-sucking vampire. But he asked me to make all these sounds, like he was really fucking me down. And that fool was hollering, 'Whose pussy is it . . . whose is it?' Do you want me to make sounds, Sean? Just in case those fools are listening at the door?"

"You think someone's listening?"

"Child, plezze, all them freaks out there. Yes. I bet they out there checking out each other. Trying to see who got the biggest piece," Marlene laughed. "When I ask them what type of condom they want to use, all of them say the Magnum," Marlene added as she showed Sean a black-and-gold condom package.

"Sho you right," Sean said.

"Why do men do that?" Marlene asked.

"Do what?"

"Check out each other's shit all the time. I did a couple of these parties before. And the whole time they be sitting out there, buck naked, talking about how big someone's stuff is. At some parties I have even seen them measuring each other," Marlene said as her delicate fingers rolled the joint. Sitting cross-legged on the bed, she took deep drags off the joint, pausing in between to ask Sean these questions he didn't know the answer to. Sean just stared at Marlene and wondered how she had gotten herself in this situation.

"I don't know. I guess it's a man thang," Sean said as he looked at his watch.

"How long you been in here?" Marlene asked.

" 'Bout fifteen minutes," Sean said.

"Well, somebody will be knocking on the door any minute. Let me finish this joint. You know, maybe I should introduce you to my uncle. What kind of guys do you like?"

"The kind that's out there," Sean said as he pointed toward the door.

"Then you won't like my uncle. He's more fish than me," Marlene said.

"That's too bad. Well, I guess it's time to go face the crowd. What was the guy's name that you thought was gay?" Sean was wondering if she could be talking about his host, Basil Henderson. Maybe he was getting ready to write a book, Sean thought.

"I don't remember his name. But he was fine. A red bone with gray catlike eyes. His hair is cut real short. But he struck me as a real asshole, Sean. You can do better than that," Marlene said.

"Maybe you're right. Nice talking to you. Be safe," Sean said as he rubbed Marlene's hands.

"I'm always safe. You be safe. It's a lot of shit out there," Marlene said.

Sean said good-bye to Marlene and opened his pants, so it would look as if he was still dressing when he walked back into the living room into the maze of half-dressed and drunk men.

He spotted Keith over in a corner talking to a friend. Sean walked over and patted him on the back and thanked Keith for inviting him.

"So how was it? You have to thank my good buddy, Basil, for the party. So how was it?" Keith smiled.

"It was nice. Basil knows how to throw a party," Sean said and smiled back.

"So I'll see you at the wedding?" Keith asked.

"Yeah," Sean lied as he left. He had no intention of attending the wedding, but with over a thousand invited guests he was certain not to be missed. Sean figured you've been to one big jock wedding then you've been to one too many.

Back home, Sean was turning the key to his apartment, when he heard his name called.

"Hey, Sean, I have an overnight package they left for you," Rodney said.

Rodney was a dancer, and Sean's next-door neighbor on the right. He and Sean were on polite speaking terms but not what you would call running buddies. Rodney was gay and had figured out that Sean was gay, too, when he saw him come in late one night, a little bit tipsy and with trade.

"Thanks, Rodney. I was waiting for this," Sean said as he took the package from his neighbor and looked at the return address. It was from Gina DeMarco's office. Sean assumed it was the additional pictures of Zurich that she had promised to send.

"You're a writer, right?" Rodney asked.

"Yeah, that's right," Sean said as he opened the envelope without looking up at Rodney.

"What kind?" he asked.

"Oh, I do all kinds of writing, but mostly I cover sports," Sean said as his eyes widened at the sight of the handsome Zurich Thurgood Robinson.

"Got something good?" Rodney asked.

"A picture of somebody I just interviewed in Chicago," Sean said.

"Can I see?" Rodney asked.

At first, Sean hesitated, but then thought Rodney's request was harmless.

"Sure, just another football player," Sean said as he handed over the photo.

"Do you get to go in locker rooms?" Rodney asked.

"Of course," Sean replied.

"Then, child, I need to get your job. I would be happier than a sissy with a bag full of dicks if I could just spend one night with the Warriors, the Knicks, or any of them teams," Rodney laughed.

Sean smiled and started to tell Rodney about the party he had just come from, but thought that would only be teasing him. He thought maybe he should become more friendly with Rodney. That it might be nice to have someone besides Anja to sit around and shoot the shit with when it came to men. When he'd lived in Atlanta, Sean had a personal trainer, Lamont Daniels, who loved sports and trained a lot of professional athletes. Lamont was also gay and he and Sean used to work out and gossip about what athletes might be gay. Lamont had told Sean on several occasions, "A dick ain't got no conscience, so every man with one could dip every once in a while." Lamont had died of AIDS three years ago, and his death had hit Sean so hard he had been slow to develop a close friendship with another gay man.

"My God. Hello, trade alert . . . trade alert. This man is fine . . . fine . . . fine. He is over," Rodney said, holding the picture out in front of him.

"Yeah, I guess he's okay," Sean said as he reached for the photo. Rodney was about to release it when suddenly he pulled it closer and said, "I know this guy. I don't know his name, but it starts with a Z."

"Are you sure?" Sean asked. He was a bit surprised that Rodney would know someone like Zurich.

"Yeah, he's a dancer. Used to dance with the Alvin Ailey company and was in a couple of videos," Rodney said confidently. "I heard he worked all the time because he was so fine and masculine-looking."

"This guy danced with Ailey? I don't think so," Sean said.

"Oh yes, he did. It was a couple years ago. I'm certain 'cause when I first moved up here, I took classes over at Dance Theatre of Harlem and Ailey. I knew all their male dancers, if not by names, then by face. Trust me when I say I wouldn't forget a body like this," Rodney said.

Sean started to blow off Rodney's comments, but he seemed so certain. If Zurich was a dancer, why hadn't he told Sean? Was Zurich in New York dancing during his year of reflection? Sean thought back to the year missing from Zurich's football résumé and how it had been obvious that he didn't want to discuss the missing year.

"Look at the picture again. You are certain this was the guy? And was he family?"

"I'm certain, Sean. And even though I didn't sleep with him, I know he was family 'cause a close friend of mine in the company used to date him. I'm sure this guy was with Ailey. So now he plays football, huh? Ain't that a trip? Now here's a sissy who really does have access to a bag full of dicks," Rodney said as he finally gave the photo back to Sean. "It looks like you didn't get the whole story, Mr. Writer."

"I guess I didn't," Sean said as he said good-bye to Rodney and opened the door to his apartment.

Inside, Sean grabbed a beer from the fridge, opened a window, and let the soft, dry night air cool his stuffy apartment. He took a seat at his desk and studied the picture of Zurich Robinson, football player . . . dancer . . . mystery man. Sean's mind whirled with questions about Zurich. Questions he was determined to find answers to.

Later that night, around midnight, Tamela's phone rang so loud and unexpectedly she woke up and reached for it in one smooth motion, saying in an angry voice, "Who is this?"

"I just wanted to make sure you gave me the real number," the male voice said.

"Like I said, who is this?" Tamela hated being startled by the phone late at night, since it usually meant bad news.

"Is that how you answer the phone? Kind of testy?" he teased.

"I'm getting ready to hang up," Tamela said.

"Hold up. Sorry . . . sorry. Tamela, this is Caliph. The policeman . . . we talked a couple of hours ago," he said.

"Yes, Caliph, what time is it?" Tamela said as she rubbed her eyes and looked for her clock.

"Oh, it's a little bit after midnight," Caliph said.

"Is something wrong with you? I mean are you on some type of medication?" Tamela half joked.

"Hey, I know it's late. But I was just sitting up here in my window, drinking a cool one, and couldn't go to sleep. So I said to myself, Who can I call? Then I asked myself who did I want to talk to the most and guess who came to mind?" Caliph asked.

"Who?"

"You. But did I wake you?"

"Plezze, now you come on. You know you woke me," she said. Lulled by the memory of Caliph's voice, she had been sound asleep with no thought of work. "But tell me why you want to talk with me the most?" She thought, *You don't know me well enough to be making a booty call.*

"I was thinking about your interview, how cute it was, and how much I enjoyed talking to you and how I couldn't wait until Sunday," Caliph said.

"I'm sorry, but it's going to have to wait until Sunday," Tamela said. She was beginning to wake up and enjoy Caliph's sexy voice once again. She didn't want to admit it but she could imagine him sitting on a fire escape, drinking a beer in one of those ribbed T-shirts she had seen Denzel Washington wear in some movie. "Like I said earlier, I was asleep."

"But it's Saturday, make that Sunday morning," he said.

"So what do you want to talk about?"

"Who said I wanted to talk?"

"Like I asked earlier, are you on some type of medication?"

"I just wanted to hear your voice," he said.

"Oh, please, don't tell me you're stealing lines from song titles?"

"Song titles? Maybe I should ask you if you're on some type of medication. Are you a big drinker?" he teased.

"No. Oleta Adams. There is a song with that title, 'I Just Had to Hear Your Voice,' I think. It's on her latest CD," Tamela said.

"Oh, I don't have that one. I'll have to get it," he said.

"So you like music?"

"Love music. All kinds."

"Like . . ." She thought music was a proper indicator of a person's worth, that it revealed a lot about them as a person.

"A little bit of everything from Tupac, Babyface to R.E.M. I might have to give my boy Tupac up since I just got out of rap rehab," he laughed. "But mostly I like the old music. You know the Motown stuff. What about you?"

"Yes, I like music. You know I like Oleta, Vanessa, Jody, Aretha, but Toni Braxton is my girl," Tamela said.

"No men?"

"Oh yeah, I like Babyface, After 7, and of course Luther. Of course I like the men."

"Hold up," Caliph said. Tamela turned on her lamp and sat up in her bed. A few minutes later she could hear music, loud music. Then she heard Caliph's voice come on the line and say, "This is for you." And then she heard Tammi Terrell and Marvin Gaye crooning "If This World Were Mine." Before the song ended Caliph came back on the line and said, "So do you like that?"

"Yes, that's nice. Thank you."

"Hold on." There was silence for a few seconds and then Tamela heard music again, this time it was Smokey Robinson's velvet voice singing "Baby, Baby, Don't Cry." She suddenly felt warm, as if the music were raising the temperature in her bedroom. She shook her loose-fitting nightgown to cool herself and thought how much she loved the song Caliph was playing. It was the first song she had ever slowed-danced to with a boy. Again, she heard Caliph's voice, saying, "This one is for me." Now she heard Marvin Gaye's "What's Going On." For the next hour Caliph played music over the phone for Tamela. Mostly he played old Motown hits from the Supremes to the Temptations and rounded out her private concert with Stevie Wonder's "Where Were You When I Needed You." After each song Caliph had come on the phone and said, "This one's for you," or "And this one's for me."

Never before had old songs made her feel so special. When he played Boyz II Men, "It's So Hard to Say Goodbye," Tamela knew her concert had come to an end.

"First of all, thank you, that was really, really sweet. Where did you learn to DJ like that?"

"In college," Caliph said.

"Where did you go to college?"

"Chicago State University, majored in criminology. Played basketball."

"Oh, that's nice," Tamela said sleepily.

"Wait, there is more," he joked.

"What?"

"Moved here from Pine Bluff, Arkansas, after high school. I know you probably haven't heard of Pine Bluff, but its about forty miles from Little Rock, known for its bad-smelling paper mills. Dreamed of playing in the NBA for the Chicago Bulls, but was too short. Wanted to play college ball for the Razorbacks, but they didn't recruit me 'cause of my color. Too light-skinned. No, I wasn't good enough," Caliph laughed. Tamela was getting the impression that he enjoyed the sound of his own voice, a sexy voice she thought.

"I still can't believe you don't have a lady in your life," Tamela said.

"Who said I didn't have a lady in my life? I do have a lady, and she's some kinda special," Caliph bragged.

"Then why didn't you call her tonight?" Tamela demanded, not wanting to believe what she had just heard.

" 'Cause it's way past her bedtime. She's in bed by eight. I think, I hope," he said.

"Oh, does she work the late shift?" Tamela said with a neck-turning edge.

"I bet you got your hands on your hips right now," he joked.

"What?"

"Never mind. I forgot. You're the smart kind."

"And don't you forget it," she said.

"Well, the lady in my life is Whitney Marie Taylor. She's my daughter, and she's seven going on twenty-five."

"So you have a daughter," Tamela said, relieved. "What about her mother?"

"What about her?"

"Is she alive? Is she still in your life?"

"Yes, to both questions. But not in the way you might be thinking."

"So now you know how I think?" She didn't know what to make of his answers.

"Naw, don't think so. But I'm not romantically involved with my daughter's mother."

"Were you ever?"

"Tamela. Are you there?" Caliph asked. She could hear him rapping his knuckles against the receiver.

"Yes, I am here," Tamela said.

"Well, wake up. Of course I was involved with Whitney's mom. Who, by the way, has a name. It's LaMonique."

"LaMonique, is she French? I mean the name sounds French," Tamela inquired without asking the real question she wanted to: Is she white?

"Naw, baby, the name ain't French, it's pure country." He laughed. Caliph knew she wanted to know if his ex was white.

"You know you're some kinda crazy," Tamela laughed with relief.

"Yeah, that's what they say. What about you? No man in your life?"

"Besides my daddy and brother, no. That's why I'm interviewing, but I don't need a man to make me feel whole," Tamela said confidently.

"Go on, girl. Now where have I heard that before? Isn't that the *Essence* magazine pledge of black womanhood?"

Tamela ignored his smart remark. "I know I'm going to be sorry for asking this, but here goes. What type of women do you like?"

"All kinds. But it's a certain kind of woman that gets my attention."

"Like?"

"I can't explain it, but I know it when I see it. But, you know, a woman like that Sonja Gantt that's on WGN. A Toni Braxton type. What about you? What type of men do you like?"

"I know him when I see him, but, you know, a brother like, Wesley, Denzel, or Morris Chestnut. You know, the guy from *Boyz N The Hood?*"

"Yeah, I know. Now you ain't got nothing against a mellow yellow-type brother, do you?"

"No. But I'm not color-struck. Well, Caliph," Tamela said, stifling a yawn. She wanted to fall asleep remembering the songs, his voice, and the way they made her feel. "If I'm going to meet you later, I better get some sleep. Again, thanks for the concert."

"You're welcome. Are you sure I can't pick you up?"

"I'm sure."

"Okay."

"I look forward to seeing you later today," Tamela said softly.

"Me, too. Good night, Tamela."

"Good night, Caliph. I'm unplugging my phone," Tamela said as she smiled to herself.

"Well, if I get the urge to talk again I'll tape it and bring it to breakfast. That way you won't miss a thing," Caliph said.

"Good night," Tamela said.

"Great night," Caliph said.

Sean had fallen asleep on his sofa and dreamed of the half-naked football players at Keith's party. When he opened his eyes a couple of hours later, he had an erection he felt was too good to waste alone. He got up from his sofa, dressed in overalls, T-shirt, and a Michigan baseball cap, and put on dark sunglasses. About fifteen minutes later, he entered a seedy adult bookstore on Eighth Avenue between Forty-second and Forty-third. On his way in, he had caught a glimpse of a good-looking light-skinned brother who looked familiar, but they were both moving so fast, Sean couldn't be certain he knew him. Not that he would ever acknowledge anyone he knew in a place like that.

He had walked swiftly past the numerous straight videos and magazines on the street level to the all-male area located in the basement. At the bottom of the stairs he stopped at an arcade entrance where a black man with a heavy West Indian accent asked him how many tokens he wanted. Without speaking, Sean pushed a dollar bill on the counter and the man slid him four gold coins like the ones used for the subway and pushed a buzzer to allow Sean to enter.

Once inside, Sean saw several men, all types, black, white, Puerto Rican, roaming through a narrow, dimly lit tunnel that extended for about the length of a block, fading into darkness. He couldn't help but inhale the stomach-turning smell of urine and masculine sex as he heard the opening and closing of doors with flashing red lights right above them. Sean knew the red light meant the video closet was occupied. Every now and then he heard the sounds of the tokens dropping in slots, sexual moans, and bodies bumping against the closet doors. As he walked with his head down, he heard men whispering to him, "Say, you wanna watch a movie?" At times he heard their voices but not their words, peppered with sexual overtones. Sean didn't see anyone who interested him, so he just kept walking back and forth along the same narrow path. Later he heard the West Indian guy yell, "Let's drop some coins, fellas, keep moving, no standing. Let's move." All of a sudden the men started to move like a herd of cattle toward the darkness and into the closets. Sean walked toward the end of the arcade where he was greeted by a tall, well-built black man, standing in one of the rooms with the door slightly ajar. He had his pants down below his waist, and was holding his very large dick, shaking it in his hands as if it wasn't attached to his body. "You want to try some of this, guy. It won't cost you that much," he smiled, revealing a mouth missing half of its teeth.

Sean gazed back uncomfortably at the man's mouth and dick. For a moment he was shocked at the behavior of some of these men, walking around with their stuff hanging out, looking for sex with no mention of condoms or safe sex. But he realized this was no place to be shocked or uncomfortable. He had come to the bookstore for sex and now that it was being offered in abundance, he was unnerved. Deep down, Sean knew he could never be satisfied with sex which was so quick and cold. So he walked into one of the claustrophobic dirty closets alone, pulled his sex out and over his warm-ups, and dropped the tokens into the coin slot attached to the tiny screen. The screen offered a preview of the choices as a tiny clock ticked off seconds. Sean chose *Black Workout Nine* and began to massage his sex while he watched several well-built black men, with that just-out-of-jail look, engaging in sex acts which defied gravity and tenderness. Just as Sean was about to reach his own climax, the tiny screen went blank. His time and tokens had run out. He put his hard sex back into his warm-ups and left the closet with the intention of purchasing more tokens. When he opened the door, he was surprised that at 3 A.M. the small movie arcade was packed. There were so many men that a line had formed at the entrance where you purchased tokens. Frustrated, embarrassed, and disgusted with himself, Sean put his sunglasses back on and headed home. It was Sunday and time to sleep.

CHAPTER 13

ONE MORE PICTURE, PLEASE

"Miss Miller, we're going to have to take a few more pictures," Kathleen Allen said. The young black policewoman had returned to Mia Miller's townhouse on Sunday afternoon along with her white partner Mike Cox.

Mia's face was void of emotion as she sat on her sofa. Her long hair looked like a tent around her bruised face. Her cheeks were puffy and swollen, the skin under her eyes looked like bruised petals, and her right eye was partly closed. She stared at the walls, but couldn't see the Jacob Lawrence painting she had taken so much pride in buying. She heard voices, but didn't know who was speaking; she saw faces, but didn't know who they were or why they were in her house. There was only one familiar face and a husky, consoling voice Mia recognized. LaDonna Woods, a stocky, chocolate-hued woman, with reddish hair and sharply defined features, sat beside her whispering, "It's going to be all right, babe.

"Mia, you need to tell the officer who did this to you," LaDonna said. "Do you think she could be in some type of shock?" LaDonna turned and asked Officer Cox.

"I don't think so. Let's just give her some time," he said. "We can do this tomorrow but it's best to try and get as much information while it may be fresh in her mind."

LaDonna had caught the red-eye flight from Los Angeles to Chicago just hours after she received a call from Mia's neighbor, Bruce Bell. Early Saturday morning, Bruce had been the one to find Mia.

She was hugging the steering wheel of her car in the parking carport they shared. He realized something was wrong when he noticed Mia's head lurch suddenly forward, then saw her throw up. When Mia lifted her head again, he could see that she had been beaten. He opened the car door and noticed that her clothing was torn and her body was shaking badly. Bruce took Mia's keys, carried her into her townhouse, and went to his house and told his wife to call the police. Bruce returned and once inside Mia's apartment he hit the redial button on Mia's phone. When LaDonna answered, Bruce asked her if she was a family member or friend of Mia Miller. He knew very little about his neighbor, but he did recall a time he once saw her in the post office mailing a package to her sister. He remembered how happy she'd seemed, sharing with Bruce about Tanya's exciting fashion career in Paris. But besides that exchange, the only thing Bruce and Becky Bell really knew about Mia was her work on television. Bruce had suggested calling the station when he found Mia, but Becky didn't think it was such a good idea. Before LaDonna arrived on Sunday morning, Mia had spent much of her time in the downstairs bathroom throwing up. Bruce had commented to Becky how Mia reeked of alcohol.

"She has been like this most of last night, but every time I suggested taking her to the hospital she shook her head 'no,' " Bruce said to the officers.

"That's fine, sir. You did the right thing. I understand her personal physician is coming over," Officer Cox said. "Can I speak with you in the kitchen, Miss Woods?"

"Just call me LaDonna, Officer Cox," LaDonna said as she and the officer walked into the nearby kitchen. Officer Allen stayed with Mia, just in case she decided to talk.

"Well, I'm sure you already know this, but the signs point to sexual assault."

"Don't you mean rape?"

"I'm not certain, but from what we've ascertained from Mr. Bell, that's what it's pointing to. At the very least it's a very bad sexual assault."

"What do you mean, you're not certain?" LaDonna snapped. "It's obvious to any fool that she was raped."

"I'm sorry, LaDonna. I don't mean to make light of what has

happened to your friend. But we need more information before we can make that determination," he said.

"I know. I'm sorry. I didn't mean to snap."

"Don't worry about it. Do you have any thoughts on who could have done this? Is she married, divorced, or dating someone steady?" Mike asked.

"No on all counts. But she was going out on a date when I talked to her Friday night. She called me right before she was leaving home," LaDonna said. "She called me because she was having problems with a former boyfriend."

"Do you know his name and how we can get in contact with him?"

"His name is Derrick Smith and I don't have a clue on how to get in contact with him," LaDonna said.

"Does he live in the Chicago area?"

"No, but I think he was here recently on business."

"Do you know who she had a date with?"

"Yes, a professional football player here in Chicago," LaDonna replied.

"For the Bears?"

"No, the other team. The new one."

"Oh, you mean the Cougars? Do you know this player's name?"

LaDonna placed her finger to her chin and replayed the last couple of conversations she had with Mia.

"I think his name was Zurich something," LaDonna said.

"Zurich, huh. That should make it pretty easy to find out if he plays for the Cougars," Mike said.

"Yeah, I'm certain he plays for them."

"Thanks, miss, we can find that information out," the officer said as he scribbled some notes on his pad and started toward the living room, where Mia was still sitting on the sofa with Kathleen at her side.

"Wait a minute," LaDonna said.

The officer turned and faced LaDonna and asked, "What was that, miss?"

"I can check my answering machine back home and see if Derrick, her former boyfriend, left his number on my machine. He had called me a couple of times trying to get Mia's number," LaDonna said.

"That would help us out a great deal," Mike said.

"I'm pretty sure that's who did this to her," LaDonna said firmly.

"Maybe Ms. Miller will be able to help us out soon," Mike said.

LaDonna went back to the living room and sat next to Mia, taking her hand and gently moving the hair away from her face. She held her friend's hand, and looked into her eyes, which darted around like pinballs. "Mia, did Derrick do this to you?" Mia didn't respond but her eyes stopped their movement.

"Just shake your head, darling. Just shake your head. Did Derrick do this?" This time Mia shook her head from side to side in a negative motion.

"Okay, Mia. So it wasn't Derrick. Was it that Zurich guy? We have to know so that we can help you."

Mia looked around the silent, shadowy room at the police officers, her neighbors, and LaDonna. They were all staring at her, waiting for a response. She wanted to sleep. She wanted them all to leave so she could be alone. But Mia knew they were not going to leave until she answered. But what was it they wanted to know? What had LaDonna asked her? A look of agony crossed her face, she wanted to cry out. Mia could feel tears pushing at the back of her eyes, but she did not cry. The back of Mia's neck and her head were both very painful. With five pairs of eyes on her, she whispered, "Yes." LaDonna gave Mia a gentle hug, then stood up facing the officer, "There you have it. It was that Zurich guy. That's who did this. Arrest the bastard before he does this to someone else," LaDonna demanded. Bruce and Becky cautiously moved closer to Mia and LaDonna.

"Okay, but I'll have to file my report and then my commanding officer will determine the next step. I'll need to come back for some additional questions and to take her statement when she's feeling better. Will someone be here besides Ms. Miller?"

"Yes, I'll be here for as long as she needs me," LaDonna said.

"Great, then let us get down to the precinct and start the wheels in motion."

LaDonna escorted the officers to the door and then came back over to the sofa as Mia stared silently ahead.

"Don't you think we should call her parents?" Bruce asked.

"No, not yet. But I'm going to do that. Right now I'm going to take her upstairs and let her get some rest. Thank you both for all your help."

"No problem. We're right next door if you need anything," Bruce said.

"Yes, please call if there is anything we can do. I will write our number down on the pad next to the phone," Becky said as she walked over to the sofa table and picked up a blank pad.

"Okay, thanks a lot," LaDonna said as she took Mia's arm. Mia stood up under her own power, looked at Bruce and Becky, and silently mouthed, "Thank you."

"No problem, you get some rest," Bruce said as he took his wife's hand and led her out the door.

LaDonna tried to get Mia to lean on her shoulder as they started to walk up the stairs, but Mia removed her friend's hand and stood on her own, balancing herself on the banister. She felt as if she could throw up again, but there was nothing left in her stomach. She looked at her friend and uttered her first complete sentence in over twenty-four hours. "I can walk upstairs on my own, LaDonna." She paused as if each word was draining her strength. "But will you fix me something to eat and bring me something to drink?"

"Are you sure? I don't have any problem going upstairs with you," LaDonna said.

"I'll be all right. I just need to get something in my stomach and get in my bed," Mia said.

"Okay," LaDonna said reluctantly and headed toward the kitchen. As she reached the doorway she called out to Mia, "What do you want to drink? Juice or coffee?"

"A glass of wine. I need a glass of wine," Mia said as she reached the top of the stairs.

It was the Monday morning after the Atlanta game and Zurich was dreaming. About Mia. She was standing silent and smiling before him. She looked beautiful. She was wearing jeans and a silk blouse with no bra, and he could see her nipples through the soft fabric. The only sounds he heard were the tinkle of her earrings as she placed them on his dresser and the rustle of her clothing as she slowly removed it. Zurich followed her lead and removed his jeans. He wasn't wearing underwear, and a look of marvel crossed Mia's face as he stood before her. His penis was large and erect. Seductively, she motioned him to her. Zurich slowly walked toward her.

Then their naked bodies touched skin to skin, like a burst of thunder, loud and shocking. Mia and Zurich merged together like an intricate puzzle. His muscular tongue slid down her body like a paintbrush. She became weak from the pleasure and fell back on the bed. He dropped his head to Mia's thighs. He kissed her inner thighs and then moved his tongue to her center. He felt her body melt as she let out soft sobs of pleasure and then loud screams calling out his name. The sobs and screams woke Zurich.

The dream was still fresh in his mind, as if it had really happened. His body was warm with sweat, his sex erect. He rubbed his face hard with his open hands, and wondered why he was dreaming of Mia. He got up from his bed and went to his bathroom. He splashed cold water on his face, then brushed his teeth. He started to turn on the shower, then he decided to call Mia. Maybe the dream was trying to tell him something. That he had left something unsaid on Friday night and early Saturday morning. He wanted her to know why he'd rejected her. He found Mia's number on his nightstand, where he had left it before his trip to Atlanta. He hoped she wasn't still mad at him and that maybe they could meet for lunch and he could explain everything to her. Maybe she would understand how he had always slept alone and dreamed his life away. How in recent years, he had not experienced sexual passion, only sexual desire in dreams. Zurich lay back on his bed and stared at the ceiling as if some mysterious force above would give him the words he needed to make her understand. Moments later, he lifted himself up, picked up the phone, and dialed Mia's number. After a few rings, an unfamiliar voice answered the phone.

"Hello."

"Good morning. Is this Mia Miller's residence?" Zurich asked.

"Yes it is. Can I help you?"

"Is she in? Can I speak with Mia?"

"Mia's not feeling well. Can I take a message?"

"Oh, I'm sorry to hear that. Will you tell her Zurich Robinson called?"

"Zurich Robinson, the football player?" LaDonna asked, her voice strong, irritated.

"Yes, I play for the Cougars," Zurich said, noticing the change in the female voice.

LaDonna suddenly went into a profanity-laced tirade, and gave Zurich, as MamaCee might say, a good cussin' out.

"You got a lot of fuckin' balls, mutherfucker! What in the fuck are you calling here for?" LaDonna shouted.

"What? Excuse me . . ." Zurich said.

"Excuse, hell. You heard me, goddammit. After what you did to my friend, you have the gall to call her! You must be out of your mutherfuckin mind!" LaDonna said.

"Miss, you must have me mixed up with somebody else. I didn't do anything to Mia," Zurich said. Was his rejection causing her this much pain?

"All I know is my friend was beaten and raped and she says you did it. I'm surprised the police haven't picked your ass up already."

"Beaten? Raped? Is she all right? Is there something I can do?"

"Something you can do? Don't be actin' dumb, you stupid-assed coward mutherfucker! Only cowards beat women, but then you know that, you coward mutherfucker. I'm hanging up on this dumb shit," LaDonna said.

"Wait," Zurich pleaded, but the dial tone droned in his ears.

He rubbed his chin as he replayed the conversation in his mind. Had Mia's friend said she had been beaten and raped? And that he had done it? There had to be some mistake. Zurich started to pick up the phone and call back, but decided against it. He was angry. He was confused. He needed to talk to someone. He started to call his father, but realized that he was driving back to Tampa from Atlanta and had mentioned possibly going to Warm Springs and surprising MamaCee. He didn't want to call there and get MamaCee worried unnecessarily. He could talk to Gina, so he dialed her number at home. Gina's husband answered the phone and told Zurich that Gina was not there, but he would beep her and have her call him right away. Before saying good-bye, he told Zurich to hang in there, that he would play much better the next game. Zurich thanked him and said he would wait by his phone for Gina's call. As he waited, he thought back to the Atlanta game. It had not been the nightmare he had dreamed before the game, but it was bad enough.

The Falcons had thrown a blitz on the first play of the game, forcing him to throw an interception that had led to the first Falcon touchdown. Zurich had lost his poise and was never able to regain it. He would throw four interceptions before the coaches pulled him and put Craig in early in the fourth quarter with the Falcons leading 42–14. The only saving grace was his eighty-yard touchdown pass after the Falcon's first score and the fact that Craig threw for three interceptions in the five drives in which he led the Cougars. The coaches told Zurich not to feel bad, that they still had confidence in his ability but they needed to work with the offensive line on their pass protection and design new plays that would allow him to run more.

The ringing phone interrupted Zurich's thoughts of the game.

"Hello," he said.

"Zurich."

"Gina. Thanks for calling," Zurich said in a harried tone.

"What's up? You sound bothered. I hope it's not that game. It's not the end of the world and you will play better against New Jersey. Am I right or am I wrong?" Gina said.

"Yeah, I know next week will be better. But I think I've got a problem," Zurich said.

"What? It's not those coaches. They aren't giving you a hard time, are they?"

"No, Gina, the coaches have been great. It's something else." Before he could tell Gina what happened, he heard call waiting beep. "Hold on, Gina, let me see who this is," Zurich said as he clicked over to his other line. "Hello."

"Zuri." It was MamaCee.

"Yes, MamaCee, how are you?"

"Well, I'm not doing that well, I woke up this morning and my legs were bothering me and you know what that means," she said.

"Naw, I don't, MamaCee, and I'm sorry but I can't talk right now. I'm talking with my manager about something really important. Can I call you back later?" Zurich said.

"Baby, that's why I'm callin' you. When my legs start to bother me then I know it's something going bad with my children. I called your father and Trey before they saw you in Atlanta. They doing fine. Talked to your other brothers. They doing fine, too. Haven't been out to the garden near the cemetery yet, but I just got that feeling that something is wrong with you in Chicago. Now tell MamaCee what's troublin' you, baby," she said.

"Trust me, MamaCee, everything is fine. I'll call you later," Zurich lied.

"Now don't you be tellin' your grandma no story, all right?" MamaCee warned.

"I'm not. I promise to call you back later," Zurich said as he clicked back to the other line.

"I'm sorry, Gina. That was my grandma," Zurich said.

"That's okay. Now tell me what's wrong. Come on now, Zurich, you've got me worried," Gina said.

Zurich told Gina about his dinner with Mia before he left for Atlanta and the scene at his apartment afterward.

"So, that sounds all right to me. I thought that woman had a boyfriend. What's the problem? She mad 'cause you didn't want none of her kitty-kat?" Gina laughed.

Zurich then told Gina about the conversation he had with Mia's friend earlier. "Now do you understand why I'm worried," he said.

"I thought they were paying that heifer good money over at that station," Gina said.

"What does this have to do with money, Gina?" Zurich asked.

"Everything. That woman wants some money from you for turning her down. I can tell a mile away what this is about. I bet you anything she wasn't even raped. This is some kinda scam. But I must admit, I'm a little shocked with her being in the media. What would she have to gain by doing something like this? To be honest it would make more sense if it were one of those Cougar cheerleaders or some shake dancer girl you football players love so much. Are you sure you're telling me the whole story? Nothing else happened when she went up to your apartment?"

"Nothing but what I've told you, Gina. That's it. True," Zurich said.

"Well, let me check this out. I know someone over at that station who might know what's going on. In the meantime, I'm going to talk with a lawyer friend of mine, just in case this woman comes for us. I was talking to him just the other day about your doing some charity work with his organization, the BMU," Gina said.

"You really think I'm going to need a lawyer?"

"I'd rather be safe than sorry. I'll just have him on stand by. You know, just in case. But listen to me, don't call her again. Just go on to practice and don't mention this to anyone. Not even your coaches or friends on the team. And please, pretty please with whipped cream on top, don't talk to any reporters. Tell them you're concentrating on your game. The last thing we need after the Atlanta game is some type of negative press," Gina said.

"Okay. I'm going to take my shower and head to practice," Zurich said.

"Yeah, do that and I will talk to you later on this evening. But don't worry, Gina DeMarco will take care of Miss Mia Miller. Am I right or am I wrong?"

"I hope you're right, Gina. This time I hope you're right."

CHAPTER 14

PROMISES, PROMISES

"Who is this guy?" Tamela asked.

"All I know from what Gina DeMarco told me is that he's a football player," Tim said.

"Who is Gina DeMarco?"

"She runs this PR firm. A real brassy-type woman. She had called me the other day about having some of the Cougars and Bears do a fund-raiser for the BMU scholarship fund. I understand she used to work with a lot of entertainment types, but now she's venturing off into professional athletes," Tim said.

"So I guess this guy is a pro football player?"

"Yeah, she said he played for the Cougars."

"Did he do it?"

"How am I supposed to know that? Gina said her client, Zurich I think his name was, went out with this young lady before he left for an out-of-town game. When he came back, he called her and some friend of hers accused him of raping this young lady. Later Monday afternoon, the policemen came by Zurich's apartment to question him, without counsel, and found panties in his dirty clothes hamper," Tim said.

"That doesn't sound too good for him, unless he's into wearing women's underwear," Tamela laughed.

"Now come on, Tamela, get serious. You said you wanted the next big case and this looks like it's going to be very big. The DA's office has become very aggressive in prosecuting cases of abuse against women. Sometimes I don't know about my black brothers, seems like they have to take everything these days. Giving us hard-working ones a bad name," Tim said.

Tamela thought, *Was this fool talking about us and when was the last time he had a conversation with one of his black brothers?* "Have they arrested him?"

"No, not yet, but the police left a message for him to come down to the station after football practice. Gina and I both agree he shouldn't go down there alone," Tim said.

Tamela leaned forward and began to tap her temples in a nervous manner. Was this case something she wanted to be involved in? A rape?

"Is the victim black or white?" she asked.

"What difference does that make?" Tim asked in an annoyed tone.

Please, God, don't let me have to read this fool. "Tim, wasn't it just a minute ago when you were talking about all your black brothers? I just wanted to know what type of man and woman we're dealing with," Tamela replied. She thought he ought to know the victim's color would make a hell of a difference.

"Now look, Tamela, I don't know a lot about either one of them. All I know is here I am trying to give you a possibly high-profile criminal case and you seem to have reservations. I can get someone else. But you can't say that I didn't keep my end of the bargain. I keep my promises."

"No, don't do that. I can handle this," Tamela said, getting to her feet. This was the chance she had been waiting for, and she was not about to let it slip away.

Tim gave Tamela a piece of yellow legal paper with the name of Zurich Robinson and those of the police officers handling the case.

"Well, I guess I should thank you, Tim," Tamela said, trying to appear gracious, even as she was beginning to question having to represent a possible rapist in a case that could bring unwanted attention toward her.

Tamela returned to her office, picked up the receiver of her phone, and held it, staring into space. She was thinking about Caliph. They had enjoyed a wonderful date on Sunday. Caliph and Tamela met

after church and enjoyed buttered grits, eggs, and ham at Gladys's
restaurant and then went to see *Jason's Lyric*. They ended the early
evening walking by Lake Michigan talking about the movie. Tamela
loved it, and Caliph thought it was okay, that the violence in the film
spoiled, as he said, "What could have been a very romantic movie
about a sensitive brother." They had talked briefly every day and
Tamela was trying to figure out whose turn it was to call. She didn't
want to appear too eager. As Desiree often said, "We're getting too
old to be eager." *I should call Desiree,* she thought, but realized she
didn't know where she was. Desiree had been laid off from her teaching job and seemed to be taking it in stride. Maybe she should call her
mother. She looked at her watch and realized her mother was teaching and that she only had thirty minutes to pick up her car and meet
her new client. She put the phone down, grabbed her briefcase, and
headed out the door. As she got on the packed elevator, one of her
mother's favorite bits of advice reverberated through her head: "Ain't
nothing to it, but to do it."

While waiting on hold for his travel agent to calculate costs for a trip
to Dallas, Sean picked up the photo of Zurich Robinson. A dancer, he
thought. He tried to imagine that same heavily padded body that
raced past tacklers leaping across a stage in nothing but a leotard.
What a fascinating bit of information this would add to his profile.
He had to know if Zurich Robinson was also a dancer, and if so, why
no one else knew it. Sean suddenly hung up the phone and called
information to request a listing for the Alvin Ailey American Dance
Theater.

"Alvin Ailey American Dance Theater," a friendly female voice
said.

"Hello. I'm a freelance writer working on a piece about one of
your former dancers," Sean said. "Who would I need to talk to?"

"How long ago did this person dance with our company?"

"I'm not certain, but I think the early nineties," Sean said.

"Do you have a name?"

"Yes, Zurich Robinson."

"Let me put you on hold for a second." Sean heard a click and
then a Muzak version of Rick James's "Super Freak." Sean had

started laughing to himself when a male voice came suddenly over the line.

"This is Terry Tyler. How can I help you?"

"Yes, as I was telling the receptionist just a minute ago, my name is Sean Elliott and I'm working on a story about someone who I think used to dance with your company," he said.

"Yes, the name our receptionist gave was Zurich Robinson. Now I've been in our publicity department for over six years and this name doesn't ring a bell," Terry said. "Do you know the exact year and if this person was a member of the main company or just a student here?"

"That I'm not certain of. Do you have a listing of your former company members and students?"

"Do you mind my asking who the story is for? Because I know most of the people over at *Dance* magazine," Terry said.

"Oh, this isn't for a dance magazine, it's for *Sports Today,*" Sean corrected.

"They've finally realized that dancers are athletes too," Terry laughed.

"Now, I wouldn't go that far, but I think they would be interested in a former dancer who is now a starting NFL quarterback," Sean said.

"Wouldn't we all be," Terry laughed. Sean could picture him snapping his fingers up in mid-air.

"So can you help me?" Sean asked.

"Well, that name doesn't ring a bell, but let me do some checking. Robinson is a pretty common name and I should remember a name like that pretty easy. As much as I'd like to think I know everything about the company somebody might have slipped through here. Let me get your name and number, and I'll do some research," Terry said. Sean gave him the information and hung up and called his travel agent back. After about ten minutes of going over fares and possible cheap hotels in Dallas, Sean hung up the phone. He'd started to look for his latest Visa statement to see how much he could spend before he reached his limit when the phone rang.

"Hello. This is Sean."

"Sean, this is Terry Tyler with the Ailey company. We spoke a few minutes ago."

"Yes, right. That was quick," Sean said. "What did you find out?"

"We definitely haven't had a Zurich Robinson here as a student or as a member of the company, but I found something that might interest you," Terry said.

"I'm listening," Sean said.

"We had a member of the main company named Zachary Robinson. He was with us from 1988 until late 1991. But I know this couldn't be the dancer slash quarterback," Terry said confidently.

"Why?" Sean asked. Maybe Zurich used an alias, he thought.

"Because I knew Zachary Robinson, and Zach has been dead for almost three years," Terry said.

"How well did you know him?"

"I knew him pretty well. He wasn't, you know, like one of my running buddies," Terry said.

"Terry, do you know where he was from?"

"Somewhere down South. Wait a minute," Terry said. Sean heard the click again and now heard the Muzak version of James Brown's "Living in America."

"Sean, he was from Tampa, Florida. Zachary Robinson was from Tampa," he repeated.

"Thank you. Look, can I ask another favor. You wouldn't happen to have a picture of Zachary, would you?"

"Sure, but he's with some other people. I'll check and see if I have an individual head shot. Give me your address, and I'll have a messenger deliver it to you."

"That would be great. Thanks, Terry."

"Glad to help out. This sounds like something interesting. Keep me posted."

"Thanks, and I will," Sean said.

Sean started to fold up several pairs of underwear, a couple of baseball caps, and jeans in preparation for his trip to Dallas when the phone rang again.

"Hey, baby brother. What you doing?" Anja asked.

"Packing," Sean said.

"Where are you off to now?"

"Dallas."

"When are you leaving?"

"Tomorrow."

"Well, I hope you'll be back by Saturday," Anja said.

"Saturday? What's happening Saturday?"

"Oh, Sean, please don't tell me you've forgotten about your promise," Anja said in an alarmed tone.

"What promise?"

"You promised to take Gerald to register for Pee Wee football up in Mount Vernon. And you told him you were going to take him to a Warrior game. Remember?"

"Oh shit, you're right, Anja. I'm sorry but it slipped my mind," Sean said.

"Are you going to tell him or should I?"

"Tell him what?"

"That you can't make it," Anja said.

"Oh, I'm going to make it. I promised him so I'll be there. I might have to change my plans, but I will be there." Maybe Dallas would have to wait, Sean thought. He didn't want to disappoint his nephew.

"That makes me feel better, 'cause that's all he's been talking about. Every night before bed he's talking about playing football and going to the game with Uncle Sean," Anja said.

"Please don't mention to him that I forgot."

"Don't worry I won't," Anja said. "Who are the Warriors playing Sunday?"

"Let's see here," Sean said as he pulled a NFL composite schedule from his briefcase. "This is great," he said.

"What's great?"

"The Warriors are playing that new team from Chicago. The Cougars," Sean said.

"What's so special about that?"

"Well, remember I just got through interviewing their quarter-back Zurich Robinson. You know, he's black, and he seemed like a really nice guy. Maybe I can introduce him and maybe take some pictures and have Gerald meet some of the other players," Sean said.

"Sean, that sounds wonderful. Now I want to go," Anja teased.

"Naw, this is the boy's day out and don't you forget about the rev," Sean teased back.

"You know I'm just playing," Anja said as she cleared her throat and then said, "And speaking of the reverend don't forget that you also promised to come to church next Sunday with Gerald and me. Remember?"

"And why did I agree to that?"

"It's Youth Day and your nephew is doing the occasion," Anja said.

"And I can leave after he's finished, right?" Sean laughed.

"Sean."

"Anja."

"Well, we can talk about that later, okay?"

"Deal," Sean said.

"Okay, I'll talk with you later."

"All right, give my little man a hug for me," Sean said.

"You got it," Anja said as she hung up the phone.

Sean looked at his half-packed suitcase and at his date book. He had planned to leave Dallas and then travel to the West Coast to interview Vince Evans. But he had made a promise to his nephew. A promise he had no intention of breaking. Besides, he thought as he pulled the suitcase off his desk, it would be nice to see Zurich Robinson and be in the Cougars' locker room once again.

Tamela met her new client right outside the police station near City Hall. Zurich was standing at the entrance with a large black notebook with Z-man stamped all over it. He had told Tamela, when they spoke briefly on the phone, he would be carrying the notebook so she could identify him. She smiled pleasantly as she approached him saying, "Mr. Robinson? Zurich Robinson . . . right?" She paused to shake his hand. "I'm Tamela Coleman . . . It's nice meeting you. This shouldn't take that long." Tamela instantly recognized him as the man in the restaurant. The one Desiree and her crew were in such heat over.

"It's nice meeting you. Thanks for helping me out on such short notice," Zurich said as he opened the large metal door and gestured for Tamela to go in first.

Tamela was struck by how tall and handsome he was close up, as she noticed his compelling dark eyes, his large, distinguished, and sexy-looking nose. He was wearing a beige cotton shirt, and his black linen pants hung limp and wrinkled. But Tamela had seen good-looking and well-dressed rapists before, and reminded herself not to be swayed by his appearance. Besides, she thought, *Didn't he know you didn't wear linen after Labor Day?*

Zurich noticed Tamela's slow smile, almost sly, and he wanted to tell her immediately that he didn't do it, but decided to wait until he was asked. She reminded him of a young lady who had tutored him in biology during his freshmen year in college. The tutor helped him to earn a B, and Tamela's resemblance to her made him feel safe immediately.

"Now I don't know what they are going to ask you, but all I want you to do is to tell the basics, like your name, where you live, you know. When they ask specific questions about your contact with the lady, leave that to me," Tamela said forcefully. "Do you know the lady in question?"

"Yes," Zurich said.

"How well?"

"Not that well. I met her when I first came to Chicago and later when she interviewed me," Zurich said.

"Interviewed you?" Tamela asked with a puzzled look on her face.

"Yes. She works for one of the television stations here," Zurich said.

"She does? Who is it?"

"Mia Miller. Do you know her?"

"Mia Miller. That's who was attacked? I don't really know her, but I know who she is," Tamela said. She wondered if Mia's status in Chicago would bring a different light to this case. She wanted to ask Zurich if he had raped her, but knew it would be unprofessional.

A few minutes later, two detectives came to the reception area and led Tamela and Zurich down a musty hallway with several doors which had black numbers on them.

"Let's go in here," one of the detectives said as he motioned Tamela and Zurich toward an open door. Once inside, he offered them a seat and asked if they wanted coffee or something else to drink. Both Tamela and Zurich responded no.

The interrogation room was small, bright, and unventilated. The tile floor was a dirty yellow, like a smoker's teeth, and smelled like a much-used dirty mop. There was a gray steel table with a phone and two chairs on both sides. Tamela and Zurich sat on one side, and the two detectives sat opposite them.

"Thank you, Mr. Robinson, for coming down and helping us out with this case. I'm Detective Dodd and this is my partner, Detective Davis," the shorter of the two white officers said.

"Let me start by stating that I have not talked in detail with my client, so I don't know how much we can accomplish today," Tamela said.

"We understand, Ms. Coleman. We just want to ask a few questions," Detective Dodd said. But before they started to ask questions, both detectives told Zurich how they had read the articles on him and had seen him play against the Bears. Both seemed in awe of him, smiling and not treating him at all like a possible rape suspect, Tamela thought as she watched their interaction. Zurich looked remarkably composed, speaking clearly about his career and looking the detectives directly in the eye.

But Zurich's insides rocked, partly from anger and from sadness. Angry that he was sitting in a police station with three people he didn't know, preparing to defend his honor. He had never been in any type of trouble in his life. Sad, too, that Mia would lie about him because he hadn't accepted her offer.

"Do you mind telling us where you were Friday night and early Saturday morning?" Detective Davis asked. Zurich was preparing to tell him he was out with Mia, when Tamela stopped him by gently touching his thigh and saying to him, "Don't answer that." Zurich followed her advice and politely shook his head yes. He liked the way she took control.

"Do you mind telling us why you left a message on Ms. Miller's answering machine saying you were sorry," Detective Dodd, the other detective, said.

"Again, I'm going to advise my client not to answer that," Tamela said as she stood up and looked directly at the officers. "Look, Officers, it doesn't look like we're going to get anywhere with these questions. Is my client under arrest?" Tamela said boldly. She wanted to say, *Look, you guys need to shit or get off the pot.*

"No, Ms. Coleman, we are still investigating," Detective Davis said.

"Well then, this meeting is over. If you have an arrest warrant, would you please contact me?" Tamela asked as she pulled out a card and placed it on the table. She looked at Zurich, who got up from his seat and started to follow her out of the room, when Detective Davis called out to him as Mr. Robinson. Zurich turned and faced him and said, "Yes, sir."

"Would you mind signing this for my son? His name is Christopher," he said as he held out a rolled-up football program and a pen. Zurich looked at Tamela for a brief second, but couldn't read her face. He gave the officer a half smile and said, "Sure," as he took the program and pen and wrote *To Chris, Always keep your head up! Zurich Robinson #12*. Tamela was thinking, *Is this guy a rapist or someone created by the Boy Scouts?*

"Thank you, Mr. Robinson. Thank you very much," Detective Davis said as he looked at the autograph like a little kid with a new prized possession. While he was looking at the program, Detective Dodd noticed the scratch on the hand Zurich had used to sign the autograph.

"Did you get those scratches in the game against Atlanta?" he asked. Zurich and Tamela both looked at the scratches and before he could answer Tamela glared at him and said, "Don't answer that," as she pulled his hand out of the officer's view.

Once they were outside, standing near the public parking area, Zurich looked at Tamela and said, "This is not going to be the end of this, is it?"

"I doubt it. I have to look over the information they have, including this answering machine message. Did you call her?" Tamela asked.

"Yes, but it's not what you think," Zurich said.

"Let's talk about this when we get together at my office. What is your schedule like?"

"I can make time for this. All I have is practice. We have a game in New Jersey this weekend. If they arrest me, will I be able to make that game?"

"Depending on the charges, if there are any, then we will need to arrange bail," Tamela said.

"Should I tell my coaches what's going on?"

"Do you trust them?"

"I guess," Zurich said.

"That's completely up to you. But I think we should see what we're up against first. I'm going to get a police report when I get back to the office. I will look it over and then we should meet as soon as possible," Tamela said.

"That's fine. When are we talking about? Later tonight or tomorrow?"

"Well, give me a chance to look the info over. Let's set up a meeting for Thursday afternoon," Tamela said.

"Can we do it after practice?"

"Mr. Robinson, you do realize that this is a very serious matter and I'm going to need your help if I am to defend you," Tamela said sternly. Didn't he realize how serious this was? she wondered.

"I know that. But I have to make practice or else I won't have the money to pay you," Zurich said.

"What time is your practice over?"

"Usually around three, depending on how much game film we have to go over," Zurich said.

"Yes, that should be fine. That will give me more time. Here is my card with the address of my firm," Tamela said. Zurich looked at the card she handed him and said, "Your office is on the same street as Gina's office. I shouldn't have any problem finding it."

"Good. But if you do, just call this number," Tamela said as she took the card and underlined the main office number.

"I need to ask you a question," Tamela said as she looked him straight in his eyes.

"Yes, Ms. Coleman."

"How did you get those scratches?" Tamela narrowed her eyes, stressing the importance of her question. Zurich felt her eyes were accusatory as if she already had made up her mind. He felt a rush of anger, but he remained cool.

"Mia scratched me. I can explain it to you now or later."

"We can talk about it when you come to my office," Tamela said.

"Ms. Coleman," Zurich said mournfully.

"Yes, Mr. Robinson," Tamela said as she looked up at him. She wanted to tell him he should save the sad-puppy-dog look for a jury if he were indicted.

"I didn't do it. I promise you," he said. Tamela continued to look at Zurich without responding. She had always prided herself on her ability to tell when someone was lying, but at this moment, with Zurich, she couldn't tell.

"We'll talk Thursday, Mr. Robinson. Try and enjoy the rest of your day."

Later Tuesday evening, Sean's buzzer sounded and he went downstairs to see one of New York's finest standing at the entrance door. A spandex-clad messenger with dreads.

"Yo, Gee. Are you Sean Elliott?" he asked.

"Yeah," Sean replied.

"Got a package for you. Sign this," he said as he gave Sean a clipboard and pen. Once Sean signed, the messenger handed him a manila envelope from the Alvin Ailey American Dance Theater.

Sean couldn't wait until he got back to his apartment before he ripped it open. There it was, a picture of Zurich wearing a form-fitting dancer's body suit and a smile. But Sean looked closer and he could see that the smile, though bright as headlights, was not the smile he had seen in Chicago. The man in the picture, though a mirror image, was not Zurich Robinson. But who was he? Sean wondered. When suddenly, the answer was clear. Twins. Zurich Robinson had a twin.

"Come in," Tamela said when she heard a knock at her office door late Wednesday. She assumed it was her secretary, Christina Martin, but to her surprise, in walked Warner Mitchell, a Yale Law School–trained second-year associate with a copy of the *Chicago Sun-Times* evening edition.

"Hello, Warner. What can I do for you?"

"You're handling the Robinson case, aren't you?"

Tamela wondered how Warner knew which cases she was handling but she said, "Yes." She wanted to say in her best bump fish tough-girl tone, *Yeah, what about it?*

"Have you seen this?" he said as he laid the newspaper on her desk, opened to page one of the sports section. Tamela leaned her face forward to read the article Warner had circled in a red Magic Marker.

Chicago police questioned pro football quarterback Zurich Robinson Tuesday about a September 8 rape of a 32-year-old Chicago woman. Robinson, a quarterback with the NFL expansion team the Chicago Cougars, was questioned at police headquarters for two hours before being released, said Chicago police spokeswoman Melanie Carrigan. No charges have been filed and the case is still under investigation, Carrigan said.

"I can't believe this," Tamela said. "We weren't even there an hour."

"So they got it wrong. But you know there will be more articles," Warner said.

"Yeah, I think you're right," Tamela said.

"Is there anything I can do to help?" Warner asked.

"What?"

"Is there anything I can do to help?" Warner repeated.

"No, I can handle this, but thanks for asking," Tamela said, wondering about his interest in her case and knowing that she needed more time to prepare for her Thursday meeting with Zurich.

"Well, I'm down the hall," Warner said as he reached for his newspaper. Tamela put her hands on top of the paper and asked, "Can I keep this?"

"Sure," Warner said as he left Tamela's office. When he was gone, Tamela picked up her phone and dialed Zurich's number. When his answering machine picked up, she said, "Zurich, this is Tamela Coleman. Have you seen the paper? The *Sun-Times*. Well, looks like we got our hands full, so I would like to reschedule our meeting for next Tuesday at 10 A.M. If that works with your schedule, please call my office and leave me a message. Keep your chin up."

CHAPTER 15

THE WALKING WOUNDED

On a beautiful autumn Sunday afternoon in New York, Zurich Robinson opened up some deep wounds. Not the wounds he suffered on the football field. Yes, the Cougars lost again. This time to the New Jersey Warriors, 38–20. Zurich had played much better than his effort against Atlanta, throwing two touchdown passes late in the game. All week, he had tried to put Mia and his troubles in Chicago out of his mind during practice and the game. On Tuesday, he was scheduled to meet with Tamela to find out what, if anything, the Chicago DA was going to do about Mia's allegations. Despite Mia's initial statement and the evidence the police had collected, Tamela told him, she didn't think they had a case, but Mia could still come after him with a civil suit. Zurich had not discussed his problems with anyone except Tamela and Gina. MamaCee had called several times, and once even left a message on his answering machine. A first for her. But Zurich assured her that everything was going fine.

After the game Zurich had a couple of surprises. Both pleasant. As he was walking toward the locker room, with his head down from the dejection of his performance, one of the Warriors' players came up behind him and tapped him on the shoulder. When Zurich turned, he was looking directly into the stunning gray eyes of Basil Henderson, the Warriors' All-Pro wide receiver. Zurich was a big fan of the sure-handed player. With a big smile on his face Basil said, "Say, Gee.

I just wanted to come up and tell you, man, that you can throw. You're going to be a good one. I wish you were throwing to me."

Zurich replied with excitement in his voice, "Thank you, thanks a lot. It means a great deal coming from you."

"Cool. Hey, we're homeboys sorta. Aren't you from Tampa?"

"Yeah, I am. Right near Temple Terrace. Where are you from, Basil?" Zurich said.

"I'm from Miami," Basil said.

"I didn't know that."

"No problem. By the way, I saw a piece in *All Sports* where some bitch is accusing you of something bad, man. How is that going?"

"Everything is going to be fine, I hope. Thank you for your concern," Zurich said. Gina had informed him some national newspapers would probably pick up the piece that ran in the *Sun-Times,* but not to worry since she was working on a plan to counter the negative press.

"Yeah, man, but be careful. Both the media and women can be a real ball buster. Look, I'm going to get a piece of paper and leave my number with your team equipment manager. Why don't you give me a call and let's keep in touch. Maybe we can hang out when we come to Chicago to play the Bears or when you guys are up here against the Giants," Basil said.

"That would be great," Zurich said.

"Cool. I'll make sure I get that number to you."

When Zurich entered the press room to talk to reporters, one insisted on asking him questions about his possible involvement in a sexual assault in Chicago. When Zurich said, "No comment under advice of counsel," the reporter continued asking questions, citing the number of black pro athletes accused of violence against women.

Zurich's eyes moved past the annoying reporter and suddenly saw Sean. Broad smiles came across both of their faces. Zurich walked over to shake hands with Sean and told him he hadn't known he was going to be at the game. Sean introduced Zurich to Gerald, who stood there wide-eyed and quiet for once, and then said, "Changes at the last minute. I have a few more questions for you. If you have a couple hours, I can get you out of this."

Zurich agreed and quickly informed Sean that he had planned to spend the night in New York City before going back to Chicago. Sean was surprised at the questions from the reporter. He had not heard about Zurich's being under investigation for rape. His subscription to *All Sports* had expired, and he had not seen the small article. He wanted to know more about this and how it might affect the article he was working on, and he also wanted to find out what other secrets Zurich was keeping.

After dropping Gerald off in Brooklyn, Sean suggested a quiet coffee shop, in midtown Manhattan, where they could get sandwiches. Once they arrived and found a small table near a window looking out on Broadway, it was Zurich who had the first question.

"How do you like living in New York, Sean?"

"Sometimes I love it and there are times when I think I have lost my mind," Sean said.

"What do you do when you're not working?"

"Well, sometimes I just go to bookstores and see what's new. You know with books and magazines. I roller blade in Central Park, and I try to spend a lot of time with my nephew." Sean was beginning to wonder who was the reporter. But he liked the fact that Zurich was interested in his life.

"Oh, he's a great kid. I really enjoyed meeting him and your sister. You guys look like twins," Zurich said. Sean thought this was the perfect opening, but he was a bit nervous considering how to ask Zurich about his brother. Maybe if he had a beer, it would relax him.

"Twins . . . hum, that's interesting. I want to thank you for what you did for Gerald. I mean the autograph and the jersey. Man, that was great. Did you see the look on his face when you gave him your jersey? I don't think he will ever be the same," Sean said.

"No problem. Glad to do it. I mean you and Gerald saved me from that asshole reporter. I wanted to say to him what part of no comment don't you understand, jerk," Zurich said.

"Do you want to talk about that?"

"I'm sorry, Sean, but no comment goes for you, too. But, off the record, I will tell you that no charges have been filed and there is not an ounce of truth to it," Zurich said confidently.

"Understood."

A waiter came over, and Zurich and Sean both ordered turkey

sandwiches and coffee. Then Sean suddenly changed his beverage to a Molson's beer. They continued their small talk about the game and about the Cougars' chances of ever winning another game. Zurich said his hopes were still really high and that he was feeling more comfortable in the NFL. He mentioned his encounter with Basil Henderson and asked Sean if he had ever interviewed him. Sean said, "No," and decided against telling him about the party where he had met Basil.

After a couple of swigs of his beer, Sean thought it was now or never, so he looked seriously across the table and said, "Zurich."

"Yeah, Sean," Zurich said as he took a napkin and wiped mustard from his lips.

"Can I ask you something?"

"Sure."

"It's personal," Sean said.

"I'm game. Ask your question," Zurich said firmly.

"Tell me about your brother," Sean said.

"My brother? You mean my brothers?" Zurich asked.

"Not your brothers. I'm talking about one specific brother. Tell me about Zachary."

Zurich didn't ask how Sean had found out about Zachary. He just looked at him and then moved his eyes around the small coffee shop and back toward Sean. His gaze became a stare, there was a respectful silence, and Zurich began to speak, as if he had been waiting for someone to ask.

"He was my best friend. He was born first. About thirty minutes before me. We were born on the same day as the first Super Bowl. January 15, 1967. Who played in that game? I know you know who played in the first Super Bowl." Zurich paused as if he was trying to remember the teams. It would take his mind away from the pain the memory of his twin brought.

"Green Bay and Kansas City," Sean replied. "It was Green Bay and Kansas City," he repeated.

"The Green Bay Packers and the Kansas City Chiefs. All my folks used to say was someday we would play pro ball or some type of sports. When we were real little, down in Mississippi and Florida, no one wanted to play football with us, so Zach and me would play against each other. I would be the Green Bay Packers, and Zach would be the Kansas City Chiefs. Sometimes we would switch. It didn't matter who won. I think we liked it better when we played alone," Zurich said as he smiled to himself. "When we played with other people, we always had to be on the same team. Sometimes I would play quarterback. Zach would be my receiver and then sometimes I would be the receiver."

"How did he die?" Sean asked.

"If you ask my father, or anyone else close to my family except my grandmother, they will tell you Zachary died of cancer. And in some ways that's true. He did have some type of cancer along with several other diseases. But the truth is my brother died of AIDS," Zurich said.

"So you're an identical twin. It must have been difficult losing him so young," Sean said. He was trying to balance his reporter's instinct to ask all the right questions with his personal feelings for Zurich, who he felt was in a lot of pain answering those same questions. He suddenly regretted bringing it up. What purpose did it serve, Sean thought, but then, he wanted to know.

Zurich had ignored Sean's comment and just started talking, dreamlike, as if he were in a trance.

"When we were around sixteen, Zach lost interest in sports and started taking dance. My father went crazy and made him stop. But Zach . . . that Zach, he didn't stop. He would sneak and take classes down at the local YMCA in Temple Terrace, which was right outside of Tampa. I was playing football there, and Zach had my dad thinking he was playing football, too. I was the only one who knew. Well, not exactly. MamaCee knew. She would send Zach the money to pay for classes and the things he needed. You know, shoes and tights. At first, I didn't understand his love for dance. I was mad at him, too, 'cause I thought only sissies took dance. I tried to talk him out of it all the time, especially when my older brothers started teasing him. Sometimes they would tease me, too, saying Zach and I were exactly alike and sooner or later I'd be taking dance lessons, too. But Zach didn't let that stop him, despite my pleas. He would say all the time, 'You, my brother, will be playing for the Green Bay Packers.' Then he would stop and say, 'No, you can play for the New York

Jets, so we can be close together, since I'll be dancing with the New York City Ballet. That way we can always be together. Zach and Zuri,' he would say.'"

Zurich took a sip of his now-cold coffee and just stared out the window. His face looked peaceful.

"All of my life it has been *we,* never *me.* Long before my mother or father held me, I'm sure Zach and I held each other as we wrestled in my mother's womb, long before we played football, or learned about things like love . . . hate. Before we knew about life . . . AIDS . . . pain and grief." His voice was soft and hesitant, as if he were choking out the words, but then it became stronger. "Even though we were different in many ways I always felt safe with Zachary. When he died, I think I went into shock, and I don't think I've ever come out," Zurich said, his voice thick with emotion. "He kept all the pain he was suffering to himself. Didn't tell me he had AIDS until MamaCee convinced him he should tell me. I think she knew something was wrong before Zach knew, kept saying something about her legs. I was living in Canada at the time, but the moment he called me I was on a plane to New York, but . . . but . . ." Zurich paused. "It was just too late . . . too late. I wondered why he didn't tell me the moment he found out. My father and MamaCee didn't handle it well. I mean, I know they loved Zachary as much as I did, at least I think they did. They loved him as much as they were able to. MamaCee had this prayer cloth she was depending on and all these homemade remedies that Zach never bothered to take. He didn't want to hurt MamaCee's feelings. They didn't come to New York to see him and then when he died, they didn't want to follow his wishes to be cremated and have his ashes spread over the field behind MamaCee's house. I became so angry at them, my father tried to explain, but I made them follow his wishes. They were not going to ignore what Zachary wanted," Zurich said. Sean now realized why Zurich didn't want to talk about his family when they first met. He was beginning to feel that maybe his own family wasn't that screwed up. After all, he was confident that if he ever got sick, both his parents, his brother, and Anja would be at his side.

"I still sometimes don't know if I can make something of this football career without my brother. Sometimes I wonder if playing football even matters. I mean I can throw a ball, I can run fast, but I can't cure cancer. I can't stop AIDS," he said.

"But look how well you're doing with your career," Sean said. "Don't you think Zach would be proud of you?" he asked as he tried to comfort Zurich's fears.

"He was always proud of me and me of him. We always supported each other even when no one else understood. I mean his death was so unfair. Things were starting to happen for both of us. NFL scouts were starting to pay attention to how well I was playing in Canada; Zach had been promoted to the main company at Alvin Ailey and was even doing some dancing in shows and videos. He was talking about going to school, you know college, so that he could teach dance one day maybe on a college level. And then just out of the blue . . . bam . . . bam," Zurich said as he slammed his palm down on the Formica table. He was silent for a few moments and then he looked at Sean. "Do you know what was the hardest part of losing my brother?"

"No, Zurich. Tell me." The waiter came over and poured water in their glasses and asked if they needed anything else and Sean mouthed, "No." And Zurich began talking again:

"Zach was living up here in New York," Zurich said as he looked out the window of the restaurant again. "Close to this place," he said. "I think he lived near here. A couple of days before he died, I was sitting beside his bed, rubbing his body with ice, because he was sweating a lot. He asked me to shave his head, so that he could look like me. You know it's funny 'cause Zach shaved his head first when he moved to New York. It was like he didn't want to be a twin anymore. But we were twins, so I shaved my head right away but only told MamaCee. And I think he was happy when I did tell him, 'cause, you know, we looked like each other again, although toward the end he didn't look like me anymore. He weighed less than a hundred pounds and there were sores all over his body. The only way I really knew it was my brother was when I looked in his eyes. The eyes were still the same. I shaved his head anyway, very slowly 'cause I didn't want to hurt him, and when I finished, we looked in the mirror and said something corny like 'twins till the end.' And then he looked at me with tears in his eyes and he said, 'Make me well, Zurich. Make me well.' "

"What did you say?"

"I told him how I wished that I could, but I couldn't. I couldn't make him well. And he said 'Yes, you can, Zuri. You can do anything. Make me well.' But all I could do was hold him. I wanted to say, 'Tell me who did this to you, Zach. Tell me who did this to you.' But I didn't. I just held him."

"Zurich, you realize no one was to blame. Not Zachary, not you," Sean said.

"Yeah, I've learned a lot about AIDS since then, I know," Zurich said sadly. After a few moments of silence Zurich said, "Two forty-three A.M."

"Two forty-three A.M.? What's that, Zurich?"

"It's the time Zachary died," he said in melancholy tone.

Sean wanted to grab Zurich and hold him or just touch his hands in support, but he didn't. He knew some men were bothered by affection, no matter how it was offered. He wanted to ask how Zachary contracted AIDS. Was he gay? And if his identical twin was gay, was Zurich also? But he didn't. This was not the place or time, he thought. He simply motioned the waiter to leave them alone when he saw him heading toward the table. He felt Zurich needed to savor the silence, and so did he.

After leaving the coffee shop, Zurich and Sean stood outside on Forty-fourth between Broadway and Eighth Avenue, preparing to say good-bye. While dusk took over the city, Zurich looked at Sean and asked, "Will you go somewhere with me? It should only take about thirty minutes."

"Sure," Sean replied quickly. He did not want the day to end. Sean thought Zurich was one of most sensitive men he had ever met. He had gotten the answers to the questions he had, but they only gave way to more questions, and feelings for Zurich that Sean himself didn't understand.

"I want to go where my brother lived. I think it's close by."

"Do you know the address?"

"Yes. It was 300 West Fifty-fifth. I think it's near Columbus Circle," Zurich said.

"Yes, it is," Sean said as he turned and pointed toward Eighth

Avenue. As the two of them started walking, Sean turned the conversation again toward Zurich's problem in Chicago.

"Are you worried about what this lady said you did to her?"

"No, not really," Zurich said confidently.

"Why do you think she's doing this?"

"You know, Sean, I really don't know. But I'm not afraid. I know what will happen will happen. MamaCee used to always tell me where there is fear . . . faith cannot exist. And the one thing I'm confident of is my faith," Zurich said. Sean simply nodded.

"What about you, Sean, have you found a good church here in New York?" Zurich asked.

"No," Sean said quickly.

"You do believe in God, don't you?"

"Of course, I'm just hiding from Him right now," Sean said.

"What? Hiding? I don't understand," Zurich said.

"It's too long a story. Maybe one day I'll tell you what I mean by that. I think we've opened up enough today. Don't you?" He hoped Zurich wouldn't pursue this topic. He was afraid talking about religion would spoil his otherwise perfect day.

"Yeah, maybe you're right. But I'm not going to let you off the hook. You can't run from God," Zurich said firmly. Sean liked the way Zurich seemed concerned about his soul.

The evening sun was going down, casting long shadows on the streets as they walked in silence. When they came up on Fifty-fourth and Eighth, Sean and Zurich waited for the light to change.

Sean looked at Zurich, whose face suddenly seemed somber as he gazed at a yellow brick high-rise across the street and said, "That's it. That's the building."

When the light flashed *Walk* Zurich and Sean crossed the street to the building where Zachary had taken his last steps.

Monday afternoon a rainstorm surprised Hyde Park, but by evening the rain had ended and the sky blossomed with a quiet pink color. The dark clouds hovering over the neighborhood had cleared to allow a pale evening light, while Tamela and her mother enjoyed wine coolers on the terrace of her parents' home.

"So this new man, you like?" Blanche asked.

Tamela smiled briefly. "Yeah, Mama, I think I like."

"So who are his people?"

"He's from down South, a place called Pine Bluff, Arkansas," Tamela said.

"Oh, Pine Bluff. They used to have a black college down there. AM&N they called it. We used to play them in football when your father and I went to Southern," Blanche said.

"Caliph said something about there being a black college down there, but he called it UAPB."

"That's AM&N. They had a good teaching program," Blanche said. Tamela didn't respond to her mother's last statement but just continued to gaze out on the neighborhood where she grew up.

"Now tell your mama what's the problem," Blanche said.

"Now who said I had a problem?" Tamela asked.

"Darling, you know I love seeing you, but when you call me at work on a Monday and say you've got something you need to talk to me about and ask if your daddy has any wine coolers in the box, then something is wrong. Besides, I can see it on your face," she said.

Tamela took a sip of her wine cooler and took off her watch and laid it on the patio table. She took a deep breath and knew it was time to share a secret she had held for years.

"Well, you know I'm working on this new case. You know the one with this football player, right?"

"Yes. I'm glad to see that firm of yours has finally realized what they have in you. Is that your problem?" Blanche wondered aloud.

"Sorta. You see, Mama, I'm wondering if I should really be handling this case, especially if it goes to trial," Tamela said.

"Why, darling? Isn't this what you've been waiting on? A high-profile case that will help you when you break out on your own?"

"Yes, I know. But without going into a lot of details, my client is a suspect in a rape and beating. A horrible rape and beating. I saw some pictures this morning of the victim and it made me sick," Tamela said.

"Do you think he did it?"

"That I don't know. He's somewhat of a mystery. I mean he seems like a nice guy, but some of the evidence the police have collected makes me wonder. Now I know as a defense attorney I am under an obligation to defend my clients to the best of my ability. That I must put my personal feelings aside," Tamela said.

"Have you talked to your police friend about this?"

"No."

"But something else is bothering you, right?" Blanche asked softly and touched her daughter's hand. Her dark eyes were full of concern, as she prepared herself to handle whatever Tamela was about to reveal. It couldn't be that bad, she thought. Her daughter shared almost everything with her. Even things she didn't want to talk about, like romance.

"It's strange how the past somehow shows up in the present," Tamela said as she looked out at the city.

"What are you talking about, baby? You know you can tell me anything," Blanche said. Tamela was silent for a few moments and then she turned to look at her mother, whose smooth brown face was unmarked by the passage of time.

"I know that, Mama," Tamela said as she took another deep breath and started to speak. "You remember Jason? The guy I dated while I was at Southern," Tamela asked gingerly.

"Yeah, baby. I remember him. He really hurt you," Blanche said as she remembered the muscular, light-skinned boy her daughter had fallen in love with during her freshman year. She had brought him home and insisted they were not sleeping together even though Blanche knew the glow on her daughter's face was not from her studies. She also remembered how depressed her daughter had been when she and Jason broke up, after her first year of law school. But both parents thought Tamela handled the breakup without much emotion. She simply put all her energies into law school.

"Yeah, he did. Well, one night during my senior year, I was over at Jason's apartment, studying," Tamela said. She looked at her mother to see if she was going to ask how late it was or had she spent the night, but she didn't say a word. "Anyhow, late that night I heard all this screaming and loud noise coming from his housemate's room. That wasn't so strange since they were always partying, especially after football games when they won or after greek step shows. They were a pretty wild bunch," Tamela said as she paused and took another sip of her drink. "But this night I could have sworn that I heard several male voices and this one woman's voice. She was crying and yelling, 'Stop . . . stop . . . stop it.' I woke Jason up and told him what I heard and he basically told me to mind my business and go back to sleep." Tamela looked at her mother to gauge her reaction but it remained the same, sort of passive, yet openly concerned. She started talking again: "I couldn't go back to sleep 'cause they were making all this racket, so I got up and pretended like I was going to the bathroom, which was in the middle of the apartment, separating Jason and his housemate's bedroom. When I walked out, I saw about four guys, all naked, standing in line, drinking beer, and shouting, 'Hurry up, man, hurry up before we have to take that bitch back to the dorm.' I could hear this female voice just saying, 'Stop, please stop,' and when all of those guys went back into the room, the door opened wide and for a second, I saw this girl's face," Tamela said as she paused. "Mama, she looked scared to death and for a brief minute our eyes met. But then one of the big guys in the room pushed her down when he saw me and told one of his friends to shut the door. I couldn't sleep that night and the cries and the noise stopped about an hour later. I heard them leave early that morning. When I mentioned what I saw to Jason, what I heard, he again told me to mind my own business, that the young lady was probably some local whore who liked to get with football players. So that's what I did, I just assumed that she knew what she was doing," Tamela said. She took her hands to her lips and was quiet for a few moments, just looking straight ahead, when her mother touched her arm and said, "Then what? What happened?"

"About a week later, there was a report on television and talk all over campus about this young girl, who I had met once when she came to one of our rush parties, who had been raped and beaten by several football players. She was a real pretty girl, light-skinned with long black hair. We started to pledge her, but some of the sisters from her hometown said she was real fast and would be trouble when it came to boyfriends, so we passed on her, but she pledged another sorority," Tamela said.

"Were the boys ever arrested?" Blanche asked.

"No, Mama, they weren't. I heard there wasn't enough evidence. The guys all said that she agreed to have sex with them and nothing happened to them. A couple of days later I heard at a sorority meeting that the young lady withdrew from school and I never heard what happened after that. And nobody seemed to care. I heard people on campus talking about it, saying the bitch deserved it for going over to

some guy's apartment that late at night . . . that she probably enjoyed it. But, Mama, I never said anything to anybody but Jason and
after a while, even he wouldn't listen to me. I kept telling him we
should go to the police and tell them what happened, but he said if I
did that I would be going alone and that he would never, ever speak
to me again," Tamela said as tears began to fill her eyes. "He said he
would say I was lying . . . that nobody was going to tell on his
boys."

"Don't cry, baby, don't cry," her mother said as she gently
rubbed Tamela's arms.

"I'm not going to cry, Mama. It's just all day . . . I mean ever
since I saw those pictures of the woman who was raped, I been seeing
that girl's face and hearing her screams and tears. I could have done
something and I didn't. I didn't do anything because I was afraid of
losing a boyfriend who was just as wrong as I was for not saying
anything. I could have helped but I didn't. And now I find myself
possibly representing a man just like those boys who raped that
young lady," Tamela said as her face became covered with tears. She
was no longer pretending to be unmoved by her confession, unmoved
by what she had failed to do.

Blanche got up from her chair and went over and held her daughter. "Just let it out, baby. Just let it out . . . cry. Everything will be
all right . . . it will be all right," she said as she rocked her daughter
in her arms.

After her good, cleansing cry, Tamela followed her mother back
into the house where she watched Blanche search for something to
eat. Tamela loved Mondays at her parents' home because her mother
always cooked huge meals on Sundays and there were plenty of leftovers for days.

Blanche set before Tamela a plate of her much-loved meatloaf
stuffed with mushrooms and bell peppers, candied yams, green beans
with smoked turkey pieces, and freshly sliced tomatoes. She made a
fresh pan of cornbread and a pitcher of lemonade before sitting down
with a cup of coffee to watch Tamela eat.

"You know what you have to do, don't you?" Blanche asked.

"Yes, Mama, but why don't you tell me?" Tamela said as she
smiled at her mother and enjoyed the first taste of the meatloaf.

"One of the things that I'm certain they taught you in law school is that there are good people and there are bad people in the world, but in this country they are all entitled to a defense. What's that phrase, 'innocent until proven guilty.' Don't you rush to judgment because of what you know some men are capable of. You went to law school to defend people, that's what you'll have to do with this young man," Blanche said.

"I know, Mama. And that's what I'm going to do. I will give my client the best defense I'm capable of," Tamela said.

"Then that young man doesn't have anything to worry about. In regard to the other matter, I think you have to forgive yourself. You did what a lot of women your age would have done under the same circumstances. And what can you do now? Try and find this young lady and apologize. I don't really think that's possible. You need to ask the man upstairs for forgiveness and then know that it's done. In times like these you have to depend on your faith for an answer," Blanche said.

"I know you're right, Mama. I've also been thinking about assisting some of the women who are raped and don't have legal counsel on what they can do. You know I've defended so many of them knuckleheads who have committed crimes against women, and I never stop to think of the women. You know if the charges are dropped against the man, those women still have to deal with their pain," Tamela said.

"What could you do?"

"You know, help them get counseling. Help them to sue some of these men, if they can't get justice from the criminal courts," Tamela said.

"That's a good idea. You could do even more when you open your own practice," Blanche said.

"Do you ever regret that you didn't go to law school?"

"No, not really. I love teaching. You know it's a very important job. Sometimes I look at the little boys and girls in my classes, and I just pray I'm making a difference. You've got to do the same thing, baby. You've got to make a difference and that means standing up to your responsibility."

"How did you get to be so smart, lady?"

"A whole lot of living, my daughter, a lot of living," she smiled.

The Tuesday morning after he returned from New York, Zurich got
the surprise of his life. He was on his way to Tamela's office to go
over his case when the phone rang. When he picked up, MamaCee's
voice reached out loud and clear, as if she were next door. MamaCee
had the type of voice that could carry for miles, no matter which way
the wind was blowing.

"Zuri," she said.

"MamaCee. How are you doing?" He was wondering why she
was calling him this early in the day. MamaCee never called during
the day when the rates were too high, saving her long distance calls
until Sunday.

"I'm doin' fine, baby. Come git me," she said.

"Come and get you? Where are you, MamaCee?"

"O'Hara. I'm here at O'Hara. I'm in Chicago, baby," she said.

"You're where?"

"O'Hara. Ain't that the name of this airport? Boy, it's big. I'm
telling you that plane ride was something else. It was so beautiful
flying up there so high, the sky was beautiful and the clouds . . . It
was like I was flying to heaven. And, Zuri, those young people on the
plane serving food, they were so sweet to me. I told them it was the
first time I was on one of them planes and that I was going to see my
grandbaby. I told them 'bout you playing for the Chicago team. The
food wasn't that good, but the peoples were so nice. I am so happy
that I brought my own food. I tried to share some of it, but I didn't
have enough," MamaCee said.

"MamaCee, what are you doing in Chicago?" Zurich asked. He
couldn't believe MamaCee was just thirty minutes away or that she
had actually gotten on a plane.

"I'll tell you 'bout that when you git here. You do have a car,
don't ya, baby?"

"Yes, MamaCee, I'll be right there. What airline did you come on?"

"Wait a minute, let me ask somebody what airline I'm at,"
MamaCee said. Zurich could hear her saying, "Come here, baby.
Yea, you. What airline is this?" Zurich could hear a voice say, "Miss,
you're at the Delta airline terminal."

"Zuri. I'm at Delta."

"Okay, MamaCee. Do you know what gate?"

"Hold on," MamaCee said. Once again Zurich could hear her talking with someone. A few seconds later he heard her say, "Thank you, baby, I bet ya'll think I'm some kinda country bumpkin, here is the gate number looking me right in the face."

"MamaCee," Zurich said.

"Yeah, baby. I'm at gate number forty-eight," she said.

"Okay, MamaCee. Wait right there. I'm coming to get you," Zurich said.

"Fine, baby. Anyhow, where am I going? One plane ride in a day is enough for this old lady. I'll be sittin' right here resting my feet till you git here. Got both my arms wrapped round my handbag 'cause I know some of these people might try and snatch it. I might even finish up this fried chicken and deviled eggs I brought. But maybe I should save some for you. I know how much you like MamaCee's fried chicken and deviled eggs, don'tcha, baby?"

"MamaCee, hang up the phone. I'm on the way."

Zurich arrived at Tamela's office over an hour late, with MamaCee in tow. He still couldn't believe that MamaCee had gotten on a plane and come to Chicago simply because her legs were hurting. But seeing his grandmother made him smile; in fact, it caused him to actually laugh for the first time in weeks.

When he picked up MamaCee at O'Hare Airport, she was sitting in the waiting area, surrounded by her bags and two white flight attendants, who seemed to be enjoying her lively conversation. When she stood up and hugged Zurich, he couldn't stop laughing, even though there were tears in the corners of his eyes. MamaCee looked like a walking curtain, in her best Sunday-go-to-meeting getup. She had on one of her church hats, with a detachable tiara, and flowers. Her shapeless floral-print cotton dress had buttons from top to bottom, and along her shoulders were gold epaulettes held together by a fake fox head. To top everything off, MamaCee had on her comfortable white ushering shoes, with stockings that stopped at her knees.

She hugged and kissed Zurich on the mouth, on his hands, as she said to the flight attendants, "See, I told y'all my grandboy was a fine thang."

MamaCee talked nonstop as they drove down the Kennedy Expressway into the city. Beginning with a story of how nervous she was flying and how Ms. Clara, the director at a hospice MamaCee volunteered for, had told her to dress up when she got on the plane. Then there was a lengthy description of Ms. Clara, her family, her life. And then MamaCee asked Zurich several questions, one after another. "What building is that, baby? Ain't you driving a little fast? Ain't people scared to be on them trains moving all fast on them little tracks?" But Zurich didn't answer her questions and MamaCee didn't notice.

Zurich was relieved when Christina promised to take care of MamaCee and showed him into Tamela's office. Maybe there, he thought, he could get a word in edgewise.

"I'm sorry I'm late, but I had to pick up my grandmother," Zurich said as he took a seat and wiped a thin film of perspiration from his brow.

"That's all right. I had something I needed to finish," Tamela said, pulling a yellow legal pad from her left desk drawer.

Zurich glanced around Tamela's office looking for a box of tissues. It was cool in the office, but a nervous sweat seeped through his shirt. Tamela's office was littered everywhere with legal books and periodicals, and a glass-topped table was covered with the three E's of magazines for black folks, *Essence, Ebony,* and *Emerge.* Behind her desk, a matching credenza and a mini-refrigerator sat before a wall covered with diplomas and family pictures.

"I haven't seen any more articles in the newspaper on this. Have you?" Tamela asked.

"No, I guess I can be thankful for small blessings," Zurich said.

"Would you like something to drink? Some coffee, juice, or water?" Tamela asked.

"Yeah, some bottled water would be nice," Zurich said.

"Would you like a glass?"

"No, I can drink it from the bottle," Zurich said.

Tamela leaned back from her desk, reached inside the refrigerator, and pulled out a small bottle of Evian. Placing a napkin around it she handed it to Zurich and asked, "So why don't you tell me what happened?"

Zurich twisted off the plastic top, took a long gulp, and used the damp napkin to wipe his forehead. He began to talk about Mia. After he had gone on for about ten minutes, Tamela said, "Tell me about the scratches on your hands."

"She was crying, kinda out of control, and I pulled her toward me. Mia pulled back and when she did her fingernails tore across my hands." Tamela's eyes narrowed and she asked another question. "Why did you invite her up to your apartment?"

"I didn't exactly invite her; she sort of invited herself, saying she needed the tape to show to her producer," Zurich said.

"Did you give her the tape?"

"I couldn't find it," Zurich said.

"How did her panties get in your dirty clothes hamper?"

"I have no idea. She did go into my bathroom to freshen up for a few minutes."

"So let me make sure I'm getting this right. She took off her panties without your knowledge and left them in your bathroom; she asked you to dance; and she placed your hands on her private parts?"

"Yes, that's what happened," Zurich said firmly. The sweat had finally stopped. Tamela felt a *nigger, plezze,* coming on but resisted.

"You're also telling me that you didn't consider this a date, but a business meeting right?"

"Yes, we were meeting to talk about the possibility of me doing some commentating on a program at the station. You can ask Gina about it. I would never go on a date the night before I'm leaving for a big game. I mean this was the first game of the season, but Mia made it seem like if I didn't do it that night, I would miss out on a big chance," Zurich said.

"So do you have a girlfriend?"

"No."

"Were you attracted to Ms. Miller?"

"Well, I don't know how to answer that. I mean she's beautiful, but that's not why I went out with her. I thought I made that clear. It was business," Zurich said firmly.

"Okay, I think I understand, but these are the kinds of questions the prosecutor is going to ask you if this thing goes to trial," Tamela said.

"So what's next?"

"I have one more question. If you weren't interested in her, then why did you call her the night or morning of your meeting and then call her again when you returned from Atlanta?"

"I just didn't want her to misunderstand me. I wanted her to know that we could still be friends even though I knew she was upset with me for rejecting her," Zurich said. He decided not to mention the dream because he didn't think Tamela would understand.

"So do you think she's blaming you because you rejected her?" Tamela felt another *nigger, plezze,* coming but she thought back to her conversation with her mother.

"I don't know."

"And you didn't take her back to get her car?"

"No, I tried but she just ran out of my building."

"I wonder how she got back to her car?" Tamela said. She took her pen and placed it on her lips, frowning, as if she was trying to figure out this mystery.

"There are always taxis sitting out in front of my building. Is there any way we can find out if a taxi driver took her back to her car?"

Tamela thought, *All right, Kojak, let me do my job.*

"Yeah, that's a possibility. I'll check on that later. Okay, I think I have enough information for now. Let me tell you what will probably happen. The Chicago Police will collect all the evidence and will present that to the district attorney, who will decide whether or not to press charges. If they don't think they have enough evidence, which they probably don't because they would have arrested you the day we went down to talk with them, the DA will have the option of presenting the evidence to a grand jury or at a preliminary hearing. They could do both but I doubt that very seriously."

"A preliminary hearing? Grand jury? What happens then? Will I ever get to tell my side?" Zurich asked.

"You could, but in most criminal cases, I don't believe in presenting a defense at a preliminary hearing. But if you have something you can tell me to prove you didn't do this, then that's considered an affirmative defense and I'd put that on," Tamela said.

Zurich didn't say anything. He just gazed out of Tamela's window, wondering how he got into this mess. He had made a promise to his father, MamaCee, and to himself that he would never get into any trouble that would land him in jail. He didn't want to be a statistic. After a few minutes, Tamela started to talk again, but Zurich didn't really hear her. A numbness set in; the thought of newspaper headlines, handcuffs, and the sound of jail cells closing cluttered his mind.

"Now at the preliminary hearing, the DA's only got to show that there's a strong probability you committed this crime. And the judge makes that determination, and a lot of that depends on what judge we get. During a trial, they have to convince a jury of your guilt beyond a reasonable doubt. That's not easy," Tamela said.

"Oh," Zurich said.

"Do you understand everything I've said?"

"Yeah, I think so. What about a semen test? Can't that prove I didn't do it?"

"Yes, it could. From the doctor's report it was hard to tell if she was penetrated and if there was enough semen for a DNA test. You could volunteer to do that, but the test takes weeks and it still might not prevent you from being arrested if they feel like they have enough evidence against you. I would like to use the test as a last resort," Tamela said.

"Yeah, I would too. So she really was raped?"

"Something bad happened. I've seen the pictures. Someone really beat Miss Miller up bad," Tamela said.

"But it wasn't me, it wasn't me," Zurich said as he got up from the chair and clasped his hands together so hard that the sound startled Tamela.

CHAPTER 16

DON'T GO THERE

Wednesday afternoon, Mia stared at the rum and Coke sitting on her kitchen counter. She knew she shouldn't drink more because she was already drunk, but she reached down, lifted the glass, and drank. After she finished, she turned up the glass and allowed the small ice cubes to slide down her tongue, savoring their rum-coated taste. She looked at the empty rum bottle and wished she had purchased two bottles the night before instead of the one.

After a week of calling in sick, she had returned to work and it had not gone well. The extra makeup and dark glasses had not helped, but caused more problems. When she walked into the station, prepared to tell the station manager she had been in an accident, Mia bumped into Cheryl. Without knowing why Mia was wearing sunglasses, Cheryl laughed and asked in a very flippant manner, "Whatsup, Miss Mia? So popular that you have to wear sunglasses in the station?" Mia didn't answer, but instead something went through her like an electric charge and without warning she slapped Cheryl. Mia was shocked at her own violence, and Cheryl appeared stunned as she ran into the ladies' room in tears. Mia had never slapped anyone in her life. An hour later, Mia found herself suspended from work for at least two weeks. She told management what had happened, how she had suffered a sexual assault, and although they were sympathetic, the general manager said he couldn't allow Mia's actions to go without punishment. He suggested that she take some time off and regroup to seek some counseling.

During the entire meeting, Mia didn't shed a tear. While her manager was talking to her, Mia wondered if women were born with a talent for crying in silence, so that after a sexual assault or beating, they could cry and not have to talk about it.

The Sunday after her arrival, LaDonna returned to Los Angeles. Mia had assured her she would be fine. LaDonna had tried to talk Mia into taking some vacation time and coming back to Los Angeles with her. When she said no, LaDonna suggested Mia call her mother and tell her what happened. Mia said she didn't want to worry her mother. But Mia was not all right, she was simply determined to get on with her life. She knew if her parents, especially her mother, found out what happened, they would be in Chicago in a heartbeat. They would baby her and try to convince her to move back home. Dallas and babying were the last things Mia felt she needed.

The Chicago detectives handling Mia's case had attempted to contact her several times, leaving notes on her door, phone messages, asking her to come down to the station to give them more information regarding her rape. But Mia had not returned their calls nor had she any plans of going to the station. She did not remember what happened that night and could not face questions as to why she said Zurich Robinson had raped her. For all she knew he could have raped her. He was the only man she could remember from that night. After three days of being alone, usually in the dark and comforted by the sweetness of rum and wine, she'd picked up her phone to call her doctor's office to see if he had called in a prescription for Valium. Before the attack Mia had seen her doctor regarding nagging headaches, neck pains, and a slight case of insomnia. When she'd asked him for Valium, he'd been hesitant, warning Mia that the drug could become addictive, but she'd pleaded with him.

"This is Mia Miller, is Dr. Smith in?" she said.

"I'm sorry, Miss Miller, Dr. Smith is with a patient," the receptionist said.

"When will he be available?" Mia snapped.

"I don't know. May I take a message?"

Mia was annoyed and the receptionist's manner only unnerved her more.

"No! Did he call in my prescription?"

"Let me check. What was the prescription for?" she asked innocently.

"Look in the file. That's what you're paid for, isn't it?" Mia said, feeling put out with the young woman's incompetence.

"Hold on," the receptionist said.

Mia was tapping her fingers nervously on the kitchen countertop when suddenly she heard a dial tone.

"Fuckin' bitch," Mia screamed. She started to call back, but instead she looked for her purse and car keys. Even though she was in no condition to drive, she needed her prescription. Besides, she thought, the drugstore was only a few blocks away. She got in her car, drove a few blocks to a cash station near the drugstore, and withdrew one hundred dollars. She decided to walk the block to the drugstore and once at the prescription department, she demanded her medication.

After searching for the prescription, the clerk came back and said, "I'm sorry, miss, but we don't seem to have one for you. Are you sure your doctor called it in?"

"Yes, I'm sure. Check again," Mia demanded.

The clerk walked back and talked with the pharmacist. Minutes later, she returned and said, "Miss, we don't have it. If you'd like, we can call your doctor."

"Call him," Mia said firmly.

Mia walked over to the magazine counter and thumbed through several fashion magazines and then returned to the pharmacy department within a few minutes. The store's harsh lighting was causing her an overwhelming dizziness and her headaches had returned as she approached the counter again.

"Is it ready yet?" Mia said.

"No, we haven't been able to get in contact with your doctor," the clerk said.

"What's the problem? This is taking too damn long. What are you people doing?" Mia questioned; her voice was rising and she warned herself to control it. But she couldn't.

"Miss, please calm down. We're trying to get in contact with your doctor. We don't even know what the prescription is for."

"I told you it's for Valium," Mia said. "You know what that is, don't you?"

"Well, then we'll definitely have to talk with your doctor and I'm going to have to see some ID," she said.

"Some ID? What the hell for? I come in this dump all the time." Mia had had it with this skinny little white girl. Didn't she know who she was? Probably not, Mia thought, as she assumed this woman was purely trailer park trash.

"It's a controlled substance, miss. Why don't you have a seat over there and just wait until we talk to your doctor," she said as she pointed to several empty chairs lined against the wall.

"Bitch, do you know who you're talking too? Don't tell me what to do. I'll sit where I damn well please. Don't make me get ethnic with you," she screamed as she shook her hand in front of the clerk's face.

"Miss, please, calm down," the clerk pleaded, as her face flushed crimson.

"Let me speak to a manager," Mia muttered.

"Just a second," the flustered clerk said.

A few minutes later the pharmacist came to the counter to speak with Mia.

"Can I help you?" the tall, white, bald man in a blue lab coat asked.

"I came here to get my medicine, and this woman won't help me," Mia said as she pointed toward the clerk.

"Miss, we've been trying to contact your doctor. He's not in. If you don't want to wait, leave your number and we can call you once we've spoken with your doctor," he said.

"Oh fuck this shit. I can go somewhere else. You ain't the only drugstore in town," Mia said as she stormed out of the store. She needed a drink.

When Mia got back in her car, she drove only one block when she saw a stop light she didn't recall seeing previously. She stopped at the light and rested her forehead on the steering wheel. When the light changed, Mia didn't move. The driver in the car behind her blew its horn. She didn't move. The car horn blew again. Mia started to get out of her car and cuss out the impatient driver. But instead she drove on and began to cry.

Day three of MamaCee's visit to Chicago and she hadn't stopped talking.

"I tell you it looks like every building in Chicago is fancy and big. I don't think I ever saw so many tall buildings. Of course you know they ain't got no building like this in Jackson. Not even in New Orleans. You know I went down there with some of my church members for a convention and the hotel we stayed in wasn't this tall. Now what did you say it cost you to live up in here, baby? And the white folks, they seem real nice. Like that man downstairs, now what is he called?" MamaCee asked.

"A concierge, MamaCee," Zurich told her for the fourth time.

"That sho do sound like a fancy-sounding job. I don't think I've ever heard of one of them," she said.

"Now, MamaCee, if you don't want to answer the phone while I'm gone, the answering machine will pick up. I'm expecting calls from Gina and Tamela," Zurich said.

"Mama don't mind pickin' up your phone, baby. You know that Tamela girl, your lawyer, she sho is a pretty girl. And I can tell she's a smart one. She could lose a few pounds though, but can't we all," MamaCee laughed. "Used to be when they was that pretty they didn't have the common sense the good Lord gave them. But yes, sir, I think she got it all on the ball," MamaCee said.

"Yes, she is smart. . . . How long do you plan on staying in Chicago?" As much as he loved his grandmother, she could be a bit overwhelming.

"Until we git you out of this mess. I knew somethin' was wrong when my legs was actin' up. But never in a million years would I believe some fast tail gal would be fool enough to claim one of my grandbabies would beat and treat a woman with some kind of disrespect. Y'all were raised better than that. My boys know how to treat women folks."

"I know, MamaCee, but everything will be fine," Zurich said confidently.

"Now I know that better than anybody. What did Grandma used to tell you all the time when you was growing up?" MamaCee quizzed.

"Always trust in God," Zurich said.

"Yeah, that too, but what did I tell your father, you, and yo brothers? Like it says in the Good Book, this too will pass," MamaCee said as she headed toward the kitchen.

Zurich smiled at his grandmother. He realized he was happy she was in Chicago to help him through this difficult time. A few minutes later MamaCee emerged from the kitchen shaking her head.

"We gonna have to git some more pots and pans. Them things you got in there ain't fit to cook nothing. I thought I told you to git one of them big ole black skillets, you know, like the ones I have back home," MamaCee said.

"Now look, MamaCee, I don't want you up here working yourself to death. We can go out to eat, and I can always call for take-out food," Zurich said.

"Take-out food? Oh no, you know I don't like eatin' no food from peoples I don't know. Three days of that stuff has been enough for Mama. I'll find a store and git the things I need. You need all your strength to play them games and help that lawyer of yours," MamaCee said as she walked into the bedroom looking for her yellow vinyl suitcase.

Minutes later MamaCee walked into the living room holding a homemade quilt. "Here, baby, I forgot, I brought this for you. I made it while I was working down at the hospice," MamaCee said as she handed him the beautiful patchwork quilt made from old towels, sheets, and even some of her old dresses.

"Thanks, MamaCee. I'm sure I'll need a quilt up here this winter. But I thought you were making quilts for the patients you worked with," Zurich said.

"Well, that's partly true, baby. I made a lot of quilts for my friends with AIDS. Matter fact I was making this one for one of my favorite ones. He was this white boy from Meridien. He was such a nice boy. His parents had turned their backs on him, and he used to call me MamaCee instead of Miss Cora like the rest of them did. I knew I was right when I told you black folks ain't the only ones who acted a fool when their children got AIDS. It was a couple of white boys and a white girl at my hospice. Whenever I walked in the place, he would call out, 'MamaCee, is that you? I smell that gardenia perfume. I know that's you.' I like it when a man knows my scent; your grandad was like that. Anyhow, I would go in and give him a big hug and sometimes rub his feet when they swelled up, which they did quite a bit, and tell him stories. You know stories about when I was growing up and then I would tell him about my family. I told him how I used to pick cotton and the white folks I worked for and how I practically raised their children. So I told him he wasn't my first white baby. But you know the stories he liked the most?"

"No, MamaCee. What stories?"

"The stories 'bout you and Zach. Oh, Jimmie Lee, that was his name, loved the stories 'bout you boys. I would tell him how you spent most of your time with me, on count your father was so busy working, or so he said. I told him how I would dress y'all up alike with outfits I made for you on that old Singer I had. You 'member that sewing machine, Zuri?" He knew to say no would only trigger an extended description of said machine, and a possible history of the person who sold or gave the machine to MamaCee. He did vaguely remember the machine, with MamaCee sitting, sewing, and spitting snuff into a can. He even remembered a navy blue corduroy outfit MamaCee had made for him and Zach.

"Yeah, MamaCee, I remember it," Zurich said.

"Well, anyhow, Jimmie Lee liked the stories 'bout how y'all tricked your father and how Zachary was taking them dance lessons and you were playin' football. I would tell him Zach use to keep us all in stitches with his jokes and imitations of different peoples in Warm Springs. You 'member that?"

"Yeah, I remember." He did. How Zach could do things with his eyes and body that always brought a smile to Zurich's face.

"What was that little bug-eyed boy that lived down the road from me?"

"You talking about Bug?" Zurich asked as he pictured the skinny boy from his and Zach's childhood who seemed to be all teeth and eyes.

"Yeah, Bug. Zach sho had him down," MamaCee laughed.

"Yeah, he did," Zurich smiled.

"Jimmie Lee told me how he wished he could meet y'all. But I told him 'bout Zach and you know what he did?"

"No, what did he do, MamaCee?"

"He cried . . . that white boy cried like a baby. Cried about my grandbaby that he never laid eyes on or knew. Only knew him by the stories I told. After he finished crying he looked at me and asked, 'How is Zurich handling this? Doesn't he miss Zach?' Well, I didn't know what to tell him. I told him how you loved your brother, but how you kinda kept things inside. How Zach always wore his heart on his shoulders, but you kept yours hidden. I said they looked 'xactly alike but they was different. But I told him nobody could mess with your brother," MamaCee said as she laughed to herself. "Yeah, you and Zach was a mess."

Zurich just stared at his grandmother. He could see tears forming in the corners of her prune-brown eyes. He was praying silently that she wouldn't start to cry. Zurich was trying to think of something he could do or say to get MamaCee's mind off sad things, but decided to let her finish her story.

"What happened to Jimmie Lee?"

"Oh, he died about two months ago. It was real sad. I was making this blanket for him and I was tryin' real hard to get through with it. So every day while I was telling him stories, I would take my thick needle and thread I use for making my quilts and just sew as I talked. So he knew how it was going to look. You see this patch right here?" MamaCee said as she pointed to an olive green patch.

"Looks like it came from an Army jacket," Zurich said.

"Yes, sir, that's where it came from. Did I tell you Jimmie Lee was in the Army? Well anyhow, he gave me a jacket of his. Said he wanted me to have it. Wasn't that nice of him?" MamaCee asked, but she didn't wait for an answer. "Yeah, the world sho has changed. Who would've ever thought that I would become friends with a white, homosexual boy from Meridien, Mississippi. Who would've thought it?" MamaCee wondered, mostly to herself.

"The world is changing, MamaCee, it's changing," Zurich said as he moved over to the window and looked out on the city. With the lights from the street and other buildings, the window was like a mirror, and while looking at his own reflection Zurich's mind wandered to what Zach might be doing right now and if he missed Zurich as much as Zurich missed his brother. For a few seconds, the presence of Zachary was so strong in the room that Zurich expected to turn around and see him. A few moments later, he heard MamaCee singing softly and then she stopped and called out his name.

"Zurich," she said. It sounded as if she was singing his name in a whispering hum.

"Yes, MamaCee."

"You didn't tell me what I should have told Jimmie Lee. How you doing since we lost Zach?"

"I'm taking it day by day. But I hope you're right, MamaCee, about what you said earlier," Zurich said as he thought about the waves of sorrow that had dominated his life since his brother's death.

"What did I say, baby? You know your grandma talks so much sometimes I forget half of what I say."

"That this will pass. That the pain will go away."

"Trust in the Lord. And this too shall pass."

Tamela knew something was up when she saw Tim and Warner huddled together in a corner booth of a nearby deli, deep in conversation. Tim, in sunglasses, saw Tamela, but looked away as she and Bettye, one of the firm's secretaries, walked in. When Tamela noticed this, she commented to Bettye, "Look at Tim over there trying to be *incognegro*." She and Bettye shared a laugh, got their sandwiches, and returned to the office.

An hour later, Tamela got a call from Tim saying he needed to speak to her right away. When she walked into his office, and before she could take a seat, Tim announced that Warner would be assisting her on Zurich's case.

"Why are you bringing Warner in on this case?" Tamela asked.

"I've told you, Tamela, just in case this becomes a civil case. Warner is much . . . much . . ." Tim paused for a delicate word. "I mean he has handled more civil litigations."

"But right now we don't even know if this is going to be a criminal case," Tamela said. *So this is what Mr. Incognegro was plotting and why Warner was so helpful,* Tamela thought.

"My point exactly. But if the DA decides she doesn't have enough evidence, then you can bet your last dollar that this young lady will be pursuing a case to net her some dollars for her pain and suffering," Tim said. "And besides, I think you and Warner will work well together."

"What does he think about working on this case?" Tamela asked. She wanted to add *like I care what he thinks* at the end of her question.

"I just mentioned it to him in passing, and he really seemed interested," Tim said. *Yeah right, do you think you're talking to a fool?* Tamela wanted to say.

"What about my request to hire an investigator?" Tamela asked.

"Do you really think you need an investigator? What do you expect to find out? And it's not really our job to find out who did this, but to defend our client," Tim said.

"Well, if our client didn't do this then somebody did. Besides I want to do some checking up on him. I don't know if he's telling me everything," Tamela said.

"Do you think he did it?"

"I'm still not convinced either way. You know it's easier to defend a person if you don't really think about their guilt or innocence. But you know I met his grandmother a couple days ago when he came in for a meeting. A wonderful lady, Mrs. Cora Robinson from Warm Springs, Mississippi. Said she came to Chicago just because she knew her grandson needed her. I just find it hard to believe that somebody raised by a lady like Miss Cora could commit such a vicious crime," Tamela said.

"Tamela, come on now. How often have we seen wonderful mothers, usually African-American, on witness stands crying about how they can't understand what happened to one of their children who's gone astray? Try every day in courtrooms all across the country," Tim said firmly.

"Yeah, I know you're right, but you haven't met Miss Cora," Tamela smiled.

Tamela went back to her office and began putting file folders in her briefcase when the phone rang.

"Tamela Coleman."

"Is this Tamela Coleman, the best lawyer in Chicago?" Caliph teased.

"I think so," she laughed. It felt good hearing Caliph's soothing voice in the middle of a busy day.

"I got a big favor to ask you," he said.

"What kind of favor?"

"It's a big one."

"I'm listening." Tamela sat in her leather chair as her curiosity took over her thoughts.

"I was caller number thirteen," Caliph said.

"Caller number thirteen? What are you talking about?" Tamela asked as she leaned back in her chair and allowed the last of the folders to rest in her lap.

"You know . . . I was caller number thirteen on the 'Tom Joyner Morning Show' and I won a prize that I have to collect this week-end," he said.

"You're kidding. I stopped trying to call in on those shows. I was always getting a busy signal," she said.

"I have a system that works sometimes. Right when I think they're getting ready to offer a prize, I dial the number and if I get a busy signal or I'm the wrong caller, I just keep hitting redial," Caliph said.

"So what did you win and what do you need me for?"

"Well, I know this is kinda early, seeing how we've only been on one date, but I won a weekend suite with room service and all at the Four Seasons hotel. And I don't have anyone to share it with me. You game?"

"A weekend at the Four Seasons . . . hum, I don't know," Tamela said. Caliph was right. This was kind of early for an overnight date. Was this some type of scheme? If it was, it showed a lot of creativity, Tamela thought, and money.

"I promise it's all aboveboard. It's a suite so I will sleep on the sofa. You know, if they don't have a sofa then I'll sleep on the floor. I'll be the perfect gentleman," Caliph said.

"Let me think about it. It's not that I'm worried about your gentlemanly qualities, but I'm really busy with my new case," Tamela said.

"How is that going?" Caliph asked.

"Fine. It's all going fine," Tamela said. She was not comfortable talking about her work with Caliph yet.

"Please think about it and you know I'm not rushing you, but I need to know soon. I just can't see spending a weekend alone in a beautiful hotel suite," Caliph said.

"Well, I'm sure you can just look in that little black book of yours and come up with somebody, Mr. Taylor." Tamela still wasn't convinced that someone as fine as Caliph would be on her like milk on cereal. She knew he had his choice of more than one woman. Unless something was wrong with him.

"True . . . true, probably could," he laughed. "But you're the one I want to spend time with."

"Why?"

"Come on, Tamela, don't go playing lawyer with me. Just let it go that I want you to share my good fortune. Why can't you women just let a brother try to do something nice?" he snapped.

"You women," Tamela said. "Don't go there, Caliph . . . you don't want to do it . . . don't go there."

"Aw, how did we get here? Let me start all over. Ms. Coleman, I was caller number thirteen, I won a great prize. A prize I would like to share with you because I enjoyed our date and previous conversations. We both said we wanted to have another date. Would you consider my request and give me an answer in the next twenty-four hours?" Caliph said in a voice alternating from serious to silly.

"Yes, Mr. Taylor, I will consider your request and get back to you in twenty-four hours or less," Tamela said as she caught a glimpse of herself smiling in the windows of her office.

"Then I'll await your reply," he said.

"Bye, Caliph. I'll talk to you."

Sean dropped off his sheets, dirty underwear, and jeans at the *Wash N Fold* two blocks from his apartment and then stopped for a cup of coffee and bagel. The morning was not off to a good start. He had received a call from his editor at *Sports Today* saying they were going to put the article on black quarterbacks on hold until the situation with Zurich Robinson was cleared up. The editor said he didn't think it was in good taste to be doing a feature that would include a guy whose career could be short-lived, or spent in a jail cell. When Sean pointed out that Zurich had not been charged with anything and that he personally didn't believe that Zurich had done anything wrong, the editor replied, "Well, I admire your confidence but given the current climate with athletes, I would rather be safe than sorry." Sean wanted to tell him that Zurich's possible case had nothing to do with other athletes, that he was different. But he held his tongue, because he didn't want to hear an I told you so, if his impressions of Zurich proved wrong.

The only good news was that Sean had a hefty cancellation fee in his contract and could move onto something else. But that was not going to be easy. Zurich Robinson had piqued Sean's interest in more ways than one. For Sean it would be difficult to simply walk away. With his country-sophisticate demeanor, Zurich Robinson was getting next to Sean. While his beautiful face and body didn't hurt, it was his innocence and Dudley Do Right charm that attracted and kept Sean's attention.

With his morning off to such a bad start, Sean was glad he was having lunch with Anja, who would, no doubt, cheer him up.

Sean walked into JR's, a midtown restaurant he and his sister tried to meet at once a week, usually Fridays, and studied the day's specials printed in red crayon on an art-nouveau mirror. All of a sudden he felt someone grab him tightly from behind.

"How you doing, baby brother?" Anja asked as she gave Sean a hug and kiss.

"I'm doing great. Boy, you smell good. What'cha wearing?" Sean said as he hugged his sister tightly. He noticed how nice she looked in a bubble gum pink pantssuit, with a black silk blouse underneath. Her hair was piled high and swooped to the left side, setting off her oval-shaped brown face.

"That's my body odor, sweetheart. You know I don't wear perfume during the week," Anja smiled.

"How's work?"

"It's all right. Let's get a table. You know I don't have but an hour. Oh, I have something for you," Anja said as she reached in her purse and handed Sean a note in Magic Marker on tablet paper. It was a thank-you note from Gerald. Sean opened the note and read the nine-year-old's printing: *Thank you, Uncle Sean, for a great day! I had fun at the game and eating hot dogs. Thank your friend for my new shirt. I love you very, very much. Love, Gerald.*

"This is really special. I'm going to save this," Sean said.

"My baby had a great time. That's all he's been talking about. How he met all these football players and he's been sleeping in that jersey your friend gave him. Boy, was he fine," Anja said.

"Tell the truth, shame the devil. He is a fine one and really nice too," Sean said as he looked at the menu and smiled to himself. Anja noticed.

"What's that smile about?"

"What smile?"

"Oh now, don't go there. I've seen that smile before. Whatsup with Mr. Football Player? Is he gay?"

"I don't know. He might be, but I don't think he knows yet," Sean said.

"How so? Now don't tell me you're going to become one of those people who thinks everyone is gay," Anja said.

"You mean they're not?" Sean teased.

"Now, come on. There's this guy that works in my department at the bank and he thinks everybody's gay. Every time a messenger comes in, he says, I bet I can have him. But when it's somebody who's not that cute and we say, 'Oswald, is he gay?' he'll laugh and say, 'Chile, I hope not, y'all can have him,' " Anja laughed.

"I don't know about Zurich Robinson, but I really think he's incredibly nice. Anyhow, if he is gay and he knows it, he's probably already got somebody. Probably another football player or some type of athlete, they stick together. Deep in the closet behind last decade's clothes," Sean said.

"So nobody won't tell?" Anja asked.

"You got it. I mean my sister is getting smart," Sean said.

"You're an athlete and you definitely know a lot of them."

"I used to be an athlete. Haven't you seen this little extra tube I'm carrying around my waist. It's not removable," Sean said as he grabbed his midsection.

"It's removable if you work at it," Anja said.

"Yeah, I know you're right. I guess I won't have that cheeseburger I was looking at. I guess it's the salad," Sean said.

"All you need to do is a few situps and walk a little more," Anja said.

"I walk almost everywhere I go. I mean I walk sometimes just to save money and to stay away from all the crazies on the subway," Sean said.

"I know that's right," Anja said.

A waiter came over and asked if they were ready to order.

"Yes, she's having the special, the beef one, and I'm going to have soup and salad, with oil and vinegar dressing," Sean said as he took the menu from Anja and handed it to the waiter. Almost at the same moment, Sean and Anja both reached for their water glasses and took a long sip of water, and then broke out in an identical smile. The smile teased their mouths, and both struggled to keep the water in place.

"There is something I need to mention to you about my nephew," Sean said.

"Uh-oh. What did he do now?"

"It's nothing he did, more of something he said. A favor he asked me."

"What are you talking about?"

"Saturday, when I took him to register for football and all the little boys were there with their fathers, there was some kind of sadness in his eyes. I mean, I know he was happy that I was there with him, but when a couple of the kids asked him if I was his father, well, the first time he said no, but the second time he said yes and grabbed my hand almost like he wanted to make sure that I wouldn't tell the truth. Later, when we were heading to the bus stop, he looked up at me and said, 'Uncle Sean, when I turn thirteen, will you help me find my father?' I mean I was shocked."

"What did you say?" Anja asked. She'd been wondering when this was going to come up with her son and how she would handle it.

"I looked at him and said, 'Do you really want that?' He was as firm as a nine-year-old can be when he said yes. I told him I would help in any way I could," Sean said.

"I know he misses his daddy, but I don't understand how he can miss someone he never knew. Maybe it's just the image of a father he misses or thinks he needs," Anja said.

"Don't you think so?"

"Yeah, I know he needs a father, but he needs a father that's going to love him and be there for him always, not one who ducks out at the first sign of a problem. I mean I will let Gerald know about his father, but to be honest, Sean, I don't know what would happen if Gerald found out his father decided not to be in his life, not me. But I realize I might have to take the blame."

"Do you know where Sean's father is?"

"The last time I heard, and that was over five years ago, he was in upstate New York, right outside Endicott. That's when he was working for IBM, but with all the layoffs they've been having, I doubt if he would have stayed in that area. I mean Jeff was a real city dweller."

"Why doesn't he want to be a part of his son's life?"

"It's really kinda stupid when you think about it. It's payback toward me," Anja said as she smiled at the server, who placed their meals in front of her and Sean.

"Payback?"

"Yeah, I thought I had told you this story. Anyhow, when I found out I was pregnant, Jeff wanted to marry me, but I wasn't certain that I wanted to get married or if I was in love with him. So when I refused, he said if I didn't change my mind he would be out of my life for good and that meant out of his child's life also. I mean I didn't know it was going to be a little boy. I think Jeff wanted a little girl since he had all brothers," Anja said as she took her first bite of food.

"Wait a minute. Are you telling me that this jerk has never seen Gerald?"

"To the best of my knowledge."

"I bet he couldn't turn his back on him if he ever saw him, if he ever spent some time with him," Sean said.

"I used to think the same thing about our father," Anja said sadly. "I used to think the same thing."

"Oh, Anja, I'm sorry," Sean said as he touched his sister's hand. He knew how she desperately wanted a relationship with their father, but his father was still being a jerk about being in Anja's life. He knew if his father saw and got to know her that he couldn't help but love her as he did.

"Oh, don't worry about it. I mean, look at me, I'm doing okay and I never had a relationship with my father. And Gerald has you. I can't tell you how much it means to me that you've taken such an interest in him."

"I love him," Sean said softly.

"I know."

"I got something else I need to ask," Sean said.

"What?"

"Does it ever bother you that I'm gay? I meant with my being so involved with Gerald?"

"What are you talking about?"

"Well, you've always been very supportive of me"—Sean paused to make sure he had the right words—"Even though I know you wished I was straight, didn't you?"

"I won't lie. But I wished you were straight so that your life would be better, not because I think being gay is wrong. I mean look at you. You're handsome, smart, kind, but you're alone most of the time," Anja said.

"I'm not all that. And I've gotten used to being by myself," Sean said.

"But back to your question. I don't have a problem with you being such a strong influence in my son's life. You are a man and not a child molester. I think Gerald can learn a lot from you on what being a man really is," Anja said.

"I'm so proud that you know being a man has nothing to do with who you're sleeping with, Anja," Sean said as he gently touched his sister's hand. She lowered her eyes and smiled sweetly at her brother and then asked, "So you've given up on love, for real?"

"Yes, I think so. I mean I know black men can make love with each other, or have sex with each other. I just don't think we know how to love each other intimately."

"The same could be said about black men and black women. I mean even when we have a man in our life, I don't think we're really intimate in the true sense of the word," Anja said.

"What do you mean?"

"I think men keep things to themselves, even when they are deeply in love. And we women tell everything, especially when we're deeply in love."

"Why do you think that?"

"What are you always saying about straight men being afraid of gay men?"

"What, the fear thing?"

"Yes, I think fear motivates so many of our actions. I mean even I'm afraid of falling in love."

"Why?"

"Probably the same reason as you. I don't want to be hurt again," Anja said.

"So you're not in love with the good man of the cloth?" He was somewhat relieved that his sister hadn't fallen for Theodis.

"Oh, I care about him deeply. But I'm not in love with him," Anja said. "Sometimes it's the little things about him that bother me the most."

"Like?" Sean wanted to know if he and his sister liked the same thing in men.

"Well, let's see, let's start with his dress. I mean every time I see him he has that *church look,* you know, jackets that don't match the polyester pants, cotton-blended shirts over those old man T-shirts, and socks you can see through," Anja said.

"Stop it . . . stop it," Sean laughed as he held his stomach.

"I guess . . . maybe my infatuation is beginning to fade," she said.

"What about the age thing? He's a little bit older, isn't he?"

"I think about ten years. But that's not really a problem with me."

"Do you ever think you were looking for a father in your relationships?"

"Oh, I don't think so. One of the things that attracted me to Theodis was his faith. I was looking for something and I thought maybe he had it. That dating a preacher was maybe a way of getting closer to God."

"Has that changed?"

"I'm realizing that he's a human being, a regular Joe when other people aren't around. The more time we spend together I see that. Like, for instance, you know occasionally, I like to use a few curse words to get my point across, force of habit. But I was trying to stop that around Theodis, that is until I realized he didn't seem bothered when he let a cuss word slip every now and then," Anja said.

"No, don't tell me the good preacher has used cuss words," Sean smiled.

"Come on now, stop messing with me."

"Then what is it? What are you afraid of?"

"I'm scared to let my heart go again on someone I know won't treat it right," Anja said.

"But that's not so strange. Look at me, despite my own personal experiences, I know that two black men, or two men period, can love each other and share a life together. But I'm scared to death of allowing myself to care so deeply for someone who can hurt me," Sean said.

"So I guess this fear runs in the family," Anja joked.

"So it's genetic," Sean laughed.

"Yeah, it's genetic," Anja agreed.

"I'll do you one better," Sean said.

"What's that?"

"It's probably the one trait we share with every human being in the world."

"I know that's right," Anja said as she tipped her glass toward Sean and smiled.

CHAPTER 17

IN MY SOLITUDE

Another week, another loss, this time a 44–0 blowout to San Francisco, and Zurich was praying for spring. The DA still hadn't decided whether to press charges, but every day at practice Zurich had to say "no comment" to the same reporter, who wanted to know if charges against him were still pending. The reporter was a former police-beat reporter who had discovered and made the police report public without mentioning Mia's name. Several other sports writers seemed annoyed and bothered by this journalist, who had invaded their territory and insisted on asking the same question daily.

Zurich needed some peace and it seemed like the only place he found it was sitting on a wooden bench in front of his locker. He hadn't shaved his head for several days, and his skull was covered with the dark fuzz of a newborn. The morning before, MamaCee had teased, "Baby, are you thinking 'bout getting one of them curls now that you lettin' yo hairs grow back?"

Yes, MamaCee was still in Chicago, turning his kitchen into a small restaurant, cooking everything from fried chicken to stuffed cabbage and sweet potato pies. She was enjoying taking care of her grandson, looking at cable television, and renting videos. She'd watched *Imitation of Life* four times in two days, crying each time, and had figured out how to work Zurich's CD player so she could listen to his *Kirk Franklin and the Family* gospel disc. She had also become hooked on talk radio, listening every morning to "The Deborah Crable Show" on WVON. MamaCee had tried several times to call in and offer her advice but always got a busy signal. Every time she heard the busy beep she muttered to herself that this was a place that could use that call waiting thing. So she just talked back to the radio.

"I told him I would go, but now I'm having second thoughts."

"Tamela, I think you should do it."

"So you really think I should go, Desiree?"

"Yes, girl. You said he seems like a perfect gentleman and sounds like from your work load you could use a night of rest and relaxation," Desiree said.

"And you don't think it's too early?" She knew it was too early but wanted someone to tell her it was all right.

"Honey, like you said, you don't have to sleep with him. It's a suite, right?"

"Yes."

"Well, anyhow, if push comes to shove you just get outta there. Get in your car or cab or whatever and you'll be home in minutes. It's not like you're going out of town or on some out-of-the-way island," Desiree added.

"Yeah, you're right," she said as she realized she was spending too much time talking and thinking about a man. There were more important things in life. "Well, enough about me and my little old life, what's going on with you? Any good leads on permanent jobs?"

"I've got an interview later this week for a part-time job teaching dance out in Evanston, and I'm talking to some people about doing some choreography. And you know, Tam, the temp work isn't so bad. It's something new every day. As long as they don't send me on a job where I have to wear a shirt with my name on it," Desiree laughed.

"I know that's right," Tamela laughed.

"Now to the important stuff. Tell me about that fine-assed client of yours. Have they arrested him yet and more important, do you think he did it?"

"No, they haven't arrested him and you know I can't talk about my case or my client," Tamela said.

"Aw, come on. Just tell me what he's like," Desiree pleaded.

"He seems like a nice man. Did I tell you I met his grandmother? She's sweet and a hoot. She brought me some of the best fried chicken I ever had up to the office the other day. It was sweet and funny. I get this call saying there's a Miss Cora at the front office with a package for me. At first, I didn't know what to do. I mean you could smell that chicken all the way down the hall. The receptionist was looking at the both of us like we were some kinda fools. But I tell you when I got home late that night, dog-tired, that fried chicken was a gift from heaven," Tamela said.

"Honey, I wish I had somebody cooking for me. Tell me, Tamela, has anyone said anything to you about my not having a regular job?"

"No, like who?"

"I was wondering, I mean I haven't talked with Karen and Stephanie since I called them and asked them was there anyone at their office who should get my résumé. I mean usually those divas will call me at least once a week to go to lunch or to the health club," Desiree said. "I can't believe they are throwing me all this shade."

"Naw, they ain't said nothing to me and if they did I would get them straight. Honey, we all living from paycheck to paycheck," Tamela said.

"I know that's right."

"How are you doing with money?"

"Of course, I need some, but I'm doing okay. I did have a little savings. And, heaven forbid, I could go to my mother for money. But these bill collectors are calling every other day," Desiree said.

"What are you telling them?"

"What I used to hear my mother tell them: 'You can't get yours till I get mine,' " Desiree said.

"All right now. Well, darling, I've got to get back to work if I'm going on this overnight date."

"I think you're going to have a great time. And just remember 'cause a brother wines and dines you don't mean you got to give it up."

"Don't I know it."

Mia sat cross-legged in the middle of her bed, looking at her reflection in a hand-held mirror. Her face was healing, the colors fading, and the contours of her normally smooth skin were reappearing. She had at least another week before she could talk to the station manager about returning to work, even though she knew she would have to apologize to Cheryl.

She was reconsidering LaDonna's offer to visit Los Angeles and thought she might look into the job possibilities out there. She was also thinking of getting out of sports and switching into regular news. She knew no matter what happened with Zurich, it was going to be difficult to go in the Cougars' locker room again.

Just as she moved from her bed to put the mirror back on her dresser, the phone rang. She had gotten her phone number changed to avoid the constant calls from an annoying reporter and the police, so she knew it could only be her mother or LaDonna. She'd started to keep her number a secret from everybody, including her mother and LaDonna, but changed her mind. She thought that the solitude of silence she had created might help connect the fragments of her memory.

"Hello," Mia said.

"Hey, girl. How you doing? Enjoying that vacation?" LaDonna said.

"Yeah, but I'm getting bored. Funny you should call because I been thinking about coming out there to visit you."

"Come on out here, girl. Have you talked with the police yet? Have they arrested that animal?" She knew Mia didn't like to talk about the incident, but as a friend she felt the need to be the voice of reason.

"Come on, LaDonna. I don't want to talk about that. What's going on out there? Got any good gossip?" When Mia changed the subject, LaDonna was certain she was deep in denial.

"Same old, same old. Nothing really big. There are a couple of movies opening soon, but not a lot happens in the fall," LaDonna said.

"You know what? I'm thinking about getting my hair cut," Mia said.

"Your hair cut? What for?"

"Oh, just to have something different. I'm sick of taking care of this mane. You know, I was thinking about getting it cut like Toni Braxton and Halle Berry," Mia said.

"Have you thought about this? Your hair is beautiful, Mia."
LaDonna knew how proud Mia was of her hair; why did she want to
cut it off?

"I haven't made any final decisions, but I'm seriously thinking
about it."

"Mia, are you sure you're all right?"

"I'm fine. Like I said, I'm just bored out of my mind." She was
getting annoyed at all the questions. If she wanted questions, she
would talk to the police.

"You haven't heard from Derrick, have you?"

"No, but I ain't hardly worried about Derrick, honey," Mia
laughed. A laugh that sounded artificial, yet Mia wanted LaDonna to
believe she was okay.

"What about the test?"

"What test?"

"Come on, Mia, didn't we agree that you should have an AIDS
test? You did say you don't remember if that asshole used a condom,
right?"

"Yes, LaDonna, I've talked to my doctor, but he said it takes
about two to three months before something would show up, so I'm
going to wait to take the test then. Why are we talking about this
shit?"

"I just want you to know I'm here if you need me. I still got some
vacation time, and I could be up there in a plane ride," LaDonna
offered.

"I know, darling, I'm fine. Look, I hear someone at my door,"
Mia lied. She was tired of talking about AIDS tests and condoms.

"Okay, call me soon," LaDonna said.

"I will, take care."

After hanging up the phone, Mia looked for the yellow pages. She
wanted to find a beauty salon for her new look. She didn't dare go to
her regular salon because she knew full well that her stylist would
talk her out of cutting or even dying her hair. When she located the
book and turned to the beauty section, a large ad for a shop called
Therapy caught her attention. The ad stated that it was unisex and
offered a wide range of services including pedicures, massages, and
even a formal dress rental. From the address Mia could tell it was in a

posh neighborhood and away from the station and her regular salon. Mia picked up the phone and dialed the number. She was impressed immediately with the telephone manner of the woman who scheduled her appointment and asked her what she wanted to get done, how she had heard about the shop, and even if she needed directions or transportation to the shop. She also suggested that since it was Mia's first time visiting the salon, she might want to allow an extra half-hour so that she could talk to a few of the stylists to discuss the look she wanted to achieve. Mia agreed and scheduled an appointment for Friday at 2 P.M. sharp.

Sean felt he had come up with a brilliant idea that might help his money crisis and allow him to see Zurich Robinson again. But first he wanted to see what Gina DeMarco thought and if she would help him. Sean picked up the phone and felt it was a good sign when she took his call immediately.

"Hi, Sean, I thought you'd forgotten me," Gina said in her normally cheerful voice.

"Oh no. I just figured you had your hands full with Zurich and all," Sean said.

"Well, it's kinda quiet right now with him. We're still trying to see what the DA is going to do and if they are going to have a preliminary hearing to see if there is enough evidence to bind him over for trial," Gina said.

"So it must be serious. When I talked with Zurich, he didn't really seem bothered by it," Sean said.

"You know that's his personality, really low key. Am I right or am I wrong? But he says he didn't do it and I believe him. His grandmother is here to support him, and he has a pretty good lawyer," Gina said confidently.

"That's good. Gina, the reason why I'm calling is to share some good news and some bad news. Which do you want first?"

"Give me the bad. Let's get that over with," Gina said.

"First, *ST* canned the story I was working on. They said with Zurich's reputation being in question that the story I outlined wouldn't fly, plus it seems like most of the black quarterbacks are having a tough year, you know Randall and Vince. Warren is playing okay, but there have been more than a hundred profiles on him," Sean said.

"So we won't get the story right now. They will come around."

"Yeah, I think you're right. Which brings me to the good news. I talked to the editor who assigned the story about another idea and he seemed interested. I proposed doing a piece on the number of black athletes being accused of crimes, like rape and dare I say double homicide, and what would happen if one of these guys, say for instance like Zurich, were falsely accused," Sean said.

"I like the way you talking, Sean," Gina said. Sean had her hooked and now he began to reel her in.

"Yeah, the story could take on different angles. You know one of the things Zurich said in our interview has really stuck with me."

"What was that?"

"I talked with him after the New Jersey game and he said how some of his teammates were quite proud of his alleged rape and beating of this woman. I think that's a chilling commentary on what black men, and especially men we've put on a pedestal, feel about black women," Sean said.

"I know that's right."

"In my conversations with Zurich, I somehow get the impression that their reaction bothers him more than the allegations. To steal a phrase, am I right or am I wrong?" Sean laughed.

"Sho you right," Gina laughed.

"So if I could get him to talk about that and his feelings, I think he could garner some sympathy if this thing goes to trial. And if *ST* doesn't buy the story then I was thinking maybe you and I could put our heads together and seek out some publications that might be interested," Sean said.

"That's a great idea, Sean. I love it! And I do have several contacts with some other newspapers and magazines. What can I do?"

"Do you think Zurich would talk to me and, if he would, open up a little more about his background. One of the premises of the story will be that a lot of this behavior goes back to that thing we call home training. And how a lot of athletes at some point go through some type of socialization to believe and expect that all women are supposed to be sexually compliant. They grow up learning that being a star includes having any woman you want, regardless if she doesn't want you."

"I will definitely talk to him about it and convince him to do it. You know his grandmother is here, and she's a real piece of work. I know she would love to talk to you. Actually, she loves talking to anybody and everybody. I mean when you meet her, Sean, it will become clear that Zurich got, how did you say it, *home training*," Gina said.

"So you will plead my case?" Sean asked.

"Of course. I think Zurich likes you. It's this one little sawed-off police beat reporter that's bugging us. Let me make sure I have your number. What am I talking about? Of course I do. Sean, let me talk to Zurich and I'll give you a call later on this evening. Would you want to conduct this interview on the phone or would you be coming back to Chicago?"

"I know he's busy with practice and all, but I'd like to do it in person," Sean said.

"Okay, I think you should. That way you can meet Miss Cora in person," Gina said.

"Great. I look forward to your call. Thanks, Gina," Sean said.

"Take care, Sean. I look forward to seeing you," Gina said.

Sean hung up the phone and smiled to himself at the thought of seeing Zurich Robinson. His smile didn't last that long when he thought about the cost involved in going to Chicago again. *ST* had only expressed an interest and was not offering an advance or travel expenses. Sean hoped he had enough miles to get a free ticket and find a cheap hotel. Sean thought about calling his mother or his older brother and asking for a loan, but quickly nixed the idea since he had always assured them that his life in New York was going smoothly. He looked around his apartment to see if there was anything he could sell or pawn. He couldn't sell his laptop, fax, or printer. But maybe he could do without his camera and the Rolex watch his father had given him when he graduated from college. All this, Sean thought, just to go to Chicago and be in the presence of Zurich. Was it worth it?

On his way home from practice, Zurich stopped at a pay phone and called Gina. He needed her help. It was late so he was relieved when Gina picked up on her private line.

"Gina DeMarco speaking."

"Gina, this is Zurich."

"Oh, I'm glad you called me, I got something I need you to do," Gina said.

"I have a favor to ask you too, but you go first," Zurich said.

"How was practice?"

"It was okay, but that jerk of a reporter was there asking me the same questions," Zurich said.

"My favor deals with a reporter, but I think it's one you like," Gina said.

"Who?"

"Sean Elliott, the guy from New York. He said he talked to you when you guys played in New Jersey."

"Yeah, I like Sean, he's good people," Zurich said. He felt Sean was easy to talk to and allowed him to say things he had kept to himself. Gina told Zurich about Sean's story proposal, and he quickly agreed.

"That was easy. Now what favor do you have for me? Let me tell you I don't know that little police beat reporter, but I can find out who his boss is," Gina said.

"No, I can handle him. It's MamaCee I need your help with."

"How can I help?"

"You know I love my grandma, but I need a break. I need some solitude. And she's not leaving until this mess with Mia is cleared up," Zurich said.

"What do you need me to do?"

"I don't know; I was hoping you had some suggestions."

"I know. How do you think MamaCee would like a day of beauty?"

"A day of beauty?"

"Yeah, I could arrange to take her to the place where I get my hair done. We could schedule her to get her hair done, nails, toes, and if we plan it right, it could take all day. Maybe we could end it with my husband and me taking her to dinner," Gina offered.

"That sounds great! But you know how MamaCee is about restaurant food. And, to be honest, I don't know if MamaCee has ever been to a beauty shop. But that sounds really nice," Zurich said. He felt a sense of relief at the thought of some private time in his apartment and the image of MamaCee in a beauty shop being treated like a queen.

"We could take her to this soul food restaurant over on the South Side. Army and Lou's has pretty good food, or we could take her to Gladys's. You've been there, haven't you?"

"Yeah, actually, I've been to both. She might like that. But who's gonna tell her?"

"I could call her and convince her," Gina said.

"Thanks, Gina. Could you do it now, like, before I get home?"

"Yeah, I can, but first I have to pull some strings at the salon. It's a really popular place and it might be hard to get an appointment. But leave it to me. I'll also check with a friend of mine, Robin, who works over in publicity at the 'Oprah Winfrey Show' and see if I can't arrange for MamaCee to go to a taping."

"That would be real cool. MamaCee loves Oprah."

"I can't make any promises, but let's keep our fingers crossed. How are things working out with Tamela?"

"Oh, everything is everything. Just waiting to see what the DA is going to do. I'm ready for this to be over for a lot of reasons. I want my life back," Zurich said as he looked at his watch.

"I hope it will be over soon, so we can get back to our game plan. Okay, let me go. I got work to do."

"Thanks, Gina. I owe you one."

"Don't worry. That's what I'm here for. Now am I right or am I wrong?"

"You know you're right."

CHAPTER 18

A Day of Beauty,
A Night of Bliss

It was Friday. The afternoon sunlight was soft, the air mild. It was the time of year when the sun confirmed the passing of summer, and the mornings and evenings were cool and comfortable, signs that fall was in full effect.

Gina made an appointment at her regular beauty salon for a day of beauty for MamaCee. The Dearborn Street salon was one of the city's most popular. Therapy pampered its clients beyond belief and operated an exclusive dress shop adjacent to the salon that sold and rented expensive evening gowns. The chatter of clients warmed the salon, as both men and women got manicures, pedicures and, of course, their do's done. The dress shop was always busy on weekends, especially during prom time.

Zurich was busy preparing to leave Saturday morning for an away game against Seattle, so Gina picked up MamaCee and took her to the salon. Once inside, Gina introduced her to Teresa, one of the co-owners, who welcomed Mrs. Cora Robinson as if she was her first and most important customer ever.

"Now, MamaCee, you are in good hands. I'll make sure someone will call my office when you're all done," Gina said.

"Okay, baby. They got your number?"

"Yes, MamaCee, it's all taken care of," Gina assured her.

"Don't worry, Gina, we'll take good care of Mrs. Robinson," Teresa said as she took MamaCee's handbag and the small paper bag in which MamaCee had packed chicken salad and deviled eggs, just in case.

"My oh my, I'm tellin' you, ain't this a beautiful place you got here? You own all this?" MamaCee asked as she surveyed the stylish waiting area with its matching gray-and-black oversized chairs and black leather sofa.

"Yes, ma'am, I do," Teresa said proudly. "Gina tells me you're from down South. What part?"

"Mississippi. A li'l place called Warm Springs. We ain't got no place like this back home," MamaCee said as she looked around. The salon was divided into black-lacquer-and-glass workstations for each stylist, with a separate area for manicures and pedicures. A bank of hair dryers and shampoo sinks, together with a dressing room, lined the far wall. "I've been doin' my own hair most of my life."

"Well, we're certainly glad you're going to spend some time with us, Mrs. Robinson," Teresa said.

"Oh, baby, call me MamaCee or Miss Cora, whichever one suits you," MamaCee said.

"Okay, Miss Cora, let me introduce you to David, one of the co-owners and the young man who's gonna take care of you."

"I'm in your hands," MamaCee said as she caught a glimpse of two young women in the adjacent dress shop modeling black-beaded gowns and checking their fit in a three-way mirror. A few minutes later, a tall, brown-skinned young man with a comb in his hands and a big smile on his face approached and greeted MamaCee.

"Miss Cora, I'm David. I'm going to be your stylist. What are we going to have done today?"

"I don't know. You the expert. What do you think we ought to do?" MamaCee said as she pulled off the flower print flop hat she was wearing. Her thickly braided hair was rolled up and held in place by several bobby pins. David took her hat and began to run his fingers through MamaCee's hair, releasing several pins and letting her shoulder-length locks free.

"Oh, you have a good grade of hair, Miss Cora. We can do some things with it. I think we should start with some coloring. Perk it up," David said.

"Uh-oh. I don't know 'bout that. What was your name again, baby?"

"David," he said as he began to unbraid her hair.

"Now, David, I like my natural color. You know this gray hair shows my age, which I'm proud of. I don't know 'bout no coloring."

"I think maybe just a little black tint will do. We can try this new color called Silky Black. Now, Miss Cora, you've got to trust me. You're such a beautiful lady. I'm just going to enhance that beauty. Will you trust me?"

MamaCee looked in David's eyes and was silent for a moment. Suddenly she broke out in a smile and said, "I can trust you. Come on, give Mama the works."

"Great," David said. He called out to a young lady in the shampoo area to come over to meet MamaCee.

"Miss Cora," he said, "this is Pam; she's our colorist. She's going to get you a smock so we can get you started. We don't want to mess up this pretty dress you're wearing. Can we get you something to drink?"

"Something to drink? What you got?" MamaCee asked as she thought about her lunch. She wasn't hungry yet, but something for her dry mouth would be good.

"Pam, why don't you take Miss Cora in the back and let her change into a smock. Let her know what we have to drink and treat her right," he said.

"Fine, come with me, Miss Cora, is it?"

"Yes, baby. But why don't you call me MamaCee."

"Okay, MamaCee. Can I get you some wine, champagne, or maybe some fruit juice?"

MamaCee put her fingers to her chin and said, "Let me think. It's the middle of the day, so I don't think I need any wine or that champ stuff. How 'bout a strawberry soda pop?"

"Oh, I don't think we have strawberry soda. We have fruit punch," Pam said.

"How 'bout orange juice. You got that?"

"Yes, I think we do. Come on with me and let's get changed. When you come out, I'll have you a nice glass of juice."

"Fine, baby. You people sho are nice," she said as she entered the private changing areas.

It was Mia Miller's first trip to Therapy, too, and she walked in with sunglasses and an attitude. For days rest and sleep had eluded

Mia. When she did manage to sleep, she had nightmares. She still couldn't recall the details of the night she was attacked. All she really remembered was a strong hand jerking her head back by her hair. Every time she woke up, Mia had nagging headaches, which she attributed to the wine she was drinking to help her sleep.

Dressed down in jeans and an oversized man's white oxford shirt, Mia checked in with the receptionist and then took a seat in the waiting area. After thumbing impatiently through a few magazines, she returned to the desk and asked just how long she was expected to wait. The receptionist told her the stylist would be with her in a few minutes. When she asked Mia if she could offer her something to drink, Mia's eyes perked up. "Yes, what do you have?"

"We have juice, wine, or champagne," the receptionist offered.

"I'll take the wine, if it's white and cold," Mia said with a quick toss of her hair and a smile without warmth. The cold smile was not for the receptionist, but in anticipation of the wine.

"No problem. I'll get it for you right away."

After Mia had finished her wine, and before she could request another glass, a tall, slender young man came to the waiting area and introduced himself. "Miss Miller, I'm Mark Young. You have an appointment with me. I think you told my booker that you wanted to get a wash and cut."

"That's right," Mia said, twirling the empty wineglass in her left hand.

"You have beautiful hair, are you sure you want it cut?" Mark said as he ran his hands through her thick hair.

"Yes," Mia said coldly.

"If you just want a new look, I can show you some styles that would look good on you, without cutting so much of your hair," Mark said.

"I want my hair cut," Mia said, emphasizing each word. She stood and placed one hand on her hip and asked, "Which part don't you understand?" Mia was using her pre-hissy-fit voice.

"Fine, Ms. Miller. If you want it cut, then that's what we'll do. Would you mind taking off your sunglasses?"

"Are we going to have problems here?" Mia asked as she slowly removed the glasses and rolled her eyes at Mark.

"Oh no," Mark said as he moved back with his hands clasped as if in prayer. "At Therapy the client is always right. Like I said, you want a short cut, then we will do it. Let me show you to the changing area." Mia turned in the direction of his extended hand. Mark looked back at the receptionist, who mouthed *bitch,* and he smiled in agreement.

"You're the sportscaster, aren't you?" Mark asked.

Without looking back at him, Mia whispered, "Yes." She'd been hoping no one would recognize her. But now that Mark had, Mia thought maybe she should try and be more pleasant. She was certain he would tell his other clients she was a bitch. She was feeling too vulnerable to deal with bad beauty shop gossip.

Mia walked into the dressing room as MamaCee walked out. MamaCee smiled at Mia and said in a loud voice, "I'm ready. What do I do now?"

"Come on over here, MamaCee," Pam said as she wrapped a towel around MamaCee's neck.

"That sure was a pretty girl that just walked in there. Is she some kinda movie star? I heard y'all have them up here," MamaCee said.

"Naw, not really. She just thinks she is," Pam whispered.

"Oh, she one of them, huh. Sounds like the white lady I worked for, BethAnn Thorsen, the original Miss Nobody-knows-the-trouble-I-seen," MamaCee laughed. "She always thought she shoulda been a movie star. Use to read all them movie magazines and them *Cosmo Something* magazines or other. I can't recall the exact name, you know, baby, the kind where they be talkin' 'bout what folks ought to keep in their 'whisperin' rooms,' " MamaCee said.

Pam seated MamaCee at the shampoo bowl and tilted her head back against the cold sink as she applied color protector to MamaCee's hair, then asked, "What's a whisperin' room?"

"Ah, you know, baby. Yo folks probably had one; it's usually the bedroom. You know where folks who married go to talk 'bout stuff they don't want other folks to know. You know, like nosy kids, nosy in-laws. Me and my late husband, God rest his soul, had two whisperin' rooms. One was the dining room, where we would sit and talk 'bout stuff over a nice strong cup of coffee. Stuff like the white folks we worked for, our kids. Stuff just 'tween he and me. And our other whisperin' room was our bedroom, you know, where we took care of our marital business," MamaCee laughed. "But you look a little too young to know 'bout that kinda stuff."

Pam just smiled as she worked the protector into MamaCee's hair. "Miss Cora, why don't you just lay back and close your eyes and let the protector sit?" Pam said.

"Okay, baby, Mama ain't goin' nowhere," MamaCee replied.

Pam allowed MamaCee's hair to set for about ten minutes and then returned to shampoo and condition it. When she finished, Pam dabbed the water and traces of conditioner from MamaCee's forehead with a towel. MamaCee looked over at Mark's station, where he was cutting Mia's hair.

"Why he doin' that?" MamaCee asked.

"What?"

"Cuttin' that gal's hair like that. She got beautiful hair," MamaCee said. "Looks like she got a good grade of hair. If I had hair like that, Lord knows you couldn't pay me enough money to let somebody cut it."

"I'm sure that's what she wanted, MamaCee," Pam said.

"Well, I'll be. I hope what's his name don't think he gonna cut off Mama's hair, 'cause if he is, then I might as well have brought my good wig with me, so I can put it on when I leave here," she said.

"Don't worry, you won't need a wig when you leave here," Pam chuckled.

Pam turned MamaCee over to David, who did clip off a few of her split ends. He rolled her wet hair tightly and then took MamaCee over to a row of five dryers. Three were already in use, so David put MamaCee in the last dryer, near the wall and the magazine table.

"Now how long you want me under here?" MamaCee asked.

"Not that long. I'm not going to forget about you. Do you want something else to drink?"

"Naw, I'll be just fine. But maybe a li'l bit later I'll have you fetch my handbag. I got some rock candy in there I might need to suck on," MamaCee said. "Keep my throat from getting dry," she said as she tapped her throat.

"Okay, just let me know. You want a magazine?"

"Naw, I'll just talk to my neighbor," MamaCee said as she looked at the empty seat next to her, but then spotted a lady in the next chair over who had smiled at her when she sat down.

MamaCee was trying to adjust the dryer's plastic helmet when Mark brought Mia over to the dryers and sat her next to MamaCee. MamaCee smiled again at Mia, who didn't smile back. Mia got up from the chair, went over to the magazine table, picked up a copy of *Essence,* and returned to her chair. Minutes later Mark brought over the plastic cup of wine that Mia had left at his workstation.

"I thought you might want this," he said and did a fashion run-way turn before Mia could thank him.

She measured the drink to make sure she had enough to last her through dryer time. Just as she was getting ready to lower the dryer back on her head, MamaCee lifted hers and said, "Baby, why you cutting all that pretty hair of yours?"

"Excuse me?" Mia said coldly. She had decided to extend her pleasantries only to Mark and not some old lady with a gold tooth who probably never ever even watched television sports. But MamaCee ignored the chill in Mia's voice and the disdain in her eyes. She wanted to talk.

"Oh, you couldn't hear me, these dryer things are kinda loud, ain't they? I said, why you want to cut all that pretty hair of yours? I saw you when you came in here with all that hair. I asked one of the peoples working here if you were some kinda movie star on count you were so pretty and when I saw that man cuttin' your hair, I wanted to come over there and tell him to stop. Don't cut all that pretty hair," MamaCee said.

Mia didn't respond. She gave MamaCee a what-is-this-crazy-woman-talking-about look as she lowered the dryer and started reading her magazine. Maybe if she continued to ignore MamaCee, she would get the message that Mia was in no mood to talk.

MamaCee shrugged her shoulders and lowered her dryer, too.

But a few minutes later, the dryer started to bother MamaCee. She lifted it from her head and looked around the busy salon for David or Pam. When she didn't see them, she pulled the dryer back down on her head and continued to look around the shop for her stylist. A minute later she balled up her fist and knocked on Mia's dryer. This did not make Mia happy. She gave MamaCee an exasperated look and MamaCee's voice, under the dryer, became unnaturally loud.

"Did you see the child that was fixin' my hair?" MamaCee asked Mia.

"No," Mia said.

"Oh, good, you can talk," MamaCee observed. "You ain't said much since you been in here, baby. I was wonderin' if maybe you were hard of hearing or something," she said.

Mia became silent again as she took one of the rollers out to see if her hair was dry. It was and she began to look around for Mark so he could take her away from this nosy old woman. Mia was about to get up from the chair to go find Mark when MamaCee launched into a story.

"Well, one thang 'bout you cuttin' your hair off is that you can be forgiven for that. You know, a young girl like you, well, your hair will grow back in no time. But an old lady like me, well, I 'spect it would take a li'l longer. That's why I told them not to cut a lot off, 'cause my hair ain't so forgiving," MamaCee said.

Mia moved forward in her chair and looked for Mark. The salon was so busy with activity that Mia assumed he was probably starting on another client. This is exactly what she hated about beauty shops on Friday evenings. You could be in there three or four hours while stylists juggled clients. Mia looked toward Mark's station and saw another woman sitting in the chair messing with her hair but saw no sign of Mark.

"That's the one thang 'bout growing old, you can't make that many mistakes," MamaCee continued, " 'cause you don't have much time left for forgiveness. But sometimes you can try to make up for mistakes, you know, by tryin' to help out somebody else." MamaCee paused and took a deep breath. It was strange, but thinking about Mia cutting her hair, and seeing other people getting their hair done, reminded her of when Zach and Zuri decided to shave their heads. At first, she didn't like it. She thought it made them look too militant. But over the years, she had learned to love their shaved domes. MamaCee thought how she had prayed to see Zachary's bald head, after Zurich shaved it for the last time. She felt tears forming in her eyes, so she did what she always did when sad memories showed up: MamaCee talked. "Take me, for instance, Lord knows I done made a million mistakes. Some of them hurt so bad that I just didn't know if I could fix 'em. But you got to try, you got to forgive yourself," MamaCee said as her voice started to change into a mournful tone. Mia noticed the change, how it had gone from annoying to sorrowful. She adjusted her body in the tight-fitting chair, and closed her magazine, using her index finger to keep her place, and started to listen. "You see, baby, that's why I'm up here in Chicago, trying to right a wrong. I flew up here, my first plane ride, 'cause the good Lord and my legs told me my grandbaby needed me. The first time that happened I didn't listen 'cause I was scared of flying in one of them big old planes, and the bus, you know the Greyhound, well, it would have taken too long. My grandbaby, Zach, he was living up in New York City all alone. You know, he had friends, but he didn't have family up there when he got real sick, and he needed his family. He thought his family didn't understand 'bout how he lived his life, but I would always tell Zach, 'Baby, ain't nuthin' you can do to make your grandma shamed of you.' But in the end his grandma did something that shamed herself," MamaCee said as tears began to slowly roll down her face. "Sometimes it's hard to accept the natural order of things, like life and death, but it's even harder when they out of step, like a child going on before his parents and his grandparents." MamaCee began making a sniffling sound as if she needed to blow her nose. Mia reached over and touched MamaCee's hand. "I like to remember my baby Zach when he was bursting with life, twirling and flipping around the field behind my garden."

"What happened to him?" Mia asked.

"Well, my Zach called me one morning and his voice was real frail, sick-like, and he said, 'MamaCee,' that's what he called me, he said, 'MamaCee, I need to see you one mo time, I need one of yo hugs and stories to let me know everything gonna be all right.' I told him it would be all right and what did he want me to do? He said he wanted me to come up to New York City, but I had to catch one of them planes 'cause he didn't think he could wait on the Greyhound. I wanted to git on that plane to come up there and hug my grandbaby, but I was just so scared, you know, thinkin' that plane was going to fall out of the sky and I was gonna beat my grandbaby to glory. So I went down to the bus station to git me a ticket to New York," MamaCee said as long, slow tears descended down her face, tears as long and slow as one of her stories.

Now completely engrossed, Mia asked softly, "Why were you scared?"

"I don't know, baby. I don't know. When I got back home from the bus station, I was packing my stuff and sanging to myself. I was sanging 'I Will Trust in The Lord.' You ever heard that song, baby?"

"No." Mia had attended a white Catholic Church and she was unfamiliar with Negro spirituals.

"Oh, it's a beautiful song. 'I will trust in the Lord, I will trust in the Lord till I die,' " MamaCee sang softly. When my legs git real stiff and ache a lot, I know that trouble is nearby and that trouble usually means my own children or my grandbabies.

"But I don't guess I did. Anyhow, 'spite my legs and my grand-baby's pleas, I got on that bus headed for New York. The first day it seem like that bus was moving so slow, I just knew I had made a terrible mistake. I just felt it. When we got to Ohio, I got off the bus and I called my Zach to tell him to hold on, that Grandma was on the way. But there was no answer at his apartment and my heart, oh, baby, it became so heavy 'cause I knew somethin' was wrong," MamaCee said as the tears continued.

Mia took MamaCee's hands in her own and asked, "What happened?"

"Well, my Zach had gone on to glory, probably 'bout the time that bus pulled into Ohio and I didn't git to give him that hug he needed before he went to meet the Lord," MamaCee said, sobbing softly. Mia reached for a tissue from the little box on the magazine table.

"Oh, look at me. Here I am in here trying to look beautiful and this old lady is crying like a baby. Now they gonna have to put some of that makeup stuff on me," MamaCee said as she tried to laugh.

"Are you going to be all right?" Mia asked.

"Yeah, baby, I gonna be all right 'cause I asked the Lord to forgive me. And then I told myself that I had to forgive me. You know, for the mistakes I made. The good Lord forgives you when you forgive yourself," MamaCee said tenderly. "And isn't it good to know that the good Lord is forgiving every second of the day?"

———

Tamela rang the doorbell of the penthouse suite at the Four Seasons hotel. Here she was, an overnight bag in tow, about to spend the night with a man she had never even kissed. Caliph opened the door, looking like a pinup for a police recruitment poster, and her knees became weak. In her head she told herself, *Don't end up with your panties on your forehead, Miss Thang.*

"Tamela, welcome to my penthouse," he said as he took her bag. Caliph took her hand and led her into the most beautiful hotel suite she had ever seen.

"Caliph, this is so nice." She looked around the plush living area, furnished with an egg-shell-white couch and matching settee and armchair, marble tables, a fireplace, and a white baby grand piano. A wood and polished brass wet bar stood near sliding glass doors that opened onto a large terrace.

"True, true. Tom Joyner, Sybil, and the Four Seasons act like they know how to treat a brother," Caliph said. He placed her bag near the bar, then seemed at a loss for words. "Can I get you something to drink?" Caliph asked quickly.

Good, she thought, *he's nervous, too.* "Sure, maybe just some mineral water for now."

"Come on, now. I've got a great bottle of wine already chilled. I know you've had a rough week. And we're here to celebrate making it through another week."

"Yes, it has been a rough week. All right, I will have the wine," Tamela said as she walked toward the terrace and enjoyed the view of dusk covering a busy Michigan Avenue and Lake Michigan in the distance. "Oh, this is exquisite. I'm going to have to start calling that radio show myself."

"If you win something like this, I hope you'll include me," Caliph said.

"That depends on how well you behave," Tamela teased. This was different, she thought, a man encouraging her to think about future dates before they had even kissed.

"True . . . true," Caliph said. "Come on over here and sit next to me; let's just talk for a minute."

Tamela joined Caliph on the sofa, where two glasses of white wine waited on the marble coffee table. Caliph handed Tamela her glass, then lifted his toward hers and said, "Here's to a beautiful lady and an evening of equal beauty." Tamela smiled back coyly and sipped the light sweetness of the wine.

"You look great in your uniform. I don't remember it looking that good at the stadium," Tamela said.

"This is my everyday work git-up. I have something else I'm going to change into later," he said as he winked and took a sip of his wine. Tamela noticed the sensual look in his eyes and felt the warm glow of the wine spread throughout her body. She felt safe.

"So how was your day?" she asked.

"It was great. I talked to my daughter two times. She was kinda upset that I won't see her this weekend, but I promised her we'd go and see *The Lion King* next weekend for the third time," he said.

"You really love your daughter, don't you?" Tamela said softly.

"True. She is my deepest joy," Caliph said. "If I could, I'd have a dozen more," he added. His words and the look in his eyes caused Tamela's eyes to mist, and she quickly changed the subject.

"Boy, this is a really a fabulous hotel. That lobby is something else," Tamela said as she looked around the room, avoiding Caliph's eyes. She reached down to press her hand into the taupe plush carpet and said, "Amazing carpet."

"True. But you can tell they don't get a lot of us in here," Caliph said.

"Why do you say that?"

"Just the way they looked at me when I walked in here. It was like I had spilled collard green juice in the lobby," he laughed.

"You know that's called pot liquor," Tamela said.

"You call it pot liquor, I call it collard green juice," Caliph laughed.

"You so crazy," Tamela said as she joined him laughing.

"True . . . true. You know this must be a real high-class joint 'cause I didn't see that many brothers working the door or carrying the bags," Caliph joked.

"Yeah, it's all right," Tamela said as she looked toward an open set of French doors and saw the edge of a bed.

Caliph gave Tamela a tour of the two-bedroom suite, informing her she could have first choice on the bedroom selection, and when they walked back into the living area he asked, "What do you want to do first? They have a wonderful health club. I've already checked it out, and there is a jazz bar in the main lobby. And you know Rush Street is only a couple of blocks away. Oh . . . oh . . . I almost forgot. We're going to have dinner served at eight. It came with the deal. It's some kind of special meal the chef is preparing just for us," Caliph said.

"I'm scared of you and the Four Seasons," Tamela said as she took another sip of her wine.

"There is nothing to be frightened of," Caliph smiled. He realized she was a little nervous and he wanted to concentrate on getting her to relax and enjoy herself and him. They finished their wine and went to separate bedrooms to prepare for dinner.

Later, Tamela emerged from the bedroom and was greeted by Caliph with an *umph, umph, umph* look on his face. Tamela wore black gauze harem pants and a black sheer pullover. She couldn't stop smiling if she tried as she gazed approvingly at Caliph, dressed in navy blue silk pants and bone knit pullover. He took her by the hand and led her into the dining area, where an elegantly dressed waiter was preparing to serve them dinner on a candlelit linen-covered dining table, with custom-built chairs. The waiter started to seat Tamela, but Caliph stopped him. He pulled her chair out and whispered, "I hope they know how to burn here, but if they don't I got backup." He sat down facing her across the table with a immense smile. The waiter poured a little wine in his glass and after tasting it, Caliph nodded toward the waiter, who filled Tamela's glass and then his. After a tasty pumpkin soup, a Caesar salad was served on beautiful beige-and-blue china. In the background, Sade's greatest hits were playing and the waiter returned to fill the water and wine glasses. Tamela started to whisper to Caliph that the waiter had great taste in music but could hear her mother saying it was impolite to whisper.

When the main course, a lemon and béarnaise-covered salmon mousse, was served, they found themselves picking at it. As they sipped their wine, Caliph slowly placed a large, warm hand over Tamela's and she smiled sweetly.

Finally, Caliph asked the waiter to remove the dinner plates and serve the coffee and brandy in the living area. Caliph gently pulled Tamela's chair from the table. When she stood, he turned her to face him, their bodies inches apart. He held her briefly and they gazed into each other's eyes. Caliph placed his hand at the soft center of Tamela's back and guided her into the living area. They sat together on the long sofa, their thighs and shoulders barely touching.

Caliph ran his fingers lightly down Tamela's arm, then back up to the softness of her neck above her top. He turned her chin toward him and, looking deep into her doe eyes, whispered, "Are you having a good time, baby?" Tamela felt a surge of heat flow from her head to her toes, as if Caliph's voice were pulling steam from her body.

"I'm having a wonderful time," she whispered back. He leaned closer and Tamela felt her heart begin to race as Caliph brushed his lips across her cheek.

"What's your pleasure, Tamela?" Caliph whispered, his full lips now close to her ear. Tamela pulled away, easing back into the sofa cushions. She felt flushed and took a deep breath.

"What's my pleasure?" she repeated.

Caliph's smile spread slowly across his broad face. With an impish wink, he got up and walked over to the entertainment area and turned off the music. "Come on over here with me," he said as he sat down at the baby grand and patted the bench next to him. Tamela walked over and eased down close to him. She loved being near him, and leaned her head against his shoulders, inhaling his masculine scent and brawny cologne.

Very slowly and delicately, Caliph began playing the piano. He moved smoothly into a jazz piece and Tamela was quietly pleased at how well Caliph played. His large fingers teased the keys softly, as though playing the piano was giving him a wonderful sensation. Tamela looked at him and asked, "How long have you been playing?" Without stopping, Caliph said, "Off and on since I was thirteen."

"You play splendidly. This is just wonderful, Caliph," Tamela said as she squeezed his right arm, then rested her hand on his thigh.

Caliph ended his concert with a jazzy rendition of Babyface's "Tender Lover," and Tamela began to melt like butter in a microwave. Caliph turned and looked into Tamela's eyes and said, "You have the right to remain silent." Taking her into his arms, he kissed her. It was a slow kiss. His full lips covered Tamela's. She thought, *This man could do this for a living.* They kissed nonstop for over ten minutes. Tasting each other, discovering each other, hands, fingers caressing each other. When they came up for air, they both broke out giggling like little kids.

"Now that was nice," Caliph said. "Who taught you how to kiss like that?"

"I was going to ask you the same thing," Tamela replied. Caliph gave her a quick peck on the lips and went over and put on a Marcus Roberts disc. They moved back to the sofa and as they sat down, Caliph's stomach growled so loud it embarrassed him. "I knew that soup and salad wasn't going to hold me for long. I'm a growing boy."

"Yeah, I'm kinda hungry too. You want to go out and get something to eat?"

"Your wish is my command and you don't have to move from that spot," he said as he picked up the phone and called room service, asking if they could heat something up for him. They promised to send someone right up.

"What are you doing?" Tamela asked.

"It's a surprise." Tamela smiled because she loved surprises. Moments later, the rich tone of the penthouse doorbell sounded and Caliph rushed into the bedroom. He returned with a brown bag, opened the door and handed the bag to the young black room service attendant. "Make sure they heat this up right, brotherman." The young man smiled and assured him he would "be back in a flash!"

"What did you give him?" Tamela asked.

Caliph placed his forefinger to his lips. "My lips are sealed. It won't be a surprise if I tell," he said. "Come over here and help me find some *mood music.*" Tamela walked over to the CD player and wrapped her arms around Caliph's waist from behind. She felt his flat, hard stomach and nuzzled her face against his back. Caliph found a Toni Braxton CD and the soulful sounds of Toni's voice filled the room. He turned in Tamela's arms and kissed her just as the doorbell rang again. Tamela pulled herself from his embrace and said, "This time I'm gonna get it." Caliph tried to grab her as she raced toward the door.

When she opened the door, the young black man was standing there smiling with a covered silver platter raised to shoulder height and resting on one hand.

"Good evening, Miss, shall I serve you at the dining room table?"

Before she could answer, Caliph stepped in front of her and said, "Naw, bro, I'll take care of it." He took the platter from the young man and pressed a five-dollar bill into his hands.

After Caliph closed the door, Tamela looked at him with a curious smile.

"What'cha looking at? You want some of what I got? Like this is some Harold's fried chicken. Straight from the South Side. And guess what? I got some hot sauce in my bag, too," Caliph boasted.

"You're something else," Tamela laughed. She loved the way he made her feel funny and sexy at the same time.

"Girl, come on, let's get busy. We got some fried bird waiting," he said as he playfully waved the dish of chicken under Tamela's nose. They sat on the floor and enjoyed the fried chicken as if they were on a picnic. Caliph had a sneaky smile on his face.

"What's that smile about?"

"I was just thinking that something is missing," he said.

"What? Some collard green juice?" Tamela teased.

"Naw. I'm talking about something to drink. You know some jug wine. You know the kind that's best served buck naked."

"You know you're some kinda fool," Tamela laughed.

"But you kinda like it, don't cha?" Tamela just looked at him, rolled her eyes, and smiled softly.

Tamela reminded Caliph of a pigtailed little girl, sitting crossed-leg on the floor, wiggling her toes in the deep carpet, oblivious to the smear of grease on the left side of her face as she put away her second chicken leg. Caliph lay on his side beside her and finished off his third piece of the spicy fried chicken. They kicked off their shoes and joked with each other about who was going to get the last wing. Tamela conceded to Caliph and began looking around for something to wipe her hands on. "Here," Caliph said, and took both her hands in each of his. He meticulously licked each and every finger, smacking his lips and giving Tamela a mischievous grin each time he finished one of them. As her fingers rested inside Caliph's warm mouth, Tamela was thinking, *Don't start something you can't finish, Mister Policeman.*

"Now what's that face about?" Caliph teased as he stopped his cleansing.

"Oh no you don't," Tamela said and wiped her face on a corner of the tablecloth. She took Caliph's face in her hand and carefully dabbed the corner of his mouth.

"Come closer," Caliph said, "I think you missed a spot." He closed his eyes and compressed his lips. Tamela leaned down and brushed her lips across Caliph's upturned mouth, then gave him a quick peck on the nose.

"You know you ain't even right," Caliph said, pulling Tamela down on top of him in mock indignation. He felt so good beneath her and Tamela felt her face flush.

"Let's go out on the terrace," she said, hoping the night air would cool her off.

Caliph and Tamela took a bottle of champagne and two crystal flutes and walked out onto the terrace. The sky was a clear, dark, and deep backdrop for a brilliant array of sparkling stars. So high above the city, Caliph and Tamela felt like the only two people in the world. Side by side, they leaned on the ornate railing that ran the length of the suite-long terrace. Caliph placed his arm around Tamela's shoulders and they sipped champagne in silent awe of the wonders of the universe.

"It's so beautiful out here," Tamela said, enjoying their closeness.

Caliph spoke in a low, sweet-talking voice, the unmistakable tone of sex. "You know, those stars are beautiful," he said, placing their glasses on a nearby patio table. "But tonight they are a distant second to you." Just as Tamela was preparing her *nigger plezze* look, he took her into his strong arms and kissed her as she'd never been kissed before. He kissed her hard, his tongue exploring her mouth, then dancing with her own tongue. He kissed her softly and the tingle that played on her lips became a rhythmic throbbing where their bodies touched.

"You really don't realize how beautiful you are, do you?" he asked in a serious tone.

"Show me," Tamela said. Caliph slowly stroked her neck, then her back, letting his hand rest on her full hips. He pressed her closer to him and felt her body tremble ever so slightly. He slid his hand across her butt, then under her blouse and released her erect nipples from the confines of her black lacy bra. Caliph paused; he didn't want to rush her. But the mere thought of his piano-playing fingers on her breasts quickened the throbbing in Tamela's body and she slid her hand between them and returned the favor, releasing Caliph's now erect sex from the confines of his silk pants. Caliph's moan was a whisper as Tamela glided her hand over his form-fitting black boxers. When Caliph caressed both her breasts, she threw her head back as a sudden weakness overcame her.

Caliph lifted her off the terrace floor and swept her into his arms. He carried her through the doors, past the dimly lit living area and the remains of their midnight picnic. Toni Braxton softly sang "Breathe Again" as Caliph placed Tamela ever so gently against the large pillows on the feather-stuffed king-sized bed. *Damn, baby, is that a nightstick you're hiding?*, Tamela thought. She stared at Caliph's body as he dimmed the lights and proceeded to undress before her. Caliph was slender, with planes of muscles stretched across his body. His arms were hard as baseball bats, his shoulders broad and his stomach flat. Caliph let his trousers slide to the floor and Tamela held her breath as he slowly eased out of his boxers. A barely audible gasp escaped her lips and she said a silent thankful prayer at the sight of Caliph's nightstick. He turned toward the teak dresser behind him and Tamela gazed at his muscular butt. When Caliph turned around, he was holding a perfect red rose from the vase on the dresser. He walked over to the bed, placing the rose next to her. "My turn," he said, his eyes the very essence of anticipation. He slowly began to undress her without ever touching her skin. He lifted her pullover above her head, slipped her bra off her arms, slid her pants over her feet, and slowly removed her panties. Caliph's appreciative smile broadened as each garment fell silently onto the thick carpeting. He kissed her penny-brown nipples and buried his face in the warmth and palmed her nice butt, soft and round.

She shivered as she felt him touch her moistness with his fingers. Caliph kissed Tamela's forehead and then her nose and lingered at her lips. He kissed her neck, her breasts, and tongued her navel, causing Tamela to moan softly.

"I found the spot," he smiled.

"Oh, that's not it," Tamela laughed.

"Is this it?" He said as he dropped to the floor and kissed her toes and tried to put her entire foot in his mouth.

"Not even close," she sighed.

He moved his tongue up to her knees and quizzed, "Am I getting close?"

"Yes."

Caliph moved up toward her inner thighs and his tongue played her body as his fingers had the piano keys, with strength and sensitivity. Tamela sensed such pleasure that she felt like a full glass of milk about to spill over the edge of the glass. Caliph planted a warm kiss where her soft hair met her legs and he kissed her along the opening of her sex as she placed her hands on his shoulders and raised her hips to meet his lips. Amid the warmth and softness, he found a hardness and he pushed his tongue up under it.

"Oh my . . . oh baby," Tamela moaned as she massaged his shoulders and ran her fingers through his hair.

Caliph stopped for a moment and looked up at her and said, "You taste sweet." He teased her with his tongue and prolonged her pleasure.

"Oh," Tamela moaned.

"Just enjoy it, baby. I'm gonna love you right," he declared as he buried his head in her lap and started to kiss her sex again. Caliph raised his head and started to kiss her breasts with an open mouth, then he took his fingers and slid them into Tamela's center, and before she realized it, she had an orgasm with Caliph's large fingers inside her. He laid his head on her breasts and pumped his own thick sex against her thigh. Sweat popped across his forehead as Tamela leaned down and placed her tongue in his ear. She sweetly kissed his chest and was rushing him toward a swift sexual sensation when he exploded like a geyser, sending creamy drops into the air and onto his chest.

For several minutes, they lay speechless in the center of the bed wrapped in each other's arms. When Caliph finally spoke, he leaned over and kissed Tamela and said, "You're sweeter than sugar." A slow smile came over her face. She was thinking, *You think that was something. Too bad you didn't have a condom. Baby, I'm like a coconut, hard to crack, but wonderful once you really get inside.*

CHAPTER 19

Until You Come Back to Me

M*ia* reread the court subpoena, for the third time, instructing her to report to the criminal court Thursday morning. She poured herself another generous glass of wine and decided she would call her lawyer first thing Monday for advice on what she should do. She did not want to appear before a judge and admit that she had been too drunk the night of the attack to tell the court anything. But what could she do? She had been raped, but had no idea who had done it. The only thing she suspected was that Zurich was not the one. Her memory of his rejection, though painful, had returned. She was hoping that her entire memory of that night would return, replacing the fragments, before Thursday. Friday evening when she'd returned from getting her hair cut, Mia had been surprised by a process server with the subpoena. She was standing at her front door, just about to insert the key, when out of nowhere the server had come up behind her. When he'd called her name, she'd turned and said, "Yes?" He'd promptly placed the white legal paper in her hands, spoiling what had turned out to be a good day. Her conversation with MamaCee had been quite inspirational, and when Mia unexpectedly found herself hugging the old woman before she left the shop, she felt as though MamaCee's powerful return hug had transferred some type of special strength. She was just going to have to use it a little bit sooner than she had hoped.

Mia picked up her glass of wine and headed upstairs to retire for the evening. As she walked through her townhouse, Mia kept touching her hair, feeling the short tight curls. She had stopped to check her front door to make sure it was securely locked. Mia opened the door and was preparing to lock it when up walked her second surprise guest of the evening. Derrick, with his six-six, Pogo-stick body, was standing at her front steps and smiling at her. For a moment Mia stood blinking to make sure she was seeing right, and when her eyes focused, she tried to close the door in his face, but not before he called out her name.

"Mia, please don't shut the door on me," he pleaded.

Leaving the door cracked a bit, Mia remained silent for a few seconds and then asked, "Derrick, what are you doing here?"

"I'm working on a project. I've been trying to reach you for weeks. Mia, please, I don't want to hurt you. I just wanted to see how you are doing," he said. Derrick was wearing a blue dress shirt, a loosened silk tie, dark blue lightweight pants, and perfectly polished black loafers.

Mia looked him directly in the eyes, which suddenly looked like eyes she could trust. If she was going to follow MamaCee's advice and start to forgive, then why not start with Derrick. She slowly opened the glass storm door, and Derrick ducked his head slightly as he walked in.

"You have a beautiful place," he said as he looked around her living room. "But I shouldn't be surprised, you've always had good taste."

"Thanks, Derrick, have a seat," Mia said as she looked into her wineglass and saw that it was half empty. She needed more. As she headed toward the kitchen, she looked at Derrick and said, "I'm out of rum, but would you like some bourbon or some wine?"

"Oh no, I don't drink anymore. Do you have some mineral water or some juice?"

While Mia was in the kitchen, Derrick stood up and walked over to admire her Jacob Lawrence painting and then moved to the sofa table and picked up a picture of Mia with Tanya and her parents. He asked Mia how they were doing but she didn't hear him, since she was checking to make sure her back door was locked and wondering if she had done the right thing by letting Derrick in. He started to join Mia in the kitchen but instead went back and sat on the sofa.

Derrick not drinking anymore, Mia thought. Maybe he had changed. Mia turned up her glass to swallow the last of her wine, while she reached in the fridge for the balance of the bottle and the apple juice she would give Derrick.

Walking back into the living room, Mia almost fell when she tripped over a throw rug separating her small dining area from the living room. Derrick leaped from the sofa and caught Mia by the arm. His touch was stern, yet soft. "Are you all right? Did you hear me talking to you?"

"I'm fine, and no," Mia said as she pulled her arms from Derrick's grasp and crossed the room to the sofa.

"I asked you how your parents and Tanya were doing," Derrick repeated as he walked over to the arm chair.

"Fine."

"How much have you been drinking?"

"Look, if this going to be the first degree, then you're going to have to leave," Mia said. He hadn't changed that much, she thought, asking questions like he had the right to know about her life.

"I'm sorry, I'm not trying to dip in your business, but your eyes are glassy. You know, I can come back later," he said. Mia was getting ready to tell Derrick he should leave, but then she realized she didn't want to be alone. She knew what she could do to make Derrick stay. She got up from her spot on the sofa and went to the arm chair; she flopped down onto his lap, and put her arms around his neck.

Derrick was surprised, but pleased, because he still cared a great deal for Mia. He was once deeply in love with her, but he had lost her love because of his mistakes and her stern refusal to forgive.

Looking in Derrick's eyes, Mia thought he looked more handsome than when she had first seen him standing outside the television station in Jackson. He had Cracker Jack–colored skin, thick curly black hair, and light brown eyes with eyelashes most women dreamed of, and a full-lipped mouth that was oversized, like a mold for lips. He had seen Mia on television the first night she appeared in his hometown. Derrick had been so blown away by her beauty that he rushed out, bought a dozen red roses, and waited at the station's back door until Mia came out. He called out her name, and when she turned to see who in her new city knew her, he placed the beautiful roses in her arms, as if she had just been crowned Miss America, and said, "Welcome to Jackson."

When Mia got back to her apartment, she'd smiled as she smelled the roses and read the card, with another "welcome" message and his home and office number. A couple of days later Mia had called, and after a breathless first date and night of passion they'd quickly become a couple. A couple heading for the altar until the night he'd slapped Mia.

"You're still the most beautiful woman, I know," Derrick stuttered. He didn't recall Mia being so aggressive.

She had not eaten very much during the day, and the wine had already gone to her head. "Hush," Mia said softly as she kissed Derrick. He kissed her back and he could taste the wine. But Mia didn't stop with the kiss. She stood up and pulled her sweatshirt and Lycra bra over her head as though they were one piece. She was used to him removing her clothing but since he was moving a little slow, Mia decided to take the lead. Derrick was shocked as Mia sat back in his lap, with her breasts flopping in his face. She started to kiss him once again as her fingers searched for the buttons of his cotton shirt. One by one, Mia undid the buttons until she could see and feel the chest she had once slept on nightly. She started to kiss his nipples, when suddenly Derrick pushed her back and said, "Mia, come on, whatsup? This is not like you."

"What's the matter, Derrick, isn't this what you want? Isn't this what you came for?" she asked as she pushed her breasts toward his chest.

"Mia, I just came to talk with you. To see how you're doing." While Derrick still loved sex as much as the next guy, it was not the reason he wanted to see Mia. He had changed, but so had Mia.

"I'm doing just fine. I just need some loving. What does a girl have to do to get laid? You can have it anyway you want it," she bragged. "You want it from the back, then I'm game for that, too."

"Mia, I'm going to leave. Maybe we can get together early next week, when you're feeling better," he said as he tried to button up his shirt. She looked at him in disbelief as he headed toward the door.

The thought of being alone brought Mia to tears. She started to cry and pleaded with him, "Don't leave me, please don't leave me."

He could hear the anxiety in her voice, but he didn't want her to fear him. He wanted her to see that he had changed.

Derrick held Mia in his arms, and said, "Come here close to me, baby girl. What's the matter?" He pulled her close to his chest and held her as if he were protecting her from the outside world. As he held Mia, Derrick realized that she did not fear him but that she was simply afraid of being alone.

For several minutes, the tears came freely. When they finally stopped, Derrick was wiping her face with a towel. Mia began to tell Derrick what had happened with the rape and her suspension. While Mia was telling him what she remembered he held one of her hands tightly as he gently stroked her tearstained face with his other hand. When he asked her who raped her, his voice was soft and urgent as if he were going to rush out of the townhouse and take care of whoever had done this to her. But Mia didn't know where to tell him to run, whom to find and punish for what had happened.

"I don't know. I don't remember a lot of what happened," Mia said.

"What are the police doing? Why aren't your parents here?"

"Please, I don't want them to know. I don't want them worrying about me," Mia said.

"What about Tanya? She would want to know, Mia. You can't stay here and suffer all by yourself. Your parents and sister love you. They would want to help," Derrick said.

"I don't want their help. I deserve what happened. It's payback," Mia said, as she expressed her inner fear.

"What are you talking about? Nobody deserves to be raped. What does this have to do with your family?"

Mia reached for her glass of wine, but Derrick stopped her and said, "You don't need this."

"Just one more sip," Mia pleaded. "I have something to tell you, and I just need one more sip."

"Trust me, Mia. You don't need this and you can tell me anything," he said firmly.

Mia looked at Derrick, took a deep breath, clenched her fists, and slowly and quietly her words emerged.

"I said I deserved to be raped, because I'm not a good person,"

Mia began. When Derrick interrupted with a firm, "No," Mia said, "Yes," and placed a hand to his lips so she could continue her story. "When I was in high school, right about the time I started drinking, my sister and I went on a double date. It was one of Tanya's first dates and the only reason she got to go was because I promised to look after her. So, when her date went home, she came with me over to my boyfriend's house. While I was back in his bedroom, making out and drinking, Tanya was sitting in the living room watching television. I didn't want her in the back room with me 'cause she didn't know I was drinking. Well, I guess I drank too much because I passed out for a little while," Mia said as tears began to form in her eyes again.

"Here, drink some of this," Derrick said as he put the glass of apple juice to Mia's dry lips. She took a sip and returned to her story. "When I woke up and ran out to see if Tanya was okay, I saw . . . I saw . . ." Mia paused as her throat thickened with emotion.

"What happened, baby? What happened to Tanya?" Derrick asked.

"My boyfriend's father was on top of my sister, raping her with a sofa pillow over her mouth to keep her from screaming. He had ripped her clothes and was yelling, 'Shut the fuck up, you little bitch, you're going to wake everybody up.' I ran over and started hitting him as hard as I could, but then my boyfriend came out, pushed me out of the way, and tried to pull his father off my sister. When I saw her face, I wanted to die. She looked like, oh, I don't know. . . . It was all my fault," Mia cried.

"What happened? Was this guy arrested? Did you girls tell your parents?"

"No, no. We just went home, sneaking in so my parents wouldn't see Tanya. And we never told anyone. It was our secret, our shame." She paused and wiped her eyes with her hands. Derrick took off his shirt and draped it around Mia's shoulders and she began to talk again. "So, you see, my rape was for a reason. It was payback for what I let happened to my little sister. And I never said I was sorry. I don't know why, but I didn't," Mia cried as she turned her face into Derrick's bare chest and let her tears begin to wash away the years of silence and pain.

———————

When Mia awoke on Saturday afternoon, she felt worse than the night before. She had the hangover from hell. Derrick was lying beside her in bed, fully clothed, smiling in a way he hoped was comforting. He gently felt the softness of her skin and leaned over to smell her hair. As his head brushed against her face and as he moved to kiss her all along her arm, Mia had a bit of her memory return. She recalled her attacker pushing his coarse hair against her breasts, and all over her skin, down to her center. But she couldn't remember his face, or who he was, and now she was certain he wasn't Zurich. His shaved head was one of the things that had attracted her to him.

"How ya doing?" he asked.

"How did I get up here?" Mia asked when she realized she had only her panties on. She didn't remember coming to bed. A small piece of her memory returned, another part vanished.

"I carried you upstairs," Derrick said.

"What time is it?" Mia asked.

"It's a little bit after twelve," Derrick said.

"Oh, wow, I've slept the day away, "Mia said as she looked for her robe. Derrick noticed this, went to her bathroom, and brought back a cotton robe that was resting on the bathroom door.

"Is this what you're looking for?"

"Yeah, thanks, Derrick. You've been here all night?"

"Yeah, I didn't want to leave you. Hey, do you feel like some breakfast? I mean we could go out, or I can get some stuff and cook," he said.

"I don't know; I'm not feeling that well," she mumbled.

"Maybe you need something in your stomach," Derrick said.

"I don't know," Mia said. She was trying to recall what she had told Derrick the night before. She remembered the tears and talking about her sister, but the night was mostly a blur.

"Well, I've made some coffee. I'll go downstairs and get you some and then we can decide what we're going to do for food later," Derrick said.

"Don't you have something to do? I mean aren't you here on business?"

"Yes, but I've already taken care of that," Derrick said as he headed downstairs.

While he was gone, Mia put on her robe and rushed into the

bathroom where she took two aspirins, brushed her teeth, and rinsed with mouthwash. She ran and jumped into the bed just as Derrick was walking in with a steaming cup of coffee.

Mia took a sip, and Derrick asked if it tasted okay. "It's fine, thanks, Derrick."

"Do you remember last night?" Derrick asked. She remembered parts, but she wondered if there was something specific he was asking about. What had she done now? She knew one thing and that was these blackouts were happening with much more frequency and that frightened her.

"Yeah, I know I made a fool of myself," Mia said.

"No, baby, you didn't. But you were in a lot of pain," Derrick said. Pain as deep as she was feeling was not something Mia wanted anyone to see, but with Derrick she was now vulnerable. She was no longer in control on the surface or otherwise. Mia sipped the coffee as if it were a lifeline.

"Mia, we don't have to talk about this, but I saw the subpoena on your counter. It has a name on it. I thought you told me you didn't know who raped you," Derrick said.

"I don't," Mia mumbled.

"But that's not what the document implies."

"I know it's a mistake. I've just got to figure out how to correct it," Mia said. She explained to Derrick what had happened with LaDonna and the police. How she had pursued Zurich, and how she had been on a date with him the night she was raped. She told him how when the police showed up to ask questions about a possible suspect, she had simply agreed when LaDonna asked if it was Zurich. She was embarrassed to tell LaDonna and the policemen she was too drunk to remember anything. Mia told Derrick how she had been drinking so much the last couple of weeks, she had convinced herself that Zurich had in fact raped her, when all he had done was to reject her offer for sex. How she'd become certain of this fact when Derrick had brushed his hair against her body the way her attacker had. Derrick listened intently, but Mia couldn't tell if he was supportive or disgusted by her actions. When she stopped talking, he finally spoke.

"Baby, I'm sorry for the hair thing. I was only trying to soothe you," he said.

"I know Derrick. You had no way of knowing. But look, it's helped my memory," Mia said as she stroked his hands.

"It looks like you got your work cut out for you, Mia," he said.

"I know, what do you think I should do?"

"Well, the first thing is you got to ask for forgiveness and then forgive yourself," he said.

"That's what she said. That's what the lady said I should do," Mia said in a startled tone.

"What lady? What are you talking about?" Derrick asked. Mia told him about her conversation with MamaCee, who she called Miss See something.

"Did you tell her what you told me?"

"No, but it was just like she knew something was bothering me, that I needed to make peace with some things in my life," Mia said.

"Sounds like my grandmother, God rest her soul," Derrick said mournfully.

"Your grandmother died? When?"

"Yes, at the beginning of the year. But before she died she got me started on the right track. Got me to face my problems and get my life together," Derrick said. He went on to tell Mia he had been in counseling for his abuse issues and had been clean and sober for more than two years. He told Mia how he realized he had a problem, not when he hit her, but when he had come close to hitting his own mother. She refused to co-sign on a loan for a new business venture and he nearly hit her, breaking a chair instead. He said the fear in his mother's eyes and the talk with his grandmother had moved his life in a positive direction.

"I don't know if I can do that," Mia said.

"Yes, you can," Derrick said confidently. "We can get you some help. I can take you to the AA meeting I've been attending here in Chicago. I also think you need to tell your sister you're sorry. And tell the policemen you made a mistake with this Zurich guy."

"Do you think I should call him and tell him I'm sorry?"

"Did they arrest him?"

"I don't know, but I know it was in the paper," Mia said.

"Well, I don't know if I would advise that. Homeboy might not be in a forgiving mood. But I'm not that concerned about him. My concern is for you and finding who really did this to you. You know, the rape."

"But I'm telling the truth, Derrick, I don't know who did this to me," Mia said as tears began to return.

"Don't cry, Mia. Let's not worry about that right now," he said as he hugged her gently.

Mia looked up at him with the tears holding in place and said, "Do you really think I can get my life back on track?" she asked softly.

"Like I know I'm holding you right now," he said as he softly kissed her hair.

CHAPTER 20

STILL ON THE THRONE

They had come so close. That's all Zurich could think of as he lay dazed under the pile of players, his own teammates and the Seattle Seahawks. He had failed to gain the one yard that would have given the Cougars a first and goal from the three-yard line, with just thirty seconds left in the game, and inches from their first regular season win. But it was not to be and the Cougars headed back to Chicago with a 14–10 loss. Zurich had been inconsolable in the locker room, and only a few teammates had offered support. It was beginning to be too much, the losing and the possibility of an embarrassing trial if the judge decided on Thursday that there was enough evidence.

When he returned home late Sunday night, just hoping for a dreamless night of sleep, he discovered he had not one houseguest, but two: MamaCee *and* Sean.

Zurich knew Sean had come to Chicago to start the story that Gina had told him and MamaCee about, but he had no idea that Sean had run into a problem checking into his hotel Sunday afternoon when his credit card was rejected. The Friday before he left, Sean had checked his available credit and had even sent a payment in overnight mail for his Chicago visit. But his pleading with his credit card's customer service rep was in vain, and she told him he would have to wait until Monday to get the problem corrected. Angry and embarrassed, Sean planned to fly back to New York Sunday night since he didn't really know anyone else in Chicago besides Zurich and Gina.

He called Gina, but got her answering machine. When he called Zurich's place, MamaCee answered the phone. After he explained that he was going to have to cancel the interview because of his credit problem, she had in typical MamaCee fashion told Sean to get himself in a cab and come on over to Zurich's place. Since he was trying to help her grandson out he could spend the night there, and she or Zurich would help him come up with the money for his hotel on Monday.

At first, Sean hesitated. As much as he liked Zurich, this was not a professional thing to do, but MamaCee had been firm, telling him it would be fine with Zurich and she was so excited to be meeting a real life reporter.

When he arrived at Zurich's, MamaCee gave him a big hug and then proceeded to cook him one of the best meals he had ever eaten. Baked chicken, wild rice mixed with sweet carrots and string beans, which MamaCee bragged she had brought up from her own garden. Sean and MamaCee connected immediately, talking about family, friends, and faith, which, MamaCee said repeatedly, would get Zurich through this mess.

When Zurich arrived late that evening, he was happy to see Sean and assured him MamaCee had been right in her invitation, though he was a little bit edgy and quiet from the loss. He asked Sean if they could conduct the interview the following morning, after he had worked out, saying he had to build up his strength so that the next time he had a fourth and one, he would make it. Sean agreed and told him he was playing well and should be proud of his accomplishments. To which Zurich responded, "I hope I'm never proud of losing."

After chatting some more with MamaCee, who had pulled out the sofa bed and climbed in with a bowl of peach cobbler and ice cream, Sean walked nervously into the bedroom. He was glad to see Zurich had a king-sized bed. Sean went to his bag in the corner of the room and pulled out an oversized T-shirt and a pair of Joe boxers that he thought would be suitable for sleeping. He went into the bathroom and changed and when he came out, he saw that Zurich had turned down the bed, so neatly that it reminded him of a four-star hotel turn-down service—the only thing missing was a Godiva chocolate on each pillow. Zurich was in his large walk-in closet, silently folding his clothes and putting them in their proper place. When Sean asked him what side he slept on, Zurich said it didn't matter, for Sean to make himself at home. Sean got in on the left side and was turning around to thank Zurich once again, when he saw that Zurich had just undressed down to his underwear. A chilly sweat came over Sean's chest. The whiteness of the underwear contrasted beautifully against Zurich's brown and impeccable body. From the back he looked like the world's greatest underwear model. It was like the underwear had been made for Zurich's ass alone, and had been carefully placed there stitch by stitch. For a moment, Sean remembered how as a teenager he had loved it when the newspaper and magazines advertised men in underwear. For several more minutes, Zurich had his back to Sean, organizing his closet so that it was perfect. When Zurich turned out the overhead light and climbed into bed, Sean felt an invisible line running down between them. Sean wanted to find a place to hide, his heart was beating so fast, and he said a silent prayer of thanks to the patron saint of black homosexuals that Zurich didn't turn around and face him in his underwear as he inhaled his sweet, virile scent.

It was dark in the room, but Sean's eyes were wide open. Zurich had fallen into a dreamless sleep and was snoring lightly. Sean smiled, thinking, *At least he's not perfect,* and then he felt his sex expanding in his own underwear. Sean got up from the bed and took his full erection into the bathroom, pulled down the toilet seat and his underwear, and in the dark, began to masturbate to images of Zurich and his white underwear with Polo stitched across the waistband. The thought of Zurich made Sean so sweaty that he even removed his T-shirt and sat on the covered toilet naked, pumping his sex with one hand, pinching and rubbing his left pec with the other, until sperm splashed over his brown thighs. Now, as he wiped himself clean with a towel, he thought he could sleep peacefully.

The next morning, Zurich was in a better mood as he and Sean enjoyed a down-home country breakfast of cured ham, grits, scrambled eggs, and biscuits made from scratch, courtesy of MamaCee. They even shared a secret smile when MamaCee came out of the bathroom and announced, "Don't nobody go in there, babies; MamaCee feels like somethin' crawled up in me and died."

After breakfast, Sean called his credit card company and found out the payment had been posted and that he could now check into his hotel. MamaCee protested, saying that she and Zurich loved the company. Zurich agreed, but Sean knew he couldn't take another night of sleeping beside Zurich without covering the bed with sweat. Sean thanked them both and made plans to talk with MamaCee again after lunch, and then to meet with Zurich later that evening at the stadium after his weight-training session.

Zurich gave Sean a ride to his hotel and convinced him that he should come running with him before their interview. Sean agreed even though he hoped it wouldn't be a repeat of the ass whipping he received when they'd played racquetball. Besides, he realized running was the one form of exercise he had managed in the last couple of years. Maybe it would be inspiration for the start of some new weight-loss program, which he knew he would need after another day of MamaCee's fat-laden meals.

After a three-mile run, Sean and Zurich collapsed on the stadium bleachers, half blind with sweat running into their eyes. The sun was down, and the dusk felt soothing as Sean and Zurich caught their breath and began to talk. Sean tried not to pay attention to Zurich in his gray cotton tank top and white spandex running tights, but he thought there should be some type of law against men built like Zurich wearing white spandex. Sean had tried to look down or off to the side while they ran, instead of noticing Zurich's backside and the thin jock strap holding the two muscles that formed his ass in place. When they sat down and were facing each other, Sean noticed the wetness isolated around Zurich's groin area, as if it were radiating some type of energy or secret signal. The contours of his muscles and the pouch of his sex glistened.

"Your grandmother is something else. I feel like I've known her all my life," Sean said. He wanted safe territory, rather than focusing on Zurich's white spandex glowing in the half-light of dusk.

"Yeah, everybody feels like that when they been with MamaCee for more than five minutes," Zurich said.

"She really helped me with something I had been dealing with a long time. You know, this afternoon, when I was supposed to be interviewing her for the piece. She turned the tables on me."

"What did she do?"

"Oh, it was a good thing, I think," Sean smiled.

"Uh . . . I don't quite understand," Zurich said, realizing that with MamaCee there was no such thing as a family secret.

"Well, she was telling me how she had raised you and your brother and almost every time she said something, she would say if it wasn't for the Lord this and the Lord that. And how God had helped her deal with your brother's death. Then I asked her something that maybe I shouldn't have."

"What was that? I know my grandmother's faith is very important to her, as it is for me," Zurich said. He didn't want to sound defensive, but he had taken note of Sean's reaction when he had talked about his faith in the past.

"Yeah, I gather that. But I've had some problems with faith and religion in my own life, so I asked your grandmother rather pointedly, where is God when it hurts?"

"Where is God when it hurts? What did she say?"

"She said He is always there, sittin' on His throne, but sometimes we don't know where to look. We're so busy with our problems that we don't see Him," Sean said.

"That sounds right to me. What happened with you and your faith, Sean?"

"Since I told your grandmother, I might as well tell you. Something tells me she might tell you anyway." Sean sighed.

"MamaCee can be like a priest sometimes. If you told her not to say anything, I doubt she will," Zurich laughed. "But then again, maybe not." Sean didn't respond. "What was it? What happened?" Zurich's curiosity had been aroused.

"There was a time in my life when I considered myself saved, I mean, I was really into the church. Bible study on Wednesday, church twice on Sunday. I really felt like it would solve my problems and some things I was going through at the time. When I gave my life to Christ, I expected the miracles they promise in church. A place where people were made perfect. So I started to pray all the time. When the one thing I was praying for didn't happen, I went to my minister and told him what I was going through. I told him that I was gay, but I didn't want to be. I thought he would help me, but he didn't," Sean said sadly.

"What happened?"

"He told me I wasn't gay and when I told him about the feelings I was having and some of the things I had done and dreamed of doing, he pulled the military stunt."

"The military stunt?"

"Yeah, right there in his study, this man I believed in and trusted pulled out his long ass dirty dick and told me if I was really gay and wanted to be saved that I needed to suck his dick." Sean paused and glanced nervously toward Zurich's face to see how he was handling his confession he had shared only with MamaCee. He hadn't been graphic with MamaCee, but she got the picture. He continued when Zurich's face gave no sign of the slightest disgust or discomfort. "I was so shocked! But it didn't end there. When I refused, this minister, the man who to me represented God, started cursing me like I had stolen something. I mean as much as I wanted to believe in God, that minister was all I had. For a long time I couldn't function, because I was certain I was doomed to hell. Living the life of the tragic black homosexual. That no matter how and for how long I prayed, I was still gay and bound for hell. I thought it was so unfair. That everything else could receive forgiveness, but not my sexuality." He stopped to see if Zurich had some type of response, but when he remained silent, Sean added, "I know that sometimes I still suffer from having those feelings that my church told me were so wrong."

Finally, Zurich broke his silence with a question. "So how long have you known you're gay?"

Suddenly realizing that he had admitted that he was gay, Sean gazed at Zurich for a moment. The expression on his face still hadn't changed—no sense of shock or judgment. So Sean answered the question, his voice softened as if he was describing a religious experience.

"I guess all my life. I think I've always known," Sean said.

"So what did MamaCee say about this?"

"She told me I hadn't lost my faith in God, but that I had lost my faith in mankind and that was okay. That it happens from time to time. That I would meet someone who would restore my faith in mankind, but it was up to me to restore my faith in God."

"You know she's right," Zurich said. He wondered if MamaCee had told Zachary the same thing, and the pain that seemed to come and go in Sean's voice reminded him of some of his conversations with Zachary about sexuality and religion.

"Yeah, for the first time in a long time, I know she's right. I mean, in a way, after that happened with the good reverend, I tried to intellectualize my religion. You know, I knew in my gut that there was a higher power. I mean when you look around you—the sky, stars, moon, and the trees—then you know that man could never do this."

"I know . . . that's where I put my faith," Zurich said.

"This is so strange. I mean I've kept what happened to me secret for over a decade and here today I've shared it with two people, two special people," Sean said as he glanced at Zurich, whose face looked as if he wanted to ask some serious questions. "Is there something you want to ask me?" Sean ventured. He knew he was going to have to take the lead if he expected Zurich to open up. The look on Zurich's face said that he wanted to talk and ask more questions, but was afraid.

"Is it hard, I mean, being involved with sports? Don't you worry that some of the players might find out?"

"Yeah, but I can't really worry about that. I try not to let my sexuality get in the way of my work. I love sports and I love writing," Sean said confidently.

"Have you ever been with an athlete, maybe somebody you were covering?"

"Yes, but it wasn't a good situation," Sean said.

"Why?"

"First of all, he was a fool. Good-looking, well built, all that stuff, you know, a dick from heaven, but he had a violent streak," Sean said.

"What happened?"

"Well, he didn't like being gay or bi as he used to say. And sometimes after we had sex he wanted to fight. He could never have sex with me unless he had been drinking. And he would only call me late at night or early morning. And he was always worried about whom I was talking to," Sean said.

"Why would you put up with that?"

"I guess I thought it was the best I could do." Sean said lamely. He had asked himself that many times, but he knew there was a price to pay for lusting after a certain type of man.

"Is it somebody I would know?"

"Know personally? I don't know, but he was a big enough name that I know you would have heard of him," Sean said.

"But you're not telling?" Zurich smiled.

"No, I'm not. Why are you interested?" Sean smiled as he looked at the curiosity on Zurich's face.

"I don't know, maybe just curious," Zurich said shyly.

"Let me ask you something. How did you feel about your brother being gay?"

"So MamaCee told you, huh?"

"Well, I think it slipped out, but she didn't seem to mind that Zach was gay. Which I find fucking amazing," Sean said.

"There were times when it bothered me. Especially the first time I saw Zach hugged up with another guy," Zurich said. "I was so mad I almost came to blows with the guy. I didn't want anybody doing that to my brother. I mean Zach had to pull me away from that guy."

"When did that happen?"

"When I came to visit him in New York. But he told me the first time he got down with a guy."

"What did you say?"

"I told him I didn't want to hear it. So I would go on talking about something in my life, but he would stop me and say if I can't talk about my life then you can't talk about yours. And I was just like 'But, Zach, how could you?' And he was just smiling and telling me how great it was."

"Why else did it bother you?"

"What do you mean?" There was an edge in Zurich's question.

"Were there any other reasons?"

"I guess I had all these stereotypes of gay people and I knew my brother wasn't like that. I mean Zach could have been a better athlete than me."

"Was there something else? I mean, besides the stereotypes." Sean felt Zurich was coming close to opening up about his own fears and how his brother's sexuality affected him.

"Like?"

"Like were you ever worried that since you guys were twins, I mean, identical twins, that you might be gay?" Finally, Sean thought, it was on the table. He felt like wiping some imaginary sweat from his brow.

"You want the truth?" As Zurich asked the question, he turned over in his mind what to tell Sean. He felt a certain degree of comfort with Sean, but realized he was not Zachary.

"Yeah. The truth works," Sean said.

"Yes. It's my biggest fear," Zurich said softly.

"Why?"

"Because of the way the world is. The way we treat people that are different. Look, I mean, I've always been in sports. And now here I am in the NFL and I know that's not allowed here," Zurich said.

"What's not allowed?"

"Being gay," Zurich said.

"You're kidding, right?"

"No. And there's the other thing."

"The other thing?"

"Yeah, my faith. The Bible says it's wrong," Zurich said. He didn't know if he actually believed that; it was just reflex, what he thought he was supposed to say.

"I've heard all that shit before. Don't you think God or whoever you believe in wants you to be true to yourself? Look, I'm not going to get into that Bible stuff with you, so let me ask you another question. Have you ever been attracted to a man?"

"What do you mean?"

"Come on now, Zurich, don't play dumb. You know what I mean."

Zurich's eyes moved around the empty stadium. For a few moments he didn't say a word. He was wondering if he could trust Sean with everything. If he answered the question truthfully, he would be sharing a secret he hadn't even shared with Zach. But suddenly the words began to emerge.

"Yes, once in college. It was this guy in one of my classes. It was a film production glass. He was kinda wiry-looking, glasses, wore dreads, but he was so smart. And when he talked to you, it was as though he was looking through you. That he was really listening to every word you said. Every syllable. We would talk all the time, about film, about sports. We even ran together. I felt comfortable with him.

And I had never felt that safe around another man, unless you count Zach and my father. Well, one night we were talking, he had just finished reading me some parts of a script he had written. And I was telling him how great it was. What a great writer he was going to be. And then, just out of the blue, he said if I asked you on a date, would you go," Zurich said as he stopped talking for a moment and stood up to stretch his large body.

"Did you go?" Sean asked. He wanted to shout, come on sit your fine ass back down and tell me the story. Don't stop now. Suddenly, as though Zurich were reading Sean's mind, he sat back down on the bleachers. He crossed his large calves, folded his arms as if he was protecting himself, and began to talk.

"I thought he was kidding. That guys didn't go on dates. But he wasn't playing and he said they did if one of them was gay and the other didn't know he was gay. I just laughed. It was a nervous laughter. Not, you're a fuckin' freak laughter. But I was nervous."

"Why?"

"Because I think I wanted to go," Zurich said.

"So come on, what happened? Did you go?"

"No, I chickened out. I told him I would go to the movies with him. That's what he wanted to do, but it wouldn't be a date. Just two friends going to the movies. But the night we were supposed to go, I stood him up. I mean I saw him pull up, walk up to my apartment, and ring the bell. But I didn't answer. I just stood in the window looking out on the night. When he was walking back to his car, I didn't move and he saw me standing in the window looking down. He just shook his head and got back in his car. He never spoke to me again."

"How did that make you feel?"

"Like a jerk. Like a stupid jerk. Almost as stupid as something I started to do recently," Zurich said.

"What was that?" Sean wondered if he was getting ready to tell him that he cruised parks and bookstores, and if he did, would that spoil the near-perfect image he had of Zurich?

"Man, just thinking about it makes me feel stupid. When this thing happened with Mia, and the way my teammates reacted, well, at first, I was mad, like I said. I was mad at her for lying and that I couldn't talk to her and get her to tell the truth about what really happened. I was embarrassed that I didn't correct my teammates, that I didn't tell the truth. But then I started to think maybe, just maybe, this is a good thing."

"What?"

"Well, it would stop some of the kidding. My lawyer had told me that since I had never been in any type of trouble, that the DA, if they pressed charges, would probably be willing to plea bargain."

"What are you talking about? I don't understand. Are you saying that you thought about admitting to something you didn't do just to impress a bunch of locker room buddies?" Sean asked. He had heard of dumb shit, but this was a first.

"Don't you see? I would no longer be Mr. Nice Guy. Zurich, the guy who's afraid of women, taking the pussy. To some of my teammates, it made me more of a man. And as quarterback you need to be respected. Come on, Sean, you've been in as many locker rooms as I have. When we're not talking about how great we are on the field, then what?"

"I know pussy, business deals, and more pussy. I also see a lot of guys checking out each other, comparing dicks and shit. You've seen it. Besides you should be respected for your playing ability. Not for accepting somebody's screwed-up idea of what it takes to be a man. Let me make sure I'm understanding what you are saying. You thought about pleading guilty to something you didn't do, just so some dumb-ass jocks would think you were just as much man as they think they are. That's bullshit, Zurich. Bullshit and you know it."

"I didn't say that," Zurich said firmly.

"I hope not." Sean didn't want to think about Zurich's current situation. He wanted to get him back to those original feelings. "Let's get back to this guy. Did you tell Zach about him?"

"No."

"Why not?"

" 'Cause he would have been mad at me for what I did. I know he would have tried to talk me into going. But I wasn't ready," Zurich said.

"How did you know that?"

"All I could think about was, what if I had a good time? What if I ended up in bed with him and then somebody busted in the door while we were doing the do? I mean I went to school on a small campus and I would have been ruined. A story like that would have followed me forever."

"So you've never acted on your desires?"

"Who said I had desires?"

"Well, you've never been to bed with a man?"

"No."

"Do you regret it?"

"I don't think I should answer that." This was getting to be too much for Zurich. He had lost control of his feelings and to a reporter, something Gina had warned him never to do. "Let's get back to the story you're working on," Zurich said nervously.

"You asked the question. Before I get back to my story, I have one more question to ask."

"Okay."

"Were you nervous sleeping in the same bed with me last night?"

"No. Should I have been?"

"No, but had we had this conversation last night, would you have slept in the same bed with me wearing only your underwear?"

"Maybe I would have worn a T-shirt," Zurich smiled as he hit Sean playfully on the arms with a balled fist.

"Man, you're something else. Naive, evasive, and scared, but you're something else." Sean hadn't determined if Zurich was telling him the whole truth, or if he had ever allowed himself to accept his truth. Sean understood that sometimes, when you are black and gay, living a lie can be the only truth accepted.

"You got another mile in you?"

"Hey, if you can do it, then so can I," Sean said confidently.

CHAPTER 21

YOU AIN'T SANGING

While reviewing the questions she had for Zurich and his upcoming preliminary hearing, Tamela listened to "The Deborah Crable Show" on WVON. Tamela was so engrossed in her notes and the callers from the show, she didn't hear when Warner walked in to discuss the case. He stood quietly at her door before interrupting her concentration.

On the radio, the host and callers were discussing gay rights and the right of gays to adopt children. One of the callers was reading the guest, a local black gay activist, the riot act. "I don't understand these people wanting special rights for what they do in bed, which, if you ask me, is unnatural and against God's law. And now they want to adopt kids and turn them into homosexuals like them, it's just wrong. Pure and simple, just wrong," the older male caller said.

Deborah Crable responded, "Caller, why do you think gay people shouldn't be able to adopt?"

"Like I said, 'cause it's just wrong. It's in the Bible. And instead of trying to get people to buy this homosexual's book 'bout adopting kids, they need to be reading one book and that's the B-I-B-L-E," he said.

"Caller, can you tell me where it states in the Bible that homosexuality is wrong and they shouldn't be able to adopt if they have been approved through the regular channels like other prospective adoptive parents? And if gay people can't look to the church and Bible for solace, then where can they go?" Ms. Crable asked. Deborah Crable always tried to get her loyal callers to stick to the facts, to be specific and brief with their comments, but whenever she did shows about sexuality, her show usually turned into a radio slugfest.

"I don't know exactly what scripture but it's in there," he said defensively.

"Okay, caller, when you find that scripture give us a call back. Thanks for calling and listening," she said.

Still unaware of Warner's presence, Tamela muttered, "Gay people raising children, what will they think of next?"

Warner cleared his throat and tapped his fist on her door, and Tamela looked up. "Warner, how long have you been standing there?"

"For a few minutes, just listening to the talk show along with you," he said as he came in and sat in one of the leather chairs facing Tamela's desk.

"Yeah, I must admit I've become somewhat addicted to these shows," Tamela said. "I can't get my morning started until I've had my coffee, my cranberry muffin, and a little talk radio."

"Which one are you listening to?"

"Deborah Crable, she's the best. Today, they're talking about gay rights and adoption and I mean these callers are giving her guests the what for." She paused and turned around in her swivel chair to lower the radio before asking, "What can I do for you?"

"I wanted to wish you luck with the preliminary hearing, but I know it will be just fine. I also wanted to know if Ms. Miller or her counsel has contacted you about a possible civil suit?" Warner asked.

"I haven't heard from her and neither has Zurich. I feel real good about our chances of having the charges dropped on Thursday. But I know you know as well as I do that a civil suit will be a totally different matter. You might have your hands full," Tamela said.

"Yeah, but I'll be ready. I've looked over your notes. Some very interesting information. I can't believe this guy hasn't had sex in over five years," Warner said.

"That's what he told me. I must admit at first I didn't believe him, but I don't know. I guess women aren't the only ones who practice celibacy," Tamela said.

"What about witnesses from the restaurant where they had dinner?"

"Well, I've talked to a couple of the waiters and one of the parking lot attendants. I've been having a little trouble reaching the other attendant who was on duty, around the time Zurich thinks Mia should have been picking up her car."

"Right. But didn't Mr. Robinson say she had been drinking quite a bit?"

"Yeah, I don't know how she was able to drive home. That's where her neighbor found her. The first attendant remembers when she showed up for dinner, but didn't provide much more information. I hope this other guy will be more help. I might not be able to use any information he might provide for the prelim, but if we go to trial, it could help you," Tamela said.

"I think you're right. So you're having a hard time getting in touch with him?"

"I've got his home address and I'm going by there tomorrow to try to see if he knows anything. Maybe I can just get him to concur with Zurich's assessment of her sobriety."

"That would be helpful. Where does he live?"

"Over in Cabrini Green housing projects with his mother. I got the information from the restaurant," Tamela said.

"You're not going over there alone, are you?" Warner asked.

Tamela looked at him and thought, *No, this white boy isn't trying to make me feel unsafe going among my own people.*

"Why do you ask, Warner?"

"It's pretty bad over there. Maybe I should go over there with you," he said unaware of how his statement might sound to Tamela. He really was concerned about her safety, even though he himself had never been to the well-known housing project. He was basing his concern on what he had seen on television and what he had read in the paper. Tamela thought Warner's going would just make matters worse. A well-dressed black woman and an equally well-dressed white man would certainly bring unwanted attention. But she wasn't in the mood to read this white man about his perception of danger.

"Don't worry. I'll be fine. My father teaches a lot of those kids. I will be safe. And if the kid has some information and doesn't want to come to our offices, then you can go over the next time." Tamela smiled slyly. She thought to herself how Warner might regret the day he went to Cabrini Green alone.

"Okay," Warner said as he started toward the door. Just as he was about to leave her office, Tamela turned the volume on her radio back up and out came the voice of a black man saying, "It ain't no black gay folks, that's white folks' stuff. They sent all the gay slaves back to Africa." Tamela started to laugh and said, "I know that's right."

"Tamela," Warner said. His voice shocked Tamela because she didn't realize he was still in her office.

"Yes, Warner, is there something else?" His tone and the look on his face captured her attention.

"Just a question," Warner said as he took a deep breath and tried to decide quickly if he would go through with asking his question.

"Okay, about the case?" Tamela asked.

"No," Warner said firmly. He had made up his mind to ask his question, no matter what might follow. "It's about the program you're listening to. Why are African-Americans so homophobic? I mean, listen to that man. They sent all the gay slaves back? There aren't any black gay people? Get real."

Tamela looked at Warner with surprise on her face. What was this about? And why would he think she could speak for all African-Americans on their dislike of gay people?

"Why would you say that?" she asked tentatively.

Warner gently closed the door, walked back over to Tamela's desk, and said, "Well, every time I've seen shows about gay rights and there are black people in the audience, they seem really adamant about their opposition. Why do they hate gay people, especially when there are a lot of gay African-American men and women?" His gentle face filled with concern.

"Warner, I can't speak for all black people, but hate is a very harsh word. I just know from a personal standpoint, I don't see the need for special rights for gays."

"It's not special rights we want. It's the right to live our lives like every human being without being harassed and prevented from being able to love who we want," Warner said firmly. Tamela looked at Warner, thinking did he say *we* and *our*? Was Warner gay? There was only one way to find out.

"Warner, are you gay?" Tamela asked boldly.

"Yes, I am, Tamela. Do you have a problem with that?"

"Oh no, I don't, I just, I mean," Tamela stuttered.

"I know, I don't look gay, right?"

Tamela didn't answer him right away, but he was reading her mind. She never in a million years would have guessed that Warner was gay and wondered why was he telling her. She had always considered Warner attractive and had once told Desiree that if she *did* white boys, then Warner would be the one to do. He was tall, with a slightly pudgy face as round as his rimmed glasses. Warner had a full head of curly jet black hair, which he wore with a part, ocean blue eyes like Paul Newman, and an olive complexion. No matter what time of year it was, he always had a healthy tan.

"Well, I'm just sort of surprised, but I still don't see the need for special rights. I mean most people who look at you, they see what I see, an attractive, successful white man. That's all you need to succeed in life," Tamela said.

"Do you really believe that? What about my right to love and the security that love and marriage bring without being attacked? Gay people are not asking for special rights. But I guarantee you I can't go to a restaurant or a movie and hold my lover's hand or kiss him in public like you can. And since we're being frank here, or should I say since I'm being frank and honest, I'll tell you something else." He paused to catch his breath. "My partner is black and deep in the closet," Warner said.

"What did you say?" Tamela asked as her mouth dropped open in shock.

"My partner is black. You got a problem with that?" He also wanted to tell her to close her mouth, but didn't. Warner got the feeling Tamela wasn't taking his announcement too well.

"Oh no, not if he makes you happy. Look, I think we should stop this conversation because I don't think there are enough hours in this day for you to get me to understand what you're saying or for you to understand how I feel," Tamela said in her trademark I Don't Want to Deal with This Now tone.

"Maybe you're right. But I would like to know how you feel. Maybe we can talk about this later because I really do want us to understand each other," Warner said.

"Okay, maybe after the case is over," Tamela said.

"Fine." He paused to consider his next words. He couldn't leave it hanging like this. At the very least he wanted to get Tamela to agree to keep their conversation between the two of them. He added as he headed out the door, "Thanks for the time and if you need any help with Thursday, remember I'm just down the hall. Why don't we finish the other conversation when we go out for drinks to celebrate your victory?"

"Okay, that sounds good," Tamela said as she looked down at her notes and turned her radio back up. They were still discussing gay rights. Tamela's eyes and ears perked up when she heard a voice she recognized.

"Baby, I can't believe I got through. I been tryin' and tryin'. Deborah, have you heard of call waiting? You need to git that, honey," MamaCee said. Tamela could hear Deborah Crable laugh and say, "I'll have my producer check into that. Welcome, Ms. Cora, to the WVON family. What's your question or comment?"

"Well, first, you got a good show. I been listening to it every day I can, since we don't have nuthin' like this down in my neck of the woods. But I'm so happy I got in today."

"Thank you for your kind words. Do you have a question for our guest or a comment?" Deborah asked again. She had a strange feeling her caller was going to be a handful.

"Yeah, it's 'bout that caller, talkin' 'bout how God don't love gay people and they all going to hell. Well, what God is that fool talking 'bout? The good Lord I know loves all His children. And I read my Bible every day and I ain't read none of them scriptures, at least not the way that fool man thinks it says. If he wants a scripture, read Romans 8, verse 1. And one more thing . . ." MamaCee paused to catch her breath.

"You've got some good points, Ms. Cora. Is that it? Do you have a question for our guest?"

"Naw, I ain't got no question, but a few choice words for that caller who said they ain't no black gay people and this is somethin' the white folks done put on us. We can't blame white folks for every thang. My uncle Frank, on my papa's side, who, God rest his soul, was one of the kindest men I've ever know, was that way. He and his friend Isaiah didn't bother nobody and they were together longer than me and my late husband, so you can just chuck the notion that this is something new, 'cause, honey, I'm talkin' 'bout the thirties and forties. Do you hear me? And my grandbaby was gay and didn't no white folks make him gay, he was born that way, and I know he's in heaven now with the good Lord," MamaCee said.

"Thank you, very much, Ms. Cora for those very insightful viewpoints. I'm like you when it comes to those scriptures. My audience knows I don't profess to be a Bible scholar, but I think a lot of it depends on your interpretation," Deborah Crable said.

"I know that's right and till the Good Lord Himself comes down here and tells us what He meant, we need to love each other no matter what, that's what the B-I-B-L-E really says. And one more thing, I think black folks needs to stop criticizing each other so much and support one another. That's the way it was in my day. That's how we got strong, by helping each other. Well, stick a fork in me, I'm done. Thanks for your time and I'm gonna pray for you, Deborah, and for some of them fool callers of yours. Pray that the good Lord will bless them with some common sense," MamaCee said as she finally stopped talking.

"Thank you again, Ms. Cora, and I guess that's as good place as any to end today's show. Thank you for calling and thank all of you for listening. Stay positive and have a blessed day."

Tamela leaned back in her chair with a pen to her mouth. She wondered about MamaCee losing a gay grandson. She knew Zurich had four brothers but he had never mentioned losing one or that one was gay. MamaCee was something else, she thought, and she had made some good points Tamela needed to think about. Maybe she should rethink her feeling about gays, especially black ones and how black people should be more supportive of each other. Tamela thought about her conversation with Warner and his black lover. What would her reaction be if that black lover was somebody she knew, or somebody she or some of her sorority sisters might be interested in. But Tamela didn't have time to think about this right now. She had to get ready for her appearance in court. She would deal with her fears later.

Sitting on the edge of his hotel bed, Sean checked his briefcase to make sure he had his micro recorder. He picked up his phone and started to dial Zurich's number to see if he could talk MamaCee into going to watch Zurich practice, but he changed his mind and instead dialed his sister's number. After the phone rang a couple of times, Sean was certain he was going to get her answering machine when suddenly he heard his sister's cheerful voice say, "Hello."

"Help!" Sean said playfully.

"Sean?"

"Yes, sister. This is your baby brother," Sean said.

"What are you talking about help? Whatsup?" Anja asked.

"I'm falling," Sean said.

"Falling? Falling for what?"

"Zurich Thurgood Robinson," Sean said, laughing.

"The football player? So he *is* gay," Anja said.

"I don't know, but I got that feeling," Sean said.

"So where are you?"

"I'm still in Chicago. Right now I'm in my hotel getting ready to go over to the stadium, just to watch him," Sean sighed.

"Oh, chile, you sound like you got it bad," Anja said.

"Yeah, sis, I do," Sean said.

"Have you told him?"

"I've told him I'm gay and he didn't run, but he hasn't confessed yet," Sean said.

Suddenly Sean and Anja heard the call waiting beep over the line. Sean knew his hotel phone didn't have this feature so he said, "Sounds like you got a call."

"Hold on," Anja said.

While she was on the other line, Sean thought about Zurich and how he should tell him he was interested in changing their friendship. He realized any relationship with someone like Zurich would have to be hush-hush and here he was telling his sister. He knew he could trust her, but he had also learned that an athlete's relationship could be doomed before it had even started if somebody else found out about it. But Sean needed to talk with someone, and Anja was it.

"I'm back," Anja said.

"Now I forgot what I was saying," Sean said.

"You were saying you found me a fine man in Chicago, he's straight, and you're bringing him back to New York," Anja laughed.

"Yeah, that's right, but I got to run one more test on him before I turn him over," Sean laughed.

"You know you're a fool," Anja said.

"Sho you right. What's this? Are you looking for a man? What happened to the good reverend?"

"Oh, brother, I think I'm going to have to let him loose," Anja said. Her voice didn't sound sad, but more relieved.

"Why, what happened?"

"Well, it's kinda funny when I think about it," Anja said as she paused, took a sip of her soft drink, and then launched into her story about the Reverend Theodis Wilder. "Sunday, Gerald and I went to church as usual, sitting on the front row like I'm the first lady of the church, so proud. We had this guest soloist, and Sean, sister could sing. I mean sang. You hear what I'm saying. She was like a combination of Jennifer Holliday, Aretha Franklin, with a little bit of Rachelle Ferrell thrown in for good measure," Anja said.

"Man, that musta been something else," Sean chimed in.

"Yes, it was. I mean the entire church was up. Waving scarfs, pocketbooks, Bibles, you name it. I mean she was singing and playing the piano. So anyhow, the good reverend got up and started looking at this sister singing and he just started shouting at her and was sweating like a greased pig. He pulled out his handkerchief and started waving it at her, just saying sing, baby . . . sing, baby. Well, Sean, sister hit a note. One of them glass-breaking notes, and Theodis started turning like a human tornado and screaming at the top of his lungs, 'sang, bitch . . . sang . . . you ain't singing . . . sang, bitch.' Sean, she kept singing but the rest of the church, chile, it got quiet. I mean we all were shocked. All of a sudden Gerald touched me and said, 'Mommy, why is the preacher cussing? Why is he calling that lady a bad name?' I thought he might start up again, 'cause it was obvious homeboy was possessed. So I grabbed my purse and my son, and we was history," Anja laughed. Sean was laughing also, spread out over his hotel bed, just picturing the scene Anja had described.

"Boy, I would have given anything to have been there," he said.

"I know you would," Anja said.

"You called it quits for that?"

"Honey, I think I was looking for a sign or a reason and that was it," Anja said.

"What did you tell him?"

"I told him, I needed some time to think about things. But trust me when I say he's history."

"So you're all right with that?" Sean asked.

"Yeah, Sean. I can still have my faith, and I will find a man when it's time. Theodis served his purpose. But, Sean, isn't that just the funniest thing you've heard in a long time?"

"Yes, it is. I wonder what the rest of the church thought?"

"I don't know, but it was silent . . . silent night . . . holy night up in that camp. But I will say one thing," Anja paused.

"What's that?"

"Sister was singing. I mean she was sanging," Anja laughed. Sean looked at his watch and realized it was time to head to practice.

"I've got to run. How's Gerald?"

"He's doing great. Doing real good with his football. Keeps asking when you're going to be back."

"Tell him I'll be back this weekend, and I'm bringing him something back from Chicago," Sean said.

"Okay, baby . . . be safe," Anja said.

"I will," Sean said.

"I mean with your heart."

"Oh, I'll be okay. You know me, I'll be over this by the time my plane lands in Newark," Sean said.

"Good, then we can go looking for a beau together," Anja said.

"That's a bet," Sean said.

"I love you, Sean, and so does Gerald. Always know that and hurry home," Anja said softly.

"I love y'all too," Sean said as he hung up the phone and smiled.

Mia stood on the deck off her guest bedroom in a new pink silk robe with burgundy piping. Derrick had purchased the robe for her before he left late Monday night and returned to Jackson. He had promised to check on her daily and said he would return in half a heartbeat if she needed him. Mia had cried softly in her pillows that night after he left, but she knew she had to depend on herself to start recovery. But she was still uncertain if she was ready for the changes she needed to make.

She took a deep swallow of the herbal tea she was drinking and then released a short sigh. The air was cool and clear, the sky cloudless, and the setting sun looked heavy. But nothing could compare to the weight on Mia's shoulders. She had not had a drink since early Saturday morning, but that was because Derrick had cleaned out her liquor cabinets. She had not talked with her attorney, her parents, or Tanya. Mia spoke with LaDonna briefly Sunday night but had told her she was doing fine and hoped to return to work within a week.

She put the coffee mug on a wooden table and breathed in the evening air, letting her mind drift back to late Sunday evening. Derrick and she had eaten takeout Chinese food on her deck and talked about a possible future together. That night she had begun to feel that maybe everyone deserved a second chance. But before Mia could look to a future with anyone, she knew she must deal with her past. She thought it was strange how new images and sounds all brought back moments that lingered in her memory. But it was one memory that Mia longed for. A memory as elusive as the scent of flowers. The memory of who had attacked her and why.

Sean was a bit surprised at what he saw in the Cougars' locker room. There was Zurich in near tears slamming his helmet against his locker, mumbling, "What else can happen? When is this crap going to end?"

Sean walked over, gently touched him on the shoulders, and asked, "Whatsup, Zurich? What happened?"

"I don't want to talk about it right now, Sean, I need some time alone," Zurich said. But Sean did not leave the area. This was his chance to show Zurich that he could be trusted, that he could be a good friend.

"We don't have to talk. If you don't want to talk, we can just go somewhere quiet. Maybe we can just go and sit in the stadium. But I'm not going to leave you alone," Sean said as he walked closer and sat on the bench in front of Zurich's locker.

"I just can't believe this crap. I just can't fuckin' believe they can do this," Zurich said as he faced Sean. His insides rocked, partly from anger, mostly from disappointment.

"What? Does it have something to do with the hearing?" he said as he lowered his voice, noticing several players starting to mill around the area. "Is that what has you so upset?" Zurich looked at Sean with eyes that belonged on a Purina puppy chow commercial. Sad, yet inviting and endearing.

"I'm not going to start against Tampa Bay. Coach just told me they're starting Craig. I mean my father might be coming to Chicago for the game and MamaCee is talking about going. Sean, she hasn't been to one of my games since Zach and I played Pee Wee football. And now I find out I'm not going to start."

"Don't worry about it. You're under a lot pressure right now. But the minute this trial shit is over, you'll be back on your game and there's no way they will be able to keep you from playing," Sean said.

"You think so?"

"I know so."

"But what about this weekend?"

"We both know MamaCee will understand, and you can just call your father and tell him. From what you and MamaCee have told me about him, I know he will understand too," Sean said. While Zurich held his head down in silence, Sean noticed a picture of an attractive football player taped on the inside of his locker. He looked familiar but Sean couldn't quite recall where he knew him from or figure out what team's uniform he was wearing. While Sean was studying the photo and Zurich appeared to meditate in silence, one of the locker room attendants came up and gave Zurich a message, saying, "This is the third time this guy has called."

Zurich took the note and looked at it, and a sweet smile came across his face as he placed the note on the bottom shelf of his locker.

"Good news?" Sean asked.

"I don't know, maybe," Zurich said.

"So, I'm not the one who cheered you up," Sean teased.

"You're doing a pretty good job. I know what you're saying is right," Zurich said as he looked at Sean. "They won't be able to keep me down for long. I'm going to get my starting job back," he said confidently as he looked toward the end of the locker room where the coaches often made decisions.

He turned back and looked at Sean and said, "Wait here for me, while I shower. That quiet time in the stadium sounds good. 'Cause I think I got something exciting to tell you."

"Okay, I'll be right here."

Zurich removed his uniform and wrapped a towel around himself. He grabbed some shampoo and shower soap from his locker and walked out of view. His locker was still open, and as Sean was preparing to get a closer look at the photo, he saw the message that identified the football player in the photo. Basil Henderson from the New Jersey Warriors. The guy from Keith's party. Sean sat on the locker room bench and wondered why Zurich had a picture of another football player in his locker. He wondered why Basil Henderson was calling Zurich and why his calling had caused Zurich to smile.

CHAPTER 22

Fat Meat Is Greasy

Tuesday night, the scent and sight of roses greeted Tamela when she walked into her apartment around 9 P.M. It had been a marathon day for her. She dropped her shoulder bag and briefcase and quickly grabbed the white note card sticking out of the roses. A big smile came across her face when she read the handwriting, *Thank You for the Best Two Days of a Young Man's Life! Let's Do It Again Soon. Peace, Caliph.*

As Tamela placed the card lightly against her breast, she thought of Caliph and the wonderful weekend they had had, and after a day such as she had just experienced, nothing would make her feel better than to fall asleep in his arms. She picked up her phone and was preparing to dial his number when she suddenly changed her mind. Wednesday was going to be another busy day. She had meetings with Zurich and needed to talk with Warner. In addition, Tamela was going to try and talk with the parking lot attendant who might be able to help the case. So maybe she should call Caliph when she could give him undivided attention and proper thanks for the beautiful roses. Just as she sat the phone back in its cradle, it rang.

"Hello," Tamela said.

"Hey, girl, did you get my message?" Desiree said.

"Oh, I haven't listened to my messages, I just walked in," she said as she noticed the red light blinking three times, indicating three new messages.

"What did you do after work? Health club? Did you meet the divas for a drink?"

"Naw, girl. I've been working. Remember I have my big day in court the day after tomorrow," Tamela said.

"Well, I knew it was something, since we hadn't talked. You got time to tell a sister about your weekend with Mr. Policeman?" Desiree asked.

"That's right, we haven't talked since then," Tamela said as she took a seat on her sofa, kicked off her pumps, and snapped open the top button of her blouse.

"So how was it?" Desiree asked anxiously.

"It was wonderful," Tamela said as she paused to find the right words to describe her weekend with Caliph. "It was sweet, really sweet. It was all that and then some," Tamela said, her voice full of delight, almost as if she were singing.

"Well, did you?" Her voice sounded as if she were about to burst with curiosity.

"Did I what?"

"Oh, don't go there. Did you do the do?"

"Yes," Tamela screamed in delight.

"Oh, not Miss I'm Not Going to Have Sex Again Until I Get Married," Desiree teased.

"I tried. But you know and I know that it's a rare thing to find a man who knows where it itches, scratches it, and then doesn't turn around and say now scratch me," Tamela giggled.

"I know that's right. So you turned in your hoe card?"

"Naw, but when he played the piano, well, it was over. I had to give it up. And to be honest, I'm sorry and glad."

"The policeman plays the piano?" Desiree quizzed.

"Yes, and he's very good," Tamela giggled. "He's really great with his fingers . . . on the piano, I mean," she added, trying to sound like a serious music critic.

"And what else can he do with his fingers . . . or shall I say play well?"

"And what?"

"If it was all that, then why on earth would you say you're sorry and glad?"

"Glad 'cause it was wonderful. Sorry 'cause maybe I did give it up too soon and because I don't know if I want to be in a relationship," Tamela said.

"So? He wants to be in a relationship. Honey, you better grab him," Desiree advised.

"He didn't exactly say that, but he was so sweet and attentive the entire weekend and then Monday a cassette of love songs that he had taped was delivered to my office and when I walked into my apartment tonight, I was greeted by a dozen red roses," Tamela said.

"Wait a minute! How did he get roses into your apartment? The policeman isn't using his pull to sneak in your apartment, is he?"

"Chile, please. I do live in a modern building where the building management accepts packages. It might not be Gold Coast, but we have our perks," Tamela said.

"I stand corrected. It sure sounds like he wants a relationship to me. Now tell me, is that fine client of yours going to jail? If not, can you hook me up with him, so I can experience some of that joy I hear in your voice," Desiree teased.

"You know I can't talk about my client, and be careful what you pray for 'cause you just might get it," Tamela said.

"I know that's right. Oh, guess what?"

"What?"

"I might have a regular job," Desiree said.

"That's great! Where?"

"It's not definite, but a position may be opening up at Hyde Park Academy. But there's a catch."

"What's the catch?"

"I'd have to teach gym and maybe a health science course. They are kinda shorthanded over there."

"So what do you think?"

"The job hasn't been offered and to be really honest, the temping is kinda fun. I mean, you hear all kinds of shit. I'm thinking 'bout hanging out on some of these temp jobs and writing me a screenplay. 'Cause, honey, the shit I see and hear in some of these offices would make a great movie," Desiree laughed. "Now I know where all the bodies are buried."

"I know that's right. And talking about buried bodies, the strangest shit happened in the office today," Tamela said.

"Ooh, more bodies, good gossip?"

"Yeah, it really blew me away. Warner, you know, the white boy that I was telling you about?"

"The fine one you once said you might do?"

"Yeah, that's the one, but cancel that thought."

"Why? 'Cause you got a new man or is he married?"

"No, 'cause he got a man," Tamela laughed.

"What, he's gay?"

"Is fat meat greasy?"

"Sho you right."

"But that ain't all. He told me his lover was black."

"Jungle Fever with a twist. Please don't nobody tell Spike Lee 'bout this kinda shit," Desiree laughed.

"Now ain't that the truth, but guess who I think it is?"

"Is it somebody you know?"

"I'm not certain, but when I was leaving the office this evening, I was going to stop by Tim's office and update him on the case. Well, just as I was getting ready to knock on the door, I heard Tim shouting at the top of his lungs, mutherfuck this and mutherfuck that. That's really all I could make out. And even though I wasn't snooping, I didn't want anybody to see me," Tamela said.

"What does that have to do with what's-his-face? The gay boy," Desiree asked.

"When I was waiting on the elevator, I saw Warner slip out from the same direction as Tim's office, obviously pissed off at somebody," Tamela said.

"Well?"

"I don't know and I could be totally off base, but those two have always been kinda chummy," Tamela said as she recalled the many times she had seen Tim and Warner leaving the office going to lunch and meetings, or so she'd thought.

"From what you told me about Mr. Tim, he's chummy with a lot of white folks."

"Yes, he is. Which is why I don't understand why he would be arguing with any of them, especially Warner, if that was him in Tim's office."

"Well, honey, and the world goes round," Desiree laughed.

"Let me go, girl. I've got to look over these notes. I can't believe I just spent all this time talking 'bout men, men, and men. I got a job to do."

"I know you'll do fine. But don't forget about your sisters," Desiree said.

"I won't. Talk to you later," Tamela said.

"I'll holler at ya," Desiree said.

Tamela hung up the phone and started to remove her clothes as she headed toward her bedroom, thinking that maybe she should have been more supportive of Desiree's idea about writing a screenplay. She knew if she expressed reservations she would sound more like a mother than a friend. As she was trying to decide if she wanted to review her files in her nightgown or in T-shirt and shorts, she thought about the possibility of Warner and Tim being lovers. If they were, what if Tim had assigned Warner to the case just to keep an eye on her. No, maybe she was just being paranoid. The thought of Warner and Tim as lovers made Tamela laugh, but then she thought, I went to bed with Tim, what if he was HIV-positive? Her mind wandered back to the night and she remembered he did have a condom on that little dick of his. One less worry for her. Besides, she thought, condoms were no longer an option. No condom, no coconut.

Just as she finished brushing her teeth, the phone rang.

"Hey, pumpkin," Blanche said.

"Hey, Mama, I was going to call you," Tamela said.

"You got my message?"

"I'm sure it's on my machine, but I haven't checked them," Tamela said.

"How ya doing?"

"Okay, just real busy with the case."

"How's that going? I haven't seen anything in the paper."

"Thursday is the big day."

"Are you ready?"

"Yeah, Mama, as ready as I'll ever be," Tamela said.

"Your daddy hopes the guy is innocent," Blanche said.

"Why?"

"So, you can talk him into coming and speaking to his players if he is."

"Aw. I'm sure Zurich would like that," Tamela said. Her voice sounded distracted to her mother.

"Are you sure you're all right? They treating you okay at the office? Are you still having reservations about representing Zurich?"

"Yeah, everything is fine. I truly believe Zurich is innocent. At first, I wasn't sure, but the more I was around him and looking at the facts, it just didn't add up. But something interesting did happen at the office today with one of my co-workers."

"Who, that guy Tim?"

"No, Warner, the guy who's also working on this case from a civil angle. He accused me of being homophobic today."

"What?"

Tamela told her mother about her encounter with Warner and how she was certain that he thought she had a problem with gay people. When her mother didn't offer support for her views, Tamela asked her mother, "You agree with me, don't you, Mama?"

"Well, sweetheart, I don't know. I've had the pleasure of working and knowing some gay people in my life and you know I'm against any kind of discrimination. Lord knows we've seen a lot in our own lives. I understand about our color being obvious, but you said something that bothered me."

"What was that?"

"You said there weren't that many gay people, especially black ones, and then you said something about where you read that only five percent of the population is gay," Blanche said and paused as she waited for confirmation from her daughter.

"Yes, Mama, that's what I read. It was an article in *USA Today* and then somewhere in *Jet*. And you know if it's in *Jet*, it's got to be true," Tamela laughed, trying to lighten up the conversation. But Blanche was not going along with her lightheartedness.

"Baby, this is something I've always believed and that is percentages only matter to bigots. That's what society has always used against minority groups so they can keep them happy with a dab here and a dab there," Blanche said.

"Mama, you're not saying I'm a bigot, are you?"

"No, Tamela. Your daddy and I raised you better than that. I just don't like to hear you spouting off statistics to back up the way you might feel about some group."

"I guess you got a point." Tamela wanted to change the subject so she quickly asked, "How's Daddy and Hank Junior?"

"I know you're trying to change the subject, but since it's about my two favorite men, I'll go along with you. For now. Both of them are doing fine. How's Caliph and when are we going to meet him?" Blanche wanted to meet this new man in her daughter's life who caused her to smile so much.

"I haven't talked to him today, but I got these beautiful roses from him."

"Ooh, he sounds like a real peach!"

"Well, I hope his daughter thinks I'm a peach," Tamela laughed, even though she was a bit nervous about meeting the other woman in Caliph's life. She had heard so many horror stories involving Daddy's little girls.

"Oh, you haven't met her yet?"

"No, but soon. Look, Mama, I've got to run. I'll talk to you tomorrow. Give Daddy and Hankie my love."

"Okay, baby. Sleep tight and when you finish with your case, think about our little talk," Blanche said.

"I will. Love ya."

"I love you, too, baby."

After hanging up the phone, Tamela set her alarm clock, pulled back the bedspread, fluffed her pillows, and climbed into her bed. Her mind wandered to her busy and eventful day; the talk and confrontation with Warner, MamaCee on the radio, Desiree, and finally her conversation with her mother. She thought about her mother's comment about percentages and realized how right she was. She rehearsed her opening statement to the judge and her request that all the charges against Zurich be dropped. She went over her arguments and even practiced a response in case the judge rejected her request. Later, Tamela was drifting off to sleep when her phone rang, but before she could move, the answering machine picked up so she decided to screen the call. After her announcement played, she heard Caliph's voice. "Hey, it's me, just checking in to see how your day went. Are you there?" His voice paused and Tamela figured he was waiting to see if she was going to pick up. When she didn't, he continued, "Well, I guess you're either out or asleep. Just sitting here, lonely, thinking about you, but I guess I'll have to shower and sleep alone. Night." Tamela began talking to her answering machine, which she did on occasion, "Good night, sweet man. You should play that song 'If You Think You're Lonely Now,' sweet peda."

In the darkness, Tamela smiled to herself thinking about Caliph and his shower. The previous weekend, he had told her how he loved watching her shower and once during the weekend, he had stepped into the stall and washed her hair, and afterward made slow, gentle love to her, scratching *that* itch. She gave herself a tight hug as she remembered every single touch of his body, and then she fell asleep.

The sounds of Barbra Streisand singing "What Are You Doing the Rest of Your Life" filled the guest room of Mia's townhouse as she sat at her desk.

It was just after midnight, and Mia gazed at a tightly corked bottle of Pinot Noir wine. She had discovered the bottle in a gift box while searching for her personalized stationery. The wine had been a house-warming gift from Tanya, as was the linen stationery.

Mia wanted to taste the wine, but Derrick had also removed her corkscrew when he left. She tried unsuccessfully to remove the cork with a butter knife, and after a few minutes she gave up and decided to write the letters she had planned all day. But who would she write first and what would she say? Tanya or Zurich? She picked up her pen and wrote, *Sometimes we forget the things that are most painful,* and then she placed the pen down on the ivory white stationery and began to cry.

For Zurich, the dreams continued. On Wednesday, however, toward daybreak, he had a different dream. He was naked, sitting in an armless chair, with his hands handcuffed behind him. He looked around the empty room, trying to free himself, when in walked Basil Henderson. Basil was also nude, and Zurich could not stop staring at his Soloflex-proportioned body. Basil's smooth skin, the color of honey, and catlike gray eyes captivated Zurich.

Basil walked over to the chair and lowered his own body in the slow rhythm of a dance, so that he was eye to eye with Zurich. They did not speak, but they were communicating with each other through their eyes. Then, as though it were the most natural thing in the world, Basil kissed Zurich on the lips. It was a long kiss, the kind of hungry, out-of-control kiss that predicted something fantastic was about to happen. Zurich wanted to resist, but he felt his sex betraying him. Basil slowly pushed Zurich's muscular legs apart and crouched between them, his lips just above Zurich's sex, not touching it, as if it were a microphone, long and thick. Zurich could feel Basil's breath coming close to his sex, blowing like a fierce, hot wind, as he struggled to free himself. Just as Basil lips brushed against Zurich's sex, he coughed and Zurich started to laugh. Suddenly they were both laughing, and then MamaCee's real laughter and coughing woke him up.

Tamela got out of bed reluctantly, sorry to leave behind the softness and warmth, but she had work to do. After showering and dressing, she went to her car and headed south toward the Cabrini Green housing complex.

Having located a parking spot in front of one of the mid-rise dirty red-brick buildings, Tamela pulled out a tablet with the building and apartment number of DeAndre Tucker. She looked at the building directly in front of her and realized it was the one she needed. For a minute, she thought about locking her purse and briefcase in her trunk, but decided they might be better off with her. She glanced around the parking lot nervously to see if there was danger lurking.

As she walked toward the building, Tamela encountered a police officer, which made her think of Caliph, and a group of three young black men, smoking cigarettes and playfully hitting each other. When she was within a few feet of the teenagers, one of them asked her if she was a probation officer. Tamela smiled and said no and then asked them if they knew DeAndre.

"Yeah, he lives right over there," one of the teenagers said as he pointed toward the building behind them.

"Thank you," Tamela said.

After waiting for about five minutes for an elevator, Tamela decided to take the stairs. When she reached the third floor, she located apartment 303A and began to knock. After a few minutes, a pecan-brown, thinly built woman answered the door. Wearing a dull pink dress, like some combination nurse–Dairy Queen uniform, she had a hurried, startled look on her face.

"Can I help you?" she said. Her dirt-brown eyes narrowed with suspicion.

"Yes, I'm Tamela Coleman, with MacDonald, Fisher, and Jackson. I'm looking for DeAndre Tucker," she said.

"Who is you? Are you the police or something?" she asked.

"No, I'm a lawyer and I just need to speak with him for a few minutes. I got his address from his employer, Mason's, the restaurant." Tamela said.

"And?" she asked.

"I've been trying to reach him for some time, but I was unable to get a phone number for him," Tamela said.

"Well, that would be hard to do since we don't have a phone," she said.

"Are you his sister?" Tamela asked. The lady began to laugh at Tamela's question.

"His sister! Heavens, no. I'm his mother," She said.

"Oh, I'm sorry," Tamela said, as she gazed at the lady who looked close to her own age. She must have started childbearing young, she thought.

"Don't be sorry. I'm Garbo Tucker. Now you sho you're not the police?"

"That's right, Ms. Tucker. I'm not the police," Tamela assured her. She went on to tell Garbo why she was looking for her son, explaining that she needed to ask him a few questions. Sensing she could trust Tamela, Garbo Tucker invited her into the apartment. As Tamela walked in behind her, she noticed the beautiful burgundy ribbon Mrs. Tucker was wearing, holding together her shoulder-length hair.

"Oh, what a beautiful ribbon that is," Tamela commented.

"Thank you," Garbo said as she touched the ribbon and then boasted, "My son gave this to me."

"Is he here?"

"Naw, he's already left or he didn't come in last night," she said.

"You know how teenage boys can be. Here, take a seat, but I don't have that long before I have to catch the bus for work."

Tamela took a seat at one of the dining room chairs and couldn't help but notice the immaculately clean living area, with plastic covers over the peach-colored sofa and matching chairs.

"Where do you work?" Tamela asked.

"I work maintenance at the Sears Tower," she said.

"Oh, that's close to my office. I can give you a ride if you like," Tamela said. Maybe if Tamela got her in her territory Garbo might give her suggestions on how to get DeAndre to help her out.

"Honey, that will be just fine. Let me get my purse," Garbo said as she went into one of the open doors and emerged with a sweater and her purse.

"When do you think I might be able to talk to DeAndre? Is he at school?"

"That's a good question I wish I could answer. Look, you give me your number, and I'll make sure he gives you a call," she said.

Tamela explained the urgency of talking with him and Garbo assured Tamela she would make sure he got the message.

The two women left the apartment and headed toward Tamela's car. While they were walking, Garbo talked freely with Tamela about her two children, DeAndre and Bridget, her ten-year-old daughter, as if they were old friends. She told Tamela that DeAndre was a good kid, but she was worried about gangs and his impending manhood.

"God knows I'm lucky that my boy has reached sixteen in this hell hole. But I keep working hard and praying that I can move to the suburbs before it's too late," she said.

"Where do you want to move?" Tamela asked.

"Out near Des Plaines or Evanston. There is this program that I'm signed up for. You know where they give you a voucher to help you get a house or a large, nice apartment. But the list is long," Garbo said.

"Good luck. I wish you the best," Tamela said as she pulled up in front of the Sears Tower. She gave Garbo a business card, and put her home number on the back of the card.

"I'll try my best to get him to call you, but I don't know if he can help you," she said.

"Yeah, I know, but please tell him it's important and it won't take that long."

"Okay," she said as she thanked Tamela for the ride and then got out of the car. Tamela headed down Michigan, to her office, to prepare for a meeting with Warner and Zurich later in the day.

CHAPTER 23

SHAKE YOUR GROOVE THANG

"*It's* going to be a cool day with the possibility of rain, Chicago. So take those sweaters and umbrellas," said V-103 Radiojock Bonnie DeShong. "And if you're not quite awake yet, then maybe this will do the trick, something new from a fifteen-year-old I think we will be hearing a lot from, Brandy, with 'I Wanna Be Down.'" Zurich rubbed his eyes, turned down the radio, and meditated and prayed for about ten minutes. Zurich prayed that whatever the day brought him, he would handle it with strength and grace. This was his big day in court. The evening before he had met with Tamela and she had told him to be prepared to be arrested if charges were filed against him. Again, she asked him if there was anything he wanted to tell her that might prove that he didn't rape and attack Mia. He started to ask her if it would make a difference if he was beginning to believe he might be gay, but he didn't. She might not accept that he was having dreams and constant thoughts of Basil, a man he had only met once.

Tamela and Zurich had decided that if he was charged, they would immediately post bail, and agree to submit to a semen sample that would prove that he was not the man who raped Mia. Gina DeMarco had sat in on a portion of the meeting and had prepared a press release stating Zurich's innocence and his willingness to submit to the semen sample and a polygraph test. Zurich was trying very hard to be confident around MamaCee, but deep down he was nervous. The night before MamaCee had commented that her legs were feeling so much better that she felt as if she could run a race. To MamaCee, this meant that everything with her grandson would be fine.

Before heading to the shower, Zurich laid out a smart navy blue suit, a white shirt, a red tie, socks, and white boxer underwear. After a warm, brief shower, he shaved his head and face and then held a washcloth under the hot water and wrapped his face in the cloth for a minute before wiping away the remaining foam. While he was brushing his teeth, he could hear pots and pans banging in his kitchen, and he knew MamaCee was up, preparing his breakfast.

After dressing, he walked into his living room and was greeted by the smell of fried chicken and the sound of MamaCee humming some gospel song. As he was walking toward the kitchen, he noticed MamaCee's suitcases sitting in front of the closet, packed. Was she getting ready to leave, he thought, or was she planning to take her suitcases to the courthouse?

"Good morning, MamaCee," Zurich said as he walked over and kissed her on the forehead.

"Morning, baby. My, don't you look nice," MamaCee said as she turned over the golden brown chicken.

"Chicken for breakfast, MamaCee, or are you cooking that for someone else?" Zurich asked. He suddenly realized that chicken for breakfast was not that unusual for MamaCee, who cooked fried chicken and waffles all the time when he came to visit.

"Naw, baby, I'm cooking this for you. Mama thought she should cook up a lot of your favorite foods before I leave. That way you don't have to be eating that takeout mess," she said.

"You're leaving?"

"Yeah, it's time for Mama to go back to Mississippi. You will be fine. The good Lord and my legs have told me so," she said.

"Have you made reservations to fly back?"

"Naw, one airplane ride is enough for this old lady. I called the Greyhound station and they have three different buses heading toward Jackson every day," MamaCee said.

"MamaCee, I kinda hate to see you leave," Zurich said, though he would welcome back his privacy.

"If you need me, Mama will be right back. But I been thinking 'bout some of my friends at the hospice and I feel like some of them need me."

"What about staying to Sunday and coming to the game? I think Dad is going to come," he said.

"I don't think so. I talked to your father late last night and he said you told him you wasn't certain you'd be playing."

"True. I did tell him I wasn't starting and tried to talk him out of coming, but he said something 'bout needing to get away and seeing you," Zurich said.

"Yeah, he talked 'bout driving up here and driving me back home, but I told him don't go through no trouble. Besides I don't like riding in that van of his. I'll be just fine on the Greyhound."

"What else you cooking?"

"Oh, baby, I made some deviled eggs, and I'm going to make you some greens and a sweet potato casserole and I'm gonna bake you a ham."

"MamaCee, you don't have to go to all that trouble. You know I have to meet Tamela in about an hour," Zurich said.

"Yeah, baby, I know and I plan to go with you. I can finish cooking some of this stuff later on. I like for my hams to cook slow anyhow. I'd like to put it in this little oven of yours before we leave."

"Now, MamaCee, you don't have to go with me. Just in case they arrest me, I would never want you to see me in handcuffs," Zurich said.

"Baby, you gonna be just fine. Ain't nobody gonna put no handcuffs on my baby," MamaCee said as she reached for a towel and wiped her greasy and flour-covered hands. Then she ran them smoothly down Zurich's shirt and tie as if she were using her hands as an iron to knock out the wrinkles. Zurich was looking at his grandmother and thinking about how much he loved her and how lucky he was to have someone like her in his life. They were both quiet, deep in thought, when the phone rang and startled them both. Zurich kissed his grandmother's forehead once again and went into the living room and picked up the phone.

"Hello," Zurich said.

"Zurich, I'm glad I caught you," Tamela said.

"Tamela, whatsup? We said ten, right? I'm supposed to meet you at ten."

"Yes, that's right. But are you sitting down?" she asked excitedly.

"No, but should I?" Zurich said as he walked over to the window. He opened the drapes slightly and stared out into the gray glare of an overcast day.

"You're not going to believe what happened," she said.

"What?" Zurich asked as he let the curtain fall back into place and took a seat on his sofa.

MamaCee had walked out of the kitchen with a pot full of sweet potatoes she was peeling, looking at her grandson.

"I got to the office early this morning, and was going over some of my notes from the hearing when I got a call from the DA," Tamela said.

"What did she want?" Zurich asked.

"That's the news. It's good news, no, make that great news. They are dropping their investigation of you. There will be no charges, and there will be no preliminary hearing," Tamela said.

"What?" Zurich said as he leaped from the sofa.

"You heard me. It's all over Mr. Robinson. You can go out and enjoy your day."

"But what happened? Yesterday you were telling me to prepare myself for a few hours in jail and a lot of bad press," Zurich said.

"I don't have all the details, but during our brief conversation I got the distinct impression that Ms. Miller recanted her story. She or maybe it was her attorney, called the DA late last night and told them you didn't rape her and that she was willing to sign a statement to that effect. This is good news on a couple of fronts, because when she signs that statement that clears you from other possible civil lawsuits we were concerned about," Tamela said.

"Oh, I can't believe this. This is great news," Zurich said.

"Well, I'm going to let you enjoy this for a while. I will give you a call later this afternoon after I speak with the DA in more detail. I just wanted to get this news to you," Tamela said.

"Thank you, Tamela. Thanks for all your help. I'll talk with you later this afternoon," Zurich said. When he hung up the phone, he let out a high-pitch shout of *yes*. When he told MamaCee about his conversation with Tamela, she began to peel her potatoes and said quietly, "See, Mama told you everything would be just fine. Now Mama know she can go home."

After Tamela called Zurich with the good news, she wanted to celebrate. But what was she going to celebrate? Once her initial excitement faded, Tamela seemed almost sad at the news from the district attorney, as if she were sorry to see the battle end so quickly. Perhaps she was disappointed that she wouldn't get the opportunity to show her stuff in the courtroom. As she sat at her desk, staring at a yellow legal pad with notes she had planned to use, Tamela could not stop thinking about Mia and the young lady from college. Sure, Zurich had not committed the crime, and she was happy he had been cleared. But someone had raped this lady and now it appeared that no one would be charged with the horrible crime.

Suddenly, Tamela picked up her phone and dialed the direct number of Karen Hedge, the deputy district attorney, who was handling the Mia Miller case.

"Karen Hedge speaking."

"Karen, this is Tamela Coleman. We spoke earlier this morning," Tamela said.

"Yes, Tamela, what can I do for you?"

"Well, I was wondering if I could talk to you about the Miller case."

"The Miller case. I thought I made it clear that Ms. Miller had cleared your client. Like I told you, she doesn't know who committed the assault, but she is certain that it wasn't your client," Karen said.

"Yes, I understand that, and both my client and I are very happy about that. And my questions don't really concern my client," Tamela said.

"Oh. Then why are you still interested?"

"Well, it's kinda hard to explain, but I saw those pictures and I was just wondering if you had any leads on who did do this?"

"I think we're back to ground zero. Just between you and me, the police are pissed that Miss Miller came forth at the last minute and said that your client didn't do it. It was the only real lead they had. I think it's going to be real hard to get them to follow up any leads that come in, because I don't think they will be so quick to believe anything Ms. Miller says," Karen said.

"Do you think she's lying?"

"What do you mean?"

"I mean do you think she knows who did it, but she's just covering up for them?"

"That's hard to say. It was impossible to get her to talk with us, after the initial investigation. But I must say when I met with her early this morning and she told me that she was certain Mr. Robinson didn't do it, I believed her. I mentioned to you when we spoke earlier, she was real sorry about the pain and embarrassment she may have caused Mr. Robinson. I mean she was crying and saying how she wished she could tell us who had raped her. But you still haven't told me why you're interested. You guys over there at that big fancy law firm aren't planning to sue Ms. Miller, are you?"

"You know, Karen, I couldn't speak to you about that. But like I said, I'm calling on my own behalf. This has nothing to do with Mr. Robinson. Could we get together for lunch sometime soon, and maybe I could explain it better in person?"

"My schedule is pretty full. And I've got to explain to my superiors why we spent almost a month investigating a man for a crime he didn't commit," Karen said.

"I understand. What if I give you a call sometime next week and see how your schedule looks? It doesn't have to be lunch. We can do drinks or breakfast," Tamela said.

"Sure, give me a call and I'll see what I can do," Karen said.

"Thanks, Karen, I'll do that."

Sean was floating in sleep, drifting through one of those sweet dreams of Zurich when the phone rang. Sean leaned over and picked up his phone and whispered, "Hello."

"Wake up, buddy," Zurich said. When he heard Zurich's voice, Sean immediately sat up in his bed and rubbed his face.

"Zurich, whatsup? What time is it?"

"Which question do you want me to answer first?"

Sean looked at the digital clock on the hotel nightstand and saw that it was a little bit before ten. He had overslept and missed calling Zurich to wish him good luck with his hearing.

"Aren't you supposed to be in court?"

"Not anymore," Zurich said.

"Have you already been? How did it go?"

"There you go with the twenty questions. Why don't you just shut up and let me talk? Stop being a reporter," Zurich joked.

"It's on you," Sean said.

"We have to celebrate; there won't be any charges pressed. From what I know, Mia had a change of heart and told the truth. I mean I was on my way to court, prepared for anything, and I got a call from Tamela. Isn't that great?" Zurich said.

"Congratulations, Zuri. You said this would all be cleared up. I guess you were right about that faith stuff."

"Like MamaCee always says, God is good all the time. I was able to get this mess cleared up without placing my body fluids in a jar," Zurich joked, even though he had dreaded the thought of having to provide semen to prove his innocence.

"So what are you going to do to celebrate?" Sean asked.

"Well, I have some calls to make. My father, Gina, and a couple other people. Plus, I want to take MamaCee out for a nice lunch and maybe buy her a new dress. She's talking about going back home," Zurich said.

"Oh no, when?"

"She said today, but I'm going to try and talk her into staying at least until this weekend. I've kinda got used to having her here," Zurich said.

"So I'm one of the first persons you called with the good news?" Sean asked as he smiled to himself. He hoped he would get the answer he dreamed of.

"Yeah, you're the first one I called. Had to share my great news with my buddy," Zurich said. Sean was silent, feeling warm on the inside at the sound of Zurich's voice and what he had just said. He started to ask him if he had called Basil Henderson, but knew that would be childish and he wanted to enjoy this moment of feeling special.

"Sean are you still there?"

"Yeah, Zurich, I'm here. Thanks for calling me with the good news. This will be a great ending for the story. Will I see you today?"

"You're coming to practice, aren't you?"

"Yeah, but I was thinking maybe later we could talk," Sean said.

"Talk?"

"Yeah, you know about the article," Sean said.

"Sure, but I think you already know too much about me, Sean," Zurich said.

"Yeah, but I want to know more. Can we talk at our special place?"

"Our special place?"

"You know, the stadium," Sean said.

"Yeah, sure. But look I've got to run. I got those calls to make and I'm going to enjoy this day."

"You do that. Tell MamaCee I said hello and I want to make sure I see her before she leaves."

"I will. Get your lazy butt up and get to work, Mr. Writer."

"Consider it done," Sean said.

Late Thursday evening, Mia was lonely. She wanted a drink, but instead she called LaDonna to tell her what had happened with her case. Mia didn't know how her friend would respond. She feared LaDonna might be upset because she hadn't come clean sooner. When LaDonna answered the phone, and after a quick hello, Mia told her she had a confession she wanted to make and would understand if LaDonna didn't want to be her friend afterwards. Mia began to tell her what she had done and ended by asking, "So are you still my friend?"

"What kind of question is that, Mia?" LaDonna asked.

"Are you upset with me for not telling you sooner?" Mia repeated.

"Look, baby. I'm your friend. I was trying to help. I was there in Chicago: I know something terrible happened to you. So it wasn't this Zurich guy. It was somebody and we just need to find out who," LaDonna assured her friend. "What did the DA say when you told her?"

"She was pretty understanding and said they would continue to investigate, but they needed my help."

"You're going to do that, right?"

"Yes, I'm going to tell them what I remember."

"That's good, Mia. That's what you have to do," LaDonna advised.

"Do you think I should call Zurich and apologize?"

"I don't think so," LaDonna said.

"Derrick said the same thing."

"Now, how did Derrick convince you Zurich didn't do it? That's the part I don't understand."

"It was his hair. When Derrick's hair brushed up against my body, I remembered the person pushing his head into my body and how abrasive it was. I don't know if I told you but Zurich shaves his head and his face is smooth," Mia said.

"Oh, yeah," LaDonna said as she remembered seeing him interviewed on television after the Chicago game.

"So it couldn't have been him." Mia didn't tell LaDonna she remembered how Zurich had rejected her advances and how she had left his apartment in a rage.

"And you don't have any ideas on who did this?"

"No," Mia said.

"Were you that fucked up?"

Mia didn't answer. A weighty silence lingered over the phone lines.

"Mia. Are you still there? Did you hear me?"

"Yes, I'm still here."

"How much did you drink that night?"

"I don't remember," Mia said softly. "Look, LaDonna, I've got to run."

"Mia, wait a minute," LaDonna said sternly.

"Uh-huh," Mia said.

"Look, Mia, sweetheart. I think you need to take a break from the drinking. You and me both like a cocktail every now and then, but it sounds like you've been blacking out."

"Don't worry, I have it under control," Mia said.

"I hope so," LaDonna said. She realized Mia wasn't ready to deal with her drinking.

"Look, I'm getting ready for bed, I love you and thanks for being so understanding," Mia said.

"I love you too. Take care of yourself."

"I will."

———

Zurich ended his day of good news by making a call. He dialed the number Basil Henderson had given him and discovered that it was a beeper number. While he punched in his home number, he wondered why he had given him a beeper instead of a regular phone, especially since his messages gave Zurich the impression he was anxious to talk with him. A few minutes after he beeped Basil, his phone rang. When he picked up his phone he heard Basil say, "Man, I didn't think you were ever gonna call me."

"I'm sorry, but you know how it is when the season is going on," Zurich said.

"Yeah, I do, Gee. I'm just glad to hear from you. How's it going?"

Zurich told Basil he was doing just fine now, as he gave him an update on his legal problems and the good news he had received earlier in the day.

"I'm glad you got that shit cleared up, Gee. You know bitches ain't shit. Always riding a brother's jock and then the moment they can't get the dick, they holler rape. Look at what happened to our boys Mike and Tupac," Basil said.

"I just think this young lady was confused. I don't think she was really trying to hurt me," Zurich said. He realized Mia might have a problem with drinking and self-esteem, and he was relieved she had told the truth when it mattered.

"Man, you better than me. I'd be talking to my lawyer right now, getting ready to file a lawsuit for defamation of character," Basil said.

"I'm just glad it's over," Zurich said.

After about an hour of exchanging general information about each other, and talking football, Basil said something that surprised Zurich.

"You know I've been thinking about you a lot. Even had a few dreams 'bout you," Basil said. Zurich couldn't believe that Basil was being so open with him. He had noticed a certain sparkle in his eyes during their brief conversation, but he thought maybe he was reading too much into the intense way Basil looked at him and the way he had looked back. He started to tell Basil that he had dreamed of him, but didn't.

"That's interesting, Gee. I've been thinking about you, too, and I'm sorry it's taken me so long to get back with you. But my grand-mother has been here and with everything . . . you know."

"Sure, man, like I said, I knew we'd have the chance to hook up sooner or later. Now when are we going to do it face to face?"

"Whenever we both have time. I'm game," Zurich said.

"So, we're both adults, we can decide when that happens," Basil said.

"Yeah, you're right! Let's look at the schedules."

"Hey, Gee, it ain't nothing but a thang. We can do this. You tell me and I'll be on a plane. You know for dinner and whatever," Basil said in a tone dripping with sexual overtones. The thought of his dream about Basil coming true made Zurich smile. When his sex began to expand, he no longer felt ashamed of his fantasies.

"Sounds like a winner to me. I'm game," Zurich said.

"Yeah, you're game. But can you handle it?"

"Handle what?"

"Now come on now. You know what time it is? If and when we kick it, can you handle it?"

Zurich didn't quite know what Basil was asking him, but he didn't care, so he said, "I can handle anything you throw my way."

"All right now, it's a lot. Be careful what you pray for. And if you keep talking like that, me and my jimmie will be in Chicago before daybreak." Zurich didn't know exactly what a jimmie was but he had an idea. He had become so sexually aroused that he felt a thin film oozing from his sex.

"I hear ya. Basil, I'll talk to you and thanks for the picture. I'll send you one real soon."

"Make sure it lets me know what you got. So I'll know if you can really *pass* the test."

"I'll see what I can do," Zurich said.

"And you know it. Be cool, Gee," Basil said as he hung up the phone.

Zurich lay back in his bed with a smile on his face and his full sex in his hands. There was something in him aching to be released. With the image of the nude Basil in his dreams and with a few quick and smooth movements of his large hand, Zurich shuddered as his body produced a glue he knew would hold him till he could see Basil.

CHAPTER 24

Never Keeping Secrets

To celebrate the news from the DA's office and MamaCee's returning home, Gina decided to give a small dinner party Friday night. With MamaCee and Zurich as guests of honor, Gina also invited Tamela, who invited Desiree and Caliph, Warner, Tim, and Sean.

MamaCee and Zurich arrived first so Gina gave them a tour of her spacious three-bedroom condo, with a formal dining room, a large kitchen, and an enclosed terrace with a great view of the city and Lake Michigan.

"Ooh, Gina, this is a nice place. I shoulda stayed over here with you," MamaCee said.

"You still can. You're sure you don't want to stay until Sunday so you can see Zurich play?" Gina said as she smiled at Zurich, who was waving his hands in the air behind MamaCee, grinning and mouthing, "no."

"That's awfully sweet of you, Gina, but I need to get back home and check up on my garden and my peoples at the hospice. But I'm gonna come back soon. What you cooking in there? Sho smells good. Now you sure I can't help out? It won't take me no time to cook up some stuff," MamaCee said.

"No, MamaCee, this is your night. All we want you to do is relax and enjoy yourself," Gina said.

"I guess I can try and do that," MamaCee said.

The doorbell rang and Gina asked Zurich to answer the door. He opened it and was greeted by Tamela and another young lady. He gave Tamela a big hug and announced, "Here she is, the best lawyer in Chicago."

"Hey, Zurich. How ya doing?" Tamela asked.

"I'm doing great, thanks to you," Zurich said.

Tamela smiled and said, "Zurich, this is my best friend, Desiree Brown." She grabbed Desiree and pulled her close to her and Zurich. Desiree had a huge smile on her face. This was a moment she had been waiting for a long time.

"Nice meeting you, Desiree. I'm Zurich Robinson."

"Oh, I know who you are. It's a pleasure meeting you. Did Tamela tell you I was your biggest fan?" Tamela was looking at Desiree with a comical cross-eyed look.

"No, she didn't, and thanks a lot. Y'all come in; Gina and MamaCee are in the kitchen I think," Zurich said as he shut the door.

"Wait a minute, Zurich. I saw Warner coming up on the elevator. He was right behind us," Tamela said. Desiree whispered to Tamela, "This is the kind of man that makes me want to give up my no-new-dicks policy."

Moments later the doorbell rang and Zurich welcomed Warner, who was alone and carrying a bottle of wine.

"Warner, thanks for coming," Zurich said.

"Thank you for inviting me and congratulations. Looks like you won't be needing my services," he said.

"Thanks, I'm real happy about that. And you'll have to thank Gina for the invitation," Zurich said as he motioned toward the light and voices that were coming from the kitchen.

"So where is everybody? I thought I saw Tamela come in," Warner said.

"Oh yeah, she's here. Come on, let's go in the kitchen," Zurich said.

They walked into the kitchen and were greeted by a spicy aroma. Everybody introduced themselves to one another, and Warner gave Gina the bottle of wine.

"Thank you, Warner. You didn't have to do this," Gina said.

"I hope you like it," he said.

Zurich walked over to Warner and told him he wanted to intro-duce him to his grandmother. MamaCee had found a chair in the kitchen and was talking with Tamela and Desiree as she drank some tea Gina had given her.

"MamaCee, this is Warner. He's a lawyer with the same firm Tamela works for," Zurich said.

"It's a pleasure meeting you, Mrs. Robinson. I've heard a lot about you," Warner said.

"All good I hope," MamaCee said as her large frame shook ever so slightly as she laughed to herself.

"Of course, it was all great. I understand you're leaving our city," he said.

"Now, young man, your name is Warner?"

"Yes, Mrs. Robinson."

"That's a nice name. Yeah, Warner, MamaCee got to get back home," MamaCee said.

"It's a pleasure meeting you," Warner said. The kitchen was well lit with bright fluorescent lights and had a huge butcher block workstation in the middle of it over which Gina seemed to have hung every kind of pot and cooking utensil imaginable. Gina was at her restaurant-size stove managing four different pots and pans. In one, she was sautéing mushrooms and shrimp in garlic butter, cooking pasta noodles in another, frying vegetables and sausage in a third pan, and boiling corn in a fourth. Over the chatter in the kitchen, Zurich heard the doorbell again.

"Gina, I think I heard the door," he said.

"Would you be a doll and get it?" Gina asked.

"Sure," Zurich said as he walked from the kitchen.

Warner made eye contact with Tamela and Desiree. He asked MamaCee to excuse him and he walked over to Tamela and Desiree, who had moved over to the corner of the kitchen. Before Warner reached them, Desiree whispered to Tamela, "Warner is fine. And speaking of fine, where is your man? I thought he was going to be here?"

"I wouldn't say he's my man, but if you're talking about Caliph, he said he would be here, but you know men," Tamela whispered.

"Tamela, great seeing you," Warner said as he walked up and extended his hand to her.

"Warner, I saw you when I came in. I'm glad you could make it. Warner, let me introduce you to my best friend, Desiree Brown,"

Tamela said. She was thinking, *Where is your man, or have you kicked him to the curb.*

"Nice meeting you, Warner," Desiree said as she placed her hand in Warner's.

"It's my pleasure," he smiled.

"Same here," Desiree said.

Just as Tamela was getting ready to ask Warner where Tim was, Zurich walked in with Sean. She decided not to be a Defective Diva after all.

"There's my baby," MamaCee said when she saw Sean.

He walked over to her and gave her a big hug and a kiss on her forehead, just like Zurich always did, and then turned around and said, "Hey, everybody. I'm Sean Elliott."

"Hey, Sean," Gina said as she placed a top on one of her pots. Wiping her hands on her apron, Gina walked over and gave Sean a kiss and introduced him to Tamela, Desiree, and Warner.

Desiree whispered to Tamela, "Oh, he's cute, too. Honey, I know I need to cool my pussy down. You didn't tell me there were going to be so many fine men here," she laughed.

"Calm yourself down," Tamela said as she looked at her watch. She was wondering where Caliph was and why he was late.

"You're not getting worried, are you?" Desiree asked when she saw Tamela looking at her watch.

"No, I'm fine. If he comes, that's great, and if he doesn't, that's great too," Tamela said.

"Yeah, right. You talking to Desiree, your triple G."

"Like I said. I'm fine. I'm going over there and talk with Miss Cora. What are you going to do?"

"I'll be over there in a few minutes. I'm going to mingle," Desiree said.

Gina made sure that everybody had something to drink and pulled down some plates from her cabinet. About every ten minutes, MamaCee would ask Gina if she needed some help and where was her husband? Gina told MamaCee that Clarence was out of town on a business trip and that Rosa, her part-time maid, would be back soon, having gone to pick up dessert.

Sean had a glass of wine in his hand and Zurich was drinking a

Diet Pepsi as the two of them walked through the living room and out to the terrace.

"So how you feeling?" Sean asked.

"I'm feeling pretty good. Seems like everything is falling into place with the exception of my job," Zurich said.

"How so?"

"Craig has really been looking great in practice this week. I mean there has been a zip to his arm that I think has even surprised some of the coaches," Zurich said.

"You're not afraid of the competition, are you?"

"Naw, it's not that. You know it's pretty hard to compete when you can't show what you can do. Besides, some might say I've had my chance. But let's not talk about me. How are you doing? How long are you staying in Chicago?"

"Hold up. One question at a time. Man, you're going to make a great reporter one day with the way you ask questions," Sean said.

"Aw, I'm sorry. I'm just glad to see you," Zurich smiled. His smile and words made Sean's palms begin to sweat, despite the coolness of the terrace.

"I think I'm going home after the game Sunday. But I'll be back if I'm invited," Sean said.

"You've got an open invite if you're talking 'bout me," Zurich said. Just the words Sean wanted to hear.

"Thanks, man. What are you doing after you finish here?"

"I've got to take MamaCee back home. Why? Whatsup?"

"Oh, I just had something I wanted to talk with you about," Sean said. He had made the decision earlier in the day to tell Zurich how he felt about him. His feelings grew every time he was in Zurich's presence.

"You want to talk about it now?"

"No, I mean, it can wait. But if you're up to it, maybe we can go over to the stadium and talk," Sean said.

"I don't know, man. It will probably be late. I'll see. But maybe instead of the stadium, we can go down by the lake instead. Let's just play it by ear," Zurich said.

"That's cool," Sean said as he placed his hands on Zurich's shoulder. Zurich looked at him and smiled. He always enjoyed his talks with Sean and he had something he wanted to share with him, too.

Inside Gina's apartment everyone was gathering around the large mahogany dining room table, where Gina and Rosa had placed a feast of shrimp and sausage pasta, Caesar salad, boiled corn, stuffed peppers, and bread.

"Gina, this looks so good, girl. Looks like you and Rosa put y'all foots in this meal," MamaCee said.

"This does look great Gina," Tamela said.

"I hope everybody likes it. We're going to do buffet-style and before we say grace I have an announcement to make and I think Zurich has something he wants to say. Right, Zurich?"

Zurich nodded his head and said, "Yeah, Gina, but after you."

Everyone lined up beside the table and piled food on their plates, commenting on how good every dish looked. Sean was between Tamela and Desiree and the three of them talked about the food. Then Tamela asked how long he had been a reporter and when his story on Zurich was going to run. Tamela was trying to keep her mind on something else besides her disappointment that Caliph had not shown up. Nor had he called her when she checked her answering machine before Gina rang the dinner bell. She didn't like the anxiety she was feeling and decided that this is what she hated about relationships, the nervousness when you didn't know what the other person was up to. She was also getting mad that Caliph hadn't just said he couldn't come or that he had other plans instead of saying he would be there and acting excited about the invitation. She didn't like the nervous flinch she felt every time Gina's phone rang or anytime someone moved near the door. Tamela wanted to finish dinner, give her thanks, and go home and mope. Another no-good man bites the dust, she thought, as she took a small bite of the tasty pasta dish, without realizing that everyone else was waiting for Gina's prayer and announcement before eating. As Tamela swallowed the food, Gina was clicking a champagne flute with a fork and saying, "May I have every one's attention?"

Gina thanked everyone for coming and expressed how happy she was for Zurich. She thanked Tamela and Warner for their efforts and Sean for his work and a new friendship. She asked MamaCee to give grace, which she quickly began because she was hungry. After

MamaCee's prayer, which was as brief as a Baptist benediction, Gina asked for attention again and said she had an announcement. She looked happy and nervous.

"I'm sorry my better half, Clarence, can't be here tonight but he sends his regards. I really wish he was here tonight, because this evening, after several attempts, we've found out we're going to have a new addition to our family," Gina said as tears formed in her eyes. Gina went on to tell her guests that they would be adopting a new baby boy right before Thanksgiving. "Everything was finalized today and that's why Clarence couldn't be here this evening."

MamaCee said loudly, "Gina, baby, that's wonderful. I'm so glad our peoples realize you don't have to give birth to be a mother."

"Thanks, MamaCee. I hope you're right," Gina said.

All the guests started clapping and saying congratulations, including Tamela, whose eyes suddenly filled with tears. So many tears that she put down her plate and rushed to the bathroom, where she cried into a pink guest towel to muffle her sobs. Why was she so upset that Caliph had not shown up? Were her feelings for him more than she was willing to admit? And why did the tears start when Gina made her announcement? Sometimes, secrets become so deep, even their keeper loses track of them. Tamela washed her face and returned to the party, although she wanted to stay in the bathroom to get in touch with her feelings, but she knew it would be childish to linger. When she walked out, Zurich came up to her and asked if she was all right and if there was anything he could do. Tamela assured him she was fine and encouraged him to go ahead with his announcement. Desiree walked over toward them, and Zurich asked her to stay close to Tamela.

When it looked as if everyone had finished eating, Gina tapped her glass again, and said Zurich had something he wanted to say. Zurich stood at the dining table, after hugging Gina and whispering, "Thanks for everything, Gina."

Zurich seemed nervous. He did not like talking in front of people, no matter how small the crowd, so he stuttered a bit and then began to speak clearly. He imagined the guests as a crowd of reporters he had to address.

"First of all I want to give thanks to my Heavenly Father, who is the light of my life. I want to thank all of you for your support tonight and for the past month, which has been a difficult one. I want to thank my grandmother, for being the mother I never had and my rock in good and bad times. The most important lady in my life. Thank you, MamaCee, and I love you with all my heart," Zurich said. MamaCee smiled as tears started to roll down her face. She became so full of emotion she was rendered speechless.

Zurich continued, "I want to thank Gina for all her help and to announce that effective immediately Gina DeMarco and DeMarco Management will be my sole agent." Everyone clapped and Gina smiled proudly as she blew Zurich a kiss. "I'm also happy to announce that Tamela Coleman will be my permanent legal counsel, and I hope I never have to use her services," Zurich said. Tamela gave a smile of surprise. Zurich had not told her his plans, but she was happy with his announcement. This was just the push she needed to follow up on opening her own firm. She looked at Warner, and he smiled without giving her any indication of what he might be thinking.

"I also want to thank my new best buddy, Sean Elliott, for changing my opinions about the press and teaching me what a wonderful thing having a friend can be. Thanks, Sean."

Sean was surprised and touched by Zurich's statement. He smiled at Zurich as a burst of chilly moisture formed all at once under his arms.

"Okay, that it. Thanks again and now I'm ready to eat some dessert and go out and win some football games," Zurich said as he walked over toward MamaCee. He leaned over and kissed and hugged his grandmother and said, "I love you, MamaCee." With her usually strong voice weak with emotion, MamaCee said, "And MamaCee loves you, baby."

After taking MamaCee back home, Zurich returned to Gina's to pick up Sean, who was drinking wine with Gina and Warner. Sean had a big smile on his face when Zurich walked in, and both Gina and Warner noticed. Moments later Gina said it was time for bed as she pointed toward the door. Before they left, she whispered thanks again to Zurich for the confidence he showed in her and told him that both the *Chicago Tribune* and *Chicago Defender* were running small articles stating that he was no longer under investigation.

"It will probably be on page ten behind the obits," Gina said.

"Just as long as they print it," Zurich said.

"Did anyone ever find out why Miss Thing said you raped her?"

"No, we may never find that out," Zurich said.

"Since that sister is in television, she needs to video tape her ass so she can see how she's acting," Gina said. "Now am I right or am I wrong?"

"Hey, what can I say? You're always right, Gina," Zurich said.

Sean, Warner, and Zurich all rode down in the elevator and talked about the party and the great job Gina had done. Before bidding good night in the lobby, Warner mentioned to Zurich that he had made a wise choice in selecting Tamela as his attorney by saying, "She's very good at what she does." Zurich thanked him, and he and Sean headed to the Oak Street beach area near Lake Michigan.

Zurich drove down Lakeshore Drive and took the Oak Street exit. He and Sean got out of the car and located a bench facing the peaceful waters where they sat for a few moments in silence. The night was quickly turning cool, and the cold air whistled. The sky was dark blue, almost black, except for a thin strip of moon along the east side of the lake. Gray clouds streamed across the sky and the shadows looked like ghosts. The visions of the clouds caused Zurich to think out loud.

"Those clouds are beautiful. You know when I look up at the sky on nights like this, I think the clouds are like cities in heaven. And when I see a thin cloud floating all alone, I sometimes think maybe it's a soul in heaven moving to another city. Then I wonder what city Zach is living in," Zurich said as he stared at the moving clouds.

"You think about him often, don't you?"

"Every day," Zurich said.

"So how you feeling, buddy?" Sean asked.

"I'm feeling pretty good. Tonight was nice, tomorrow MamaCee will be on her way back home," Zurich said.

"You're going to miss her, huh?"

"Yeah, I will. You know tonight when I was taking her home, I asked her if she would be upset if I ended up being more like Zach," Zurich said. Sean assumed he meant if he was gay like Zachary and he realized this might be as good an opening as he would get.

"What did she say?"

"She said, you're already like Zachary! MamaCee said I've picked up a lot of his ways, like the way I lick my lips and arch my eyebrows. I thought that was pretty interesting."

"What do you mean interesting?"

"You know, interesting that I'm becoming more like him every day. I think that's cool 'cause my brother was very brave and honest. I always admired that about him."

"From what you've told me about Zach, I'd have to say you're right. He must have been a very brave man living his life openly as a black gay man."

"Yes, Zach was very brave," Zurich said softly.

"So you don't have any concerns about becoming more like your brother?"

"No, I don't think so," Zurich said. There was a little self-doubt in his voice, which Sean noticed.

"You don't sound too certain, my friend," he said as he slapped Zurich on the knee. His body felt as solid as marble.

"Sean, can I ask you something?"

"Sure, you can ask me anything," Sean said.

"How is it?"

"How is what?"

"Being gay . . . I mean I know we've talked about it, but how is it? Do you think you can be happy?"

"I think you have to work at it. I mean it's tough, but there can be some joy. I think gay people are looking for the same thing everyone else is looking for. Love. And don't all of us deserve love?" Sean was telling himself, now is the time, tell him how you feel. But a part of him was still fueled with fear.

"Yeah, I think we do."

"Have you ever been in love, Zurich? I mean really in love?"

Zurich paused for a minute and then looked at Sean and said, "Yes, once. I was in love with this young lady, Rosalind Shepard, when I was in college. She was wonderful. I think I could have married her."

"What happened?"

"Well, after about two years of a wonderful relationship, sexually and emotionally, Rosalind became saved and closed up shop. After she graduated, she went to work as a missionary in Africa."

Sean thought, *Great, at least he has had sex.* He was beginning to wonder if Zurich was a virgin in every aspect.

"You know what's funny?"

"What?"

"How people somehow always think sex and religion are not compatible. That the two can't coexist," Sean said.

"Isn't that what the Bible says?"

"Oh fuck, Zurich, don't go to that Bible stuff. Think about it. If not having sex would assure us a place in heaven, don't you think everyone would stop doing it?"

"Man, that's deep. I hadn't thought of it that way," Zurich said.

"I think our sexuality is a gift from God. It's how we use it that becomes the problem."

"You never really answered my question. I mean about being black and gay."

"I guess for me there's no way around it. I think the problems come from closer to home than a lot of us want to admit."

"How so."

"It could be easy to blame the problems of being black and gay on society as a whole, or the white gay community. But the truth of the matter is, we . . . meaning black gay men, could solve all our problems if we treated each other better. If we really truly believed that we deserved love in our life and that we could give that love. I mean real love to each other. Two black men loving each other completely, no matter what, could be a powerful thing," Sean said.

"Maybe that's what I'm afraid of," Zurich said.

"What?"

"I mean if I accept the fact that I might be gay, then I could at least look forward to having love in my life. I mean Zach had plenty of lovers in his life, but I don't know if he ever had true love," Zurich said softly. This was the time Sean thought. Now he should tell Zurich that he could have love in his life. That he already had someone who loved him. Sean could hear his heart beating and feel his palms began to sweat. He took a deep breath and reached deep down for the strength he needed to tell Zurich he was falling in love with him. His mouth opened, but the words wouldn't come out. It was silent but for the waters rolling up to the shores and the sounds of seagulls. When Sean finally got the courage he was searching for, Zurich spoke.

"I think I've found someone," he said. Did Sean hear him correctly, did he say he had found someone? Maybe Sean wouldn't have to bare his soul. Maybe Zurich was getting ready to do it for him. Sean felt as though he was watching a romantic fairy tale unfold before his eyes.

"You've found someone?" Sean quizzed as he moved closer to Zurich. As he looked at Zurich and then over at the lake, Sean felt pure joy running through his body.

"Yeah, Sean, I think I'm falling for this player from the New Jersey Warriors. I mean we've only talked on the phone a couple of times, but I've had dreams about him. Sexual dreams and he said he'd had the same dreams about me. We're getting together next weekend, and if he feels the way I think he does, then I'm going to give it a try," Zurich said firmly.

Sean didn't answer. He was in shock. It was as if his heart had stopped. His fairy tale was turning into a horror film. He wanted to take Zurich and shake him and scream to him, "It's me, you fool. I'm the one that's in love with you. That dumb, pretty jock isn't going to do anything but hurt you. He can't love you like I do." But he didn't say a word. His stomach was all mixed up with the incredible sensations of love and a sick feeling in the pit of his stomach. He didn't look at Zurich. He just looked straight ahead at the water. Sean wanted to run into the water and swim in the ocean of self-pity, sorrow, and lost opportunities he felt. Zurich noticed the far-off look in Sean's face and asked him if he was all right. He nodded his head in a yes motion. Then Zurich asked him if he had any advice for him and his new love.

Very softly Sean said, "Make sure you protect your health. Make sure you protect your heart."

When Tamela finally got into bed around 1:30 A.M. Saturday morning she couldn't sleep. She still had not heard from Caliph. She had called his number several times and kept getting his answering machine, but she didn't leave a message. Tamela was worried that something could have happened to him at work. She started to call the station where he worked to see if there had been reports of any type of accidents, but decided not to. About 2 A.M., she got up to make herself some warm milk to help her sleep, when her phone rang. Tamela raced into her bedroom preparing to pick up her phone when suddenly she stopped herself. Instead of picking it up, she turned up her answering machine. After her announcement Tamela heard Caliph's voice, "Tamela? Are you there? Pick up . . . pick up, baby." Tamela didn't pick up—instead she talked to her answering machine.

"Pick up, baby. You messing with the wrong one. I'm not your baby."

Caliph continued talking into the answering machine, "Tamela, if you're there, please pick up. I'm sorry I couldn't make it. But I ran into a problem." The answering machine tape clicked off. Tamela continued talking to the machine, "Yeah, I bet you ran into a problem. What's her name? What's your problem's name, Caliph?" Tamela was getting ready to walk back into the kitchen when the phone rang again. She didn't pick up and after a few moments she heard Caliph's voice again, "Tamela, please, baby, pick up the phone. I need to explain what happened. I'm sorry I missed the party. I really wanted to see you tonight. Please pick up the phone . . . baby," Caliph pleaded.

"Please . . . baby, please. Negro, you need to stop begging 'cause I'm not the one," Tamela said as she slowly turned the volume down on her answering machine and went to the kitchen to warm her milk. While in the kitchen Tamela didn't want to admit to herself that she was relieved that Caliph was okay. Instead she thought, *Negro didn't have the decency to be in an accident.*

The morning MamaCee left Chicago, Zurich had another question for her. So a couple of exits before reaching the bus station, Zurich turned down the radio from the gospel station MamaCee was listening to and asked, "MamaCee, are you sure you wouldn't be disappointed if I turned out to be just like Zachary? I mean, in a certain way."

"What are you talking 'bout, baby? You are like Zach. I told you that the other night. You two will always be one and the same. And just like all my babies, I will love you no matter what."

Zurich wanted to ask another question and avoid a long story, which he knew might not be possible with MamaCee.

"When did you know Zachary was gay?"

"Mama always knew. But one day when I came home, dog-tired from cleaning up my white folks' house, Zack, who was 'bout thirteen then, was sitting in the kitchen looking all sad, like somebody had told him it no such thing as a Santie Claus, and my kitchen was not cleaned up. It was a mess. You member how you boys could mess up tryin' to fix somethin' to eat and I knew it was Zack's week to clean up the kitchen and take out the garbage. You musta been playin' sports or somethin'. But instead of jumpin' on Zack for not doin' his work, I asked him what was wrong," MamaCee said.

"What did he say?" Zurich asked.

"Hold on, baby. Mama gonna tell you. He took my hands and said, 'MamaCee, I got something to tell you and I hope you won't be mad or sad about it.' So I asked, 'What's the matter, baby?' Then he said, 'I don't know how to tell you this,' and so I said to him with a laugh, 'Ain't nuthin' to it but to do it.' So he looked at me straight in the eyes and said, 'MamaCee, I think I'm gay. Do you know what that means?'" MamaCee paused and looked at Zurich.

"What did you say to him?" Zurich asked.

"I looked at him and I said, 'Yeah, baby, Mama know what that means, but I got a question for you.' So anyhow, I put my hands on my hips and asked him, 'What does you bein' gay have to do with my kitchen not bein' clean?'"

"What did he say?" Zurich asked as he gave his grandmother a gentle smile.

"He didn't say nuthin', me and my grandbaby just busted out laughin' and huggin' each other."

Zurich placed his hand in MamaCee's and clasped it tightly and said, "Thanks, MamaCee, I needed to hear that."

MamaCee tightened the grip of her grandson's hand and smiled. MamaCee was thinking how proud she was of him and how delighted his mother and brother would be of him and his noble strength. As Zurich located a parking space, he realized how much he would miss MamaCee. How there was something comforting about her powerful presence and stories for any occasion.

CHAPTER 25

IF IT AIN'T ONE THING, IT'S ANOTHER

It was like a dream. The Cougars were trailing the Tampa Bay Buccaneers, 24–0, at halftime, nothing new to the Cougars and the thirty-five thousand fans who had gathered to see them play. At the beginning of the second half, the coaches pulled Craig, who had been hurt slightly on the last play of the first half when one of the Buccaneers' defensive linemen hit his right shoulder as he prepared to release the ball. Zurich was determined to make the most of his second chance and led the Cougars to two quick touchdowns in the third quarter.

With the score 24–14, and less then ten minutes left in the game, Tampa Bay was driving for a score when Cougar safety Roderick Smith intercepted a Tampa Bay pass and returned it seventy-eight yards untouched for a Cougar touchdown, slicing the lead to 24–21. The Cougars saw a light. But the light dimmed, and four failed drives later, the Cougars had one last chance. With less than twelve seconds remaining, and the ball on the Cougar forty-two-yard line and fourth down with nine yards needed for a first, Zurich dropped back and passed. It was a beautifully thrown ball, a perfectly run pass route and a marvelous catch by Mario, who leaped like a gymnast doing a high-bar routine and came down with the football in the end zone, landing on two Buc defensive backs.

A stunned Tampa Bay team was standing on the field and sidelines with their mouths hanging open. They had lost to an expansion team. The sparse Cougar crowd suddenly took on the sound of more than one hundred thousand plus, thoroughly enjoying Zurich's coming off the bench in the second half and orchestrating a cinematic finish worthy of any sports highlight show.

The Cougar team went wild, lifting Zurich, Mario, Roderick, and the head coach briefly to their shoulders and showering them with Gatorade. The atmosphere in the locker room was pure bedlam, as if they had just won the Super Bowl, not just their first regular season win. The Cougars had finally tasted the nectar of winning and it was sweet. Later that evening, after several interviews and calls from his father and MamaCee, Zurich dialed Basil's beeper and punched in his number. Moments later, like clockwork, Basil called.

"So you showed them what you could do," Basil said.

"Yeah, Gee, I guess so. I still can't believe it," Zurich said.

"Man, I saw that final pass on the 'NFL Today'. I would have given anything to catch a pass like that," Basil said. He was trying to forget the Warriors' loss earlier in the day and the fact that he didn't catch a single pass.

"I haven't seen it yet, but when I threw it . . . man, it was like I was in a dream and Mario, what can I say, my man made a helluva catch," Zurich said as he lay on his bed, moving his throwing arm in a passing motion as he replayed the final play in his mind. He didn't know that Basil's team had lost or about his lackluster performance. Zurich was too excited at his own accomplishment, one he hoped might make the cover of some national sports magazine.

"So are you and this Mario guy tight?" Basil asked. There was a sound of envy in his voice.

"Yeah, we're tight. We don't hang out a lot. I mean Mario is into chasing the women," Zurich said.

"I heard that," Basil said.

"What did you mean when you said tight?"

"I mean does he fuck around?"

"I don't think so. I told you I don't think of my teammates in that way. And none of them have ever come onto me that way," Zurich said.

"Zurich, that's the way you should keep it. Like I said before, it wouldn't hurt you to be seen with some women. Sooner or later your coaches and other teammates are going to start to wonder," Basil said.

"Start to wonder? They know I'm pretty quiet. I don't think any of them would ever think I'm gay," Zurich said. He didn't know what difference it made what he did in private.

"Don't say that!" Basil said sharply. Zurich is really new at this, he thought, and this naïveté both excited and annoyed Basil.

"Don't say what?"

"Man, don't ever say you're gay. If you start to say it then you'll believe it and start to act that way," Basil said.

"Man, I'm just talking to you. What's wrong with me saying it to you?"

"Like I said, when you say that about yourself or even think it, you might start to act that way. Trust me, Zurich, it's not a good thing," Basil said. He knew of two former NFL players who were cut after rumors regarding their sexuality surfaced. The owners blamed the cuts on the salary cap, but Basil knew better. He felt his sexuality never came into question because he always had more than his share of women. All types of women, black, white, and Asian.

Zurich wanted to know why Basil was reacting this way, but he wanted more to enjoy his victory.

"Well, man, I'm going to talk to you later. I need to call another friend of mine," Zurich said.

"You didn't say anything to that sportswriter about me, did you?"

"Man, you need to chill. I'm trying to enjoy my moment, and I wanted to share it with you. But you're tripping," Zurich said.

"Look, man, I ain't tripping. I'm just trying to make sure rumors don't keep me out of the Hall of Fame. I was open with you 'cause I thought you were cool. I don't need any nosy-assed sportswriter in my business," Basil said.

"Sean's not like that. Anyway, I don't know anything about your private life, Basil. I'm just trying to get to know you. Like I said, I just thought I'd call and share the day."

"I know, man . . . I'm sorry. You're right, I need to chill," Basil said.

"When is your new place going to be ready so I can call you at home?" Zurich asked.

"In a couple months. When you need to talk just beep me," Basil said.

"No problem. Look, I'll beep you tomorrow," Zurich said.

"Keep it hanging."

"I will," Zurich said.

Zurich's mood had changed drastically since he began his conversation with Basil. He realized Basil was trying to keep his private life private and so was he. But these interrogations were getting a bit tiresome, Zurich thought.

Zurich picked up the phone to give Sean a call. He was surprised he hadn't seen him in the locker room after the game and that he hadn't at least received a phone call of congratulations. When the operator at the Lenox Hotel answered, Zurich asked for Sean's room.

"Can I have the guest's name?" the operator asked.

"Sean Elliott," Zurich said, wondering why the operator was asking since Sean had been in the same room for over a week.

"I'm sorry, sir, but Mr. Elliott checked out yesterday."

"Are you sure?"

"Yes, sir."

"Thank you," Zurich said. That was strange, he thought. Sean hadn't said anything about leaving Chicago so soon. And why hadn't he told Zurich? Zurich thought back to early Saturday morning when he'd dropped Sean off after their talk. He had said very little after Zurich told him about his interest in Basil. When Zurich asked him if everything was all right, Sean had said things were okay, but mentioned some problems with his nephew. Maybe that's why he had gone back to New York so suddenly. Now Zurich felt bad. Sean had been there for him, and when Sean needed him, Zurich felt he spent the time talking about Basil. He had forgotten that earlier that evening Sean had mentioned that he had something he needed to talk with him about. Maybe he needed to borrow some money or maybe just needed a friend.

Zurich picked up his phone book and located Sean's New York number. He dialed the number, and after a couple of rings Sean's answering machine picked up. After the announcement, Zurich said, "Say, Blackman. You missed my big moment. How come you left town without telling your buddy? I mean what's up, Sean? Give me a call. I'm home. Alone."

Sean sat on his bed with his remote control, changing channels every few minutes. So Zurich was worried about him, he thought, as he listened to his answering machine. But Sean didn't feel like talking. He had not missed Zurich's big day. Having taped the pass that had won the game for the Cougars, he had seen his second-half heroics several times. But Sean was in no mood to celebrate. He wanted to be alone.

Sean felt lost in a deep sadness, knowing that love, something he had always wanted, and needed, was gone before he'd even had the chance to enjoy it. Zurich had found love with someone else. Sean knew that love was a terrible gift to offer when unwanted.

Mia was unaware of the Cougars' victory and Zurich's heroics. She spent most of the beautiful autumn Sunday on her deck, reading a copy of *Acts of Faith,* an inspirational tome LaDonna had sent her days before. After reading the book cover to cover Mia went inside to call her friend and thank her for the very special gift. It was just the thing Mia felt she needed to face Monday, when she was to return to work. When LaDonna answered the phone, Mia said, "Thank you . . . thank you . . . thank you . . . thank you," without even saying hello.

"For what?"

"For *Acts of Faith*. Honey, it's just what I needed. It is one of the most special gifts anyone has ever given me, LaDonna. Thank you."

"Oh, Mia, I'm glad. I can't tell you how many days that little paperback book has gotten me through," LaDonna said.

"It's just what I need to get me ready for tomorrow," Mia said.

"So you think you're ready, Mia?" LaDonna asked. She and Mia had not talked in great detail about her return to work.

"As ready as I'm ever going to be," Mia said.

"Have you thought about what you're going to say to Miss Cheryl?" LaDonna asked.

"Not really. I think I'm going to say something like I'd been under a lot of stress and I'm sorry," Mia said.

"Do you think the general manager might have told her what happened to you? I mean you know how newsroom gossip can be."

"Well, I'm not going to think about that. I'm going to assume that she doesn't know. I will just say I'm sorry. She will probably accept my apology and we will go on with life like it used to be," Mia said matter-of-factly.

"You really sound cool about this."

"What can I do? I was attacked. I got over it! I have to go on," Mia said.

"Hold up, miss. This is LaDonna you talking to. You don't have to play that tough Cleopatra Jones act with me. I've never been through what you've just gone through, and I don't know if I could handle it as well as you have. Especially since they haven't found the creep. I just want you to know that I'm here if you need me."

"I know, LaDonna, and I love you for that. Let's change the subject. I'm going back to work tomorrow and I'm ready. I'm tired of sitting at home watching my hair grow," Mia said.

"So how is that going?"

"How is what going?"

"Is your hair grown back?" LaDonna asked.

"Oh yes, girl, it's almost longer than before," Mia said.

"Damn, girl, then I'm going to the shop and get my hair cut off and then maybe I can let go of this weave," LaDonna said.

"You're a fool. I'm so happy I have you as a friend. I should never be depressed," Mia said.

"That's what I'm here for," LaDonna said. "The pretty girl's best friend, LaDonna Woods, at your service."

"Now you know I'm kidding," Mia said. She didn't want LaDonna to think she didn't appreciate her friendship. Mia knew she could be a piece of work.

"I know you're kidding, Mia. I'm just glad that I can cheer you up," LaDonna said.

"Are you sure? Because I don't ever want to take you for granted. I don't know what I would do without you," Mia said seriously.

"I know, Mia. Now don't keep going on or else you're going to make me all mushy. Let's change the subject. When's the last time you talked with Derrick?"

"This morning. I told you how he calls every morning just to wish me a good day. I mean he really has changed."

"Are you thinking about giving him another chance?"

"I don't know. I know I have some things to work out. Besides, I don't know if he wants to get back. I think he's concerned about my well-being. He ends every conversation by telling me there's an AA meeting going on every day in Chicago."

"Have you given AA any more thought?"

"No, Miss Derrick. I told you I don't need AA. I'm going back to work, I got *Acts of Faith,*" Mia said proudly.

"I know that, Mia, and I'm happy for you. But it's only a job and a book. Sometimes it takes something more to heal."

"Who said I needed to be healed?"

"We all need to be healed, Mia. And if we're truly blessed the healing will never stop," LaDonna said.

"Tamela, this is Caliph and this is call number twenty-five. I tried to explain why I missed the party. My baby was sick. What could I do? Will you stop acting like a baby and at least tell me to leave you the fuck alone. Just let me know you're all right," Caliph said into the answering machine. Tamela didn't pick up the phone but she did answer Caliph. "I don't care if you call twenty-five hundred times and yes you should get the message and leave me the fuck alone so I can start to answer my phone."

Tamela didn't want to admit it, but she was enjoying hearing Caliph squirm. Maybe now he knew how she felt on Friday night when she was worried sick about him. Tamela decided to take a shower and pay her parents a surprise visit and then maybe talk Desiree into going to a movie provided she didn't bring up Caliph.

When she got to her parents' house, her mother was in the kitchen, putting Sunday's dinner in plastic containers. Blanche was surprised to see her daughter on such a beautiful autumn day, when she figured Tamela would be spending the day with her new beau.

"Look what the cat done drug in," Blanche said as she stopped her storage of leftovers and gave her daughter a hug.

"Mama, is that any way to greet your daughter and best friend?" Tamela said as she hugged her mother back. She needed a hug.

"Darling, you know I'm playing with you. I was thinking about you at church, wondering where you were," Blanche said.

"Yeah, I didn't make it today. I had a rough week, so I decided to sleep in," Tamela said. Maybe church would have started her day off better, she thought.

"Oh so, it's like that now. We find a man and all of sudden we're sleeping in," Blanche said, knowing how much her daughter enjoyed her weekends. Tamela always got up early on Saturdays and Sundays so that she could make the most of the day.

"Don't go there, lady. My missing church had nothing to do with a man. Especially since I don't have one," Tamela said sadly. Noticing the change in her voice, Blanche turned to face her daughter with a puzzled look on her face. Tamela didn't look directly at her mother as she grabbed a red apple from the fruit bowl sitting on the counter. After taking a bite of the apple, Tamela looked at her mother and said in an exasperated fashion, "What?"

"What nothing! What do you mean you don't have a man? Don't tell me you've let Caliph go before your daddy and I got the chance to meet him? He sounds so nice," Blanche said.

"Yeah, he's history. I can't hang with liars," Tamela said.

"What happened?" Blanche said as she put the last of her food in the refrigerator. She walked over to the kitchen table, took a seat, and then pulled out another chair, patted it, and said, "Come on over and sit here and tell Mama what happened."

"Aw, Mama, I don't want to talk about it," Tamela said as she shrugged her shoulders like an annoyed teenage girl.

But Blanche was firm. "Tamela Faye Coleman, listen to your mother. Come over here and talk to me," Blanche said as she once again patted the flower-covered vinyl chair.

Tamela took a few more bites of her apple and then asked her mother, "Do you have anything to drink?"

"Is this an iced tea, lemonade, or wine cooler conversation?"

"Probably a wine cooler, but maybe lemonade will be better," Tamela said as she slouched in the chair. While Blanche was fixing lemonade for her daughter, Tamela told her about Caliph's missing the party and how she felt he had lied about where he had been. She didn't mention how worried she had been when she didn't hear from him.

"So why do you think he's lying? Did you call all the hospitals to see if his daughter was sick? I mean, honey, get a grip. A lot of men don't even know when their children are sick. He's just a concerned parent. And you're just being spoiled and stubborn," Blanche said.

"No, I'm not, Mama. He could have called," Tamela said.

"But from what you told me, he did," Blanche countered.

"But it was hours later. What would it have taken just to call and leave a message? He had the number for Gina's."

"Hello, daughter of mine. The man's child was sick. Once when you were sick with the flu and I stayed home with you, I was so worried I forgot to call the school and tell them I wouldn't be there. And your father was the same way when Hank Junior had the mumps and when you had the measles," Blanche said.

"Why are you taking up for him, Mama? You haven't even met him. Caliph is smooth, and he's typical," Tamela said.

"Typical what?"

"A typical up-to-no-good black man."

"Wait a minute! What have I told you about stereotypes?"

"Mama, you don't understand," Tamela said.

"I guess you're right. I don't understand how you can dismiss someone you obviously care about just because you think he lied. Not that I endorse lying, but people, both men and women, tell little lies every now and then. It sounds like Caliph really cares about you. There is something more to this. And if we have to sit here and drink lemonade until we get sugar diabetes then so be it. But you gonna tell your mother what's really bothering you," Blanche said firmly.

While her mother was making lemonade, Tamela sat at the table and started to wonder if she could tell her mother what was really bothering her. *Well, lady, you might not want to hear what's really bugging me, but if that's what you want, then I'm going to give it to you.*

Blanche brought two glasses of lemonade to the table and sat one in front of Tamela with a certain force. She wanted to get Tamela's attention. When Tamela moved her eyes upward at her mother standing over her, Blanche looked back at her daughter and said, "Talk," as she kicked off her house shoes and sat in the chair facing Tamela. "I'm listening and I'm prepared to give up '60 Minutes' and 'Murder She Wrote.' " She enjoyed a sip of the sweet-tasting drink and took a deep breath and said, "Here goes nothing." Tamela was thinking, *Here goes everything, no more secrets.*

"The reason I think I'm giving Caliph such a hard time is because I'm afraid. I'm afraid of falling in love and being hurt again," Tamela said.

"Hurt again? What do you mean, baby?"

"Well, I know we didn't talk about it a lot when I broke up with Jason. I mean I just put on my tough-girl act and pretended like it didn't matter, but it did. Mama, I loved Jason a great deal and when we broke up it hurt." Blanche touched her daughter's hand, rubbed it softly, and said, "I'm sorry, baby. Why didn't you come and talk to your daddy and me? We thought you were handling it pretty well."

"I guess when I look back on it, I did. But with Jason, I thought it was my only chance to have what you and Daddy have. You know, a nice house, good jobs, and children."

"You can have all that, baby, it just doesn't have to be with Jason," Blanche said.

"But I can't, Mama. Jason took all that from me," Tamela said sadly.

"What do you mean he took it all from you?"

"When I was in college, I found out the hard way that Jason was completely unfaithful to me. He was sleeping anywhere he found a hole . . . oops," Tamela said as she put her hands over her mouth in embarrassment. She wanted to say, *Anybody who wanted it could've had a sample of that crooked fat dick of his.*

"We can suspend the mother-daughter rules for this conversation. Tonight I'm Blanche Coleman, best friend. Tamela, you're thirty, say what you want. How did you find out he was sleeping around on you?"

"I got a call from the student infirmary," Tamela said. Blanche's face suddenly turned serious. What was her daughter getting ready to tell her and was she prepared for it? "Mama, please don't look that way," Tamela said as she reached and grabbed her mother's hand.

"Why did the infirmary call you, Tamela?"

"It seems like Jason had given several young ladies on campus an STD. Rumor had it that he had also passed it on to one of his fraternity brothers," Tamela said in a matter-of-fact tone.

"What kind of disease?"

"Well, it seems he was an equal-opportunity spreader of diseases.

He had given one young lady the clap and his frat brother, too. That was never really confirmed, but he had given me and two other young ladies, including one of my sorority sisters, chlamydia."

"What?"

"Chlamydia, Mama. You know what that is, don't you?"

"Yes, darling. I've heard of it. They have a cure for that, don't they?"

"Yes, Mama. *If they catch it in time.* The other young ladies had found out almost a year before I did. Jason had told them to go and get themselves checked out, but he didn't tell me. When I went to see the doctor, he told me he could give me something to take care of it, but I might be infertile," Tamela said as tears began to form in her eyes and her lower lip began to tremble.

"You mean you can't have children?"

"Yes, Mama, that's what I'm trying to say. It's something I haven't told anyone. Not even Desiree. And then along comes Caliph, sweeping me off my feet, and telling me how much he loves children and how he wants to have a million of them," Tamela said as tears started to make their descent down her face.

"Are you certain?"

"I think so, Mama. Let's just say before AIDS came around, I didn't always insist on protection 'cause I wasn't worried about getting pregnant. And that's what the doctor told me at school. I never mentioned it to Jason. I think my sorority sister is the one who told the doctor that I was sleeping with Jason."

"You could always adopt," Blanche offered. She needed time to think of what to say to ease her daughter's pain and concern.

"Yeah, I know, but probably not with Caliph. You see, Mama, I have to give him up now before I fall in love. Maybe there is some man out there who doesn't want kids who could love me," Tamela said. She was determined not to go through a sob session, and she took a long gulp of her now ice-free lemonade.

"I know what we need to do and that's get a second opinion. It's been years. And I'm not bad-mouthing my school, but, honey, that was a doctor at Southern and medical science has made all kinds of advances. If it's the good Lord's will then you will have children somehow. But I still don't think you should give up on Caliph. Date him for a while and if you fall in love, then you're just in love. Don't go into this relationship with some self-fulfilling prophecy that it's not going to work," Blanche said. "Be honest with him."

"But I want what you have, Mama. I want to have love in my life like you and Daddy," Tamela said.

"And you can have that. Look, nothing is promised. I had no way of knowing when I gave up my dreams of going to law school to marry your daddy and help him get his master's degree that our love would last. He could have traded me for a younger model anytime. And I would have had to live with that. We never know what's going to happen when we deal with emotions. The only control you have when it comes to love is how you love another person; you can't control how they feel about you."

"I don't know, Mama. I'm just so scared," Tamela said.

"Then be scared. That's okay. But don't run away from love. Give this young man a chance. And the rest will work itself out," Blanche said.

Just as Tamela was getting ready to tell her mother she wasn't certain she believed her, Hank Senior walked up behind her and gave her a big hug, rubbing his itchy face between Tamela's chin and neck. It both scratched and tickled her. "How's my pumpkin? Mama didn't tell me you were going to be here."

"Hey, Daddy," Tamela said as she got up from her chair and hugged her father. While she was hugging him, Tamela started to cry.

"Now, now, baby . . . stop crying. It's going to be all right. Didn't you hear? You don't have to cry . . . our team won," Hank Senior said.

"Fool, what are you talking about?" Blanche asked.

Hank winked at her as he said. "That's why my pumpkin is crying because she thinks the Cougars lost again. But they won. That Zurich fellow has been playing great since he hired my daughter as his lawyer."

Blanche and Tamela just looked at Hank, Senior as if he was ocean deep crazy. But Hank knew full well what he was doing. He knew his daughter was not crying about some sporting event. Whatever it was he knew Blanche would let him know later that night when they prepared for bed. Right now, he wanted to lighten up the mood, to make his wife and daughter smile. After they both repeated what he had just said about the dumb game, they did exactly what he wanted. They started hitting him playfully as they both stopped crying and began to smile.

When Tamela got home, Caliph was standing in her lobby. He didn't look happy.

"Caliph, what are you doing here?" Tamela asked. Caliph didn't answer her. He walked over to her and looked directly in her eyes and said firmly, "Don't say a word until I'm finished. First off, I'm not into playing games, so this phone shit has got to cease."

"Wait just a—" Tamela started, but Caliph took his large fingers and put them on her lips and repeated his warning.

"Don't say another word till I'm finished. I'm sorry I missed the party, but Whitney was sick and I forgot to call. Look, I care a great deal about you, more than I'd like to admit, but I love my daughter more than life itself. When she hurts, I hurt. I wasn't thinking and I know I should have called. I knew you might be worried. But when you see your child hurting then your mind just goes blank. I do have room in my life for you and for Whitney, but you've got to work with me. You have to tell me when you're scared, because I'm scared, too. I want to be there for you, but I need to know you're behind me and that we're not going to play games and you're not going to compete with my daughter. You got to be honest with me and I promise to do the same. But you have to decide what you want. I know what I want. I want my daughter to be healthy and have me in her life always. I want you in my life also. Now you might tell me I can't have both. But that's what I want. It's on you now, Tamela Faye Coleman, it's on you. And another thing," Caliph said as he moved closer to Tamela and gently kissed her on the lips. He took his finger and touched the end of her nose, smiled a sexy grin, and said, "Just so you'll remember," and then walked out the door. Tamela was stunned as she thought, *I guess I been read!*

Round midnight Zurich's phone rang. He thought it might be Sean or Basil wanting to be talked to sleep. So he was quite surprised when a female voice greeted him with an abrupt "Who is this?" when he said hello.

Zurich's first thought was that the woman sounded white. Proba-

bly some groupie, he thought, but how did she get his unlisted number?

"Who's calling?" Zurich asked.

"Look, don't play with me," she demanded. "Whose number is this?"

"Miss, if you tell me who you are and how I can help you, then maybe I'll share that information with you," Zurich said.

"I know some bitch probably lives there, but you better tell her to stop beeping my husband," she said.

"Miss, I'm the only one who lives here," Zurich said.

"Are you sure?"

"The last time I checked," Zurich said.

"Do you know my husband?"

"Your husband. What's his name?"

"I'm Vickie Henderson, Basil Henderson's wife," she said. Zurich was pissed. So this is why Basil only had a beeper number. The jerk was married, not between houses like he said.

"Yeah, I know Basil and I did page him earlier tonight," Zurich said.

"Oh, do you play with him?" Vickie asked.

"No, but I've played against him," Zurich said.

"Then I'm sorry. I'm just checking. I'm sure you know how some women are. They don't have any respect for relationships. And I was just checking. I mean Basil usually never leaves here without his beeper. But tonight when he went running . . . well, I'm sorry. Please, I'm sorry, what was your name?"

"Zurich."

"I'm sorry, Zurich, for bothering you. Can we keep this just between you and me? I mean Basil doesn't need to know I've been checking up on him," Vickie pleaded.

"No problem, Mrs. Henderson, your secret's safe with me," Zurich said as he hung up the phone and yelled in the darkness of his bedroom, "Basil, you're a jive mf who just got busted."

Tamela couldn't sleep. At around three A.M., she got up from her bed and went into her living room, where she sat cross-legged on the floor and enjoyed the stillness of the apartment. After a few minutes,

Tamela hit the play button on her stacked stereo system and Anita Baker's melodic voice filled her apartment. As she listened to the music, she thought of her surprise meeting with Caliph. How firm and definite he had been in his comments.

Tamela knew she had jumped to conclusions. She wanted to tell him about her fear of falling in love with such a handsome man. How she was certain that after he won her heart he would revert to his man shit, not calling, missing dates, lying, cheating, and showing her disrespect. Tamela knew her pride couldn't stand for that; being alone would be better.

But what if Caliph was different? Maybe his being a father to a little girl had changed him for the better. Tamela realized that if she surrendered to her fears, she might never have love in her life again.

Suddenly Tamela stood and started to pick up the phone to call Caliph when she heard Anita sing a song called "I Apologize." The words in the beautiful song conveyed what Tamela wanted to say to Caliph. So instead of calling him, she taped the song five times on a blank cassette, and wrote on a plain white index card: *When I look at my list of needs and wants, I find you on both. Let's talk.* She placed the card and the tape in an envelope and climbed back into her bed.

The next morning on her way to her office, Tamela stopped by Caliph's apartment and placed the envelope on his car between his windshield wipers. Later that afternoon, via messenger, she received the same envelope at her office, with Caliph's name scratched out and her name written with a black Magic Marker. Nervously she opened the envelope and pulled out an After 7 CD single with the song "Till You Do Me Right." And on the back of the attached index card she read: *Tamela, Listen and learn and then let the games begin. Your man who is ready to protect and serve, Caliph.*

CHAPTER 26

WHEN YOU SMILE

Thanksgiving sneaked up and passed. The Cougars were in the middle of another losing streak, but Zurich was playing well. His personal life was still a ball of confusion. Basil was trying to convince him that his marriage was dead and to go on a trip with him after the season was over, but Zurich was not convinced of either. Still mildly depressed, Sean was putting final touches on a story proposal entitled "Violence and Latent Homosexuality in Professional Sports." Looking for work and his nephew kept him sane. Tamela, back with Caliph but trying desperately not to fall in love with him, was busy with her caseload at the firm and checking out office space in preparation for opening her own offices, while Mia was adjusting to a new set at the station that required her to stand rather than sit behind an anchor desk. She was still drinking, though not as much as before, a couple of glasses of wine a week, and trying to accept the realization that she might never remember who attacked her. MamaCee was back at the hospice every other day, instead of once a week, falling in love with new friends.

The Wednesday after Thanksgiving, aware that Sean seemed depressed after returning from Chicago, Anja talked him into an evening on the town, her treat. She had bought great seats to see Vanessa Williams in *Kiss of the Spider Woman* and made reservations at the popular B. Smith's restaurant, located near the theater, for afterward.

The show seemed to cheer Sean up, probably since he was a big Vanessa Williams fan. But toward the end of the second act, Anja looked over at her brother to comment on how good it was, when she saw tears streaming down his face. Anja didn't say anything; she simply gently rubbed his hands and laid her head on his shoulder.

After the musical, Sean and Anja enjoyed the night while they were walking up Eighth Avenue to B. Smith's. It was cool, and the sky was clear. When they reached the restaurant and were waiting to be seated, Anja asked Sean why he had been crying. "It was just so sad. I mean with the gay character being killed just when he had finally found love," Sean said.

"But it's just a story," Anja said.

"Yes, but stories come from real life. It just made me realize that as a gay man, I may never find true love, and if I do, it might be too late," Sean said.

"Too late? What are you talking about? Where are you going?"

"Let's just enjoy the rest of the evening, Anja. Let's not get deep," Sean said. They were seated in a booth in the packed establishment. It was an open and airy restaurant, accented with calm pastel colors and golden walls. The room shimmered with the sounds of glassware, dishes, and patrons in lively conversation. Sean was gazing at all the happy couples at the silver and black bar, while Anja studied the menu.

"What are you going to have, Sean?" Anja asked. Sean had not looked at the menu.

"Oh, whatever. You order for me," he said.

"Come on, Sean, cheer up. I'm going to order champagne."

"What are we celebrating?"

"Just me being here with my brother and one of my most favorite people in the world," Anja said.

Sean didn't respond but continued to stare at the couples at the bar and the surrounding tables.

When their meals arrived, Sean still seemed preoccupied with sadness. Anja was trying to lighten up his mood with a few jokes and some of Gerald's latest antics on the football field. "You should really see him play, Sean, I think he's really going to be good," Anja said.

"He's not ignoring his studies, is he? I mean sports can't be the end all for all little black boys," he said.

"Come on, lighten up. It's only Pee Wee and Gerald isn't even ten years old. Aren't you the one that got him interested in the first place?"

"I'm sorry," Sean said as he picked at his tasty seafood pasta.

"You're still thinking about the play, aren't you?"

"Not the play. Just about love and Zurich," Sean said.

"When was the last time you talked to him?"

"I haven't talked to him since that night I left Chicago. He's left several messages. I've returned a few of them. But I always call when I know he's not going to be at home. When I'm certain he's at practice or away at a game," Sean said.

"Why do you do that? Why are you playing games with him?" Anja asked.

"I'm not playing games. He's probably really happy with Basil Henderson and I don't want to mess that up."

"Do you know that for sure? Didn't you say that Basil guy was married?"

"I think he's married," Sean said.

"Do you think Zurich knows that?"

"I don't know; come on, let's talk about something else," Sean said.

"Tell me why you just can't be friends?"

"Maybe someday we can be friends. But I still feel like I'm in love with him and if I talk with him or see him, it will only make matters worse," Sean said as he played with his food.

"If you want to talk about something else, then I got something that might shock you," Anja said.

"What? Is it about Gerald?"

"No."

"What then?"

"I've met someone," Anja smiled.

"Who is it? But please don't tell me it's another minister," Sean pleaded.

"No, but I did realize how special this person was at church," Anja said.

"What church, Reverend Theodis's church?"

"No, Sean, you know I stopped going there months ago," Anja said.

"Well, then, who is he? And does he have a gay brother? Stop teasing me." Maybe Anja was getting ready to tell him a story that would make him laugh. Something that would make him forget his blues.

"Who said it was a he?" Anja asked slyly.

Sean stopped his fork in mid-air. His mouth fell open so wide you could have pushed a wine bottle through it. Anja was smiling a cat-who-ate-Tweety-Bird grin, satisfied that she had finally rescued her brother briefly from his doom-and-gloom mood.

When Sean finally closed his mouth, he looked at Anja and asked, "What did you say?"

"You heard me correctly. I said, 'Who said it was a he?' "

"Is it a woman? Is my sister bumping pussies?" Sean smiled.

"Yes, it's a woman and her name is Marilyn and no we ain't as you so politically incorrectly said bumping pussies," Anja said. "At least not yet."

"Come on, tell me 'bout this. How did you meet?"

Anja told Sean she had met Marilyn Dodson at the bank, where she had just been hired as an assistant vice president after graduating from Wharton School of Business. They had become fast friends, and one day when Anja mentioned she was looking for a new church, Marilyn told her about a great church she attended in Brooklyn. She invited Anja during one of the weekends Gerald was staying with Sean.

"You mean the weekend after Halloween?" Sean asked as he remembered one of the last weekends he hadn't constantly thought about Zurich. Being with his nephew had taken his mind away from his *Love Jones*.

"Yes, that's the weekend. Anyway, Sean—the church Marilyn took me to was wonderful. I mean it was the best church I've ever been too. You'll have to come with us real soon. Get this, Sean, it's a gay church, and the majority of their congregation is black or Hispanic," Anja said as she took a bite of her fish.

"Okay, that's all well and good, but tell me about this Marilyn woman."

"She's wonderful. Smart and beautiful in her own way," Anja beamed.

"Is she gay?"

"Yes and quite proud of it."

"But, Anja—I still don't understand. Are you telling me that after a couple of church services with some wonderful lady—you've become gay?"

"No, Sean, I know you know better than that. All I'm saying is I'm keeping my options open. I'm just saying I feel wonderful when I'm with her. And I've had fantasies of being intimate with her, that's all."

"What does she think about all this?"

"Marilyn's very understanding. I mean we've talked. I've been honest about my feelings for her. I also told her I've never been with a woman, and I don't know if I could. Right now, I'm just enjoying our friendship. And I'm never saying never. That's the way you should look at your relationship with Zurich," Anja said.

"My situation is a little different. But, boy oh boy, how the worm turns. So maybe we share more than a genetic trait of fear," Sean said.

"Maybe . . . maybe not," Anja smiled.

Zurich dialed Basil's beeper number and punched in his home number. A few minutes later Basil called back.

"Whatsup, Gee?" Basil said.

"Hey, guy. How was practice?"

"Cool. What about yourself?"

"It was okay. It's going to be tough this week against Pittsburgh," Zurich said.

"Yeah, man, they're tough. I think they're going to the Super Bowl," Basil said.

"Yeah, I think you're right," Zurich said.

"So whatsup? Have you made up your mind? Are you going to meet me in Hawaii?" Basil asked eagerly.

"That's why I called. I think I'm going to pass. I've decided after the Super Bowl to spend a lot of time with my grandmother. I want to convince her to let me build her a house, right alongside her place now. If she won't move into it, then maybe I'll stay there during the off-season," Zurich said. He knew he was just rambling and Basil wasn't listening. Zurich had figured out that the only way to get his undivided attention was to talk about Basil.

"You've chickened out. You're still scared," Basil said.

"No, it's not that. But I'm still not convinced you're going to be able to just leave your wife and I'm not so certain you should," Zurich said.

"What the fuck are you talking about? I told you that bitch is history and it has nothing to do with us. I'm just waiting on my lawyer to get back with me on what she wants," Basil said.

"I've just been having second thoughts. I've explained to you how I'm still discovering things about myself and as much as I enjoy talking with you and all, I think I need to take things slow," Zurich said.

"That's on you, man. I've laid it out there, man. It's on you. I'm not going to beg. And right now I've got something to take care of," Basil said in a terse tone.

"I know," Zurich said and then suddenly he heard a dial tone. Did Basil hang up on him? He waited a few minutes thinking maybe he had been disconnected by accident, but thirty minutes later he still had not heard from Basil. Zurich dialed his beeper number and waited another thirty minutes before he picked up his phone again, and this time he dialed Sean's number. He got the answering machine again and when the beep sounded he left a long message. "Sean, this is Zurich. Why haven't you returned my calls, man? I miss talking to you. I miss seeing you. So much has happened and I really need to talk to my buddy. I want to see you, man. Maybe you can come here or after the season we can meet in Atlanta. I know I'm rambling . . . MamaCee says hello . . . call me."

After leaving the message, Zurich realized Sean might not call back, so he unplugged his phone, put in five CD's, and climbed into bed. When Sean got home after his evening with Anja he saw his answering machine light beeping. When he hit Play and heard Zurich's voice, he immediately hit the Stop button. He was already in the dumps, hearing Zurich talk about how wonderful Basil was would send him over the edge. And he was trying to hold on.

———

Tamela wanted to scream, but instead she ordered another white wine. It was Thursday evening and she was having drinks at Houston's with Dante X, a Chicago attorney with whom she was considering sharing an office suite. Dante was married, but it was obvious to Tamela he was a professional flirt. Every time she saw him, he was always commenting on how good Tamela looked and how he'd be happy as a pig in slop if he could share an office space with her and whatever else she wanted to share.

Dante always ended his comments with this lewd sucking sound he made with his teeth and was constantly touching his private parts as if he was making sure they were still there. His office was in a prime location, directly across from the Sears Tower, and Tamela had already pictured how her new stationery would look with the well-known address on the letterhead. But after one drink with Dante, Tamela knew her search for suitable office space would continue. She wanted to tell him to stop sucking on his teeth and *get a real last name.* If he was so worried about that little dick of his being detachable then he should replace it with one that came attached to a body with brains. She knew it was time to go when Dante leered over her shoulders and said, "Look at this fine high-yellow mama walking in here. Good googly moogly, would I like to taste some of that." Tamela didn't look to see who he was talking about. Instead, she got down from the bar stool, and picked up her purse and briefcase, and said, "I would love to stay here and engage you in a battle of wits, but it's obvious you're unarmed." She didn't wait for a response and as she headed toward the door, Tamela bumped into the woman Mr. X had been talking about.

"Excuse me, I wasn't looking where I was going," Mia said with a flustered look on her face.

"Oh, no, excuse me," Tamela said as she stared at Mia and wondered if she knew who Tamela was. But it didn't appear so, since Mia just smiled and walked toward the hostess station of the restaurant. Tamela was debating whether or not to go over and introduce herself, when she noticed the beautiful burgundy ribbon holding together Mia's thick ponytail. The ribbon looked familiar, and Tamela's thoughts were now clouded with why the ribbon caught her attention, when Dante walked up beside her and whispered in her ear, "Now I understand why you wouldn't give me no play. I saw the way you're checking that sister out. If you're a dyke, we can still deal. I like to watch," he said as he smiled and made that sucking sound with his teeth. Tamela wanted to slap the smirk from his face, but instead she smiled and said, "I would call you a retarded mother-fucker, but I see no reason to insult your mother." With a smile of satisfaction Tamela walked out of the restaurant.

Mia spotted Derrick waving at her from a table located near the back of the dark restaurant. She walked up and kissed him on the cheeks as he stood up and hugged her.

"So how long you in town for?" Mia asked as he pulled out her chair.

"Just a couple of days. You're looking great. I saw you on the news. I like the new set," he said as he poked a chip into the spinach dip he had ordered while waiting for Mia.

"Thanks, I'm still getting used to it," Mia said. The waiter came over and asked Mia if she wanted something to drink. She wanted to order a wine spritzer but she didn't want a lecture from Derrick. She was certain he wouldn't understand her plan for getting alcohol out of her life slowly.

"I'll have a cranberry juice with club soda," Mia said, without looking in Derrick's direction.

"How was your Thanksgiving?" Derrick asked.

"It was okay. My mother came up and we had a good time, but I had to work," Mia said.

"How is your mother?"

"She's fine. We really had a good time," Mia said.

"Have you told her what happened?"

"Not yet," Mia said as she looked over the restaurant menu.

"When are you going to tell her?"

Mia placed the menu down on the table and looked at Derrick and said, "I'm working up to it. My parents will go crazy when they find out. And since the case hasn't been closed yet, I just don't want to burden them. I'm not certain I will ever tell them. Derrick, look, I'm happy to see you, let's not spoil it by talking about the assault and my drinking," Mia pleaded.

"So, you're still drinking?"

"No, not really. Just a glass of wine every now and then with people at work. You know it's expected."

"You could always do what you did today," Derrick said.

"What's that?"

"Order a cranberry and club soda. It looks good and it tastes wonderful," Derrick said.

"Derrick, I'm taking everything slowly. One day at a time," Mia said.

"That's what you have to do. It's one of the things you learn in AA," Derrick said.

"Please not that AA stuff. I'm a personality in this city. If I ever feel I need help, then I'll go away and get help," Mia said.

Derrick could tell he wasn't getting anywhere with Mia, so he decided to change the subject. He realized as much as he wanted to help Mia it was up to her to admit that she had a problem.

"What are you doing for Christmas?" Derrick asked.

"I haven't seen the work schedule yet. If I'm not working, LaDonna and I are talking about going skiing," Mia said.

"With the Black Ski Summit?"

"No, we're thinking about going on our own, maybe someplace like Utah or Aspen," Mia said. "What about yourself?"

"I'm going to spend it with my family. But I might be interested in a ski trip if I was invited," Derrick smiled.

"You never know what Santa Claus is going to bring you," Mia smiled. It was her sweet smile that Derrick loved. The type of smile he hadn't seen from Mia in years. Maybe, he thought, it was a smile of a new beginning.

Friday evening, just as Tamela was preparing to leave her office and meet Caliph for dinner, her office phone rang. Christina had already left for the evening, so she picked up her phone thinking it might be Caliph.

"Tamela Coleman, speaking."

"Tamela, this is Karen Hedge from the DA's office. You got a moment?"

"Sure, Karen, what can I do for you?"

"You called some time ago about Pede Morris, right?"

"Oh yeah, I'd forgotten about that," Tamela said as she sat on the edge of her desk.

"Well, I've looked over the file. I think I'm prepared to drop the charges if he completes a counseling workshop on violence," Karen said.

"That's great. Thanks, Karen. I'll talk to Pede and his mother this weekend. I'm certain they'll agree."

"No problem, I'm sorry it's taken me so long to get back to you, but we're still swamped over here."

"The tough life of being a public servant," Tamela said.

"You're telling me. Okay, and I still haven't forgotten about our lunch. Have a good weekend."

"You too," Tamela said. Just as she was getting ready to say good-bye, she remembered bumping into Mia and something that had been bothering her. "Karen."

"Yes, Tamela."

"Have you gotten any new leads on the Miller case?"

"No, she still doesn't have her full memory on the evening back. To tell you the truth I don't know if we will ever solve it," Karen sighed.

"I have something I think you might be interested in," Tamela said.

"I'm listening."

Tamela told Karen about her meeting the valet parking attendant's mother and the ribbon she was wearing. She explained it was very unusual-looking and how Mrs. Tucker said her son had given it to her and how she had seen Mia with the same type of ribbon a couple of days before. She also mentioned that the last time anyone had seen Mia, it was in a cab heading back to her car parked in the valet lot. Tamela went on to tell Karen how DeAndre never returned any of the calls she left at the restaurant and wouldn't talk with her investigator or Warner.

"I don't know if it means anything but you might want to check it out," Tamela said.

"Yeah, you never know. This sounds interesting. Thanks a lot," Karen said.

Tamela hung up the phone with a feeling of satisfaction that her information might help Karen and Mia.

CHAPTER 27

IF GOD IS DEAD

The night before the first day of December, Sean couldn't sleep. He had a lot on his mind. He was looking at entering a new year with his life in disarray. It was becoming more difficult to find work and he was facing the prospect of returning home. He still found himself thinking about Zurich, but hadn't talked with him. Sean was hurting, and he needed help. He felt there was only one place to turn.

About 3 A.M. Sean got up from his bed and put on a pair of warm-ups, a heavy sweatshirt, and his Cougar baseball cap, a gift from Zurich. He went to the rooftop of his apartment, a place he had been only once before, when the building manager showed it to him. A cloudy sky shielded the stars and moon, and a crisp breeze chilled his face. Sean sat down on a wooden crate under a lamp the color of candlelight, as he looked out on the city. The city seemed motionless, except for an occasional taxi moving slowly down the street. The rooftop was peaceful, and Sean wanted peace. Sean began to speak as if he were in a private conference with someone who had all the answers. He looked toward the sky and began to talk out loud to God.

"Hey, God, remember me? Titus Sean Elliott, your boy. Of course you do, you're God." Sean paused for a moment because he felt silly talking to the sky, when he noticed the clouds moving, revealing a full moon, and a wave of emotion came over him. Man couldn't do that, he thought, and he started to talk to God once more. "I've been hiding from you for quite some time, but you know that. I won't bore you with my life and what's been going on with me, 'cause you already know. I just need some help here. I need some questions answered. I want my life to work. And I know you can help me."

Sean paused and took a deep breath and began to talk again. His voice fell into a rhythm, a potent mix of strength and vulnerability. "I'm trying not to let the obvious control me. You know, my being black and gay. I have learned to live with it. I want to love it. I guess you in all your wisdom know how I can do that. I want love in my life. Is that selfish to pray for? Don't I deserve love in my life? Isn't it one of the best gifts you gave us, your children? If it's not Zurich, then make sure it's someone who loves me. When I was hiding, I knew you could see me, and I know now you were protecting me. Protecting me when I got too drunk to care. When I brought home people who could have taken my life. Protecting me from all the diseases. Thank you. I want to be a better person. I want to do more to make you proud of me. I want people to understand that you knew what you were doing when you made us all so different from each other. But I don't understand why we, meaning all your children, don't understand that. Why do we spend so much time hurting each other? I want to know why we all can't have the same amount of joy in our life, and if we must have sorrow, then why can't that be equal, too? I know you're the boss and maybe something else is going on in heaven that I don't know about. Is everybody I meet down here one of your children, or does Satan have just as many? Why can't you just come back here, just one day, one hour, a minute, and explain it all to us. Why all the different colors? Why do some of us love different? Why do some of us feel things that people we love can't understand? Would it be too much for us to know? I think if we knew, then things might be better down here." Sean let out a loud sigh as he felt his time was almost up, but he had a few more things he needed to say.

"You know I love you . . . that I believe in you. You know what's in my heart. I'm sorry I was hiding. I was hurting. I'm not going to do that anymore. I'm not going to let the people who claim they represent you take away my faith. I won't let them do that. They can't have my faith. But can't there be joy in faith, joy in love. I know you love me. I know that one day I'll have love right here," Sean said as he punched his fists toward his heart. "I love you, Lord, and I know you love me. If I have to be alone here on earth, then please don't let me be lonely. Show me the way and I will follow. I won't hide anymore. And when it hurts, I'll know that you're there, ready to soothe me, when soothing is what I need. Thank you, Lord, and tell everybody, hey. All my friends. Tell Zach hi and for him to give Zurich a clue. Okay . . . I love you. I believe in you. And I will talk to you again real soon. Peace out, God!"

Tears began to roll down Sean's face, and the cool wind dried them. Talking to God made Sean feel strong, sure of himself. He took a deep breath of the cool air, and suddenly, he knew who he was and what he wanted. He felt cleansed by his talk and the wind seemed to vitalize him with a surge of hope. He had the feeling of satisfaction that came from making a positive step in life, a big step. Sean blew a kiss toward the sky and moon and went back to his apartment and slept.

When the arctic wind blows off Lake Michigan, it becomes hard to remember the power of the sun. It was the second week of December, and as the city prepared for Christmas, Mia Miller and Tamela received an early Christmas present. Mia got the call Monday evening, and Tuesday morning Tamela's phone rang.

"So was it the ribbon?" Tamela asked.

"Yes and no," Karen said. "Let's just say it was the ribbon and the Rolex."

"The Rolex? I don't remember a Rolex," Tamela said.

"We didn't know anything about it either. Ms. Miller had forgotten she was wearing the watch the night of the attack. When I went to meet Ms. Tucker, she was wearing a Rolex watch. When I mentioned how nice it was, she told me her son had given it to her. I got back to my office and called Mia, and asked her if she had a Rolex. She said, 'Yes,' but the next day she called and said she couldn't find it and forgot the last time she had it on," Karen said.

"So what happened?" Tamela asked with an excited voice, as if she was getting close to the end of a tough mystery.

"Well, I went back to see Ms. Tucker, told her my concerns about her gifts, and mentioned how possession of stolen property was a federal offense." Karen paused. "And the next morning she was in my office with her son. He confessed to everything."

"So he admitted raping her?"

"DeAndre said Mia invited him into her car to drink. When he got in the car, he said she began flirting with him and didn't have on any underwear. When she asked how old he was, he told her, and then Mia told him to get out of her car. He didn't take that so well."

"What did Ms. Miller say?"

"I didn't go into a lot of what DeAndre said. I just told her we found her watch and we were pretty certain the thief was the same man who raped her. We have a written confession from the young man, so I don't know if we will need her testimony. His mother was adamant about him telling the truth."

"What's going to happen to him?"

"It's hard to say right now. He's only a seventeen-year-old. Not like that's an excuse. But I'm going to see what I can do. He was very remorseful, but we just can't let it slide," Karen said.

"Does he have an attorney?"

"I'm sure the court will appoint one. Why do you ask?"

"I'm going to see what I can do. I met his mother and I was really impressed with how she was trying to keep her family together. I want to see if I can help," Tamela said.

"I'm sure she'd appreciate that," Karen said.

"Thanks for calling me. We still have to do lunch," Tamela said.

"Let's give it a shot at the beginning of the year."

"I'll give you a call. Merry Christmas, Karen."

"Thanks a lot. Merry Christmas and Happy New Year to you also."

CHAPTER 28

MERRY CHRISTMAS, BABY

On Christmas Eve, a sudden snowfall silenced the city. Small flakes flickered in the darkness, dancing on a cold wind, like a magic carpet. Tamela and Caliph walked down a quiet tree-lined street near her apartment building to enjoy the beauty of the surprise. A serene wind caused the trees to sway as if they were slow dancing.

"This is beautiful," Tamela said as she and Caliph stopped in front of a triplex townhouse decorated from top to bottom with thousands of tiny red, green, and white lights. The snow appeared lavender when the lights hit it.

"Yeah," it's nice. This reminds me of my neighborhood down South at Christmas. People didn't have a lot of money, but they sure made it feel like Christmas."

Her hands covered with mittens, Tamela brushed snowflakes from Caliph's face and asked, "So, how you doing?"

He touched her cold cheek and tucked a wisp of her hair under the red skullcap she was wearing and in his trademark humor quipped, "I ain't brand new, but I'll do."

"You'll do just fine," Tamela said as she kissed his cold lips.

"What do you want for Christmas?" Caliph asked. He had already purchased a stunning set of pearls to replace the fake ones he had seen her wear.

"I already have it," Tamela said. She thought, *Now I know you got me something, don't make me take back that leather parka I bought.*

"What do you mean, you already have it?"

"I'm happy. I've got my health. In March, I'll have my own practice. I have you. What more could I want?" Tamela smiled.

"So you're really going to open the door to your own office? I'm so proud of you," Caliph said.

"Thanks to Zurich Robinson and Gina DeMarco, my dream—my professional one, that is—will come true."

"You think you and Gina will be good officemates? I didn't think you sorority girls liked to mix it up," Caliph teased. He was talking about Tamela's plans to share an office in the old Lincoln Park townhouse Gina was converting into space, and the fact that Gina was an AKA and not a Delta like Tamela.

"Oh, that's college stuff. I think Gina and I will do just fine. Two strong black women, making our mark in the world. But I've been thinking about asking somebody else to join me," Tamela said.

"Who?"

"Warner," Tamela said.

"The white guy who works in your office?"

"Yes. What do you think?"

"It sounds cool to me. But you don't sound like you're sure," Caliph said.

"Well, you know I told you he was gay."

"And?"

"And? Is that all you have to say?"

"What does him being gay have to do with his lawyer skills? You've said he's a great lawyer, didn't you?"

"Yeah, he is. And he mentioned to me that he admired me for striking out on my own and how he wanted to do the same thing. I don't even know if he would consider going into the practice with me. But let me ask you something," Tamela said.

"I'm listening," Caliph said.

"What would you do if you had a gay partner. Could you handle that?"

"Well, you know we do have gay policemen. And if he or she pulled his or her weight as my partner, it wouldn't make a bit of difference to me," Caliph said firmly.

"I guess you're right," Tamela said.

"Of course I'm right. You're talking 'bout a business partner. Not somebody to share your bed. I got that covered," he smiled.

"You're right. If things with my practice go the way I expect, I sure could use the help of somebody like Warner. And in the process learn something," Tamela said.

"You know, I coulda helped you solve the Miller case, if you'd asked me," Caliph said.

"I know. But to be real honest, I didn't know when I started the case I would become a detective. I'm just happy I was able to help."

"How do you think the young lady is doing?"

"I don't know. I watch her on television and she looks fine. But you never know. I hope she's doing all right."

"Me, too. You ready to go home?" Caliph asked.

"Sure, let's go," Tamela said.

After they walked a couple of blocks, holding hands in silence, Caliph asked Tamela if she was nervous about meeting his daughter, Whitney, later on Christmas Day.

"No, should I be?"

"I'm telling you, you two are going to love each other right away," Caliph said.

"Are you nervous about meeting my folks?" Tamela asked. Blanche had been planning as if Harry Belafonte and Billy Dee Williams were coming just to see her. She had called over a hundred times reviewing every single detail of the menu and what she was going to wear. Tamela had jokingly warned her mother, no wool scooter skirts with matching vests.

"I'm actually looking forward to meeting your people," Caliph said.

"It's been quite a fall," Tamela said.

"Yeah, it has. But meeting you made it worth it every day," Caliph said.

"Even with the hard time I gave you?"

"I wasn't bothered; I knew you'd come around."

"Oh, you did? How so?"

"We were made for each other. Soulmates."

"You think so?"

"I know so."

"So you spending the night?" Tamela asked as they came to the door of her apartment building.

"You want me to?"

"You know I do. But I realize you have to play Santa Claus in the morning."

"Yeah, I do. Got to fix that training bike," Caliph said.

"My alarm clock works."

"Oh it does?"

As Tamela slipped her key in the lobby door, she looked at Caliph and smiled, "But if it doesn't, we could find something to do all night to make sure we don't oversleep."

"And you know it," Caliph said. While waiting for the elevator, Tamela and Caliph noticed they were standing under mistletoe. They shared a sensual smile until Caliph brought his mouth to hers, and their lips brushed gently as she took his tongue into her mouth like nourishment, like love. When they took a minute to breathe, Caliph whispered in her ear, "Merry Christmas, baby. Caliph's gonna treat you right."

When Mia left the Channel 3 studio on Christmas evening, she had every intention of going home, crawling into her bed with a good book and a bottle of champagne. It was the holidays and a little bit of the bubbly would be all right, she thought. In a couple of days she would be heading home to Dallas, and she was still trying to decide what she would tell her parents.

Mia was relieved they had found the guy who attacked her, but it did not solve the internal struggles she was still dealing with on a day-to-day basis. She was using sleep and work to fill the empty spaces in her life and learning that pain had its comfort. After DeAndre was arrested, another memory of the night came back to Mia. And even though she couldn't recall his face, she remembered his man-child smile, his kettledrum voice, and his offering Mia some of the rum he had in a silver flask. Mia had a memory of saying, "No, you're too young," and how DeAndre in anger at her rejection had hit her hard. The pain had been indescribable. Mia had seen showers of stars cross her face and then she'd passed out. When she awoke, daybreak had come, and Mia pulled her dress back on her shoulders and drove home.

Just as Mia was placing her keys into her car, she heard a voice call her name. For a moment she felt nervous, her heart racing and her mind frozen. When she turned around, she saw Derrick walking toward her with his arms filled with roses, a dozen red and a dozen white.

"Derrick, what are you doing here?" She was surprised to see him, and she walked quickly to give him a hug and a kiss on the lips.

"Merry Christmas, Mia. I woke up this morning and you were on my mind. I dropped off my family's presents and caught a plane," Derrick said. "These are for you," he said as he placed the bundle of roses in Mia's arms.

"Oh, thank you, Derrick. These are beautiful," Mia said as tears began to form in her eyes.

Derrick noticed this and asked, "What are those tears about?"

"All day I was thinking how alone I was. And now . . . you. Well, I'm just a little bit surprised," Mia said as the tears rolled sideways off the corners of her eyes. Her eyes were wide, balancing her tears. She was thinking of Derrick's kindness and gentleness, two qualities she had always desired in men.

"What are your plans? I know you don't cook. But what say we go back to your place and let me cook you up a Christmas omelet? You do have eggs, don't you?"

"I think so, and that sounds like a great idea," Mia said. When she said yes, Derrick's face expanded in a smile of the purest pleasure. Mia gazed at his smile and his eyes as if in a trance. Mia wanted that same joy and pleasure, so she asked Derrick how he had come to this point in his life.

Derrick replied, "I admitted to myself that I was powerless over alcohol, that my life had become unmanageable. That I had to seek and enjoy the miracle and blessings in each day." At that moment, Mia realized she needed to admit that she, too, was powerless over alcohol. And yet the realization was not painful. It seemed to give Mia a sense of peace she had not known in years. After so much fear and pain, her face relaxed into the relief of knowing the pain was over for now.

She smiled at Derrick and asked, "Did you rent a car?"

"Yeah, it's right over there," Derrick said as he pointed to a green Neon.

"Then follow me," Mia said. Just as she was getting ready to turn over the ignition, she called out Derrick's name. When he turned, Mia smiled and said, "Thanks, Derrick. Merry Christmas." Derrick softly touched her face and asked, "Where did that smile come from?"

"It's my miracle," Mia said. She had rediscovered her smile, and even though it faded when she got into her car, she knew her smiles would return. She looked at the red roses as a symbol of passion and thought of Derrick, and then smelled the white roses of hope and thought of herself. The flowers evoked another memory for Mia. On Christmas Day, Mia recaptured what it was like to be happy.

When Sean arrived at his apartment Christmas evening, he felt a sense of peace. He had spent the day with Anja and Gerald, playing Santa Claus for his nephew. They had ended the wonderful day by joining Marilyn for an inspirational service at the Unity Baptist Church in Brooklyn.

Since his rooftop conversation with God, Sean's love affair with sadness was over. He was looking forward to flying to Atlanta the next morning and spending the rest of the holiday week with his parents and his brother. He couldn't wait to watch the football games, and maybe put back on some of the weight his depression had melted away, with his mother's good cooking. The last thing on his mind when he turned the key to his building's entrance was an unexpected visitor.

"Hey, Blackman," he heard a resonant voice say. When he turned around he saw Zurich Robinson standing in front of him looking fantastic. He was wearing a navy blue cashmere overcoat, with a tomato red silk scarf tucked neatly inside the coat.

"Zurich?! What are you doing here?"

"Merry Christmas, buddy. Our last game was yesterday in Philadelphia. I decided to take the train up and surprise you," he said.

"How did you know where I lived?"

"Remember, you gave me a card when we first met. I also talked with Gina a couple of days ago to make sure I had the right address," Zurich said.

Sean was in a state of shock. He had thought of Zurich a lot, but didn't think he would see him again so soon. He wanted to make sure he could keep his feelings intact, but here Zurich was standing before him. He didn't know what to say, so he decided to stick with safe ground.

"Did you guys win?"

"Yeah, 27–24," Zurich said proudly.

"That's great! Congratulations," Sean said.

"Aren't you going to invite me in?" Zurich said.

"Huh?"

"May I come in?" Zurich asked as he gestured to the building and pulled his coat closer in, as if he were cold.

"Oh, sure," Sean said as he hurried to pull open the door, and Zurich followed him in.

"How long have you been standing out there?" Sean asked.

"About thirty minutes. I got here about five o'clock, and I checked into the Crowne Plaza over near Times Square," Zurich said. Sean started to ask why he wasn't staying with Basil, but the new Sean wasn't bitter.

When they reached Sean's apartment, he looked at Zurich and said, "I'm in shock. I can't believe you're here."

"I felt we left some things unsettled. I mean, you left Chicago so quickly and wouldn't return my calls. So I had to come to you," Zurich said. He wanted Sean to realize how much he meant to him.

"But on Christmas? What about your family?"

"I'm going home tomorrow. MamaCee is down in Tampa. Can you believe she caught another plane? I spoke with her and my father this morning and they understood when I told them I had something real important to take care of," Zurich said. Sean wondered what could be so important that he had to fly to New York on Christmas Day to discuss. Sean took Zurich's coat and hung it in his small closet. When he turned around, Zurich was standing very close to him with a big smile on his face. He had on a red turtleneck and blue jean overalls. He looked cool and sexy. He had a thin shadow of hair on his head and a day's growth of hair on his face.

"Gimme some love?" he said as he opened his arms toward Sean, who hesitated. After a moment of awkwardness, he said "Sure," and Zurich held him tightly in a powerful embrace of muscle.

After an endless moment, Sean pulled back from the hip-hop hug and looked at Zurich. Silence connected them. They felt each other's presence without touching. Finally, Sean said, "Come on, Zurich, tell me what this is about. What are you doing in New York?"

Zurich looked at Sean and said "Well, where should I start?" as he took a seat on the sofa.

"It's on you, Zurich," Sean said as he sat down next to him.

Zurich began to talk slowly, telling Sean about his discovery that Basil was not the dreamboy he had hoped. He told him how Basil's constant disrespect for women and gay bashing soured their alliance before it had even started. Zurich confessed that he had decided that if he was going to have a relationship with a man, it would be with someone who knew who he was and what he wanted. When he made that statement, Sean stopped him and asked, "Do you know who you are and what you want, Zurich?"

"Yes," he said firmly.

"And what is that?"

"I want a loving relationship with someone who I can talk to. A relationship that's God blessed and God honored. Somebody I can trust my deepest feeling with. Someone who will share my successes and my disappointments. I want somebody who will be patient with me when I'm slow. I want a friend. Someone like you," Zurich said.

"Are you saying you're gay? Because that's what I am. I'm not interested in having an intimate relationship with someone who's not like me. A proud, black, gay man. I don't mean the person has to be leading the Gay Pride parade, but he has to be honest with himself and with me. He has to know that being gay is more than having sex with each other," Sean said.

Zurich licked his lips and moved his eyes downward, and then looked up at Sean. "It's hard to accept I'm gay, Sean. But it very well may be my reality. What I do know is that I have strong sexual attraction toward men. I had those feelings with Basil. But that was just about lust. I'm interested in more. I want a complete relationship, with someone I like and am sexually attracted to. Someone like you," he repeated.

Sean couldn't believe his ears. Had Zurich said someone like him?

For an instant he wanted to say, You can't want me. I'm not good enough, fine enough, for you. But that was the old Sean's negative thinking, so the new Sean spoke. "Well, I'm not looking for a quick trick. I've made a decision that the next time I sleep with someone, it's going to be with someone I love. I like what you said about a relationship being God blessed and God honored. I have very strong feelings for you. I have since our first conversation. But I'm not in love with you. At least not yet," Sean said. Sean knew his statement wasn't totally true. He did love Zurich, but he was afraid of revealing too much in case this was all a dream. He was afraid of being hurt again, yet found it impossible not to believe Zurich.

"I know. I'm just sorry I didn't realize sooner that you care so much for me. I don't know if I'm in love with you, but I think I could be. I do already love you as a friend. I think it could grow into more. That is, if you're willing to give me a chance," Zurich said softly. After his statement, Zurich felt a wall inside him collapse; all the years of holding himself taut, protecting himself from the possible hurt and the rejection Zach had faced, were gone.

Zurich turned to Sean and began to gently brush his eyebrows with his fingers. Sean couldn't recall anyone ever touching him there and so he asked Zurich what he was doing. Zurich smiled and said, "Because this is like kissing you." Sean closed his eyes and enjoyed Zurich's touch.

Zurich and Sean talked long past midnight. Zurich suggested that the two of them rent a car and drive to Atlanta and then on to Florida. Both agreed the long trip would give them a chance to get to know each other. They talked about the obstacles that faced them, about the fact that neither of them was prepared to leave the homophobic confines of professional sports. They agreed to give a relationship a chance. They would start slow, building on their friendship, so that no matter what happened, they would have a friendship. They made a commitment to always tell the truth about their feelings, to not hold things inside. They said that faith, not organized religion, would be first and foremost in their relationship. They would use their faith to empower them, not as a tool for guilt.

Zurich and Sean sat on the sofa for a time, silent. They weren't touching, but there was an energy between them, like an electrical charge. Then, without any notice, Zurich placed his large hand over

Sean's hand. The suddenness of his move made Sean flinch. But the contact with his body was warm, like the sensual drive of jazz music. Sean looked at Zurich with a smile of complete understanding, and Zurich returned his smile. With dawn a few hours away, Zurich asked Sean if he could spend the night and Sean said yes.

He pulled out his sofa and they undressed in silence in opposite corners of the room. When Sean saw Zurich standing before him bare-chested in white Calvin Klein underwear, he thought, *If I can make it through this night without lust taking control, then we've got it made.* True love had a chance.

They exchanged a smile as they pulled back the covers, and Zurich got in on the left side of the bed. Sean looked at him and asked if music would bother him and Zurich said, "No." Before climbing into bed, Sean turned his radio to Wendy Williams on Hot97, who was in her usual perky mood, singing along with Donny Hathaway's "This Christmas." Sean slipped in beside Zurich and placed him inside his arms, their legs twisted together. Zurich's body felt warm, his skin smooth over heavy muscle. Sean whispered in Zurich's ear, "Thank you."

Zurich turned to face Sean and smiled and said, "Night, Blackman. Merry Christmas." He pulled Sean close to him and said, "I'm not that good at this," and then he kissed him.

EPILOGUE

Zurich discovered passion was like a river, it had to go somewhere. Tamela learned that secrets were like seasons, they changed. Sean discovered when religion doesn't work, faith will. Mia learned that demons can be destroyed one day at a time. MamaCee already knew. All you had to do was listen.

About the Author

E. *Lynn Harris* is a former computer sales executive with IBM and a graduate of the University of Arkansas–Fayetteville. In 1991, he made a career change that resulted in the best-selling novel *Invisible Life* and generated a sequel, *Just As I Am*. Both novels were nominated for the Outstanding African American Novel by the American Booksellers Association Blackboard List. His writing has appeared in *American Visions, Men's Style, Essence, Go the Way Your Blood Beats,* and the award-winning anthology *Brotherman: The Odyssey of Black Men in America*. A devoted Arkansas Razorbacks fan, Harris currently divides his time between New York City and Atlanta, where he is completing his memoirs and the *Invisible Life* trilogy.